don't close your eyes

Holly Seddon is a full-time writer, living slap bang in the middle of Amsterdam with her husband James and a house full of children and pets. Holly has written for newspapers, websites and magazines since her early 20s after growing up in the English countryside, obsessed with music and books. Her first novel *Try Not to Breathe* was published worldwide in 2016 and became both a national and international bestseller. *Don't Close Your Eyes* is her second novel.

don't close your eyes

HOLLY SEDDON

CORVUS

First published in hardback in Great Britain in 2017 by Corvus,
an imprint of Atlantic Books Ltd.

1 2 3 4 5 6 7 8 9

A CIP catalogue record for this book is available from the British Library.

Hardback: 978 178649 217 3
Export trade paperback: 978 178239 671 0
E-book: 978 178239 672 7

Printed in Great Britain

Corvus
An Imprint of Atlantic Books Ltd
Ormond House
26–27 Boswell Street
London
WC1N 3JZ

www.corvus

For my friends.

CHAPTER ONE

Present day

ROBIN

Robin drags in the stuffy air with thin breaths, puffs it out quickly. Dust dances in the foot of a sunbeam. Robin tries not to imagine those tiny specks filling her lungs, weighing her down.

Outside, the Manchester pavement is grey and wet but the air has a freshness, a flirtation with spring. Robin won't feel this. She won't let the damp tingle her skin. It won't slowly sink into the cotton of her faded black T-shirt.

A bus rushes past the window, spraying the front of her house and its nearest neighbours with a burst of puddle water temporarily turned into surf. But Robin doesn't see this. She only hears the gush and the disappointment of the woman whose jeans got 'fucking soaked'.

Robin did not go out yesterday and she will not leave her house today. Bar fire or flood, she'll still be inside tomorrow. Just as she has been inside for these last years. Until a few weeks ago, everything in Robin's world had been fine and safe. A cosy shell. She spends her days clocking up the recommended ten thousand steps a day on her pedometer, watching television, lifting a metal graveyard of weights and aimlessly searching the internet.

Robin is careful and controlled. She only answers her door by prior appointment. Online groceries arriving outside of designated slots get lumped back to the depot by irritated drivers. Unexpected parcels are unclaimed. There is an election soon, but Robin is not interested in discussing politics with earnest enthusiasts in bad suits shuffling on her doorstep.

Someone is knocking on her door right now. They were polite at first but now they're building to a crescendo of frustration. Robin stares forward at the television in grim determination, jaw jutting ahead. The screen is filled with bright colours and mild voices. Television for toddlers. The minutes are filled with stories of triumph in simple tasks, of helping friends or learning a cheerful new skill. There is no baddie, there is no guilt or fear. Everyone is happy.

As the knocks grow a little more frantic, Robin deliberately takes a deep breath. She focuses on her chest filling and expanding, and the slow seeping of air back out between her teeth. Still she stares doggedly at the screen.

SARAH

My child has been torn from me and there's nothing I can do. Four days ago she'd walked off happily holding her uncle's hand and that was the last I'd seen of her golden hair, doe eyes and tiny pink nose. Violet was smiling and oblivious, waving to me while I sat at my own dining table and heard accusation after accusation with no right of reply.

Jim was flanked by his parents. We'd just eaten a 'family lunch' that I'd spent all morning cooking. Instead of letting me clear the plates, as I usually would, Jim had cleared his throat, nodded to his brother to take Violet away, and started reading out his list. Line after line, like bullets.

For a moment afterwards we all sat in stunned silence until Jim looked at his mum and, on seeing her nod of encouragement, said, 'Let's not drag this out. You need to pack your things and get out of here. We've found you somewhere to stay until you get on your feet.'

I was marched upstairs, hands on my back. They watched me while I packed my bags, then Jim and his father escorted me from my home and into a taxi, where I spent fifteen minutes dumbly staring out of the windscreen, too shocked to even cry.

As the blood drained from my skin, I went over and over the list Jim had read out and tried to make sense of it.

1. Jealousy

I thought he was going to say more. But he'd said the word 'jealousy' alone, quietly and firmly, without taking his eyes off the piece of paper in his hands.

At that point I still thought the whole thing might be some kind of joke. His mother and father at the dinner table, his normally pally younger brother in another room with Violet.

But no punchline came. Instead he just carried on reading his list. His parents sat there with their hands in their laps, curled in on themselves while their son made terrible claims about me. About me and our almost-four-year-old.

Jim thinks I was jealous of his affection for Violet. Jealous of their bond, which was apparent from the earliest days. Jealous that he would come in from work and say 'where's my girl?' and mean her. Our little baby. And even though I had nourished her all day, run ragged trying to do everything in the house single-handed while my koala baby stuck to me, covered my ears and bitten my lips when she'd screamed, as soon as she saw Jim come through the door at 6.15 p.m., up her little arms would shoot and she'd make monkey-like straining noises as she tried to reach him.

I wasn't jealous of her. If anything, I was jealous of him. I wanted her love all to myself but I didn't begrudge their bond, I loved to watch it. Love in action. A hard-working, loving man, our comfortable home, our beautiful little baby.

All lined up in a row, like dominoes.

CHAPTER TWO

1989

ROBIN

Robin drags the toes of her patent shoes along the wall. Just because she's small doesn't mean she should be dressed like a stupid little doll. Sarah's the one who likes to look shiny and neat. Sarah's the one who turns herself this way and that in the mirror and admires her golden hair like Rapunzel. Their mum and dad would love it if Robin acted more like Sarah. The thought of it fills Robin's mouth with sour spit.

'Robin!'

'What?'

'Don't spit on the floor. What's wrong with you?'

Robin scowls up at her mother. 'I had a bad taste,' she says and, without thinking, carries on scuffing her shoes along the wall.

'Robin! What the hell are you doing?'

Whoops.

'Nothing.'

'Those are brand new, you naughty girl.'

Her mother stands with her hands on her hips, legs apart. With the sun behind her, her silhouette is sharp but really her mum is quite soft.

'They're too shiny,' Robin says, but she knows she's already lost the argument.

Sarah stands to the side of her mother, affecting the same look of concerned dismay. Even though they've spent the whole day at school, Sarah's hair is still in perfect plaits. Her gingham summer dress is clean and she doesn't have an ominous line of black muck under her nails. Robin's own dark brown hair had burst out of its band before the first playtime. There's so much of it, the curls in a constant state of flux, that no hair bobble stands a chance. In a few years' time, Robin will have cut it off in sharp clumps with the kitchen scissors, but not yet.

Robin and Sarah are still lumped together as one: the twins. But in reality they could scarcely be more different. Blonde and brunette; tall and tiny; rigid and rowdy.

When they were very little, their mother Angela – Angie – had done the usual twin thing. Matching bonnets, dresses and shoes. But Sarah had been so much *longer* and acted so much *older* – almost from day one – that the coordinated clothes only highlighted how different they looked. There were even times – as had gone down in Marshall family folklore – that perfect strangers had argued that the girls could not possibly be twins.

'I should know,' her mum would say with a pantomime sigh. 'I had to squeeze them both out.'

'My little runt,' Robin's dad, Jack, calls her as she sits by his side on the sofa, swinging her feet that are yet to reach the ground. Or when she spends long Sundays contentedly passing him bits of wood, nails or glue in the garage while he fixes something that her mum would prefer to just replace. 'I'm not made of money, Ang,' he says. 'Ain't that the truth,' she replies with another of her sighs for show.

Robin and her sister have just started walking home from their first day of the new school term. Their heads sag on their shoulders, lunch boxes rattling with sandwich crusts. Their talking fades into yawns and complaints. The first day back is always tiring after six weeks of playing and watching TV. They won't usually be collected by their mum – they're big girls now, turning nine next month – but this is a first day back 'treat'. Robin has already been told off twice, so she can't wait to be left to trudge her own way back tomorrow, albeit with her sister acting as nominated adult. Amazing the difference that sixteen minutes can make. 'I'm the oldest,' Sarah says all the time while Robin rolls her eyes. *It would be different if I was taller.*

Robin frowns. Up ahead, there's a shiny black BMW parked partially on the pavement, its hazard lights blinking on and off. The mums who have younger kids in buggies are huffing loudly as they exaggerate how hard it is to negotiate this intrusion to their paths. The driver's door springs open and a woman glides out. She has bouncy, shiny hair and wears an expensive-looking coat. 'I'm so sorry,' she says in the general direction of other mothers. 'I didn't know where to park.'

As the women ignore her, the shiny, bouncy BMW mum sees someone and waves excitedly. It's the new boy from Robin and Sarah's class. He runs up to her, his backpack bobbing up and down. His hair must have gel on because it doesn't move. He climbs into the front seat, the car eases off the pavement and whooshes away almost silently. Robin is unimpressed.

SARAH

There is a new boy in our class. He's as good-looking as Jordan Knight from NKOTB and as quiet as a mouse. He has blond hair and dark eyes, cheekbones like a model from an Athena poster. Our new teacher, an elegant old lady with long silver hair called Mrs Howard, who Robin says is a witch, made him stand at the front of the class and introduce himself. His ears went pink and he opened his mouth but nothing came out. Eventually Mrs Howard pursed her lips and said, 'This is Callum Granger, he's new to the school. I hope you'll make him very welcome.'

I wrote 'Callum' in my exercise book and drew a heart around it so I'd remember his name. As if I'd forget.

At lunchtime, I saw him sitting on the friendship bench by himself. His knees were clamped tight together and he was reading a book, *The Ghost of Thomas Kempe*, while he ate an apple. The boys skirmished around nearby, kicking and stamping on a tennis ball, but every time they got near to Callum, he'd just tuck his knees out of the way and continue reading.

'Hi,' I'd said, smiling in as welcoming a way as I could manage. 'I'm Sarah.'

'Hi,' he'd said. 'I'm Callum.' I thought for a moment that he might extend his hand for me to shake.

'Do you know this is the friendship bench?' I asked.

His ears had gone pink again but he said he didn't realise.

'It's where you sit if you're feeling lonely and want to play with someone,' I explained. I always find it a thrill to explain the rules and rituals of our school. I've been here since I was four and I know all of them.

I offered to show Callum around. He looked at his book, closed it carefully around a bookmark and followed me as I showed him the field where we have games, the leaking swimming pool that isn't used any more, the caretaker's shed that's haunted and – to make him laugh – the outdoor girls' toilets. He went pink again.

He told me that he'd moved to our village, Birch End, for his dad's new job. His dad is something important at a cola company in Reading, but Callum probably can't get any free pop because his dad doesn't like to be asked for things. He sounds very strict.

It's home-time now and Mum has already had to tell Robin off. She'd been scraping her new shoes along the wall and I'd chosen not to tell on her but then she'd started spitting for no reason and Mum had to tell her off. I don't know why she does these things because she always gets caught. It's like she wants to get in trouble. I don't know why anyone would want to get in trouble. Everything's so much nicer when you're good. I try to be a good girl, *always*.

Dad calls me his little swot. Mum calls me her golden girl.

Mum likes to pretend that she's really fed up of Dad and he likes to clown around and call Mum things like 'her indoors' or make jokes about nagging, but I think they still like each other. They'll curl around each other on the sofa when we watch *Stars in Their Eyes* or *Roseanne*, Mum's blonde hair fanning over his chest, his hand resting loosely on her leg. When we're in the car, they talk nonstop like they've not seen each other for weeks, and Robin and I give up trying to interrupt them to ask for more Opal Fruits. We play 'eye spy' or 'yellow car', where whoever sees a yellow car first yells 'yellow car!' and punches the other one on the arm. It always ends in tears but while we're playing it, my sister and I laugh maniacally and press our noses to the glass and it's the most fun in the world. My sister drives me crazy, but if there's one thing she always knows how to do, it's have fun.

CHAPTER THREE

Present day
ROBIN

From Robin's bedroom window on the second floor, she can see into nine separate flats behind her house. If she moves down a floor and balances herself on the window sill in her spare bedroom slash gym, she can see another three flats on either side. Each of the apartments that face her back wall has three windows facing out, filled with lives she doesn't know. Zoetropes stacked on top of each other, showcasing the effortless movement of people as they drift and glide in and out of the windows.

It's mid-morning now, so most of the windows are empty, on hold until the evening. In a top-floor flat, a cleaner pushes a mop around briskly. Her bright top swings around her large body like a circus tent. Her shoulders shake; she's either listening to music or remembering it. In the bottom right-hand flat, the old lady is doing her usual chores. Bright yellow Marigold gloves on, navy tabard protecting her no-nonsense nylon clothes.

In the apartment at the dead centre of the building, a man and woman are both home. Mr Magpie. Robin's special one.

Mr Magpie isn't his real name, of course. He is Henry Watkins and his wife is Karen Watkins. But before Robin knew this, Mr Magpie – named so for the prominent grey streak that sweeps down the side of his otherwise black hair – had already formed an important part of Robin's day.

Every morning, Robin watches, breath held, until Mr Magpie and the little boy (whose name wasn't available online, so was called Little Chick) comes out of the flats' communal garden, shaking the night rain off the boy's scooter and working their wiggly route down the cobbled alleyway that separated the two rows of yards and gardens.

Saying, 'Good morning, Mr Magpie' is a fundamental part of the day. Once that is out, the day can begin. But until that point, there could be no tea, no toast, no steps, no weights, no comforting kids' TV, no nothing.

There are other essentials too, of course, that slot together to make Robin's day. The steps. The weights. The sorting and careful disregarding of the post. The hiding. And the watching. Always the watching. *When I don't pay attention*, Robin thinks, *people die.* Unlike most of her 'what if' thoughts, this one carries a certain truth.

Robin hadn't intended to see anything untoward in the Magpie house over the last few weeks. She was only watching to keep them safe. Robin hadn't wanted to meddle. The Magpie family had been all that was good in the world. Loving, caring, normal. That was what Little Chick and Mr Magpie deserved. Magpies mate for life. They're supposed to mate for life.

So when Robin saw Mrs Magpie and her friend walking along the alleyway, talking animatedly, hugging, kissing, and then more, she couldn't look away. An impotent anger rooted her to the spot, behind her curtains.

She watches now. The oblivious husband and a ticking time-bomb of a wife, picking fights and pointing her finger.

Downstairs, the post has fluttered to the mat and the letterbox has snapped shut again. Robin is about to go down and collect it up, organise it – unopened – into the neat piles she's been building. But just as she steps out onto the thickly carpeted landing, the knocks come. Robin waits. It could be a charity worker with a clipboard, a politician or a cold caller selling thin plastic window frames. Or it could be someone else. The only way to know – short of flinging open the door and allowing all that outside to rush in – is to wait.

Knock knock. Still they land politely, but they don't stop.

Knock knock knock. More urgent now.

Knock knock knock knock knock. Rapid, sweating effort. Now Robin knows it's 'someone else'. The eager caller, the angry caller, the nameless, faceless man at her door. She stays on the landing, and counts the time it takes for him to give up. Thirty-seven seconds. His determination sets her teeth on edge.

SARAH

2. Lies.

I understand why this was on the list. I did tell Jim a lot of lies. From the outset, I omitted. Then omitting turned to spinning, which turned to outright fabrication.

Jim and I had met at work, not long after I'd moved to Godalming in Surrey. My first job in a long time, flushed with drive.

When Jim asked me about brothers and sisters, I said I didn't have any. And my parents were dead. That first lie felt like the right decision for a very long time: *I don't have a family.*

He talked about his family and his gentle hopes and I knew he was the right man. I moved in. And oh my god, I could breathe. I could smile. It was normal and wholesome and good and I'd managed it.

The lies flowed, and then hardened. So many questions came that I hadn't reckoned on. There were gaps to be filled, and they had to be filled on the hoof. Once you tell one lie, you've chosen your path and there's no going back.

I chose Jim. And I chose to be nice, normal Sarah, living in Godalming. And, most importantly, I chose Violet.

Jim and I had to learn how to be together, in our shared home. There were some awkward spots while we adjusted but our girl transcended those. She'd been born early, needed extra care. I loved her instantly.

While the house slept, I had gazed at the little rag-doll baby with the skinniest legs I'd ever seen. My baby. I whispered it over and over like a mantra. 'My baby, my baby, my baby.'

My first night with her felt like a gigantic prank. This incredibly small, painfully delicate creature was being left with me. No instructions, no-one from the hospital coming to inspect the house, no-one watching my every move.

I watched Violet's miniature veins, pulsing with her heartbeat. A tiny light blinking on and off. The held breath between pulses became more normal and less frightening, until I relaxed and started to believe we were all safe.

I couldn't always stop her crying at first. And in the early months, I often cried with desperation in the small hours when there was no point waking Jim, because what could he do besides watch me being tired?

But we got there; I got there.

And it wasn't bad. It wasn't just this desperately tough time of night tears and warm milk. It was often a feat of endurance but all underpinned by a tidal wave of love.

When he said number two on the list, 'the lies', I didn't know what Jim meant. He said the word quietly, like it was a curse word.

I'd raised my eyes to his. 'Lies?' I'd said. 'What lies?'

I should have said 'which lies?' because there were so many. They'd spilled out of me like blood.

CHAPTER FOUR

1990

ROBIN

Robin and her sister are staying at Callum's house tonight for the very first time. Ever since their parents became friends with the Grangers – a chance meeting of the mums in the local hairdresser's a few months ago tumbling into firm friendship – weekends have been turned on their heads. There are no more Saturday dinners on laps in front of the telly for the Marshall family. Saturday afternoons are for baths and hair washes, Saturday evenings are for sitting around a table while the adults talk about boring stuff and make jokes that seem designed – annoyingly – to deliberately exclude Robin, Sarah and Callum.

Hilary – Callum's mum – cooks things she's seen on *Masterchef* with Lloyd Grossman or *Food and Drink* with Michael Barry. There's often a 'coulis' or a 'jus'. Robin misses having Saturday night Chickstix or pizza. Callum's dad spends the evening talking about money – how much he has, how much he expects from his 'bonus', what he's going to spend it on – and Robin's mum does a really irritating loud laugh and then all the next morning she and Robin's dad argue because he won't – can't – buy the stuff that Drew Granger buys.

Normally, the evening ends with a wobbly car ride home, the girls buckling up nervously, the air thick with warm, boozy breath from the front. But the police have been clamping down and using breathalysers more and their dad says it's not worth it because if he loses his licence, he can't do his job. Robin's suggestions to just stay at home instead of go to the Grangers' were ignored, so instead they're sleeping over.

Although Robin would always rather be in her own house, eating her own food and wearing jeans instead of the dresses she gets wrestled into, there is a frisson of excitement about the night. She and Sarah will be top and tailing in Callum's room – he has a bed even bigger than Robin and Sarah's parents – and they've been promised a film before sleep. Robin's hoping for *Labyrinth* but Sarah will probably stamp her feet for something like *Grease 2* or *Dirty Dancing*, the three of them given a note of permission and a quid to go and rent something from the video section of the petrol station. Maybe an extra note of permission to get Robin's dad some cigarettes too.

Callum is going to sleep on the floor next to them on a fold-out bed, willingly giving up his usual digs for the girls he now spends much of his free time with. Listening to them talk, fascinated by the easy flow of conversion, in-jokes and bickering so abstract to an only child.

SARAH

I've been so excited all week. I love going to the Grangers' house. Everything is new and warm and soft to the touch. They have three toilets. One is downstairs and Hilary calls it 'the cloakroom', which makes us smirk a bit because a cloakroom is where you keep your coats and wellies. Sometimes Robin and I pretend that we're going to wee by the coat-rack at our house.

One of the toilets at the Grangers' is in the main bathroom, which also has a shower and a bath – I'm gagging to have a go in the shower; I've only ever had one at the swimming pool in town and that's like a dribble of spit. And then the last one is in Drew and Hilary's bedroom. It's called an 'en suite' and our mum is desperate for Dad to put one in their room. 'Where am I s'posed to put it?' Dad says, laughing at her. 'In the wardrobe?'

I'm looking forward to spending time with Callum. Robin is always pretty good fun, not that I'd tell her that, but she's a bit less manic and crazy with Callum. And she doesn't show off by kicking me or doing disgusting things when he's there.

At school, Callum circles Robin and me carefully in the same way we move around each other. There's only one class in each year, so we're all in the room together whether we like it or not, but it's an unspoken truth that we'd have the mickey taken if we played with each other. Boys don't play with girls and sisters don't play with sisters. Almost right from the start of school, Robin and I acted like we had an invisible force field around each of us so we couldn't get too close. It's protection, I suppose. Some people think twins are weird and some twins *are* weird. They close ranks, turn away from other people and make up their own languages. We don't do any of those things. Our mum says that when we were small, we used to sleep in the same cot. We'd be put down at opposite ends but, in the night, we'd wiggle around until we were next to each other. And when we started school, it took us a little while to realise the unspoken rules. So on the first day, we'd sat down together in the classroom that we'd gone into holding hands. I suppose it makes me sad that we're not like that any more. I don't think Robin really wants much to do with me, and I don't really know how to tell her that I enjoy being her sister and I like it when we get on.

Perhaps it's because we're not identical twins, quite the opposite. In fact, if someone looked in at us playing with Callum, they'd think he and I were related. We're both tall and golden-haired; he carries himself upright like a dancer and I try to do that too. Robin is small and dark-haired, she's bone-skinny and her clothes never seem to fit her right so she's always tugging at them and yanking them up or down.

Callum is different at his house. When we're playing in our respective groups in the playground, he's at the quieter end of 'normal' boy behaviour but he seems okay, unburdened. When we're in the woods or a country park or the beach, pooling flasks and picnics, the mums rubbing suncream on whichever skin is nearest, he's fun and playful. He does his funny little shoulder-shaking silent laugh freely. But when we're in his house, Robin says he's like an old woman. He fusses and flaps. If Robin picks something up, he goes red and hovers near her like he'll have to rescue it. She is clumsy, but she's not *that* bad. 'You don't understand,' he says. 'Even if she drops it, it'll be my fault.'

We arrive at the Grangers in our old Rover. The mums do this kind of stagey air kiss now. It started as a joke but now it's a habit. I notice that my dad has to gear himself up for the night. He sort of takes a breath and puffs his chest up as we knock on the door. His other friends aren't like Drew Granger. They're gardeners like Dad or bricklayers or thatchers. They don't really talk they just crack jokes and buy rounds in the local pub. Standing at the bar with their crusty work trousers on and tapping their cigarettes on chunky ashtrays. With Drew, it's all talking and sort of jokes but not the same, nothing with a punchline. I think we're here more for Mum. She and Hilary are the friends, everyone else fits around that. He'd never say it, but Dad would do anything for Mum, and she seems to like this new life of cordon bleu food and wine that makes her chatty and shared days out. I like it too.

CHAPTER FIVE

Present day

ROBIN

Snap. Flutter. Crash.

The post arrives a little earlier than usual but it will be dealt with in the same way. Flyers and junk will be placed in the recycling box, lying dormant until Robin can summon a surge of nocturnal energy and rush it all out to the brown wheelie bin under a protective night sky. The bills will be filed away in trays in the office/spare room still in their envelopes, most recent at the front. Everything is paid by direct debit, but Robin is belt and braces; she likes the feel of a hard copy. Generally that will be all, but sometimes a white envelope will sit among the rest, looking shiny and *other*. It will not be opened. It will not be filed. It will be picked up gingerly and placed on the pile of identical white envelopes, up high on the unused wardrobe where they can do no harm.

Robin is not alarmed by bills. Bills get paid. Robin has money; the pot has diminished but there's enough to last a while longer.

She was – nominally still is – the lead guitarist of a British rock band, Working Wife. A string of top-twenty albums, a handful of singles that caught the imagination of the radio programmers and burst out of their niche, plenty of insertions on compilation albums through the noughties. Somewhere, she might still be hanging on a bedroom wall or two, her guitar slung over her shoulder, her lip curled. Maybe even the picture of her from *FHM*, when she was featured – in her trademark shorts and vest, sulky in make-up she didn't want to wear – among the gaggle of bare bottoms. The headline: 'WEIRD BUT WOULD'.

What would those once-keen fans think if they could see her now?

Having filed the post – no white envelope today – Robin hovers by her bedroom window at the back of the house; the front is out of bounds. One of her curtains moves ever so slightly in time with her breath. She tries to keep it still with her fingertips but it just spreads against the glass. She does the same to the other curtain so at least everything is equal. She swallows hard and ragged, does it again to keep things even.

In the Watkins/Magpie house, the adults are lying on the sofa in the back of the room. The little boy is sitting at his miniature table in his room, tongue poking out in concentration as he builds something out of Lego. It's a mishmash of coloured bricks, slabs of roof jutting out. He sits back to admire his work, smiles and gets down carefully to go and paw through a stack of soft toys, pulling out something small that looks like a bunny. He lifts a few of the roof slabs from his Lego building to carefully place the toy inside when something makes him jump and he knocks the building to the floor, his little hands covering his face in defeat.

Robin looks into the main room to see what spooked him, and sees the adults in the kitchen, gesturing wildly and obviously arguing. It looks like Mr Magpie has a phone in his hand and he's shoving its screen at his wife's face, pointing at it as she tries to grab it. The little boy appears and the adults spring apart and affect casual poses so disingenuous Robin feels embarrassed. All couples fight, but there's more to this. The man just needs to open his eyes to the full picture. Robin is determined to help.

A young guy is moving into the ground-floor flat underneath the Magpies. He has a stream of helpers, and he is directing them as they cart boxes and bags around.

He's kind of handsome, smiley, but his features are loose and baby-like.

There are different types of boxes. Half of them are brand new and have the name of a packaging company on them, the others are bashed-in and all different sizes. Robin wonders if he's moving out of a relationship, if this is his new 'bachelor pad' and he's putting a brave face on everything.

The boxes in Robin's dining room have the name of the removal service she found over the internet. They are all lined up, logos facing out, like a football team having a one-minute silence. One day, she'll be brave enough to open them. To let their grief spill out into the room. But not today.

SARAH

3. Neglect

This one, I knew as soon as Jim said it. It was old. Over three years out of date, but even at the time, I'd known it wouldn't be forgotten. It was the look he'd given me that day. More of a pause, like he was taking a mental picture and filing it away. But he didn't say anything more, he'd had a lot going on at the time and was only starting to surface himself.

I'd fallen asleep while I was looking after Violet. The night before had been rough. She couldn't settle, didn't want to feed, didn't have wind. I'd paced the house, jiggling her with increasing frustration. Jim had gone to bed, marching wearily up the stairs and falling into bed so heavily the mattress had squealed. Violet eventually relented and I grabbed a few hours of fitful rest, her cries echoing around my skull long after she'd stopped. The next day I shuffled around like a zombie while Jim went off to work as usual, the lunch I'd made him tucked under his arm.

I'd laid down on the sofa, daytime TV chatting to us both. The cushion under my head, the warm sun through the window. My little baby with her baggy tights and pretty little dress had been contently kicking her squishy legs next to me, her plump pink hand wrapped around my finger.

My eyes were open. The next second, they were springing back open. I'd been woken up by the cry as she hit the floor.

'But she shouldn't have been able to roll over yet,' I'd spluttered in disbelief to Jim as he rushed in through the door after my hyperventilating phone call.

'That's not the point,' he'd said, and I'd shrunk. 'My poor little girl!'

'I wasn't blaming her,' I'd said to his back as he whisked her off, gently cooing her cries away. He didn't answer me.

Later that night, Jim nudged me awake in the flickering light of the TV set. Violet lay asleep on his chest, mouth open, eyes scrunched shut. She'd been glued to him ever since he'd rushed back.

'We should have gone to the hospital to have her checked,' he'd said. Before I could answer, he'd asked, 'Do you fall asleep when you're looking after her a lot?'

I tried to explain. Sleep when baby sleeps, that's what they say. It should have been okay. I'd put her in the Moses basket from now on, it wouldn't happen again. He nodded slowly, looked back to the blue light of the screen.

While I shakily packed up my things four days ago, watched by the awkward parade of Jim's family, I'd asked pointlessly, 'What did you mean by neglect?' I just wanted to hear him say it. Because it really seemed like such a small and common thing to fall asleep like that, and I wanted his voice to shrink it back to size for him and for them.

'When Violet was younger, sometimes you'd stare into space ignoring her, she'd cry for you and it's like you hadn't heard. She'd need her nappy changed, she'd be sore and you would fucking – sorry, Mum – fucking ignore her, Sarah. That's what I mean. I caught you. I caught you once and I told myself it was a one-off but it wasn't. Because I caught you again.'

I'd lowered my eyes, zipped up my holdall and left the room. *My god*, I'd thought, *I really believed that I'd managed it.*

CHAPTER SIX

1990

SARAH

Our dad is a gardener.

'Landscape gardener and tree surgeon,' he's started to say because he had this long talk with Drew Granger who 'sells big ideas' for a living. Drew Granger told him that you can call yourself anything you want and people will believe you. That if you say your services are better than anyone else's, and if you look confident enough, you can charge more. Dad didn't seem sure but Mum got some new leaflets printed up that made it sound like Dad had been trimming the lawns of mansions with nail scissors all his life and he started to get more work from big houses on the outskirts of the village.

Mum's never really taken an interest in the actual gardening side of things. Like me, she likes a nice green lawn or a pretty flower, but it's not something she's obsessed with. Robin likes gardening. I think it's because she's allowed to get muddy and dirty if it's with Dad in the garden. It's funny because I would have thought Hilary was the same as me and Mum. She has flowers on her dining table and neat little flowerbeds outside their modern house, but the thought of her so much as kneeling down, let alone *touching* soil, is at odds with everything I've seen so far. And yet the last time we went to Wellington Country Park, I noticed that Hilary had dropped back to ask Dad something about soil acidity and hours later at lunch they were still nattering away about seedlings and polytunnels and the best secateurs for roses.

There was something I struggled to read on Mum's face. Gardening wasn't her passion but Hilary was her friend, and maybe she was jealous that Dad was leaning over the beer-garden table to talk to Hilary, that he seemed so excited that someone besides Robin was finally interested. Mum was sitting next to him, but had to make do with listening to Drew Granger tell her why it was the best time to get an Access credit card and that the economy was booming and she and dad should sell our house and buy something bigger. Mum muttered something and they both looked at Dad and then started laughing. Robin knocked her knife onto the floor near me and when I dropped under the table to pick it up, I thought I saw Mum and Drew's feet untangling.

ROBIN

Robin didn't want to like Callum. He was 'boy Sarah' and her sister was everything that Robin wasn't. The girls clashed a lot, as sisters do. But there was something else with Callum, something she couldn't help but be drawn to. A look in his eye, like he had seen something amusing that he couldn't dare to share. Or like he knew something secret and had zipped his mouth shut. Like maybe, if he really trusted you, he might unzip it.

At school, the kids had their own clusters of friends. Callum was tall and poised, and when he wanted to, he could jump into a football game and dribble, kick, header the ball perfectly well. But, most of the time, he preferred to read or chat about books or television with whoever might be nearby. His ability with the ball and his height meant that the other boys – the loud, fast, brash boys – afforded him space to do both.

When the Marshalls and the Grangers got together outside of school, Sarah would practically perform for Callum's approval. The three kids would climb trees or make up spur-of-the-moment, complex, ever-changing games, but Sarah seemed to care the most. And yet. Robin noticed that Callum's shoulders seemed to shake more at the things she herself said and did. He'd never say anything cheeky or rude to his parents, but if Robin back-chatted her mum or dad, Callum would practically vibrate with excitement, his eyes wide.

This thing had started with Robin's mum and Hilary, but the two families had soon squished together to form a new shape. Despite herself, Robin started to look forward to staying over at the Grangers', watching films or learning card games like Shit Head that they had to play in late-night whispers.

She noticed that the lines were blurring with the adults too. The mums were still the organisers, the confidantes and the ones who met up the most without the others, but the adults were more of a group. Sometimes, Robin's dad and Hilary would even pair up. Hilary had turned up at the Marshall house once in jeans and a sweatshirt, hair tied up in a scarf so that he could take her to the nursery he bought his seeds and soil from, and help her with her garden. And Drew and Robin's mum started to have their own little smirks and jokes. Robin noticed that her mum had started to repeat things that Drew had said, as if they were the gospel. Or she would begin sentences about money or shopping with: 'Drew says...' Robin didn't like that and expected that her dad wouldn't like it either, but it looked like he hadn't noticed.

CHAPTER SEVEN

Present day
SARAH

4. Anger

Anger was number four on Jim's list. 'Everyone gets angry,' I'd said quietly. They'd ignored me. It wasn't fair. I worked harder than anyone to crush those feelings. Even as a child, I'd always tried very hard not to get angry. I'd make a fist, bite the flesh of my cheeks, think about ponies. I wanted to be described, always, as 'a good girl'.

But Violet, Violet *is* a good girl. She could push my buttons with the endless questions, she could drain my patience with the odd tantrum, but she didn't make me angry. Not really.

I think it took about six months to really slide into clichés – hard-working man who just wants some peace and quiet when he gets home; frazzled woman, alone all day with the endless demands of a child. I remember reading an article somewhere that highlighted all the ways caring for an infant compares with mental torture. It's impossible to be your best self in those conditions, and it's the time you most want to be.

Violet was not a *difficult baby* but babies are difficult. The constant noise, the sudden escalations in volume, the never-ending roller coaster of needs and wants, of juggling risks and teaching lessons and pleading for just a few moments of silence in which to think. Thinking, before kids, is just something you do. Afterwards it's a luxury.

Today's parenting is about gentle and reasonable negotiation. When Robin and I were little, my mum would just tell us to shut up. Or if we were bickering she'd suddenly swing her arm back from the front of the car and clobber whoever's knee was nearest. But that stuff doesn't work now. Jim didn't see the balancing act and the diplomatic effort. Jim went out to work and returned to a cooked meal and a bathed, fed baby whose toys were packed away. That I was exhausted was neither here nor there. We both had our roles: mine was twenty-four hours a day care-giver; Jim was sensible, caring dad.

And Jim is a good man. No matter how I angry I am with Jim, I can still see that. From the Jim I first met to the Jim keeping our girl from me today, he's always been a good man. He thinks he's doing the right thing, for the right reasons.

Jim has a slight stoop because he's apologetic for his height, and dark brown hair that's thinning on top and just-grey at the sides. He's good-looking, I think, in a kind of understated way. Is that a backhanded compliment? Maybe.

I had no right to complain about any of his foibles and any of the difficulties that come from round-the-clock parenting. It's what I wanted. It's what I want. But I wasn't perfect, and there were times that I slipped. Shouted. Grabbed rather than cajoled.

'Can you just get your fucking shoes on, Violet, please!'

I know I shouldn't have said it and certainly not in front of him. Jim had rushed into the hall and ushered me off to the kitchen like some kind of bouncer.

'I'm sorry,' I'd said, looking at my feet. 'I just got frustrated.'

'You're an adult and she's a little girl; you need to control yourself.'

And that was that. Another card marked.

ROBIN

The apartment block that Robin's house backs on to is a classic red-brick Mancunian monolith. It has its own rhythm, almost tidal. Hundreds of breakfasts every month, hundreds of dinners. Iron filings drawn out of the door in the morning by a big magnet just out of sight, swept back home at night. Lots of lights turning off for bed, dark blocks appearing in the place of lit windows, one after the other.

But the ones who linger in late yellow light, whose blue screens stay flickering long into the early hours, those are the ones Robin notices. Hundreds of worries, hundreds of nightmares. And as she watches them, the lone colours in a sea of dark brick, the quiet little faces at windows, those are the people Robin falls in love with and watches carefully from a distance, with concern.

Mr Magpie is a night dweller. Last night, as Robin took slow and heavy blinks, she had watched as Mr Magpie walked out from the main room, opening the door to his boy's room slowly and then standing at the side of the bed. He'd squatted, held his hand near his son's head but stopped short of touching him. Probably afraid to wake him up. Instead he'd sat down next to the bed with his back to the wall and rested his own head on the edge of the pillow until his wife had come home, teetering on pinprick heels and collapsing onto the sofa. Mr Magpie had crept back out, stood over her drunken form. Eventually, he'd pulled her up by the arm and hustled her away. No doubt to bed.

The flat above his was occupied by a young woman who would sit hunched at her laptop every night, occasionally getting up and coming back with a bowl of cereal. Robin wondered if she was a student; she would sit with one pyjamaed leg under her for hours on end, tapping away at the keys.

Below and to the right of the Watkins/Magpies live an old couple, who often wear their coats inside for ages after returning home. Perhaps it takes a long time for the heat of their living room to thaw the Manchester chill in their bones, thinks Robin. Perhaps they just like their coats. Her coat is a kind of teal colour and she wears burgundy gloves and a purple hat. When they get inside, she comes into the kitchen where Robin can see her more clearly, takes off her hat and gloves, rubs her hands together and fills the kettle.

Later, the old lady will generally reappear in the kitchen without her coat. She'll slip a blue tabard over her shoulders slowly, drag unyielding yellow gloves over her hands and wash up with the precision of a surgeon.

For months after Robin had first moved in, Mr and Mrs Peacock – named for her coat – just seemed like cold, old people. Robin watched them only if there was nothing else to do, no-one else to watch, all the daily steps done.

And then one evening in late spring, the sun still high in the sky and with his shirt sleeves rolled up to the elbow, Mr Peacock had carried two dining chairs out to the shared garden, one-by-one. The couple had eased themselves into the chairs, drinking what looked like gin and tonic, clinking their glasses together. After taking his first sip, he'd placed his drink on the floor by his slipper and pulled something out of his pocket.

Mrs Peacock had smiled girlishly as her husband played a harmonica, his hands and mouth working fast, like a zip, up and down the instrument.

Watching the Peacocks often made Robin think of her own parents and how they could never be like this.

— —

At times, Robin's pacing can turn to prowling. Frantically churning over ideas as she stalks the house. Memories can collide, fray, rejoin all wrong. She feels anxious, antsy, unable to settle.

This kind of itch used to get scratched in the studio, or channelled into sketches of lyrics.

When Robin had moved to her current house in George Mews, she'd told herself that it was to recover from the strangling fears she'd given into, and that her recovery would be set to music. She'd do a Bon Iver, just in a three-bedroom terraced house in Chorlton instead of a log cabin. She'd ordered numerous bits of kit, most of which were still boxed. She'd searched the internet for the perfect pen and writing pad, secondhand copies of the guitar magazines she'd first learned from. She'd written nothing, recorded nothing, had no ideas.

Instead, walking ten thousand steps filled her day and hundreds of squats, burpees, press-ups, deadlifts and bench presses pushed her limbs to shaking point.

The rest of the empty hours were simply spent watching. She catalogued and reviewed, compared what she'd seen from one day to the next, one apartment to the next. Most of the time there was nothing much happening. Just day-to-day life. Straining pasta or potatoes into colanders. Washing up. Women and men sucking their tummies in and turning this way and that in the reflection of the nearest window.

When the flats lie still and Robin's limbs are too heavy to stand, she watches TV, silent guitar next to her, hand draped over it like a special stuffed toy.

Sometimes she finds herself tapping out a tune, but then faces from her childhood flash across her mind and she catches herself. The tune disappears, scrunched away along with the memory, and she throws herself into pacing again or lifting weights in her spare room. If nothing else works, she takes one of the sleeping pills she bought online and climbs under her bed where she feels cocooned. That feeling of safety, wrapped up and hidden, has been chipped away at recently. Signs were getting harder to ignore.

The frantic knocks had come again today. A dry fear coating Robin's throat as she accepted that this was not a random visit, not a parcel for a neighbour, not a well-wisher. Stuck in her house for years on end had given Robin an acute eye for patterns. And this was one pattern she could not ignore. Someone had tracked her down, and they weren't taking silence for an answer.

CHAPTER EIGHT

1991

SARAH

Downstairs, we can hear the top notes of music and bursts of laughter. The warmth of merry adults rising up. It's the same every weekend, to the point where Robin and I think of Callum's room as 'our room' now. He doesn't seem to mind, although I've noticed he hides things on top of his wardrobe so Robin can't break them when she gets overexcited. For some reason, no matter whose fault anything is, it's always Callum's fault as far as his dad's concerned.

Tonight, Robin had smuggled Penguin bars, leftover Easter chocolate and Golden Wonder crisps from our kitchen cupboards at home to Callum's room. When we'd been put to bed by our mums, Robin opened up her rucksack and tipped it all out on the bed. Callum was immediately panicked. 'I can't eat in my room, my dad'll kill me if he finds that stuff!'

'But he won't find it if we eat it all,' Robin had assured him. Still, he'd got up quietly and wedged his desk chair under the door handle to buy us more hiding time, just in case.

Robin launched into a feeding frenzy. She was two-thirds of my size but she could eat like a lion. And now, within ten minutes of finishing, she's whimpering and holding her tummy.

'You can't throw up in here, it'll go everywhere,' Callum says.

'Help me take her to the bathroom,' I say.

'No,' Robin sobs. 'I want to go home.' She looks smaller now, shrunk back down to size and tugging at her pyjama bottoms to hold them away from her skinny little belly. Only sixteen minutes' difference, but she looks like she belongs to a different generation. It's my time to shine. I love looking after people and taking charge of this kind of situation. I give Callum triage duties: 'Get a cold compress for her.'

'A what?' He pulls a face.

'Some wet toilet roll,' I explain in a matronly way.

He creeps down the hall to the bathroom and returns with a dripping pad of loo roll, which we hold to her forehead like her life depends on it. While she whimpers, Callum and I help her along like a wounded solider, holding her hands and stepping three abreast down the thickly carpeted stairs.

I can hear music, 'Midnight Train to Georgia', and the low rumble of our dad's snoring. He sleeps like a dying fish, mouth gasping and breath catching in his throat and burbling back out. When mum chides him, he says, 'You know you love my cat purrs, Ang.' I don't think she does. We get into the living room and on the large leather sofa that forms part of the new three-piece suite, I see Dad lying with his feet up on the armrest, one arm flopping towards the floor and his flapping fish mouth open in the dim light. There's zero point trying to rouse him, this is Mum's domain. Where is Mum? Or Hilary – she'd do. *A mum* is what we need.

We thread our way around the furniture and towards the connected dining room. No-one at the table, the stereo playing obliviously, its graphic equaliser bubbling up and down. It's a new piece of equipment and the CD player is the jewel in the crown; apparently you can put jam on the CDs and they'll still play. Robin's been desperate to test the theory, Callum draining white every time she even steps near the stereo. There's still no sign of Hilary as we enter the dining room and wind our way through to the shiny white kitchen.

As we wedge into the connecting archway, Robin slumping dramatically like she's taken a massive heroin overdose, I see Mum.

It doesn't make sense. She's pressed against Drew Granger in the corner of the kitchen. He's leaning back on the corner cabinet – the one that has round pull-out shelves that I think are the coolest things I've ever seen – and Mum is facing him. I can see his knee poking out through her parted legs. Her skirt is hitched up and she's holding onto his shirt like he's rescuing her.

'Mum,' Robin whimpers, and I don't think she's really seen the full picture. Callum and I look at each other and Mum and Drew pull apart like a zip.

'What's wrong?' a voice behind us says. I spin around. Hilary is coming into the kitchen from the hall, hair in curlers and wearing a dressing gown.

Callum says nothing, Robin moans and clutches her belly, and I just watch, confused, as the two mums start moving around the kitchen like practised colleagues, sorting Robin out and ferrying me and Callum back up to bed.

'Where's your Andrews antacid?' Mum calls after Hilary, who is chivvying Callum and me along the hall towards the stairs.

'Top cupboard on the far left,' Hilary calls.

Am I in *The Twilight Zone*? Did I just imagine seeing my mum cuddling up to Callum's dad, while my dad snored on the sofa?

ROBIN

Sarah and Callum are already awake and Robin opens her eyes slowly to the sound of their low talking. She swivels her head around and sees the bucket next to her side of the bed. She sits up, remembering her bellyache from last night and feeling starving hungry now.

'What time is it?' she says groggily.

'Nearly nine,' Callum says, reading the time from the radio alarm clock on his desk.

'What are you two talking about?' Robin asks, irritated that they've been chatting without her *and* managed to wake her up in the process.

'Last night,' Sarah says.

'What about last night?'

'Nothing,' Callum answers. 'We've got a variety pack downstairs and you can have the Frosties if you want, Robin.'

Robin nearly falls over getting out of bed in a hurry and rushing out the door.

Downstairs, the girls' dad is still wearing the clothes he fell asleep in last night, his socked feet are still on the armrest but now he has a pillow under his head, tucked under there in the night by his wife. Their mum is in her nightie, nudging their dad to give him a pint glass of water with something white and bubbly at the bottom of it.

'Morning,' her mum says, but she doesn't look directly at her daughters or Callum.

'Morning,' they trill in unison, just as they do at school. ('Good morning, Mrs Ho-ward.' 'Good morning, ev'ry-bod-y.')

Hilary and Drew are in the kitchen. He's drinking coffee and looking at a big newspaper, and she's cooking bacon and sausages that fizz and spit in the pan. The adults' bottles from last night have been stacked neatly in a box as Hilary has recently taken up recycling.

'Why the hell aren't you dressed?' Drew Granger suddenly explodes at his son. Sarah and Robin look down awkwardly at their own night clothes and cross and uncross their legs nervously.

'I'll go and change,' Callum says quietly.

'How are you feeling, Robin?' Hilary asks gently.

'Okay. Hungry.'

She's not sure what she's said wrong, but Robin notices Drew Granger frowning and ruffling his paper. Their mum is watching from the archway through to the kitchen; she's changed out of her nightie double-quick and is wearing a new summer dress that sticks to her body.

'Very nice,' Drew Granger says to her, and she smiles and looks away. Hilary carries on turning the sausages and Robin's tummy rumbles loudly.

CHAPTER NINE

Present day
SARAH

5. The bruises

When I first held Violet, I'd never seen skin so new. She was almost see-through and so soft you could barely feel her. She smelled of milk and talcum powder, at once ancient and fleeting.

Until she filled out from all the creamy milk, Violet had scrappy red legs that folded up like a frog. She wore the smallest nappies and I felt like I was dressing a doll made of egg shells when I had to navigate the fabric over her tiny wrapped fist.

She was a little dollop of innocence and her easy trust stirred up a near-murderous rage in me, just imagining that there was some generalised evil that could seep under the door and touch her. We loved each other immediately. I know that wherever she is, whichever familiar room she's waking up in, she still loves me. And that the love she's feeling must be tinged with pain and confusion, because I'm not there. And I've always been there.

I have never deliberately hurt Violet. I have spent the last three and something years chasing away any pain she might be at risk of, at least kissing it better when I didn't manage to prevent it. Hugging her tiny body as it bucked with the force of tears.

— —

Again, no explanation. His expression was almost goading. 'Just try to deny it,' his raised eyebrows said.

I couldn't deny it. She did have bruises. Every kid has bruises. She didn't have bruises as a baby. She picked up a few murky smudges on her legs when she first started toddling, but those were not the bruises in question. The bruises I think he was referring to were from last year, when Violet was two and a half. The truth is, I don't know how she got them. And I realise how bad that sounds.

We were at a big adventure playground in Bracknell Forest with a bunch of other kids and mums from our local toddler group. We'd car-pooled, Violet and I in the large people-carrier of a woman I'd never even spoken to before, grappling for conversation that crash-landed in silence three-quarters of the way there. The woman had twin boys, a little younger than Violet but bigger and louder. Little tanks. The back of the car was rowdy until all three fell asleep just as we pulled in to the car park.

The adventure playground was organised into different sections, and a bank of picnic tables ran alongside the fenced play equipment, benches stuffed with women and a few men, hands wrapped around plastic cups of coffee or decanting tea from flasks. I stood holding the fence of the playground, watching Violet's every move as she tentatively followed the others up cargo nets and down slides. It was a world away from our little village park, and Violet looked more daunted than excited. She seemed eager to leave almost as soon as we arrived.

One of the mums had tapped me on the shoulder and offered me tea from her flask. It was a kind gesture and I turned to smile at her as she poured it for me. We had a brief conversation about how awkward we both found these events. 'Us shy ones should stick together,' she'd said and I felt a little shiver of kinship.

She went back to her table but when I looked back at the playground, I couldn't see Violet. She wasn't on the cargo net where she'd been moments ago, and she wasn't on the slide where she'd been before that. The big twins were there, snot-nosed and oblivious. The other children who'd been near her were there, playing and feuding, but she wasn't. I was immediately frantic. My head whistled with fear.

'Where's Violet?' I'd shouted to the twin boys, who ignored me. I ran to the cluster of mums, grabbing one of them by the arm. 'Have you seen Violet?' I asked. They shook their heads and looked concerned. A couple of them joined me to look. 'Which one is she again?' a redheaded mum asked. I found it near impossible to describe her. I saw her when my eyes closed, I lived for her, but I couldn't put any of it into words.

'Don't worry,' the mums had all said, rubbing my back and gathering me up in their energy. We covered all of the ground. I was desperate, spinning uselessly on the chipped bark. Suddenly, I turned towards the cafe and saw a woman holding Violet tightly. I ran over, heart pounding, and tried to rip Violet from her arms.

'Hey,' the woman had cried, 'what are you doing?'

'She's mine!' I'd cried.

'Are you her mum?' she'd asked. 'She was lost.'

'I only looked away for a second,' I said, outraged but near sick with relief. I'd stroked her hair, kissed her cheeks. She was still shaking and sobbing. 'Where did you go, darling?' I'd asked her.

The woman who'd had her was hovering but I barely noticed. Violet just hugged into me, her tears soaking into my coat.

'She was wandering around by herself and she was crying and hurt,' the woman said, her hands on her hips.

Violet must have thought I'd gone somewhere when she couldn't see my face. I felt unbearably guilty at prioritising a conversation with someone whose name I didn't know. A conversation long enough for Violet to fall off the cargo net or run into something or slip off a slide and not know where I was. She had blueish-green marks all up her legs and the side of her arm, but it wasn't the bruises that upset me. It was the feeling that I'd put anything or anyone before her that stayed with me. I vowed never to do that again. After all, I knew how that felt.

ROBIN

It was just some knocks on the door, Robin had told herself last night as she tried to sleep, duvet tangled in her legs. Just a few knocks. And what harm could someone knocking on the door do? Robin lived in a busy suburb of Manchester, on a bus route and with the front of her house facing a popular green. There were witnesses everywhere, there were hundreds of people whose very presence should stop anyone even trying something dangerous. So why hadn't she just opened the door?

Tomorrow, she told herself, she would open the door if he knocked. More than that, she would fling it back and say, 'Yes?', phone in her hand, ready to call the police if there was any need. And surely there'd be no need.

The decisiveness calmed her at first, but the thought of the door opening, the rush of daylight, the face of someone angry and desperate emerging ... She had climbed under her bed before she knew what she was doing, tugging her duvet down after her.

She swung through these loops often. The logical part of her taking charge, then the broken part of her swinging a wrecking ball through all that sense. There were so many things that a reasonable person would have done differently over the years. A reasonable person would open her own post, would open her own door, would sleep on top of her own bed, would leave her own house, wouldn't count her daily steps, would watch normal adult television and not seek out the nursery comforts of *CBeebies*. A normal person wouldn't believe that she holds other people's mortality in her scrawny hands. Wouldn't take responsibility for strangers as if that could bring anyone back.

A normal person would just live, without analysing every decision before, during and after she made it. But, Robin accepted, maybe she'd never been normal.

She pushed open the door of the 'gym' – one of the first-floor spare rooms – lay down on the weights bench and tried to focus on the bar of metal over her chest. At least working out was a fairly normal thing to do, even if she did do it for hours on end, getting stuck in loops of round numbers and having to keep things equal and burning her muscles to oblivion.

The hole she was in had opened up in LA, California. The band were in the city to work on their fifth album, which was an indulgence designed to inspire.

Robin had gone outside to get some fresh air – air warmer and grittier than in the air-conditioned room she'd just left – an unexpected arrival the day before still pressing on her mind. Then she saw it. A triple drain. Three drains in a row. She walked around it, slid into the road to avoid it, just like she had as a teenager when it was a pavement in Berkshire rather than a sidewalk in LA.

Why did that old phobia kick in then? She didn't know for sure. The letter, perhaps. It's ugly words pasted onto cheap lined paper, sitting in her hotel room.

The drain thing was just a stupid habit from the 90s, a kind of socially contagious fear. An urban myth of a superstition that no-one could actually explain or find a history for when pressed. *But why are all these teenagers in the suburbs lunging into the road to avoid triple drains? And why are double drains lucky? None of this makes any sense.* No, it didn't. It didn't make sense in the south of England and it certainly didn't make sense in the San Fernando Valley nearly twenty years later where there were far more frightening things near that studio than three manholes in a row.

But that was it. The final trigger. The Pavlovian bell that had her up on her tiptoes, walking carefully to the top of a landslide of panic attacks and weird rituals, hurling herself down it with furious determination. The more she tried to grasp control any way she could get it, the more slippery her life felt.

From avoiding triple drains, it was a hop, skip and a jump into washing her hands three times every toilet visit, carrying antiseptic wipes, sprays and alcohol hand rub (LA is amazing for germaphobes, she couldn't have been better placed). Soon she was obsessed with security in the hotel, checking the small balcony on her room repeatedly, pulling back the curtain to catch someone standing there, fully expecting to see eyes every time.

Where once the band's drummer, Steve, had only to give or receive one loaded look, the shared shorthand of the hungry and the wanting. Where he was used to being pulled inside her suite – always larger than his – and used willingly and secretly (he was only the drummer, after all), now he was left outside in the hall.

By the time the band arrived back in England, three-and-a-half-star album in the can, tour dates looming, Robin was a nightmare to be around. She was a nightmare to *be*. She barely scraped through a shortened rehearsal at the Manchester Apollo. Too busy trying to stop herself curling into a ball to notice the anger on the others' faces.

Steve avoided her eye, lest she mistake it for that hungry look. Alistair, the bassist and singer, talked to her mostly via text message or pushed notes on hotel paper under her door, with dissolving courtesy and an increase in passive-aggressive question marks.

Her days revolved around strict milestones of hand-washing, swallowing, lock-checking, nail-cutting and knee scratching. Red-raw all over, her fingertips throbbed constantly and she could barely hold a conversation because she'd be frantically scheduling the next hour, day, week and month in her head. Of course, Robin told none of this to her bandmates, manager, tour manager, driver, A&R contact, press officer or anyone else. What she did instead was nothing. She just stayed in her hotel room, doing all of this stuff, thinking all of these things. Or worse, sat with everyone else but contributed absolutely zero.

The band started the UK tour in Manchester.

In Manchester, it finally snapped.

Robin never managed to leave.

The morning of the first gig, Robin had gone to ground. She'd tried to get out of the show that night with minimal fuss, texting various people to say she'd lost her voice and had a high fever. A session musician would have to do.

A few minutes later, there was a knock on the room door. Before Robin had a chance to get up, Bev the tour manager was yelling. 'Bollocks, Robin, I'm not having any of this shit today.'

Robin had laid down on the floor, not replying.

'Enough of it, Robin. If you're well enough to text, you're well enough to play.'

Robin texted:

Told you, lost my voice so can't answer, please don't be so hostile.

'Fuck off, Robin, no-one expects you to open your mouth but you're part of a machine, we can't just lose a big chunk of the machine a few hours before you're all due on.'

Bev had paused. Probably weighing up whether to try to bash her way through the faux-mahogany door.

'Look, love, it's the first show, you're bound to feel a bit funny, but it's only the small room and it'll be a friendly crowd. Relax, yeah? You just have to try out some of the new stuff and play the faves. It's nothing to worry about, Robs.'

Robin hadn't replied. After decreasingly patient 'interventions' from pretty much everyone in the band and staff, a brief chorus of 'fuck you, then', 'bollocks to you, Robin' bubbled up and then, finally, the footsteps stomped away. Robin stood back up, still wearing an extremely thick hotel dressing gown and single serving slippers with the hotel crest on. She picked up the note on hotel paper, Alistair's handwriting:

When will you grow the fuck up, Robin?

She breathed in and out hard, that creeping gruesome feeling that she could never quite fill her lungs enough, and then lay carefully on the floor again, eyes wet and hot, and counted every bead on the cornice until she fell asleep.

It wasn't the first time everyone had been angry with her. But whereas she'd thrived on it, courted it and rolled it up into a big boulder as a kid, this anger crushed her. Sat on her chest, stole her voice. And now, over two years later, she sometimes had to say things out loud to herself just to check she still had a voice.

'Good morning, Mr Magpie.'

CHAPTER TEN

1991
SARAH

Dad's working on an old oak at a big house about an hour's drive away. It's a specialist job that keeps him out of the house more than I'd like. There's something unbalanced about our place when he's out of the house until late. Like there's a missing tent peg so the fabric flaps a bit and lets the wind and rain in. Mum's not the most patient person at the best of times, she always seems to be irritated by something. I find myself tiptoeing around even more so I don't get caught in the crossfire between her and Robin sniping at each other. But this time, she's quiet. She doesn't sigh dramatically and talk about all the things she could be doing with her life instead of standing there in front of us refereeing our squabbles. She doesn't chase Robin up the stairs, threatening to smack her legs for being cheeky. She doesn't complain when we ask what's for tea, every half an hour until teatime. She just says, 'Oh, um, not sure,' and things like that.

It's warm for spring. The heavy orange skies stretch out overhead, filled with the perfume of new grass. It's nosebleed weather and I've had three today already. There are bright splatters all over my gingham dress. I'm standing in the school office holding a soaked tissue under my nostrils and the school secretary is telling me to lift my head back.

'No.' The teacher with the first-aid certificate rushes over. 'Don't hold your head back like that, just keep it still like this. Here's a fresh tissue.'

'I was thinking of the carpet,' I hear Mrs Woolacombe – the secretary – grumble as she sits back down by her desk and takes a bite of her sandwich.

They've been trying to call Mum but there's no answer. I convince them that she'll be in the garden and just won't have heard the phone. The secretary looks at me, my dress and the carpet. 'If your mum's not there,' she says, 'you need to come straight back.'

I'm giddy from being out of school, the lunchtime sun on my arms. I feel alive with the rushing sounds of the adult world all around me as I run home, nose throbbing.

I get to our front door, freshly painted green by Dad, something Mum's been asking him to do for years. It's not locked, and I guess Mum's probably in the garden lying on a sun lounger with oiled legs and a Twix.

I close the door quietly, hoping to get to my room to change clothes before telling her about the blood on my dress. As I step towards the stairs, I hear a noise in the living room. It sounds like Mum's laughing, or maybe singing, but sort of faster than usual and not in tune. And then I hear another noise. It's like a grunting sound, like a dog might make while it snuffles around, smelling things in thick grass. I stand still, and catch a tiny drop of blood working itself loose from my nostril.

I touch the banister, thinking about making my way up, but I can't help myself and I have to look. I tell myself that I'm checking everything is okay. But I'm not, I'm curious and a bit frightened, and I just can't stop myself from pushing my eye up to the gap between the open door and the frame, and looking in. It's dark. I hadn't noticed the curtains had been tugged shut when I walked past the front of the house. There's no light on, just the orange glow of the outside framing the curtains.

Drew Granger is lying on the sofa and there is a fan of blonde hair spreading out under him. He's topless, pink-skinned, and his trousers are loose around his middle. I can't see most of my mum, just her hands and arms clasped tight around his back, and the new summer dress in a pile on the floor.

He's tall and broad, kind of barrel-shaped, but not fat. Just *big*. My dad is narrow, wiry. He says he's built like a monkey, which is good for climbing trees. Drew Granger is more like a gorilla: hairier, bigger, louder. Powerful.

I've never seen anything like this before. The only man I've ever seen naked was my dad, and only occasionally. When I needed a wee and he was in the bath, or the time the washing machine flooded the kitchen first thing one Saturday. Robin and I had started screaming and yelling, and Dad had appeared out of nowhere, stark naked, to turn off the water.

I don't like the size of Drew Granger. I don't like how he swamps my mum and I really don't like the fact that she seems to like it so very much. My poor, narrow monkey dad. I think of him shinning up the old oak, working so hard for us, and I feel tears welling.

I hurry back to the front door and out onto the little front garden. I rush out of our road and back through the village. I return to school still holding the wrinkled red tissue to my nose that I'd left with.

'No-one was in,' I say to Mrs Woolacombe without meeting her eye.

ROBIN

Something's up with Sarah but Robin doesn't know what. Seeing her sister distracted by something secret is disconcerting, and it chews at her thoughts more than Robin would have expected. Normally Sarah is a fountain of criticism and do-goodery but she's barely sniped at Robin for days and hasn't told on her all week. Instead, Robin notices that Sarah is spending more time in her room than usual and is obviously avoiding their mother. One curious effect of this, which Robin's not sure if she likes or not yet, is that her mum is spending more time with Robin.

So far this week, Robin has had a hair-cut – her mother agreeing for once that she could have it shorter than her shoulders – and even though there were some cross words in both directions, Robin was even invited to go to Safeway to do the weekly shopping. A treat disguised as a chore, the real bonus being able to choose a comic and some sweets at the till, while having the illusion of a say over dinners for the week ahead:

'Hot dogs, Mum?'

'Good idea, I'll do toad in the hole, Robin.'

Her dad's not quite himself either. He stares at the TV but doesn't laugh at the funny bits. He left some dinner uneaten earlier this evening and it was a mixed grill. That's his favourite. Even Sarah raised her eyebrows back at Robin as she noticed their father's half-finished plate on his tray. Her parents don't seem to be bickering either, it's like they're both holding their breath all the time. Normally Robin's mum would have stood over her dad demanding to know what was wrong with the pork chop, fried egg and sausage that had been so uncharacteristically ignored. But she didn't seem to notice.

As her dad moved his leftovers around the plate with his fork, resting his cheek on his free hand, Robin asked what the plans were for the weekend. She was hoping for a beer garden where she, Sarah and Callum could run wild, and not the worst-case scenario – a craft fair, which her mum had started to like.

'I'm not sure yet, Robin,' her mum had said, and Robin and Sarah both noticed that their dad had stopped pushing his food around and was looking at his wife. He didn't look surprised, exactly, but there was something odd about it.

Now Sarah is in her room again, having an early night. The idea appals Robin, who would rather chain herself to the sofa with her eyelids prised open than willingly go to bed. The doorbell chimes and the three remaining Marshalls look at each other. Eventually her mum sighs one of her dramatic world's-end sighs and heaves herself off the sofa to go to open the door.

'Hiya,' Robin hears her mum say. 'You want to come in?'

There's the tell-tale mwah-mwah of stage kisses, but without the effort or humour they used to carry. Just air now.

'Hi, Jack,' Hilary's soft voice reminded Robin of women from coffee adverts.

'Alright, love,' her dad replies, flicking his eyes at Hilary briefly and smiling, then looking back at the screen.

The two women go into the kitchen to talk. Their blue-grey cigarette smoke seeps under the closed door, and the sound of the kettle springs on and off for the next couple of hours. It worked out very well for Robin, as her dad generally didn't remember to put her to bed if she kept quiet enough.

Hilary is about to leave now but she comes into the living room and quietly asks Robin's dad if their plan to go to the garden centre at the weekend was still on. Robin's ears prick up, practically standing on end when she hears her dad confirm that, yes, that's still a definite plan, when just a few hours ago her question about the weekend had been brushed away.

'Perhaps we could all get lunch afterwards,' Hilary adds, looking at Robin.

'P'raps,' says her dad.

No mwah-mwahs at all as she leaves.

Robin's dad suddenly notices the small child curling into the corner of the sofa, watching TV that she didn't understand. 'Come on then, squirt, off to bed,' he says, seeming to come to life for the first time that day.

That weekend, they didn't have lunch together. Callum came round to the Marshalls' house and he, Robin and Sarah stayed inside watching *The Chart Show* and *Carry on Camping* while her mum went window shopping and their dad went to a garden centre with Hilary. And her parents had still not bickered by then. Something was up.

CHAPTER ELEVEN

Present day

SARAH

6. Too much control

What does that even mean? As he'd said it, I noticed that Jim's mother was nodding slightly. I doubt she even knew that she was moving her head, but it told a story. I'd always had self-control. It had often disappointed me that it was the women who'd looked down at that.

My appetites, my inclinations.

After slipping just once, I'd cultivated that control and was proud that it had seen me through. Perhaps he had meant too much control over Violet. Who can control a three-year-old to excess? They're the Wild West of children. No longer babies, no longer easy to pen in a cot or highchair but too young to reason with. Besides, Violet is a good girl, she doesn't need control. Our boy, my boy, he'd be the little rascal. The one beyond my control.

I had always said I wanted two children. I hoped for a girl and then a boy. Jim had always wanted two children as well. He said he didn't mind if they'd been boys or girls. I said I didn't mind too.

There was a lot I had to learn in preparation for a relationship with Jim. A lot I had to unlearn.

I tried to be attentive but it was hard to know what that normally looked like. I hadn't had the best examples.

Jim liked to eat with Violet as soon as he got in from work. He liked to do her bathtimes and bedtimes – the evening shift, he called it. He liked to strip out of his work things, shower the day off, and get into his joggers and T-shirt ready for dinner. His at-home uniform. He didn't really like my cooking as much as he'd politely suggested in the beginning and started making more and more requests, remarks. It was hard to keep up. I often made mistakes. Not just with the food.

I still get it wrong, even now. The more I tried to fix things after the list was read out, the worse I made it. Eventually I had to stop and regroup. Refocus. At first, I just span my wheels and sprayed mud all over myself.

It's been four days since the list was read out.

The first night away from my home had been sleepless and bewildering. I wasn't in the bed I'd woken up in that morning, nothing smelled the same. The following day, I didn't need to get up at the sound of Violet's call. I had no use.

The pull to her was as strong as ever though. I stayed away most of the day, trying to do as I'd been told. But I couldn't. I'd shown up at my home with a teddy bear for Violet. The lights were off, the house was empty. My key no longer worked. The sheer speed of this project chilled me. The taxi had started rolling back out of the close we'd lived in but luckily the driver saw me running after him. It was obvious where they'd be. I wondered how long it had been planned and when Violet's Trunki suitcase must have been packed behind my back. While I was washing and folding her clothes, was Jim squirrelling them away? I tried not to think about it, tried to swallow away the burning rage in my chest. I even asked the taxi driver to swing into the petrol station so I could buy flowers for Jim's mother. Habit.

When we pulled up at Jim's parents' home, Jim's car was on the drive. Had he booked the day off work in advance or called in that morning? The logistical questions made my head swim. I'd asked the driver to wait this time, knocked on the door more sharply than I'd intended. When Jim's mother answered the door, I could hear my girl's laughter bursting out of another room. I handed Jim's mother the flowers and asked to come in. She'd stared at me, this woman who had once told me how grateful she was for my care of Jim. Of Violet. Now she stared like I'd asked to see her kidneys.

'Please?' I'd said again, my voice cracking.

Violet's laughter had stopped, and she'd called my name and come running to the door. She was wearing a new pink dress, her wavy golden hair bouncing as she ran towards me, her eyes ablaze. I'd managed to grab at her to hug her just as Jim skidded into the hall behind her and whipped her away.

'No!' I'd called. 'Please!'

'You need to leave, Sarah,' his mum had said, looking down at both our feet.

'But you said you wouldn't keep her from me.'

'We said you needed to get help and then perhaps...' she'd started, raising her face to look at mine just briefly. Tears rolled hot. I didn't have the words so I balled up my fists, crushing the flowers I'd bought so bits of them tumbled onto the mat.

'You need to go, Sarah. If you don't...' She'd taken a deep breath and whispered, 'We'll need to get the police involved and I'm sure you don't want that.'

'I just want Violet. I've not done anything wrong,' I'd cried, louder than I'd hoped.

'If you think you've done nothing wrong,' Jim's mother had said, suddenly matching my volume, 'you're madder than we thought.'

The taxi driver had dropped the chit-chat and driven me back to the B&B in silence. I'd leaned my head against the car window so my jaw vibrated with the engine and the tears traced zig-zags on my face.

I tried again yesterday. Jim and his parents watched from the window as I hammered on the door until it bounced in the lock. When I tried again today, Jim had come outside, grabbed my arm and marched me back to the taxi like an unruly drunk.

I went to the bank before I could talk myself out of it, drained his account with the card he'd given me for shopping, took out the small sum that I'd saved in my own account, packed all the money into my holdall and caught the bus to Guildford.

I stepped down from the bus at the train station, went inside with my holdall.

The man behind the counter smiled at me, and it was the first smile I'd received in a while. Through streaming eyes and a breaking voice I said, 'I need a one-way ticket to Manchester.'

ROBIN

Robin was four thousand steps into her pacing when she stopped by the curtain in the top bedroom. She's still standing there, on pause. There have been no knocks today, and somehow the anticipation is worse than the reality. Will it be more aggressive today? Will the knocks rain down for longer? Will whoever is knocking appear at the back door instead? Will they wait until after dark and climb up onto the roof of the kitchen, tease the window of the spare bedroom open with gloved fingers, drop silently to the floor like a cat and stalk around her house while she sleeps?

She couldn't sleep last night. Lay awake until the early hours, battling to keep the thoughts of the past out, failing to keep the fears of the present in check. In the end, she pulled herself off the bed and, rather than climbing under it, headed to the 'gym' bedroom to tire herself out with kettle bell squats and miles on the static bike.

It had worked, of sorts. After cycling nowhere for fifteen miles, she'd made it to two hundred and eighty squats, pausing briefly every twenty, closing her eyes for the last two sets. It was an equal number at least, round and smooth. She'd shuffled back out of the spare room-cum-gym, into a hot shower and then up the second set of stairs and into the top bedroom. There she'd given up any pretence of a normal night, wrapped the duvet around herself and crawled under the bed.

Now afternoon, her knees are still aching and her sore leg muscles feel hard and inflexible. Robin leans at the window, resting one hand on the sill to stare out the back of her house. She sees that the Magpies are both at home but no sign of their little boy. It's unusual for both the Magpies to be home before teatime. Just the briefest of glance at their body language, the way they're circling each other, shows that everything is wrong.

She looks away, scans up to the student woman but her flat is abandoned, an empty cereal bowl still on the table from the night before. No sign of the old people, Mr and Mrs Peacock, but the young guy Robin had watched moving in recently is leaning against the garden wall smoking. He stubs it out on the wall, drops the butt and walks slowly back inside.

Robin flicks her eyes back to the dead centre and watches the Magpies. They're still circling each other just behind the window, pieces of paper and small items being tossed about. Mrs Peacock has now been shaken loose, perhaps from the shouting that doesn't reach the distance to Robin. The old lady is standing outside her flat, broom in her hand motionless, head craned.

It's nothing new. But it's probably entertaining enough for a bored pensioner. Robin's in no position to judge. She tells herself that she's acting as a kind of custodian, watching over the lives opposite. But whenever she examines that claim for long, it falls apart. If she was really just a caring witness, she'd spend more time worrying about the young mum looking after the baby by herself, pacing at night with it red-faced and screaming. She'd worry about the old people, the elderly woman caring for herself and her husband, who is looking increasingly frail and keeps wandering out of the flats, only for Mrs Peacock to round him up at the last minute and coax him back inside.

No, Robin's interest is not solely benevolent. Mr and Mrs Magpie were an important part of her coping strategy. They were true North. They were good and wholesome, a reminder of what normal families look like. She doesn't want to see them as Henry and Karen Watkins, another screwed-up couple. It's knocked Robin's whole system out of whack confronting the idea that maybe every single family is as fucked-up as the next.

CHAPTER TWELVE

1991

SARAH

Ever since I saw Mum and Drew on the sofa, I've been seeing the ghost of that image everywhere I look. The new clothes Mum is wearing, the looks Drew gives her in those clothes, the way Hilary is wearing less make-up, like she cares less, the miles-away look on Dad's face. A look that says maybe he knows. The two families still meet up but there's a strange feeling, like we're on the edge of a cloud but the rain never falls. One mean word and everyone might start barking like dogs.

I can't help but think back to that weird night when Robin got sick from eating too much, when Mum and Drew were smooshed together in the kitchen and Dad was asleep on the sofa. I know that when adults drink they get cuddly but it's all sticking together in my head and I don't like it.

Callum is being odd too. He's been quiet and a bit nervous ever since we met him but now it's on overdrive. You say hello to him and he jumps. He looks on the brink of tears if an adult uses a loud voice near him. In class the other day, he ran out after Mrs Howard yelled at some of the boys for doing something disgusting. He wasn't even sitting near those boys but, if I didn't know better, I'd have thought he'd wet himself.

When we did PE, I noticed he had these yellow and green bruises all up his legs and arms. Any other boy and I'd have thought it was from rough and tumble, or football.

We went to the Grangers' house last weekend and stayed as usual. Normally we get to sit at the table and have dinner with the adults. Even though I don't really understand the jokes and especially don't understand it when talk turns to Drew Granger's work or money or politics, I enjoy being near all that chatter. It's like I can feel the edge of another stage, the one just out of the corner of my eye. Teenage years, adult life. I like to think that one day I'll cook cordon bleu food and have a table-top plate warmer and a husband who has a job that people don't understand.

It was different last weekend though. We didn't eat together – us kids were given our dinner first. It was paella, which Robin had picked at suspiciously, dragging the alien prawns to the side of her plate and lining them up like murder victims. We were even allowed to take popcorn upstairs – normally we have to sneak it up like burglars. Drew had called Callum over to him first, whispered some rapid rules into his ear while holding onto the back of his neck in a way that made Callum wince. Out of concern for Callum, we ate that popcorn more carefully and slowly than any children in the history of time.

We watched *Labyrinth* and I tried to sing along to all the songs like Callum and Robin did, but I could never remember all the words. When the film ended, my hurt pride made me snappy and Callum went pink trying to referee me and my sister and keep us quiet enough that none of the adults would come up. By which I think he really meant his dad. I don't know what that's all about. His dad is definitely more demanding and – in Robin's words – stuck-up than my dad but he's always friendly to me. I don't think there's anything wrong with rules or with trying to keep nice things in good condition. (And they have a lot of nice things.) But that's not a popular opinion so I keep it to myself. Besides, I don't exactly think Drew's a great man, certainly not a great husband, not after what he did with my mum.

I still can't shake the picture of that day when I had all those nosebleeds a couple of months ago. I've never even caught my mum and dad doing that. It's not like I'd want to see that, but at least it would be normal. Other kids at school have heard their mums and dads, and one boy even saw them 'doing it' in the bath ('They looked like sea monsters') when they thought he was out playing, but no-one has ever mentioned seeing their mum with someone else's dad. I don't risk saying anything to anyone.

Tomorrow is Saturday and the Grangers are coming to our house to stay. I don't really know why because our house is smaller and it means all of us kids have to stay in Robin's room while Drew and Hilary will sleep in a single bed in my room. It's funny because Mum didn't seem that sure it was a good idea either, but it was Dad arguing that it would make a nice change and then flattering her about her cooking.

'You just want to be able to go out in the garden with bloody Hilary,' Mum said later as she appeared in the doorway, hair all scratched up into a bun and Marigolds on her hands. She's paranoid about the state of the house.

'Give over,' said Dad and he seemed cheerful, but then Mum gave him a sharp look like she was about to argue and Dad stopped smiling and stared at her until she left again muttering: 'I hope it's nice enough for Queen Hilary.'

It's Saturday night now and we're in Robin's room. Under her bed is a pit of broken toys and dusty, abandoned bits of paper. I feel bad for Callum, who is on the floor next to the jumble, lying in a sleeping bag and coughing. We're talking about the school holiday and how we'll spend the summer. Robin thinks we'll go down to Dorset but something tells me we won't. Granddad died last year and I think we'd be too much for Nana on her own, but who knows. Dad had cried so much when his dad died that I thought he'd throw up. I was embarrassed for him and sad like a deep well had opened up in my chest and I had to drag something heavy over it as quickly as possible so the rest of me didn't fall in.

Callum says that they always go abroad in the holidays. That his dad doesn't consider it a proper holiday if it's not over eighty degrees and a plane ride away. He says it's strange that his mum and dad haven't mentioned going away; they usually book something for the next summer straight after they get back from a holiday. Robin says he should ask his dad where they're going on holiday, or at least ask why they're not going, and Callum looks at her like that's the most bizarre suggestion he's ever heard.

'You don't ask my dad anything,' he said after a moment, 'you just wait for him to tell you what to do and you make sure you do it.'

It's Sunday morning now and we're sitting up in bed playing Boggle. Robin's furious because I'm beating her, even though she never tries hard with her spellings at school so of course I'm going to do better. We're doing best of three, but she's changed it to best of five and if this carries on then the winner (i.e. me) is never going to get to play Callum. It's supposed to be a tournament but it's turning into a tantrum.

The smell of bacon and toast has taken over the whole house and I suggest we call it a draw so we can go and eat something, and Robin, who is definitely not really drawing, says, 'Hmm, okay, but you know I would have won.' I see Callum turn away, smiling.

ROBIN

Say what you will about my mum, thinks Robin, *but she can cook a breakfast*. Her mum may not do all that poncey food like at Hilary and Drew's house, but her bacon and eggs are legendary.

When Drew Granger compliments her on the full English she's placed in front of him, she giggles and compliments him on his taste in return. Her dad pauses for just a moment but says nothing. If he was going to compliment her mum, it would look too staged now. Drew beat him to the punch. Robin wonders if her dad is just so used to these fry-ups that he forgets they're remarkable. He's been eating them for a lot of years now. Robin puts her knife and fork down to count on her fingers, one, two, three ... 'Twelve years!' she exclaims, spraying chewed-up baked beans and egg onto the table in front of her.

'Robin!' her mum shouts, and she looks more tearful and embarrassed than angry.

'Come on, squirt, you know how to eat nicely,' her dad says.

Robin decides she's on to a losing thing and apologises, wiping the food away with her jumper sleeve as the corners of Drew Granger's mouth tip downwards and Callum goes red.

'I was just working out that you and Dad have been together for twelve years,' she adds, looking at her parents and expecting some kind of ripple of warmth. Parents normally love being told that something they've done is extraordinary. Twelve years of going to sleep with the same person in your room, spending every night and every weekend with someone and staying friends, that *is* extraordinary. Sarah and Robin fall out after one night of top and tailing, and even Callum has snapped at them both in close quarters before. But none of the adults seem to like what she's said so she tries something different because nobody is talking any more and it makes her feel weird.

'How long have you two been together?' she asks Hilary but it's Drew who answers with a joke. 'Too bloody long!' Hilary and Robin's dad make a couple of polite 'hmph hmph' noises but her mum throws her head back and laughs. She laughs so loudly it's more like she's shouting 'HA HA' in a speech bubble like a character in a book. The kids wolf their food down after this and, after Callum asks for permission from his dad, they slide off their chairs and bound upstairs.

After Callum is shouted down and the Grangers leave, her dad asks Robin if she wants to come into the garage to help him with something. She runs down and out of the back door so fast she skids a bit and grazes her knee on a bit of gravel. She doesn't even slightly cry, and hopes her dad notices how brave and hardy she is, but he's doing that far-away look again. Just as they're about to go into the garage, he grabs her hand and says, 'Be quiet, squirt. Look over there, there's a couple of fledglings.' Robin squints to see two brown shapes bobbing about on the lawn and a larger bird watching them from a tall branch. 'Starlings,' her dad says, but she knew that anyway. 'Poor old mum bird,' he adds.

Inside the garage, he starts to take off the legs of a chair that used to sit with the others in the kitchen. It got scuffed over the years – they all did – so, one-by-one, he's sanding all the bits of each chair and polishing them again. The dust smells like Christmas, all woody and sweet, and Robin can't help but feel calmer in the semi-dark room with her favourite parent. They work silently, Robin rubbing her chair parts diligently with sandpaper wrapped around a block of wood. She hears her dad open his mouth a few times, his dry, dusty lips audibly parting, but every time she looks up expectantly, he closes them.

Eventually they're called in for sandwiches. While her dad packs away the tools in their special cases and canvas pouches, he says, without looking up, 'I know you think Mum's on your case a lot, but it's just because she loves you and wants you to be the best that you can be.'

'She's never on Sarah's case.' Robin is surprised to hear herself say in a choked voice.

'Yeah but your mum and Sarah are peas in a pod, aren't they, girl. And you and me are alike. So you're always going to butt heads with Mum. Doesn't mean she doesn't love you, it just means that, y'know, it's a bit easier for her with Sarah and it's easier for me with you. But you're a good girl in your own way, Robin,' he says, looking at a deep cut on his hands. 'So remember that.'

It's nearly the end of term and school rules have gone out the window. The whole school piled into the hall on Friday afternoon, filing into neat lines and sitting cross-legged like matches in a box. The headteacher played them an old Disney film through a projector, and even though they could barely hear anything, the excitement crackled over the hall like electricity running through wires.

That night the girls slept over at Callum's again and the adults plain forgot about the rules there too. At night they ate pizza out of the box, collected from the takeaway by one of the dads. They watched films in Callum's room until they fell asleep, no-one knocking on the door with a five-minute warning, no kisses goodnight from the mums.

The next day, the adults huddled around a special filter coffee machine in the kitchen where they talked in low, hungover voices. The unattended kids were allowed to drag all the spare bedding onto the lounge floor and hide in the blanket fort they made, eye holes focused on the TV. Callum let Sarah choose the film, much to Robin's disgust. Thankfully she chose *The NeverEnding Story* and not something lovey-dovey.

Robin had never thought about it before but Callum seemed to take a lot of pleasure in making sure everyone was okay, in offering to give other people their way. He let the girls slide backwards into the fort first, waited as they settled into their chosen spaces before straightening the blanket carefully and wedging himself in however he could.

He always offered to fetch them drinks. He listened patiently to their fights and, without taking sides, offered a suggestion that always seemed to flatter both their interests. Often not his own though. At first, Robin thought he was a kiss-ass. Sucking up to Sarah and showing off to the adults, but she noticed he was like this more when it was just the three of them, and if he was ever thanked for anything – like just now – he'd glow pink and change the subject.

'There's something going on in there,' he said, gesturing to the kitchen and lowering his voice. 'My dad was yelling at my mum the other day and my mum was crying and saying Dad had done something wrong and she *never* says that, even when he ... well, anyway. I heard your mum and dad's names too—'

'What?' the girls both asked, a shot of excitement and fear sparking between them. Adults falling out with each other was a riskier, more raw thing than when kids feud. Both girls were moths to the flame whenever it happened. They had to be dragged away from gawping at drunks scrapping outside pubs, they automatically walked towards teenage lovers in the midst of world's-end showdowns, they rubbernecked car crashes on the motorway, hands pressed to the window and sliding to whichever side was nearest.

Before Callum could stop them, they'd scrambled free from the bedding and had headed to listen at the kitchen door. If Callum had only brought this up to stop them from thanking him for his kindness, it had backfired.

'You two are fucking mad,' their dad was saying, his voice that weird whispered shout that only parents can do.

'Jack,' their mum said, 'keep your voice down, you're shouting.'

'I'm not fucking shouting. You don't know what shouting is. And what the fuck has that got to do with anything? After what you've just said, you've got a nerve telling me how to bloody react.'

'Now, Jack,' Drew started.

'Don't.' Their dad's response was as swift and sharp as a thrown knife.

'Jack,' the girls could barely make out Hilary's voice. 'I need some air. Do you want to come into the garden with me?'

A scrape of chairs, no words. The back door closed again, a swelling silence. The girls held their breath, looked at Callum, who was jiggling nervously behind them.

'My head's banging,' they heard their mum say finally.

'Mmm,' grunted Drew. 'Well, you were three sheets to the wind last night, eh?'

A subtle laugh, a sigh.

'Are we doing the right thing?' they heard their mother ask, in the voice she uses when red reminder bills fall through the letter box.

'Don't wimp out on me now,' Drew said with an edge. 'Look at them out there. Those fucking roses.'

This obviously meant something to both of them as they laughed and then sighed. Now more silence.

'This is boring,' Robin said, an unease in her tummy that she wanted to crush. 'I'm going to fix the fort.'

With relief, the other two followed her and worked quietly and diligently until it was all neat again.

CHAPTER THIRTEEN

Present day

SARAH

7. The Blood

I've arrived in Manchester, the city my twin heart beats in. I've never been here before, never had a reason to, but as soon as I found out Robin lived here, my mental map widened and the pin beckoned me. It's taken months for me to shake myself onto a train and it's taken this horrible separation from Violet to give me a reason, but I'm here. And for a rainy city, it feels like I'm bathed in a pool of light. Hope, I suppose.

But there's a lot to do now. For a start, I don't know exactly where my sister lives. Secondly, she isn't expecting me and I don't know if she'll be happy to see me. The last time we met she was hurt and confused, and I was hurt and confused, and we span away like two positive charges, the way we often did.

It's been a long journey, and I feel the brain fog that comes from ending the day in a different place to where you started the day. The first train from Godalming to London was half-empty. I spent the first ten minutes rocking up and down the aisle, carefully choosing a seat. But the bullet-shaped train from London to Manchester was packed. A queue two people deep shuffled its feet outside the chemical toilet at any one time.

I've never been north of London before. As kids, the furthest we'd go was to stay with my dad's parents – Nanny Mary and Granddad Joe – in Dorset, where they'd retired.

We'd drive down in the old Rover, sick as dogs despite the Joyriders tablets. Nanny Mary would wrap us up in tight hugs as soon as we'd arrive, making us sickly drinks with the SodaStream and wiping her eyes about how tall Robin and I had got, even though Robin never got tall in her life.

On those Dorset days, we'd skim stones and eat chips that tasted totally different to Berkshire chips, and Dad would say it was because of the ozone. Robin's hair would go so curly in the sea air that she'd look like a lollipop and she'd always get the burps. I loved the seaside. I loved the salt stains on my shins from paddling in the sea, loved collecting pretty little shells and pebbles, arranging them on my bedroom window sill when we got home or filling little bottles with them. My favourite gems to find were tiny pieces of glass that had been buffed into hearts or diamonds by the waves.

My first holiday with Jim and Violet was also to Dorset. To a little village near Charmouth, with a thatched pub and an ice cream hut on the beach that was only open four afternoons a week. It wasn't a deliberate nod to my childhood, of course; we'd just found a good deal online for a holiday flat and it was only a few hours' drive from our house if we left after rush hour. We looked forward to it for weeks, imagining ourselves paddling and walking on the sand with a newly toddling Violet. I bought a lemon sundress for me and a matching one for Violet. I wrestled her into hers the weekend before we left to check it fitted; I still have the picture I took of wearing it. I can't look at it now.

Throughout the evening before we left, Violet developed a summer cold. By the end of our sticky car journey the next day she was a pulsating red orb of snot and tears. The holiday was a long week of having to deal with a sick toddler in a flat without our stuff and nowhere near a pharmacy. A week we spent looking forward to being back home, with Calpol, and nostalgic about the sea.

We only really went out on the last day. Jim insisted on visiting the thatched pub nearby and drinking a pint of ale in the sunny beer garden. I didn't want to go but couldn't begin to tell him why. Who doesn't like beer gardens? Probably only my sister and I. And I couldn't tell him that either. I sat on the bench seat nursing my orange juice and distributing Fruit Shoots to a still-peaky Violet.

But anyway, the blood. Like so many stories, this one starts with my mum.

When we were little, she always had music on, pop music or golden oldies. I can't help but think that helped Robin's eventual career but I'd never dare say that.

In summer, Mum would carefully unfold a stripy sun lounger from the shed, like a safe cracker, angling it just so. She'd drag the kitchen radio out through the window, lead dangling, and rest it on the white picnic table. She'd turn it up loud and lie with her skirt hitched, oiled legs gleaming. When she'd finished reading her magazine, drinking Typhoo tea or 7-Up, she'd spring up and grab whichever one of us was near enough, put us on her hip and dance.

Robin would kick to get down but I would wave my arms, shake my hair, giggle. I loved those moments. She was the best fun in the world in those moments, our blonde hair mingling together, our laughter colliding. I'd just wanted Violet to feel like that about me, that was all.

So one day, I found a music channel playing old songs from the 80s, the kind I'd danced to several decades before. I'd got up from the sofa and started dancing, waving at Violet who was looking at me quizzically. When Kim Wilde came on, 'Kids in America', I sprang over and plucked her from her playmat where she'd been arranging her teddies and dolls. She gave in to it, started to laugh. We jumped sideways and up and down. She copied my exaggerated moves. I copied hers.

Her dimples were so deep and her smile so big that her whole face changed shape as I gazed into it, laughing and kissing her nose. That little nose. We swung each other around and around. As the song changed to Glenn Medeiros's one-hit wonder 'Nothing's Gonna Change My Love For You', I put her little feet on my feet and took big sways, which she found hilarious. She'd thrown her head back laughing, her shiny hair – getting so long – had swished from side to side.

At the peak of our fun, her face smacked into the door. She didn't knock into the wood hard but she'd caught the edge and split her lip. A thin red line of blood pointed from the door to the television like an accusation while the music blared on and surged into adverts.

She barely cried as I hugged her and cleaned her up but I bawled.

I cried because she might have ended up with a tiny scar; little lips are so fragile. I cried because Jim would be upset and we would probably have a clipped exchange of cross words, and that always unnerved me. But mostly I cried because we had been having so much fun. And I'd felt so free.

To my surprise, we hadn't had cross words when Jim came home. That evening he'd scooped her up to brush her teeth, noticed Violet's lip and asked me the story. After listening, stroking her hair while I told the story, he'd gone off to do bedtime. I'd heard him ask her to tell the story again as they disappeared up the stairs. 'We were dancing, Daddy. It was funny...'

A little later, Jim had come back downstairs. 'Nice bedtime,' he'd said. Then he'd put the television on and got some papers out for work.

And a few months later, there it was on the list. He hadn't believed my version of events – or hers. Number seven:

The blood.

ROBIN

The Magpies had been fighting a lot recently. It seemed worse at weekends, their house turning into a pressure cooker. The little boy seemed to know when to clear out of the way – just as Robin and her sister had as kids – but the flare-ups were getting more frequent.

Perhaps, Robin had thought, Mr Magpie needs a little help to see what's going on under his nose. To shake his cheating wife loose so he could get on with parenting his kid. Right now, they were feuding in a directionless, painful circle. Far better to cut it at the root, cleanly. The longer it goes on, the less healthy everyone becomes, as Robin knows all too well. The last time she tried to steer the course away from disaster, it had been ham-fisted and messy. This time would be precise.

She'd ordered a gift to arrive when she knew they would both be home. Something for Mrs Magpie, to encourage Mr Magpie to ask some tricky questions. Underwear, something sexy but classy. Something that said 'hotels and anticipation' rather than thanks for the random bunk-up. She'd dredged her memory for moments of desire, of being desired, and for the gift message she had chosen:

The thought of your body in this drives me crazy. x

The email had just come through to the dummy address, the parcel had been signed for. Now Robin watches from behind the curtain as the parcel is opened in the kitchen and the fight begins.

Robin sips her tea and wishes she could hear what was happening. She can see the little boy covering his ears in his bedroom, feels a pang of guilt.

But it hasn't worked. There's still an edge, Mr Magpie hangs back away from his wife and accepts an awkward hug only briefly, but she's still there. They're still together. The champagne-coloured silks have been put back in the box, bundled up. Robin knows without even checking that her card will be refunded in a few weeks, the box returned under the guise that it must have been intended for someone else.

Maybe he hadn't asked the right questions or jumped to the right conclusions. Maybe he'd chosen to accept a flimsy lie over the painful truth. Either way, she'd got away with it again. The lies were deepening and Robin hadn't saved them from the inevitable. Poor Mr Magpie, it would only get worse.

CHAPTER FOURTEEN

1991

SARAH

After a few long weeks of not doing much, we finally get to meet up with Callum and his family. It's halfway through the summer holidays, and Robin and I have been kicking about at the park or riding our bikes around the woods that curl around the back of our village. There's a rumour that a farmer lives in the middle of the woods and he once mistook a child on a bike for a dog coming to eat his hens, and that he shot the child dead. I used to be terrified of this until Robin pointed out that no-one telling the story ever knew the kid's name, which was very suspicious and, anyway, if a farmer had done that, he'd be in prison right now.

Every time we go to the village playground I hope we'll see Callum there, but we never do so we don't get to play our intricate three-person games and have to make do with stunted versions. Sometimes, other kids from school come and we all squint into each other's faces and bark out instructions for games or compete to see who can jump off the swing when it's going the highest. It's always Robin; I don't know why anyone ever bothers going against her.

But today, we're finally doing something different. It's a Friday, which is weird, but Dad is home and he and Mum have been locked in their room all morning. When they come out, Mum is wearing one of her good dresses but she looks like she's been crying. And, actually, Dad looks like he has been too. They squeeze each other's hands, just a tiny squeeze when they don't think I'm looking, and then we get into the car to drive to a beer garden in a nearby village.

We arrive and park up at the other side of the car park to the Grangers' BMW, even though there are spaces nearby. We go through the wooden fence and into the garden and I see that Callum is dressed in a shirt and jeans and has gel in his hair. He has a coke and he's taken the straw out and laid it next to his glass.

He looks at Robin, tries to catch her eye but she's too busy nagging Dad for a coke and a bag of crisps to pay attention. He looks at me and, for a moment, we share a look that makes my tummy feel funny. I want to ask, 'What? What is it?' But he bites his lip, sees his dad watching him and shrinks back down.

My mum and dad stand awkwardly at the table while me and Robin clamber over the bench seat and wedge in next to Callum.

This means that Mum and Dad have to perch either side of us, so, without saying a word, there's a big reshuffle among the adults and it ends up that Mum and Drew are sitting opposite us and Dad and Hilary have wedged in at either side of us kids.

'Are you okay?' I ask Callum. 'You look a bit weird.'

He looks at his dad again. 'I'm fine,' he says. 'Oh, I brought you both these.' He opens up the kitchen paper I'd not noticed on the table in front of him and points to a collection of little baby strawberries, their delicate juice turning the paper pink. 'I grew them at home, with Mum.' He shares them out carefully; he's learned that perceived injustice is at the root of almost all sibling fights so he takes pains to give the same number of fruits, of approximately the same size, to each of us. Robin scoffs hers in one go but I eat them slowly, try to show how much I appreciate it.

A big fuss is made of going to buy drinks, with both the dads staring each other down. Eventually Drew Granger stops insisting and just walks inside, and my dad follows after him. I notice that the mums aren't talking to each other, when usually they're talking at the same time. Instead, Hilary asks me about my dress – it's a cream embroidered one that I love and am almost too big for – and, noticing that Robin is in jeans and a T-shirt with a dinosaur on it, asks if she likes dinosaurs. Robin looks at her like it's a ridiculous question. 'Everyone likes dinosaurs,' she says. Now it's Mum's turn; she compliments Callum on his smart hairstyle and he goes so pink he glows. When the dads come back with two trays, we're all relieved.

'Who wants to start?' says Mum. We all look at her. Dad looks away first and studies his hands so Drew Granger half stands up like he's a teacher but then sits back down. 'I'll do it,' he says.

All of us kids take a drink of our pop. I've taken my straw out like Callum, but when I see how much the line of Robin's drink zooms down when she sucks, I reconsider and dunk my straw back. Still we wait.

'So,' Drew Granger says, and it sounds like he's going to run some kind of meeting. 'We all have some news.'

I notice that Hilary is shaking a little and she reaches for Callum's hand. I've seen them do this before, especially when Drew speaks. I notice that our usually laidback dad is fidgeting and irritable. He picks at a knot in the wooden table, shuffles his feet around so his cord trousers make a swishing sound. He doesn't stop, even when Mum gives him a look. If anything, the swishing grows louder.

'We've all been friends for some time,' Drew says, 'and we've got to know each other very well. And sometimes, when people become friends, they get to know each so well that they realise that, actually, they should spend more time together.'

This is strange to me, because we've spent far less time together in the last few weeks but the memory of Mum and Drew on the sofa makes my stomach churn. I don't know what he's going to say but I don't like where it's headed. Robin is clueless; she slurps the last of her coke and burps.

'Is this about you and Mum snogging?' Robin asks and everyone gasps.

'What?' Dad shouts.

'In the kitchen, when I had a bad tummy,' Robin says, chasing ice cubes around with her straw. The adults all look at each other, Dad looks like he's going to pop.

'Are you fucking kidding me?' Dad shouts, and he stands up now. 'You did that in front of our kids?' He points his finger at Mum and I notice Drew puts his arm around her briefly before he stands up and faces my dad eye to eye.

'Calm down, Jack,' Drew says. Callum grasps his mum's arm and she puts her hand over his.

'It's too late to rake over the details,' Mum says. 'Please calm down, Jack.'

'Calm down?' My dad's eyes suddenly get wet and it's like he's taken by surprise because he sits down heavily and just stares at Mum.

'Yes it is, Robin,' Hilary finally says in her creamy advert voice. 'It is about that. Your mum and Drew realised that they liked each other quite a bit and that they had a lot in common.' She took a deep breath, looked at Dad just briefly. 'So, *eventually*, they told me and your dad about it. And we were very shocked.' Hilary looks down.

'We were fucking fuming,' Dad hisses, looking Drew Granger in the eye and then turning to Mum. 'And we were very pissed off that they'd been running around behind our backs.'

Hilary reaches across all of us to tap Dad on the hands and he stops jiggling his leg and looks down again, his eyes even wetter than before.

'Well,' Hilary says, her own tears starting to slide through her make-up. 'We all talked about it. And that was very tough. We weren't sure what to do for the best. And Jack and I started to spend a bit more time together while we were working out what we could do.'

I start to feel sick. Robin has stopped moving the straw around and is glaring at Mum. Callum has just wiped his eyes on his shirt and now does it again. I feel my heart get quicker until I can hear it banging.

'You can't help who you fall in love with!' Mum exclaims dramatically and we all look at her.

'No,' Drew Granger says in a bellicose grunt aimed at Dad. 'You can't, Angela.'

'We talked about what should happen and how to make it work best,' Hilary continued, ignoring them. 'And the more Jack and I spent time together, we stopped talking about how angry and sad we were, and we started to realise that we liked each other too. We have lots in common, like the love of gardening and things...' I see my mum roll her eyes just slightly and I think, *No, you don't have the right*, but I squash the thought down.

'How long has this been going on?' Robin asks. 'All this falling out of love and falling for each other stuff?' Her eyes are black and narrow, and she's staring at our mother like she could leap across the table and bite her.

'That's not what's important,' Drew Granger says.

'No, course not,' Dad says spikily, but when Drew opens his mouth to say something, Mum must have done something under the table as he looks at her suddenly, and then flashes her a quick smile.

'The thing is,' Mum says, 'there's been a lot to consider. But we've decided that we can't carry on as we are and that Drew and I want to be together.' I look at Robin and Callum, aghast; their pale faces stare back at me. 'And Dad and Hilary have decided that they would like to see if they can be happy together too,' Mum says, like she's reading from a script. 'So we're going to have to make some changes.'

Callum folds into his mum, he's crying openly now and I notice that Drew is looking at him like there's a sour taste on his own tongue.

'It's okay, darling.' Hilary rubs Callum's arms and Callum whispers something about his dad and Hilary whispers something back, something that sounds like 'never again' and rubs his arms and back even more.

ROBIN

When Robin had woken up this morning, it was just like every other boring day in the holidays. But now she would like nothing more than to crawl back through time on her belly, sit on the sofa in her nightie watching *Why Don't You?* and enjoy the feeling that everything was the same as it always had been.

Now nothing was going to be the same. Her parents had just told her, here in this beer garden, that everything was changing. Her mum was moving out and going to live with Callum's dad, and Callum and his mum were going to come and live with her dad.

'But where will he sleep?' she asked, refusing to use Callum's name so that the plan seemed less definite. 'There's no room.'

And that's when they split the twins' world apart.

'Are you going to let her get away with this?' Robin cries at her dad, snot and tears running down her crumpled-up face. 'She can't take Sarah away from us. If Mum wants to run off with *him*, let her go. I want Mum to go! I hate her! But she can't take my sister.'

As Sarah hears about her new house and her new room and her new life and the weekends that they'll all see one another and the pony she'll maybe get and the new bedroom set she can pick from the catalogue, probably, she lifts her hands to her ears and covers them. Robin pulls at her sister. 'Tell them you don't want to go!' And Sarah curls herself even tighter into a hard little ball. When her mum reaches across the table, Sarah shrugs the touch on her shoulder away. When her dad reaches along the bench to stroke her hair, she suddenly screams at him: 'Get off!' Robin starts to cry and thrash about. Callum climbs away and sits the other side of his mum, clinging to her like a limpet. He'd got what he wanted. He was getting away from his dad. He'd not said it often, but he'd told the girls a couple of times that when his dad is angry, he hurts Callum.

'Like, smacks your bum?'

Robin had said the first time, in a mocking voice.

'Kind of,' Callum said. 'Not really.'

'My mum smacks my bum all the time,' Robin had said, in a disinterested voice that stopped the flow of conversation that first time.

The second time it came up was during one of the earliest sleepovers. Callum had winced as he turned over on the Z-bed and after some coercion from Robin, showed us a huge purple and yellow bruise on his hip. 'He thought I was being disrespectful,' was all he'd say, 'so please don't make him angrier with me by dropping any food on the carpet.' Even Robin had put her stash of crisps away then.

This split, this is the realisation of a dream for Callum. Away from his dad but still with his mum. But for Robin and Sarah, this is a new nightmare they'd never considered.

Her dad grabs Robin's wrists and pulls him to her, hugging her and restraining her at the same time.

'You don't understand,' her mum says as she climbs out from the bench and walks around to Robin, trying to hold her shoulders. Robin wriggles free and turns into her dad, rubbing her face into his top and grabbing the fabric in her fists. She'd never felt so angry and the red heat of it was pouring from her eyes and her heart.

After a moment, her dad gently pushes her away but holds her in front of him so she can see his face. 'This wasn't just Mum's decision,' he says, but the tears are balling up in his eyes like when his dad died and when he looks at his daughter, they fall fast down his face.

'This has been a long time coming, love. And it's not just Mum who realised that something wasn't right and that we weren't happy. We've not been happy for a long time, not really.'

'You pretended to be happy then! You're just horrible liars!' Robin cries, breaking free of her father's grip. She notices that, rather than look to her mum for back-up, he looks past her to where Hilary is now standing with Callum. But it's Drew who speaks.

'Now, Robin,' he says, 'you need to be a big girl about this. We've all sat down and talked it through and we've decided that this is the best thing for everyone.'

'This is best for you and Mum, not me and Sarah. Or Dad. Or Callum. Or Hilary. So fuck off!' Robin shouts and Drew Granger looks like he's been shot in the head. Then he looks outraged. 'Fuck off! Fuck off! Fuck off! Fuck off! Fuck—' she keeps shouting until her dad pulls her back to him and she cries until she's burned out and yawning.

Drew Granger's face is red. It's highlighted even more by the yellowness of his hair. He's twitching and pursing his lips. Callum slips behind his mum like he's trying to crawl away undetected.

'Why can't *he* stay with you and Sarah stay with us?' Robin asks, jerking her thumb at Callum who looks down at his feet and continues to sob.

'He needs to stay with his mum, Robin,' Drew says.

'Why?' Robin shouts.

'It'll be fun,' her mum says to Robin, 'you always said you wanted a brother.'

'Yeah, not instead of my sister!' Robin shouts.

'Well you did say that sometimes,' her mum says, and she tries to laugh but her dad looks at her like she's terrible and Hilary leaves Callum for a moment to crouch in front of Robin and say: 'I know it's hard to understand, Robin. I know you're very upset about your mum leaving.'

'I'm not,' Robin says. 'I hate Mum. She started all this and now she's taking Sarah away.' Her mum chews her lips but her eyes fill with tears.

'You'll still see Sarah a lot,' Hilary continues, trying to touch Robin's arms but she swings them away. 'And you'll stay over there and Sarah will stay over with...' She falters. 'With *us* and we'll try to make it the best it can be. And you do get on very well with Callum, don't you, and you'll be able to have fun together too.'

'I don't want him, I want my sister,' Robin says, quieter now but with chest-bucking sobs every little while. 'He's just some boy. I don't want him in my house.'

Quietly, to the side of Robin, Sarah speaks in a low voice to her dad. 'Please don't make me go, Dad. Please let me stay.'

'She can share my room,' Robin says louder, 'and Callum can still come then, I don't care.'

Her dad looks over at her mum, a look of pleading on his face, but she mouths, 'I'm sorry.'

Drew shakes his head. 'We've worked this all out,' he says. 'Let's not get it all messy again.'

Robin figures that if she just makes it 'messy', then maybe they'll work it all out differently. So she keeps screaming and yelling everything she can think of. If she can just keep this going all day, they'll have to just go back to their houses and rethink it all. But it doesn't work that way. Instead, like they'd already talked it through, her mum goes in Drew's car back to the Grangers' house alone for the night, and Hilary and Callum pile into the Rover and go back to the Marshalls' house. Before the cars leave, there is an exchange of overnight bags. Sarah's is not one of them; she will stay until the end of the next week, pack her things and prepare for her new home. Robin is desperate not to let this happen. But no-one seems to care.

CHAPTER FIFTEEN

Present day

SARAH

8. The internet searches

This was the one that stopped my heart. The last item on the list: the internet searches. The false comfort of an empty room. Free to spend a child's nap time at the screen with no little eyes peeping over your shoulder. How liberating, to be able to really dig in, to be able to allow your brain free rein to go off in any direction, scratch itches, get answers and snap the computer off if you reach saturation point.

With no thought – well, I certainly never gave a thought – to repercussions. I never considered that there would be any record, those lines of code recording every scraggly, knotty thought I'd tried to smooth out and tie up neatly.

I would never have thought to look at Jim's internet search history. I would never have cared. I wouldn't even look now, except perhaps to understand what his intentions are.

But he'd certainly gone through mine. Him, his parents, his brother. Raking over every absent typed doodle and whim. Not to mention every deliberate and hard-typed word.

'Angel cake recipe'
'Calories burned sleeping'
'Vitamin E deficiency'
'Homemade face masks'
'How to hide effects of child trauma'.

ROBIN

Springtime has definitely brightened up Chorlton, but it seems to have illuminated dust rather than uplifted everyone.

The Magpies are arguing again. They've been at it for a good hour. This isn't just sniping, this is hammer and tongs. A wall rattler.

Robin notices it's caught the attention of Mrs Peacock, the old lady from one of the ground-floor flats. She's repeatedly walking in and out from her apartment's patio doors to the garden, shaking rugs and bashing them, shuffling back out with hair brushes and working out fistfuls of old hair for the birds to use for nests, disappearing back in and coming out with a welcome mat to bash.

The Magpie fight started at the table by the window. It was a sedate summit with mugs of hot drinks that snowballed towards animated gestures and hair tugging, then on to pacing and hand-waving and finally descended into the kind of shouting match that, even though Robin couldn't hear it, was the kind where neck veins bulge and things are screamed that can never be truly packed away.

A few times now Mrs Magpie has held her palms up, an attempt at peace that is dashed away by her husband. At one point he grabbed her hands like he could scrunch them up and toss them, letting them go just as angrily.

When he stormed out of the kitchen for a few minutes, the woman had immediately started jabbing frantically at her phone, shoving it quickly back in her pocket as the kitchen door flew back open.

Robin's heart beats loudly as she watches, adrenaline surges as she grows more and more angry with Mrs Magpie for choosing to play around with something so precious, to risk her son and husband's happiness so callously.

Eventually the Magpies go to fume in different corners. Downstairs from them, Mrs Peacock goes back inside, absorbed into the belly of her own apartment.

The adrenaline and rage is still crackling through Robin's knotty muscles and she kicks open the door of the 'gym' and slides onto the bench. The rack above her is loaded from the last session and she lifts it to untether the barbell and pulls it hard onto her chest. Robin shoves the metal bar up again as high as she can. Her muscles sting as she holds the weight for a few seconds over her body, before pulling it back down. Her stomach gurgles; she can't remember when she last ate.

Staying home twenty-four hours a day has a curious way of scrambling body clocks. Without ever feeling the sun on her face, except filtered through a window, Robin's days and nights are artificially painted on. She takes daily supplements of Vitamin D and tries to stick to normal bedtimes and meals. More normal than when she'd been on tour, anyway.

Manchester does not enjoy an embarrassment of seasons. It's grey for two-thirds of the year. But even when the summer slaps stickily against the window panes, an air conditioner keeps it at bay. Its clicks and gurgles, a companion on hot nights.

She tries to respect the night, to sleep through it. Otherwise it coats her in a heavy tar, an anxious blackness everywhere through which her eyes squint to see ghosts. When she can't sleep, and exercising doesn't help, she roams nervously, watching the house lie still like a film set. It reminds her of abandoned sets from music videos she'd once, awkwardly, 'starred' in. The glamorous idea of which was crushed with the reality of standing around for hours, watching people fiddle with lights.

It's when she's alone at night that she finds it harder to forget. With no sunlight to bleach things, every memory is framed by a black background. Faces from the past sit next to her, silent and accusing.

One of the first purchases Robin made when she moved into George Mews was a new laptop. A shiny Apple MacBook that had felt heavy on her knees after years of using a phone for everything.

Still fooling herself she was holing up to write new material, she'd installed GarageBand and used the tutorial. Only used the tutorial. Instead of writing songs, she had multiple browser screens open, Googling in all directions depending on which lane her mind had wandered down. Robin frequently and guiltily searched for 'Working Wife', her bandmates and finally her own name. She'd watched herself slide down the 'Robin Marshall' search results, slipping on to page two and then settling on three, replaced at the top by two characters from *How I Met Your Mother*.

And sometimes, unable to stop herself, she would search for the names from the lower branches of her family tree. Some with key dates alongside them, some without. The results never changed.

CHAPTER SIXTEEN

1991

SARAH

I moved in with Mum and Drew the weekend after the beer garden sentencing had been handed down. Until then, because Callum was already there, I slept in Robin's room. There was a sleeping bag on the carpet but we lay curled up together in her bed until we got so hot and sticky and she got so wriggly and sleep-talky that I quietly slipped out from the duvet and onto the floor.

On the Friday night before I moved, she'd cuddled up to me, draped her leg over me and told me she was sorry that I had to go and she had to stay. I said I was sorry that she had to stay and had to have a boy living with her. That night, we fell asleep together and when I woke up I wondered if that's how we'd slept when we were in Mum's tummy but I had to stop thinking about it because my heart felt like glass as it hit the floor.

I'd never moved before, I'd lived in the same house my whole life. I didn't want to pack up my room, I didn't want to take the toys and teddies I'd had since I was tiny; they belonged surrounded by the same things they'd always been surrounded by. Dad tried to help but that made it worse. He seemed so gangly and awkward folding my things, and he kept having to go off to do little errands and jobs. I knew he was upset and trying to hide it so I tried not to make him more upset. I told him I was fine.

Robin came and sat on my bed for a bit, and Callum went with his mum to go and collect the rest of his things. When they got back, he hid his stuff in Dad's room – Dad and Hilary's room, I should say – until I was out of the way. A straight swap.

I was collected in the BMW. They arrived five minutes early and I felt cheated. The bags were loaded into the boot and foot wells by me and Mum while Drew stayed in the driving seat with the engine running. Robin, Callum, Hilary and Dad all stood on the front lawn and waved me off. My dad slowly bent in two as the car slid away.

It only took that one short journey to learn two important things. One: That Dad had agreed to let one of us go so he could keep one of us – if he hadn't, the courts would probably have let Mum take us both. Two: That Hilary had given up her claim on the Granger house so she could keep Callum. No-one had let anything go to keep me, from what I could gather. Even though I was the good girl who always tried her best. Over the following week, Mum tried to tell me that she'd wanted it to be like this, but I think she realised how badly her behaviour had come across that day in the beer garden, and she didn't want to lose her remaining ally besides Drew.

It's the week before we go back to school now. I've spent most of the time that I've lived here lining everything up in my new room, picking the new furniture that – I think – Mum made Drew buy me as a bribe, and then rearranging it all again. Last weekend, I went to stay with Dad. That doesn't sound right. I wonder if it ever will. I don't *stay* with my dad, my dad is not a separate thing. Him and Mum and Robin, we're all something connected, we're all supposed to be on the same sofa, eating the same tea. But now Callum sits on the sofa where I used to sit, and I don't know what they've had for tea. Not last night, or the night before, or the night before that.

When I stayed last weekend, I slept in Robin's room again because Callum is now permanently in mine. So I shouldn't say it's mine – it's his. My room is in the bigger house on the new estate with the Next wardrobes and new stereo that I don't listen to because Drew doesn't like any noise that isn't his.

The first week after that horrible day in the beer garden, Hilary and Callum had felt like guests. The house had felt full but in a temporary way, a swelling. They hadn't known where things were. When I went back, things had moved and there were new things too.

I noticed that Robin was still snippy with Callum. He would gradually inch closer to her, like you would with a cat that scratches, and she'd pretend she hadn't seen him. Over the weekend we gradually found our places, started to play together like we used to. Sometimes, though it feels painful to say it, sometimes it was more like the two of them playing and me just watching. When Callum saw me looking over as they played this made-up word game they have where they change the first letter of people's names to 'B' – it's really stupid – he came and sat next to me.

'Are you okay?' he asked.

'I'm fine,' I said, being deliberately sour and then regretting it when he looked hurt. 'Sorry,' I said. 'I'm fine. I just, y'know, I just find it hard sometimes.'

'With my dad?'

'With all of it.'

'But ... is my dad okay with you? Like, does he—'

'Your dad's fine with me,' I say, wanting the attention back on the fact they keep leaving me out. 'Staying here with you two, it's just, I...' I grind to a halt. What's the point?

Mum keeps cooking stuff that she never used to cook at home. Drew has given her a credit card and she's bought armfuls of cookery books and new clothes. She's planning the food for the weekend as Robin and Callum are coming to stay. She's talking about frittatas and Caesar salad. I don't know why because she knows full well the kind of food that Robin likes and it is not frittatas and Caesar salad. So if she really is planning things to be nice for Robin, she's going about it completely the wrong way. I'm not going to warn her though. I may be the only one still on her side, but I'm angry enough not to show it yet.

ROBIN

The first time that Robin and Callum went to stay at the Granger house with Sarah, it had been a disaster. Their mother was so keyed-up and anxious about it that she ended up burning dinner – some gross quiche thing that made Robin gag – and then, after she'd served it up and they'd eyed it suspiciously, she'd yelled at them all. Drew Granger had told them off: 'Angela went to a lot of trouble over this meal,' he said.

'Sorry,' Callum had said, his hand shaking on his glass.

'Well, she shouldn't have,' Robin said. Drew's brown eyes had flashed black. 'And her name's not Angela, it's Angie. She hates being called Angela.'

After the first few weekends of all three children occupying either one house or another, the adults had another of their secret summits and it was decided that it would be one weekend with all three in the Marshall house, then a weekend off, then a weekend with all three in the Granger house, then a weekend off, and so on. Robin was perfectly happy not to see Drew Granger so often, but as much as she hated the weird poncey food her mum kept burning, she wanted to see her mum. She didn't want to speak to her, or make her smile. She didn't want to be told off by her or even be hugged by her – she was still too whirled up inside about everything for that. But she wanted to be near her, just for a bit. Like she'd always been near her.

She wanted to be with Sarah too. Just with her, on the sofa watching TV like they always did, or going to the shop to pick up something for their parents and buying a ten-penny bag of sweets to split with some of the change. The Granger house was too far from the centre of the village to do that, but at least the estate had a little playground with a rubber floor so they could play there and hurl themselves off onto the bouncy floor that Robin said was designed to make breaking bones impossible. Even though the others knew that wasn't true, they went along with it.

For the first few months of the new plan, things started to settle. The kids were still sad, and confused. The three still talked in whispers about when things might change on their heads again, but they got used to it. Got used to adults living with them whose first name they used. Mum and Drew. Angie and Dad. Jack and Mum. Dad and Hilary. Not simply 'Mum and Dad'.

It was their last year of primary school. Kings and queens of the playground. They scattered from each other as they always had, but when they could work together or play together without recrimination, the girls did. After school, Callum and Robin would walk home like the twins used to, and Sarah would be collected by her mum in a nearly new BMW with a soft top. A gift from Drew, one that complemented his own. On the block-paved drive, after Drew got home from his commute, the cars sat side by side: his n' hers.

At first, the walk home with Callum was a stilted affair. Where once Robin would have scrambled up and walked along the railings on the wall, she simply dragged her lunchbox so it made a loud noise. They didn't speak, just walked in silence like they were on shift work, just getting it over with.

Then, one day at school, Mrs Howard had a heart attack. Right there in front of the class. It didn't happen like on films. She didn't clutch her chest and go purple, or make a big fuss. She stopped what she was doing, fanned her face like she was hot, held onto her left arm and bent over slightly like she felt sick. She'd sat down a bit heavily in her worn fabric chair behind the desk and beckoned Sarah over, telling her to hurry to the office to call an ambulance.

A great ripple of excitement spread through the class, staring goggle-eyed as their teacher – just a year or so off retirement – sat there worrying that she might die in front of twenty-five ten- and eleven-year-olds. Before the ambulance arrived, the headteacher had bustled in and taken the class into the school hall where the lunch things were still being packed away, and they sang hymns while trying to look out of the window to see the flashing lights as the ambulance screamed onto the playground next to the junior classrooms.

That day, walking home, Robin and Callum couldn't help but talk.

'Sarah loved it, did you see?' Robin said to Callum.

He smiled a little. 'Yeah, she really did.'

Robin was torn. Sarah was a goody two shoes who loved to insert herself into any kind of drama and showcase her skills at calming things down. But she didn't want to laugh at her twin after everything that had happened.

'Don't take the piss out of her though,' Robin snapped.

Callum reeled back in surprise. 'I wasn't.'

'Just make sure you don't.' She felt bad, and also like she had a surge of energy to burn, so when they got to the recreation ground by the cricket pitch, Robin grabbed Callum by the coat and dragged him to the swings, and they found that, even without Sarah, they could play pretty well together after all.

CHAPTER SEVENTEEN

Present day

SARAH

After leaving the Surrey B&B to come up north, I'm now staying in a similar place called Cornell Lodge. It's cleaner and smaller than the last one, and the couple running it are friendlier. The room in Surrey had been arranged by Jim's mother, and I had a strong suspicion that the beady-eyed landlady was reporting back to her. It was hard to know whether my sadness and shock were making me paranoid, or whether she really was going through my bag when I went out. I kept everything that mattered with me at all times, just in case. One thing in particular I could never leave in my room, it was with me at all times no matter what. Something Jim didn't even know existed, something he wouldn't know about until it was too late.

The room I'm in here in Manchester has pale lemon walls and sun streaming in the window. It's pleasant enough and has a little bathroom for me to be sick in most mornings, when it all gets too much. I have a stack of pastel-coloured towels and a kettle in my room, with a handful of tea bags, sachets of Nescafé coffee granules and pots of long-life milk. I've restricted myself to one coffee a day. I'm trying to do this right.

I've calmed down and started to think clearly. I'm not exactly relaxed. There is still something twisting and broken in my chest without Violet, but I've started to feel like this is all possible. Like

I could stay here, in this busy city I'd never considered before. Like Violet could come here too.

I have a plan. The first part, the toughest part, will be finding my sister. Robin holds the keys to everything that follows. She has money, she has energy and she has a place for me to hide.

Nobody knows I'm here, that's important. I'm untraceable. Tomorrow I'm going to buy a cheap pay-as-you-go phone instead. I can use the B&B's WiFi on that if I need to. I'm not one of those people who lives online and what I used to use the internet for, I'll never risk again.

ROBIN

Both the Magpies are home but there's no sign of their son. It's unusual for both of them to be home this early, the sight feels jagged and uneasy. Robin's watching in mute, but the woman in the flat to the left of the Magpies isn't. She's standing, hip cocked towards the Magpie flat, holding her baby in her arms and craning her neck – it's obviously a barnstormer.

Mr Magpie had seemed to fall for his wife's lies when they opened the expensive underwear Robin had Napalmed into their kitchen, but since then they'd fought almost every time Robin had seen them. She watched as the husband swung between head-hanging defeat and chest-beating rage. Perhaps Mrs Magpie was doing the decent thing and telling him the truth about her infidelity, leaving? Do people ever do that outside of a mea culpa, being caught in the act?

The Magpies are face to face and clearly shouting. Robin can't see their mouths but she can see the way their backs are moving, propelling angry sounds from their chests.

Suddenly, Mr Magpie looms towards his wife with his fist raised, just as someone hammers hard on Robin's front door, and she drops to her aching knees and rolls under the bed, fighting to breathe.

Robin hadn't seen Mr Magpie's fist smash into his wife's face but she continues to feel sick hours after, reliving what she saw. Sick that he'd finally noticed what was happening under his nose, in his house. Sick that maybe he'd pulled Robin's gift into the fray, that it might have been the tipping point. That Robin could very well have pulled a man's fist back and driven it into another woman with her meddling.

Robin had watched them arguing so many times, but this time had felt different. A higher gear. The woman backing away, the man jabbing his finger, the fist, and then the knock had come and Robin had dived out of view.

She'd hidden under the bed, replaying the scene over and over in her head, which worked fairly well at blocking out the sound of the banging on the door.

She couldn't see much when she'd resurfaced a few minutes later, couldn't see Mrs Magpie or check for bruises or anything. As she stared into the empty kitchen, Mr Magpie had suddenly stormed out into the garden, sending the back door to the apartments flying so hard that Robin ducked as if it was going to leap up and hit her.

She'd sat on the floor, catching her breath, trying to catch her imagination. Half an hour or so later, she'd heard the sing-song giggles of the little boy outside, poked her head up and saw Mr Magpie's frown. The little boy seemed oblivious, scooting ahead towards home without his father pulling him back gently like he usually did. The little boy dropped his scooter on the ground and they disappeared into the back door, Mr Magpie looking around anxiously before closing it.

It's the evening now, but it took hours for the twin horrors of witnessing a man punch his wife and being hunted down by a determined visitor to recede. Her heart had beat more frantically all day, and every little sound or feeling seemed to add to the groundswell of panic that began with the argument in the opposite flat and rolled into the beating of her door by someone with hard intentions.

This person – The Caller, as she'd started to call him – was coming again and again, trying different times of day to trick her. It was affecting her routine, and she needed her routine to cope.

Music used to help. Before. If she woke up in a panic and the pacing just wound her up tighter, she turned to her lifelong friend. Fill the house with sound and fury. Build a wall of drums and strings.

And now The Caller has ripped all that away. She couldn't listen to music that would be heard on the street, that would give the game away and say: 'I'm in! Just keep knocking and you'll get me in the end!'

Who would want to wreak that much fear on someone already riddled with the stuff? Robin had an inkling but refused to follow that thread. Knowing would be worse, it always was.

And she couldn't play any of her guitars to fill the wide open silence, her own music poisoned with memories. She couldn't even pick up the 50s-style Hayride Tupelo, its thin maple neck weeping to feel hands around it. Nor the old acoustic Eastman that for years she wrote the main bulk of Working Wife music on, only transferring it to dirty electric when she'd got it sounding clear and sweet. Nor the gorgeous Duesenberg picked up in Berlin, 'Caribou Narvik Blue', a cross between a mad cowboy's shirt and a tropical bird. Gathering dust painfully. Unfairly. And certainly not the Fender 56 Strat. She certainly didn't deserve to touch that sunburst body. Didn't deserve to hear the precise wail of its notes, the grind of its chords. How he, the unmentionable he, would have loved to even touch it, let alone play it. How he deserved to, far more than she did. How cruel that something purchased on another continent, with a royalty cheque ten years after she last saw him, could make her miss him more.

Her guitars had been gathered from around the world the way some people collect postcards. Now guilt, fear and silence hold the poor, beautiful things hostage like animals in a zoo.

She especially missed music this evening. The rain lashed at the windows, the city outside was irascible and jumpy. Drivers beeped, teenagers fought, kids screamed. And, inside, the dishwasher beeped and imaginary clocks ticked. Everything was irritating. She misstepped on the stairs, stubbed her toe. She screwed up the order of her washing, doing dark day clothes when it was time for light night clothes. She realised too late, the water rushing into the drum as she clawed at the door. Kicked it with her stubbed toe. Refused to cry. Cried.

She needed a blanket of sound to muffle the rush of dark feelings but headphones weren't the same, and with this Caller, they weren't safe either. A wide, deep bass line through a big dirty speaker, that's what she needed. And guitars like claws on a blackboard. But that doesn't scale down, it just withers.

And now she scratches herself seven times on the left arm – good, satisfying scratches. Tries to do the same on the right, for balance, but her left hand is so much weaker that the scratches waver and her skin drags. By the time she gets seven good scratches, her right arm is pink and lined all over. The pain blocks the thoughts of what she saw in the Magpies' kitchen, the image a constant ticker tape at the top of her mind. His fist. Her fear. Scratch. Scratch. All over again.

Robin looks in the mirror while she brushes her teeth, carefully, before bed.

She doesn't look very different to the way she's always looked. Dark curly hair, chopped and sitting around her ears. She has very dark eyebrows – like Elizabeth Taylor, her mum used to say, generously – and dark brown eyes. She has the palest skin she's ever seen.

She's wearing a dark grey Motörhead T-shirt with some black jersey shorts, no socks. Her left arm dangles while the right brushes. A tattoo peeks out of the short sleeve, a 40s-style pin-up girl with a rockabilly fringe and a guitar. The stockinged feet are all that's visible.

On her right arm sits the first tattoo. The one that really hurt. A quote from *Labyrinth*:

'It's only for ever, not long at all.'

CHAPTER EIGHTEEN

1992

SARAH

My mother knew the call was going to come before Drew did. He'd been nervous – I'd never seen him nervous before – and was laying down the groundwork for a rebuttal. 'I didn't want the job anyway,' that kind of thing, but laid on thicker, and polluted with business-speak.

When the 'headhunter' had called him months before, he hadn't stopped going on about it. It was a win in itself, it seemed, to be someone whose head was hunted. And by America, no less.

'The land of opportunity, Sarah,' he'd said the first time, his hand on the small of my back like he was going to swivel me somewhere and show me a chart of opportunities. It's all they – we – talked about for weeks.

'But I've got a clear path where I am,' he said to Mum as he drove us around the M25 in the overtaking lane. 'I've done all the groundwork for VP so it would be reckless to start again somewhere else.'

'But what if the Americans want to take you on as a VP now though?' Mum had said, a slight twitch of excitement in her eyebrows. Until moving in with Drew, I'm sure she had no idea what a VP was. I'd never even heard of a director.

He seemed to like this idea. Pondered it a while as he took the junction signposted 'Lakeside', a big out-of-town shopping centre in

Essex that Mum had wanted to visit ever since it opened a couple of years before.

'Hmm,' he said again. 'You're a smart cookie, Angela. Your mum's a smart cookie, Sarah. Okay, worth hearing them out, yes?'

'Yes,' Mum had said, a smug warmth in her voice.

They'd spent that trip around the strip-lit shopping mall talking themselves into a frenzy, imagining how much bigger the mega malls of America would be. You know, *if, if.* They nudged each other at every American shop or fast-food place, even though Drew would never have agreed to go into a fast-food place. Instead, wherever we were, we had to seek out the kind of cafe that's called 'Ferns' and has indoor plants and a large non-smoking area, and sells jacket potatoes with fancy fillings like 'prawn delight' rather than beans and cheese.

Well, he got the job, as Mum had known he would. He could have been terrible at his job for all she knew. She'd never even met someone with Drew's kind of job before, so she saw him as the absolute pinnacle of people with that kind of job even though she had nothing to compare. And perhaps her resolute faith and fandom bolstered his confidence so much it became self-fulfilling. Who knows.

ROBIN

She'd been told about the toilet rule. She'd forgotten the toilet rule. At Robin's home with her dad, if one of them goes for a wee in the night, they don't flush the chain. It's a small house and the noise of the old cistern chugs and rattles, waking everybody up. The Granger house is loaded with modern toilets, and the rule is different. If you go to the toilet at any time, you flush the chain. After the first time Robin stayed, Angela had pulled her to one side in the morning, spoke urgently and seriously about something so trivial Robin had actually laughed.

'I'm serious, Robin, if you go for a pee in the night you need to flush it, okay?'

'Alright.'

But she'd forgotten. She'd forgotten a stupid rule about flushing the stupid toilet. She barely remembered dragging herself out of bed in the night, sitting on the loo in her nightie, blinking in the bathroom light, washing her hands and then slipping back under the crackly feather duvet.

The next morning, she was woken to the sound of Drew shouting, 'Fucking animal!'

She didn't realise that she was the animal.

Her mother had rushed to him. 'What's going on?'

'Look at this,' he was saying. 'It's disgusting!'

'I'm sorry, I was in the en suite,' Angela had started to say but he cut her off.

'Don't you take the blame, gorgeous, this isn't your fault. You told her the rule, right?'

'Yes,' Robin's mother said emphatically, 'you know I did.'

'It's bloody disrespectful.'

'I'm sorry.'

'I told you, it's not you who should be sorry. Robin!'

Robin had walked slowly into the bathroom and was greeted by a scene of such drama and over-reaction that she couldn't help smirking. 'Why are you two looking at my wee?'

Drew had looked at her in astonishment, looked back at Angela with the same open mouth. 'So you admit it?'

'Admit what?' Robin had asked, the smirk wavering.

'That you urinated all over the place and just left it for us to find?'

'I ... no, I went to the loo in the night, I didn't—' Robin didn't know how to find the words to explain something so obvious.

'Robin,' her mum said in her parents' evening voice. 'We were very clear about this rule, weren't we?'

'Yeah, I guess.'

'About flushing in the night, remember?'

'Yeah, I mean, I just forgot, it's not the same as at home.'

'Goddammit!' Drew had shouted, slamming the wall with the heavy side of his closed fist and making Angela and Robin jump. 'You've not even said you're fucking sorry!'

'I'm sorry,' Robin spluttered. 'I just forgot.'

'Well,' her mother said, more to Drew than her, 'just make sure you remember next time, okay? Or we'll have to start punishing the rule-breaking.'

I don't even want to be here, Robin thought as she walked back to the bedroom to tug her clothes on ready to go home. *Home.* As she'd left, she heard Drew call her a 'bone idle little shit'. Her mother's silence upset her more than Drew's insult.

So when Drew and Robin's mum had asked to come around a few days later, Robin had thought it was so that they could tell her dad that they didn't want her to come to stay any more, after she'd got in trouble.

I'll be glad if they don't want me over there any more, Robin thought, though that wasn't exactly the truth.

But they didn't want to talk about that. The adults had gone into the living room and perched on the new sofas that Hilary had chosen. The gardening business was doing a little better now that she was helping out, sending out the invoices and talking to 'clients'. They'd celebrated with a pair of two-seater sofas from Debenhams and a new kettle that lit up when it boiled.

'These are new,' Robin's mum remarked, rubbing her hands along the sofa cushion briefly. 'They're nice,' she added, smiling quickly and disingenuously at her former friend.

'Thank you,' Hilary had said.

Callum and Robin had listened at the door as the adults started to talk. Gone were those conversations interspersed with bursts of laughter. Now they all used their parents' evening voices all of the time.

They listened as Drew told Hilary and Robin's dad about the job he'd been offered.

Robin and Callum had looked at each other. Why was he telling them this? Why would they care?

And then it became clear why.

'And they've asked us to relocate to Atlanta.' There was a pause.

'Atlanta in America,' Robin's mum added.

Behind the door, Callum looked at Robin and Robin stared back. What did this mean? Was Sarah going to come home? Where would she sleep? It didn't matter, Robin decided, they'd make it work.

There was a heavy pause from inside the room.

'And Sarah?' her dad said, finally.

'The company will pay for an excellent school for her,' Drew started to say.

'In America?' Her dad had interrupted.

'Yes,' Drew and Angie answered in unison.

'But you can't take—'

'We can, Jack. You know we can.' Drew was speaking louder

now. Using his business voice that he spoke with on the phone to *get things done.*

Robin burst into the room.

'You're not taking my sister to America,' she said, pointing her finger at Drew, her eyes filling with tears. She span around. 'Dad! You can't let them. It's bad enough that you let them take her away in the first place, you can't let them do this.'

Callum hovered in the doorway but didn't say anything.

'We'll talk about this later, squirt,' her dad said, quietly. But she didn't leave. Her dad looked back at Drew and Angie. *Angela* as she apparently liked to be called all of a sudden.

'You can't just take my daughter out of the country,' he said at last, Robin nodding frantically. 'And what about Robin? And Callum, for that matter. When do they see Sarah? When do you two see *them*? How can you leave your kids?'

As the questions flowed, the conversation got louder and more confusing. Things were being said that the kids had never heard before, accusations and threats. The upshot was this: if Robin's dad fights to stop Sarah being taken abroad, he risks losing both of them. The mum always keeps the kids, everyone knows that.

'At least this way,' Hilary had said later, when Robin's dad was out doing an errand (i.e. telling his worries to a pint or five), 'we can arrange it so Sarah can stay in holidays and you two can go and stay over there sometimes.' She saw the look on Callum's face. 'Maybe,' she added, 'if you wanted to.'

'I don't want to,' he said quickly. 'But that's not what I'm worried about. What about Sarah, Mum? She shouldn't be going with him. No-one will be able to check she's okay.'

'What do you mean?' Robin asked, looking between both their faces but they ignored her.

'Cal,' Hilary started but he shook his head.

'Can't she come and live here?' he said, his eyes wide and desperate. 'This is her home too, isn't it? I can sleep on the sofa or ... or she can share my room! Why are you and Jack letting her go?'

'You know it's not that simple, darling. Jack doesn't want her to go at all but Angela is Sarah's mum and—'

'So she's going to keep her safe, is she? Like you kept me safe?' Robin had never seen Callum so openly upset, had certainly never heard him questioning his parents or arguing. For once, she didn't wade in. She just watched.

'You know what your father's like, Callum,' Hilary said, growing pink, her words hurried. 'He will fight tooth and nail—'

'Then *Jack* should be fighting harder!'

'It doesn't *work* like that, Cal!' Hilary's eyes were filling up with tears and as soon as one broke free, Callum stopped arguing and apologised, turned and walked rigidly from the room and up the stairs.

Robin followed him up to his room and knocked on the door. He was sitting on the bed, arms around his knees in a spiky triangle.

'What was that all about, Cal?' she said.

'It doesn't matter.' He didn't look up.

'It does matter, actually. Sarah's my fucking sister!'

'This isn't about you, Robin.' Callum looked up slowly, held her gaze. Robin said nothing but stepped back. 'I know you might find it hard to believe but the whole world doesn't revolve around you.' He looked back down, hugged his knees tighter.

'What did your dad do to you, Cal?' Robin asked quietly, stung by the precision of his words.

Callum didn't look up, didn't say anything, just stared dead ahead until she left.

SARAH

Drew's on 'gardening leave' now. A full two months off before he can start working for the competitor that he's moving us to America for. I thought that meant we had two months before we left but I was wrong. An estate agent and an interested family walked into my room this evening. Mum hadn't mentioned they'd be coming. The estate agent apologised to the family when she found me in there. I've only just got used to this new house, this new life, and now it's all going to change again. And no-one has asked me what I think about that. Not even Dad. He's just going along with it so Mum doesn't take him to court and take both of us. I'm pretty sure Drew wouldn't want Robin living with us anyway, he's always happy when she and Callum go home after visits, but I don't say anything. I notice that not once has anyone asked if he would *want* to take Callum. He's not even mentioned that he'll miss him. 'I have you now,' he says.

Mum is spending a lot of time in the evenings calling 'real estate people' in Atlanta but not – as I've asked several times – any schools yet. 'Drew's company will take care of that,' she says. 'They'll pay your fees for somewhere really good. Not like that falling-down shithole you're in at the moment.' I don't remind her that her other daughter goes to that school too, and no-one's offering to pay her school fees.

I don't want a cola company to decide where I go to school. I don't want any of these 'golden opportunities' at all. I just want to go back to my old house, and for everything to be the way it used to be.

One evening, sick of the giddy excitement at home, I stuff some clothes into my bag and tiptoe down the stairs and out of the house. I don't leave a note. I don't need to, any fool could work out where I'm going.

I walk the path to my old house with new eyes. Knowing all of this will be a memory soon makes it fresh and vital. Past the sweet shop, past our old primary school, the cricket field with the nearly finished pavilion being painted white.

I turn into my old road, see the house looking smaller than it used to. Hilary is on the front lawn, knees on a pad and rose secateurs in her hand. She has her hair swept up behind a silk scarf and looks straight out of another time. A more glamorous time, even wearing gardening gloves.

'Hello, Sarah,' she says, jumping a little as she notices me. 'What are you doing here? Not that it's not lovely to see you,' she adds in a hurry.

'I just...' I trail off, feel my throat tighten and my eyes fill. 'Is Dad here?' She shakes her head ever so slightly. 'Or Robin?' Her head shakes again, the perfect scarf slipping just a fraction. 'I'm sorry, darling, Callum and Robin are out somewhere. Maybe they're at the cricket field? Did you want me to come and look with you?'

I stand there, staring up at the house.

'Or you could come in?' she says cautiously. We don't speak for a moment, but there's no option really besides walking in.

Hilary doesn't use as many words as Mum. Mum repeats herself, embellishes her own omnibus re-telling, talks over people and uses three adjectives when one would do. Hilary sits, listens, leaves such a gap that you almost fill it with embarrassed supplementary small talk, and eventually asks a small, precise question or makes a small, precise observation.

I finish commenting on something and nothing that's changed in the kitchen when she waits for several breaths and then says: 'How do you really feel about going to America?'

It's the 'really' that does it and I start to cry.

'I know I have to go,' I eventually say, and she doesn't correct me. 'I just wish everything was simpler.'

She purses her lips like she's chewing the remark I've just made, tasting it, and then nods. 'Yes,' she says, 'me too.'

We sit in silence and wait for me to stop crying. As I dry my eyes, almost sad that the tears have stopped because the relief was so sweet, she says to me: 'It's important that you know how much your dad wanted you to stay here too.'

'Did he?' I blurt out, angrily. 'Because he didn't even ask me if I'd like to.'

The pause grows, two breaths, three. 'No, he didn't. He didn't ask you because the possible answers were too painful. If you said you didn't want to stay with him, his heart would have broken. If you said you wanted to stay, and he knew your mother would fight for you and win, his heart would have broken.'

I open my mouth to speak, to protest, but there's nothing to say so I just let myself cry again but it doesn't offer the same relief as before.

Hilary insists on driving me home. She doesn't question my stuffed rucksack, but tells me I can come back anytime. It's still my home. But it's not. I let myself in around the back of the house that is currently my home. Mum and Drew are still in the kitchen, looking at brochures for new homes in Atlanta.

'Have you been playing in the garden?' Mum asks, without looking up. I leave a Hilary-length pause but it's wasted on them. 'Yeah,' I say eventually. 'I've been playing in the garden.'

'I love this breakfast island,' Mum says, pointing Drew's attention to the shiny paper in her hand. I head to my room.

ROBIN

The thought of Sarah leaving the country, especially with a man like Drew Granger and all the hinted complications that he would be packing with him, seemed too unreal. Robin just couldn't imagine it. She couldn't picture Sarah on a plane, or using dollars, or eating American food for tea while Robin would already be in bed.

Robin has never left the country. Some of the ritzier kids at school had gone to the Algarve or the Costa del Sol, but Dorset had been their holiday destination and anything outside of that was alien.

She'd heard of New York, where the ghosts and the ginormous Stay Puft Marshmallow Man live. She'd heard of Hollywood, where the films get made and all the celebrities live. And she'd heard of Washington, D.C., where President Bush lived, the bloke who liked war. She had not heard of Atlanta. She had not even heard of Georgia.

Robin didn't want to go live in America, and she certainly didn't want her sister to go to live in America with that man. As much as she didn't want to lose her twin to the big gobbling mouth of the States, it also cut her in a way she'd never admit to anyone that her mother hadn't even asked her. All those years of feeling she wasn't the favourite and her mum didn't really like her; she'd actually assumed she was imagining it because doesn't everyone's mum like them? But, no, she was spot on. And her mother was going all the way to Atlanta, Georgia to prove it.

'You can come to visit,' her mother had said and it sounded more like a warning than an offer.

Although Drew had tried to dissuade them – 'It will be stressful enough, it's not a good idea' – they'd all gone to Heathrow to wave them off the following month. 'Over my dead body,' her dad had glowered, 'am I missing out on saying goodbye to my girl.'

When her dad, Hilary, Callum and Robin had arrived at the terminal just after six in the morning, Drew, her mum and Sarah had already checked into their flight and were waiting to go through to Security. Sarah's face had no colour in it. She gripped her new cabin bag – one that matched her mother's new cabin bag – with white knuckles. A bumbag on her hips was bursting with 'sucky sweets' for the take-off and landing.

The company were paying to fly them business class. Something that didn't mean anything to Robin or Sarah as neither had flown before, but that seemed to be more exciting than the move itself to their mum.

Every airport goodbye in films, Robin had thought, involved a last-minute plot twist. A declaration of love or a change of heart. Maybe her mum would change her mind. Maybe she'd move back in with her dad, and Sarah too! But one look at her mum's face, the Christmas-morning glee, and it was obvious that this would not be like a film.

Her mum tried to hug Robin, while Drew patted Callum on the back and shook his hand, which was the strangest thing Robin had ever seen a dad do. Callum shrunk back to his mum's side afterwards and they sat on a luggage trolley and waited while Drew went to buy a coffee and the Marshalls said goodbye. Sarah hugged her dad, and Robin hugged them both. At first, the early morning strangeness, the adrenaline shot through the girls and they found themselves laughing, but it quickly turned into sobs. Howling sobs. Robin looked up at her mum – standing just to the side – and realised that she was sobbing just as hard, mascara running down her face in streaks and dripping from her jawline onto her new camel-coloured mac. When Robin realised her mum didn't care about the coat, she relented and reached for her. Her mum pasted herself against their bodies and wrapped her arms around both her daughters. Her parents touched their hands together behind their girls, as they'd done so many times. Breaking them off only when Drew came back with two miniature coffees in paper doll's cups – 'expressos', Angie called them, '*espressos*', Drew corrected.

Her dad and Robin watched until her mum and Sarah had disappeared up the escalators to have their new cabin bags searched. Afterwards, drained, they all got back in the car and went to a Little Chef for breakfast, which no-one really ate.

And that was it. Robin's sister really had gone.

CHAPTER NINETEEN

Present day

SARAH

It would be easier if I could just call my sister. It would be a lot easier if I had her address. I know I had her mobile number once but the last number I have for her doesn't work and I stopped giving out my number when I moved in with Jim. Sim card removed, the phone from my life with Jim switched off and tucked in my bag, only kept at all for the hundreds of photos of Violet. The hundreds of photos I can't stand to look at.

I got my new phone earlier and the young man in the shop showed me how to block my number when I made calls, just in case.

Most of the clothes I've brought with me aren't fit for purpose, so I've had to get more. After picking up my new mobile, I visited a charity shop opposite the phone store. I left with two carrier bags full of loose-fitting clothes. I disappear into them. They're baggy, dark, chosen for their price and ease of cleaning and air-drying. They'll last as long as my plan does.

I have worked out how many more nights I can stay in the B&B before I need to have moved onto the next stage of the plan. I run the plan over and over in my head, like a mantra; it calms me as I fall asleep.

I felt better this morning, I didn't throw up. I'd slept almost through the night and woke up only to use the loo and check that my envelope of money was still safe.

I nibbled at the cold toast from the rack and asked one of the ladies who run the place if I could have some scrambled eggs on toast 'well-cooked', but then my stomach rumbled so I caught her arm and she smiled unexpectedly when I said, 'actually, can I have a full English?'

It's mid-afternoon now. If I was at home, at my old home, I'd just be putting Violet down for a nap ready to tidy up the lunch things and prepare for dinner. With ingredients chopped and ready, in bowls like on TV cooking shows, I'd have sat at the computer and gone to the Mum Talk online community that I joined when I first found out about Violet. I'd scour the posts. I'd write down improved recipes for homemade playdough, or roll my eyes at the complaints about lazy husbands and boyfriends, interfering mother-in-laws, sibling fights. I'd memorise phrases, concerns, pleasantries. I'd say things out loud so they'd sound natural when I used them at the doctor's surgery or the toddler group.

I try not to think about Violet. What she's eating, what she's wearing. Whether Jim has gone back to work, what he's told his colleagues. I wonder if Jim has tried to prise information from Violet. What would she say? The truth, I think. We've always told her to tell the truth, even when it's difficult.

Like me, Jim and his family will also be quietly planning the next stage. Just like they planned the first. They have already outlined their case against me. Now they're setting up her new life and routine so that even now, *I* would be the disruption to her status quo and not her status quo.

Jim's mother will be her new stay-at-home carer, no need for safe and sensible Jim to pause his safe and sensible job. They have money. The house is in Jim's name.

I have no claim to any of it. The only piece of paper worth anything is Violet's birth certificate and that is in my old home, behind changed locks. As if that's enough to keep me out. Not once I'm mob-handed. Not once I have my twin on my side again.

ROBIN

While Robin watched from the various windows, there were flurries of change in the apartments. After the boiling rows, it looked like Mrs Magpie had finally left her husband and taken the little boy with her. She'd been back a few times briefly, but never for long. Cautious visits after a life together. After they leave each time, Mr Magpie remains. He's stopped going to work as far as Robin can tell, rarely leaves.

It's a battle for Robin not to feel sorry for a man who beats women. She watches his husk in a dressing gown, sees him sitting on his son's bed in the box room next to the living room-cum-kitchen. Robin reminds herself that what she saw may have been the tip of a very dangerous iceberg. That it's a good thing that the family are apart. But the way the lights in his eyes go out every time his son leaves, that's hard to ignore. Especially as Robin's gift may well have played a part, and not in the way she intended. Robin hates infidelity, hates blurred lines, but violence trumps it all.

He didn't ask to be her symbol of normality and goodness, and he didn't owe her his routine. But watching him clatter around his empty flat, troubling each room in turn, never seeming to sleep, not dressing until late – if at all – also feels like an injury to her. Feels like he's pulling her down even further with him.

Mr Magpie, possible wife beater and god knows what else. And yet every day, still, 'Good morning, Mr Magpie.'

He spent hours in his son's room this afternoon, staring out of the window but seeing nothing. Not noticing Robin staring back from behind the curtain in her gym room.

She's seen more of him in these last few days than ever before. He lurches from periods of deadly stillness to frenzies of activity, flashing past the windows with hammers and tools, or standing on stepladders fiddling with things on the ceiling, the view of which is cut off by the top of the window. Robin recognises it all too well. The lost filling their hours with important missions that mean nothing and are rarely completed.

After the arguments in the kitchen, a heavy question mark has sat over the Magpie family. While tuning out her own pressing concerns, quite literally in the case of the drumming on her door, Robin has found herself running over spools of old film in her head. Scenes witnessed in the Magpie house, newly soured from the recent activity. Robin has watched this family for over two years. Watched their son turn from a bundle in their arms to a scooting, laughing zip of colour through the alleyway. Watched their Christmases and their birthdays, their milestones.

Months ago she'd watched Mr Magpie sobbing, his broad shoulders shaking, as he took down a cot and replaced it with a bed. Watched the little boy jumping on his new mattress that first bedtime. Later saw the boy sitting up with his nightlight on, Mr Magpie slipping into the room to reassure him and sleep next to him on the floor.

So many times she'd watched and thought what an attentive man, what a good father. Envied the simplicity of the pure love, the solidity the boy could take for granted. Robin had seethed, wondering how Mrs Magpie could cheat on a man like that. A man Robin doesn't really know. A man who is standing in his kitchen right now with a large kitchen knife in his hand and testing the weight. He's dropping it into his flat palm, holding it up to the light, staring at it like it offers some kind of solution.

CHAPTER TWENTY

1993

SARAH

We've been in Atlanta now for six months. The first three we lived in an 'executive serviced apartment' paid for by the company, which meant that someone came in every day to empty the bins and there was a gym in the basement where Mum spent a lot of time while Drew was at work. She'd met some of the other executives' wives and was surprised to see that Americans weren't all overweight, like we'd been raised to believe.

The whole of Atlanta feels like a building site. They're preparing for the Olympics even though it's still years away. And they're building even bigger houses and even taller towers. Drew says it's a 'boom city', which sounds dangerous. All in all, it feels a very long way from Birch End.

I liked the apartment we stayed in. I liked the huge fridge that had a special chute just for ice. I liked that we were on the sixteenth floor of the building – the highest I'd ever been – and when I opened the electric curtains with a special button, I could see out across a city that was glittering with glass, the cement mixers and diggers out of sight on the ground.

I was sad when we moved out but I was awestruck by our new house in Sandy Springs. It could have gobbled both my old houses and still had space. Three of the five bedrooms have their own bathroom. I have a wardrobe that you can walk into, and even after

I'd hung all my clothes up, there was about eight foot of railing left empty.

The school that the cola company found for me is very small. It's for students from around the world, and there are three other cola kids in my class of twelve.

I notice the other cola kids smirking at me when I get told off for misunderstanding things. At my old school, I'd known all the rules. I was like an encyclopaedia. I showed prospective pupils around.

But here, here I get everything wrong.

I was due to fly to England two weeks ago. Apparently, March in Atlanta is usually chilly and very rainy. But the morning before I was due to leave – my second-ever flight and the first on my own – snow started to fall. It fell and fell and fell. We tried to set off for the airport early, Drew begrudgingly lined up to drive me as Mum doesn't like driving on the right. There was at least two feet of snow on our front garden – yard, as our neighbours called it. We tried to get to Drew's car. I couldn't drag my suitcase through the heaving drift of white.

We went back inside to watch the news and work out what to do. The newsman said that the airport only had four inches of snow on it, but that the roads were 'treacherous'. My flight was cancelled. The power went out. When the electric came back on, we watched the National Guard on TV as they handed out bags of fruit to stranded motorists. By the end of the day, fifteen people had died in the snowstorm.

Mum said she'll rebook the flights for the next school holiday, which seems like a year away. I wanted to call my dad and let him know about the blizzard and that my flight was cancelled but the phone lines were down.

Robin answered when I finally got through.

'What the fuck happened?' she said. 'Were you trapped in the snow?'

'Not exactly', I said, too sad to match her agitation. 'But it snowed really badly and the planes couldn't take off.'

'I'm gutted', she said.

'Me too', I'd whispered. A sob lodged itself in my throat, which I tried to swallow back down as my mum came near the phone.

'Is that England?' she said. 'Let me talk to them.' But I wrapped myself in the phone cord as I turned away, and she stepped back.

'I'd never seen Dad so excited', Robin said, her voice calmer then. 'We got to the airport early.'

'I'm sorry', I said. For the weather, for the electricity, for Dad, for Robin, for me.

The day after the snowstorm, when Drew and Mum had to cancel their child-free plans, I expected to be in trouble. When Drew had knocked on my bedroom door, I inched a little further away where I was sitting on my bed working on my algebra.

'If I hadn't been here to take you to the airport', he said, really seriously, 'I'd have driven to work and got stuck. Maybe even killed.' I didn't know what to say but he warmed to the idea and grabbed my hands in his. 'You're my guardian angel, Sarah. My good-luck charm.'

He's said it since, and I've started to like it. He's finally noticed that I'm a good girl.

'I booked that flight', Mum had huffed after one of his bouts of praise, but he'd ignored her.

Drew is tall, like Callum. Like me too. He's broad and strong. He plays golf but no other sports so I guess it's just luck. Mum has to work at it. Drew has sandy hair and dark eyes. I guess he could have been my dad. Maybe if I let that happen, I'd be happier. Maybe he is my dad now.

At school, I'm Sarah Granger, but I'm not allowed to tell Robin or Dad as 'Jack'd blow his stack'. Americans are more traditional, Mum says, and everyone at Drew's work thinks they're already married. 'We're as good as,' she says, looking at Drew with a look I never saw her give Dad. More like the looks Dad used to give her. Longing.

Sarah Granger. A new name. A new dad. A new life.

ROBIN

'Happy Sarah and Robin day!'

It was eight o'clock in the morning for Sarah, but Robin had been awake for six hours already and was full of birthday bounce.

'Thank you, happy Robin and Sarah day,' Sarah said, her voice muffled and a little sleepy.

'What did you get?'

'I don't know yet,' Sarah said, laughing a bit. 'Mum's at the gym and Drew's gone to work.'

'Oh.' Robin flickered her eyes at Callum, who was perched on the stairs but didn't know how to interpret the look.

'What did you get?' Sarah asked in the space that had opened up.

Robin took a deep breath and then launched into it. 'Some T-shirts from Dad and Hilary, Lemonheads CD from Cal, ten pounds from Phil in the pub that he gave Dad last night, and Dad says he probably won't remember and not to say thanks or he might ask for it back. And a box of make-up from Mum,' Robin snorted. 'Did you tell her to send that?'

'What do you think?'

'If she asks next time, tell her I want—'

'She never asks, you should just tell her what you want.'

'Yeah, right.'

'What else?'

'The best bit … drum roll, Cal!'

'Yeah?' he replied softly, while at the other end of the line Sarah strained to hear.

'Do a drum roll, please,' Robin commanded and Callum slapped a fast beat on his knees.

'I go-o-o-o-t...'

'Yes?' Sarah chided, a toss-up between amused and annoyed.

'A guitar.'

'Oh, nice. I thought you had a guitar?' Sarah asked.

'Yeah, I've got Dad's old acoustic guitar, but this is a proper guitar. An electric guitar with – I'll have you know – an amp and ... drumroll again, Cal ... a whammy bar.'

'Oh great. What's that?'

'It's like a stick screwed into the guitar and you pull it when you play a chord and it makes it go—' Robin launched into an impression of vibrating rock guitar noises and Callum smiled to himself and walked off into the kitchen to leave her to it.

Callum had been playing the guitar a while longer than Robin. He'd had piano lessons since he could first sit up on a stool and because of his early exposure to music and hours of excruciating practice, Callum found it easy to pick up other instruments. He learned guitar methodically, as he had the piano. As he did everything. Robin thought she'd have a go too. She'd picked up her dad's scruffy old acoustic guitar from the garage, got Callum to tune it, and started learning how to play along with him by ear.

Sarah had had to endure an audio update every phone call since, but Robin improved rapidly between the calls.

Robin's dad was shaken when Sarah couldn't come because of a snow blizzard in Georgia. He'd been playing it cool but casually mentioning to Robin the things that they would do during her stay, picking up presents for her with Hilary's help, making a little truckle bed to slide out from under Robin's so Sarah had her own proper bed to sleep in. Practical dad stuff. When he'd gone to the airport, driving faster than Robin was used to, he'd bounded out and practically run in to Arrivals. Her plane was not on the board. He worried he'd gone to the wrong terminal and went to ask someone who worked there. When he found out she wasn't coming at all, he'd looked at Robin aghast, like he was waiting for his daughter to know what to do or say. What could she do? What could any of them do?

Robin was glad Hilary was waiting for them when they got home from the airport. Hilary was good at extinguishing drama. She'd hugged Jack and Robin, made tea, called the airline.

Robin had cried into her flannel in the bath for an hour, then sat on the sofa scowling through her wet hair.

'Come on,' Callum had said, linking his arm through Robin's and tugging her into the hall to put on jackets. 'We're going to the petrol station.'

'Why?'

'Wait there a sec.' He'd thundered up the stairs, his long legs and big feet barely fitting on the steps. A few moments later he was back down, patting his back pocket.

They trudged through the village in silence, icy water running down Robin's neck. Everywhere she looked Robin saw something that had changed since Sarah left, something she could have shown her. The new white wood cricket pavilion, which someone had already drawn a dick and balls on in marker pen. The big rock that had been dug up at the quarry down the road, seemingly at random, and stuck out in front of the village hall. A sign said it was 'probably over a million years old'; the vagueness of the claim creased Robin and Callum up every time they read it. '*You're* probably over a million years old,' they would often say to each other, out of the blue. Sarah could have joined in on the joke.

The wind was biting, but there was no snowstorm here. The idea of her sister being stuck in some kind of extreme adventure while they just trudged past the million-year-old boulder seemed to make no sense.

'Right,' Callum said, as they pushed the door to the petrol station mini-shop open.

'Yeah?' She'd glowered.

He pulled two folded notes from his back pocket.

'Where d'you get that cash?' she asked, accusingly.

'It's the rest of my Christmas money,' he said, and before she could interrupt to ask more questions, he added, 'we're going to buy every guitar magazine they've got and whatever's left will buy as many bags of sweets that we can cram in before we puke. Okay?'

She'd smiled then, for the first time since the ride to Heathrow.

'You don't have to do that.'

'I know. I want to.'

'You're alright, you are.'

'And you're probably over a million years old.'

CHAPTER TWENTY-ONE

Present day

SARAH

I use the computers at Sale library, a big red-brick building with glass doors. I'm allowed thirty minutes, and use them as wisely as I can.

I search the web for Robin but there's nothing new. I search Twitter, an alien territory for me, and find several accounts from people with similar names, many of which were unused or had laid dormant for a long time. One account 'RobMarshallGuitar' looks promising but is far more likely to be some middle-aged, male, potbellied heavy metal fan than my sister.

I searched 'how to find someone's address' but the results were mostly American or talking about IP addresses. Just as I'm about to leave, I look for 'RobMarshallGuitar Manchester' and the one search result for a review website. A scathing verdict on a curry house – The Spice Room – in Chorlton, which hadn't followed the specific instructions about delivery. Could it be?

Just before my library computer time runs out, I find the address of The Spice Room and head back to the B&B where I put on an extra jumper and then ask at reception which way it is to Chorlton.

If this curry complainant was really Robin, the frustrating thing was that she hadn't been happy and wouldn't have ordered again. I couldn't call up as Robin Marshall and ask for the usual, check the address they have. No gifts from god like that here, it would take more effort. I need to remember to eat, to keep my blood sugar stable, and pop into a corner shop for a Mars Bar, something I haven't eaten since I was a child.

The walk to Chorlton will take at least an hour. 'It's fine,' I say to the concerned B&B staff, 'I've got nothing better to do today.' I've got nothing better to do full stop, not until I can move on to the next step.

ROBIN

It's 20th March. For the seventh year running that means something. And for the first time in seven years, Robin has been too distracted, too haunted by the ghosts of the present to feel the anniversary looming.

Last night, she'd sat in her bedroom in the dark, curtains open. Under her bedroom door, she'd propped a chair to keep it closed. An old trick Callum had used as a kid, when he was scared of his dad getting in. Taking out his fucking 'executive stress' on his little boy. With the lights off and the curtains open, Robin had a clear view over the roof and into all of the flats opposite but no-one could see her.

She had a flask of coffee at her feet, a phone charger and a torch.

She'd stayed curled on the window sill, her only company the strangers opposite. Mr Magpie had looked over once. She thrust her chin up, glared at him angrily with a steeliness that wobbled when she saw that he was holding his son's soft toy in his arms like you'd cradle a baby.

Robin awoke hours later with her forehead pressed hard against the glass and the morning sun leaking under her eyelids.

She sat up with a start, confused by the shape of her own body. She was utterly exposed, framed by the window and on full display like the Amsterdam window prostitutes she'd laughed at while on tour. She dropped out of sight, checked her phone. It was eleven minutes past six. And it was Sunday 20th March.

A thousand years ago or seven. The length of time didn't make a difference, the bruise of guilt and sadness was permanent. It came at her as hard as it ever had, while she crouched on the floor of her bedroom and stared at the date on her phone.

She'd been coming off stage at a festival in Melbourne when she got the call. It was still summer in Australia, everything was pink and orange and sticky. Mums and dads and toddlers had watched the band play from the shade of parasols, a polite audience in the morning before the real fun started.

Adrenaline still coursing, Robin had been wringing her T-shirt out with one hand and checking messages with the other. There were several missed calls from UK numbers and texts from Robin's sister asking to call back. Robin hadn't known that Sarah had her number.

Sickness mingling with adrenaline, Robin called the old house and left a message on their BT answering phone – the one they'd bought when she was about eleven and had collected all the family's calls dutifully ever since. Sarah called back a few minutes later. It would have been around midnight in Berkshire.

'Hello, Robin,' she'd said.

'Hi,' Robin had said. She knew it was bad news. You don't get a flurry of calls and texts from a family you barely see if it's good news. 'Is it Dad?' she'd asked.

Sarah had made a little strangled sound. 'I'm sorry, Robin. It is. It's Dad.' She'd started to cry without clearing anything up. 'We didn't want to tell you while you were away, but then he got pneumonia and it all happened so fast.'

Hilary took the phone from her and started to speak in a strangled voice. 'Darling, we didn't expect it to happen this way. I'm so sorry.'

Still knowing nothing much, Robin sank down to rock on her heels. 'What's happened?' she asked, unsure if she really wanted to know. Couldn't she just go back on stage, stay there for ever and hide from whatever Hilary was about to say?

'A few weeks ago, he found out why he's had some breathing problems. He had a terrible cough and it wouldn't shift. You know what he's like: he had to be strong-armed into the doctor's but, well, they found something.'

'Cancer?'

There was a pause and the slight break in Hilary's voice as she said, 'Yes, cancer. It was in his lung.'

'Was? Have they taken it out? Did he have an operation? Can I see him?'

'Oh,' Hilary said. 'I'm so sorry.'

There was a brief exchange of words the other end that Robin couldn't make out.

'Robin.' Sarah again. 'Look, you were away and we didn't want to worry you. We were going to call you as soon as you got back and get you round to see him so he could tell you everything himself.'

'Were?' Robin said, covering her eyes from the pink sun.

'He got ill really quickly. He was home and it all happened fast. We thought it was just a cold, that he'd be okay for a while yet. But—' She broke off and in the background Robin could hear, 'No, it's okay, I can do it, let me tell her.'

Sarah carried on, her voice catching. 'He died, Robin. I'm so sorry.'

'My dad's dead and I've missed my chance to say goodbye? My dad's dead? Dad's dead?'

'Yeah,' was all Sarah said. Robin stood up again, kicked the dirt with her boot and squinted at the sky, realised people were watching her. 'I have to go.'

The adrenaline had fully seeped away, leaving Robin standing in waves of heat, walking on the cracked pinky-red soil of the VIP area, hot phone in her hand. Her dad was dead. She behaved badly. You think you know how you'll act when a loved one dies, you might even have run through it in your head, tried it for size, imagined every angle of it to test how much you really care, how quickly you cry at the thought. You're wrong. You don't behave like that. Every time it happens, you behave differently, and never in a way that you would like.

She didn't cry right away but had sat on the earth for a moment before leaping up because it was too hot. She had found her way to the VIP beer tent and asked for a bottle of water, drained it, asked for a beer, drained it, and then threw up. She didn't tell the rest of the band until that night, when they gave her awkward hugs and bought her more drinks. Alistair, who'd known her dad the longest, stayed up drinking and smoking with her. Cried a few tears too.

Over the next few days, as Robin trudged silently through pre-planned photo ops and interviews, there had been text messages with times and arrangements coming through as they were arranged.

The funeral. A week away. Which had seemed like ages, until you factored in a twenty-four-hour flight time, with stops.

Robin still did the press stuff – no-one said she could miss it and she was too numb to ask. She'd sat next to the others, staring blankly, laughing robotically, giving slow and stop-start answers. In the middle of a radio show as she was asked how much she'd enjoyed the Melbourne music festival and started to cry, Alistair wrapped an arm around her to muffle the sound.

The flight from Melbourne to Sydney was fine. The flight from Sydney to Hong Kong was fine. Then there were a few hours to kill, time for Robin to buy a black outfit for the funeral. She'd never picked something like that for herself before. She'd walked into the main shopping bit of Terminal One and panicked. It was almost all designer clothes, beautiful handbags on pedestals in the middle of shops and delicately lit mini-boutiques where no other customers were wearing jeans. She went into Gucci because she vaguely knew that they did clothes in black.

She found a black dress and jacket, bought them without trying them on and forgot she needed shoes. Walking to find coffee and lunch or breakfast or whatever time meal it was because she was out of sorts, the only shoe shop she could see was Jimmy Choo. At least she'd have a proper neat outfit, she'd thought, even though it was extravagant and uncomfortable.

The flight from Hong Kong to Heathrow was delayed. As the gate opening time slid further away, Robin and others waiting had been put up in hotel rooms near the terminal. Some people's giddiness at the bonus stay was palpable. Others, like Robin, who were bored skinless of travelling, trudged onto the airport minibus like they were headed to the executioners' block.

For the next twelve hours Robin lay in bed wearing an old T-shirt and knickers, eating room service, drinking beer from the mini fridge, watching weird TV and just weeping.

She'd thought of her dad up a tree, where he'd spent most of his waking adult life. She thought of his concentrating face as he worked, of the green patches he always had on his work trousers, of his hair, which was grey and curly but plentiful. She thought of his giddiness when he spotted a rare bird, dragging them out to see even though no-one shared his interest. How they'd laughed when he pointed to a Blue Tit or Great Tit, and he'd pretended not to notice.

Robin had tried to count how long it had been since she'd seen him in weeks and months. The months ran to years. She wept so hard that she got a migraine and nearly missed the rescheduled flight.

When she finally touched down in England there was an hour and a half to go before the funeral started. She'd joined the long shuffle to get through Security and tried to call a cab before realising that she didn't know any local numbers. In desperation and post-migraine exhaustion, she'd called and asked a PA from the record company to arrange a car. She'd explained it was for her dad's funeral, that she was running late and needed to get there fast. With forty-five minutes left to get to Birch End, Robin stepped into the arrivals lounge to find a chauffeur holding her name on a thick pink card.

He'd taken the trolley loaded with suitcases, three weeks' worth of gig outfits and off-duty clothes, wordlessly pushing it through the sliding doors towards the car park, the freezing cold slapping her cheeks.

They'd sent a fucking limousine.

The thing Robin knew about limousines, besides being ostentatious and broadly less safe than any other cars, is that they're slow.

With no other options, Robin had struggled into her dress and new shoes in the back of the limo, in the slow lane of the M4. She'd texted everyone whose number she had to try to explain, to plead with them to wait. She eventually rolled up, taken almost to the church door – past the hearse – just as Sarah and Hilary were giving up and going inside. Robin had stepped out carefully in pinprick shoes and tottered slowly up the last of the cobbled path.

'I'm so sorry,' she'd said, reached for Hilary awkwardly to try to hug her and ended up pulling her black handbag from her shoulder.

'Are you drunk?' Sarah's eyes had widened.

'No, new shoes,' Robin said. 'I didn't have much notice,' she'd added to Hilary, still cross that she'd been kept in the dark for weeks. Cross that Sarah was living so comfortably in a shared past that Robin had been excluded from, had no place in. Furious that Sarah had not once asked if she was okay. To have lost their dad without saying goodbye, a luxury Sarah had awarded herself.

'You're here now,' Hilary said. She had blusher on the sharp ridges of her cheeks, pale lipstick and no eye make-up. Her eyes were red-rimmed. Robin thought about the way Hilary had looked when they first met, and wondered why she hadn't noticed the changes over the years.

Robin pays close attention to everything she can see now. She can't see much but she studies it like it's her job. She'd learned just how much can fall away and fall to pieces when she closes her eyes. Looking back, there were so many signs that her mother and Drew Granger were sneaking around but when the split came, it still knocked her for six. And Callum, his smile only loosely masking the mess below his surface. But she'd accepted his smile and demanded his attention, instead of the other way around. Lessons learned in the hardest ways, she wouldn't make these mistakes again.

Over the last few days Robin had continued to watch Mr Magpie roaming his empty flat, refusing to close her eyes and look away.

Watching in mute, Robin imagined the awkward exchanges when Mrs Magpie dropped the little boy, saw the change in the man when his son was there.

Mr Magpie was getting thinner, and slower. There seemed to be a light on all day and night. Robin would stir to go to the loo, or, unable to sleep, she'd go to work out in the early hours, and there'd be a yellow glow in the kitchen or a blue glow from the lounge area behind. Sometimes she'd see a man's shape in the little boy's bedroom, when the little boy wasn't there.

CHAPTER TWENTY-TWO

1994

SARAH

Everything in Atlanta is huge. The supermarkets with shelves so high I get dizzy looking all the way up, cars that seat seven or eight people, towering offices. And the portions of food, my god. Burgers bigger than your head. Chicken and biscuits with jug-loads of gravy. Even alligator steaks.

In the last year, I've had many biscuits and gravy, and grits, iced tea, I even tried the alligator steaks. My favourite place to go is The Varsity, which claims to be the world's biggest drive-in.

When we go to The Varsity, I always wonder what Robin would have. She'd probably go for the triple-stack bacon cheese burger because her eyes are always bigger than her belly. And she'd have Sprite and a fried peach pie.

At first, Robin and I talked on the phone every Sunday and it would often be about food. Mum would perch awkwardly on the stairs and interject whenever I said anything she thought Dad might seize on as reason to take me back to England.

The calls are more like every other Sunday now. Our days don't fit together, England is full of lunch before we've had breakfast, but it's easier to find things to talk about when it's been a bit longer.

'What did you have for lunch?' is how most of our calls start.

'Sandwiches,' Robin generally says. It's enough for me. From that I can picture the kitchen table, the radio on the side sticky from the cooking oil in the air. I can picture Dad holding his tea with two hands, Robin and Callum doing impressions of whatever thing they're obsessed with on TV. I can picture Hilary fluttering about, never really eating much.

'What did you have for breakfast?' Robin will ask.

'Pancakes with bacon and syrup, Fruit Loops and freshly squeezed orange juice,' I'll lie. It's always toast, if it's anything.

I always speak to Dad after Robin. He tells me about the birds he's seen in the garden, or a joke he's heard on Steve Wright. He'll ask about school, and I'll tell him it's okay. I tell him I have lots of friends, list the names of people who in reality either hate me or ignore me.

After the last call, I said goodbye, handed the phone to Mum and then crept upstairs to the bathroom to listen on the phone by the loo.

'You promised you'd send her over last holiday and I'm still waiting.' Dad's voice always changes when he's speaking to Mum.

'We're not made of money, Jack.'

'*He* earns plenty and he doesn't pay shit towards his own son so the least he can do is buy Sarah a plane ticket home.'

'Oh, you want to talk about contributing, do you? Well, how about you put your hand in *your* pocket, Jack.' Mum says Dad's name like it's an insult. 'And Sarah's *home* is here, by the way. You agreed to that.'

'We're raising Robin *and* Callum and every penny I earn goes towards them and this family. You know I don't have plane money, Angie, that's bang out of order.'

I'd heard this argument so many times that they'll never get past it on their own. A few nights ago when Drew came to tuck me in, I decided to try a new tactic.

'Look how long your hair's getting,' he said, as he sat on the bed. 'Shame your mum cuts hers off – you could be sisters.'

'Drew?' I said, but he'd already launched into his night-time routine.

'Who's my girl?' he asked.

'I am.' I smiled, despite myself.

'You're my *guardian angel*,' he stressed, as he always does. 'Don't you forget it.'

'I am your girl,' I said carefully. 'And I love being here. But I would really like to see my sister soon, just for a bit.' I'm always careful not to say that I miss my dad; it shakes loose ugly adjectives that I don't like to hear. Drew had looked down, and for a moment I worried that I'd crossed a line. That I'd see his frequent flashes of angry lightning break into a full storm. The kind I've only seen once or twice, and which caused my mum more problems than me.

'You miss England?' he said.

'I miss my sister,' I reiterated, in case it was a trap.

'I was an only child,' he said, looking into the corner of the room. 'I only ever had myself to rely on.' I worried that he'd launch into one of his questionable stories about the school of hard knocks and we wouldn't talk about me visiting after all, but he sighed. 'I'll get you a plane ticket to see your sister,' he said. Before I could thank him, he added, 'But I want one thing in return.'

'Anything,' I said, but I didn't know what I could possibly have that he'd want.

'Come and sit on my lap and give me a big hug.'

This seemed fair. I threw back the covers and climbed onto his lap and wrapped my arms around him. He smelled the same way he always did. A mixture of sandalwood and whiskey, and just a bit like the air freshener in his car. He held onto me, his scratchy face rubbing up against mine. I thought he might kiss my cheek but he pushed my head down a little and kissed the top of my head, and then lifted me off him and onto the sheet, and left in a hurry.

The next morning, he told Mum he thought it was time I went to England for a visit. As he bustled out the door without looking at me, he handed her his gold card and told her to book me on a flight as soon as possible.

ROBIN

Sarah is due to land at Heathrow the next morning and Robin has been sorting out her bedroom for hours. There needs to be space to pull out the special bed that their dad made, and it's still pretty hard for Robin to kick a path through the room.

Callum doesn't need to tidy his room, but he's done it anyway 'in solidarity'. He finished ages ago and is lying face-down on her bed, possibly asleep. He's grown in the last few months. Uncurled. His socked toes touch the bed frame and his head isn't far off the other end. His height was only part of the reason that he'd been accepted and encouraged into the friendships and in-jokes of older boys at school. He'd almost never seemed young.

Robin was still small. Robin would always be small. So she just shouted louder so no-one ignored her. 'Foghorn', Callum called her.

'Are you going to help or what?' she shouts at Callum's back, which rises and falls gently.

'Help with what?' he laughs into her pillow, without looking up. 'You're making a good mess all by yourself.'

'Oh, fuck off, Cal,' she huffs, but there's a teary edge to it so he scrambles to sit, cocks his head to one side and surveys the scene.

'It's not that bad,' he says. 'Look, let's get all the rubbish in the bin bags and then take them down to the bin, which'll clear some space. Then we'll put all your dirty clothes in the laundry bin – hang on, do you have a laundry bin?'

'Somewhere,' Robin says.

'Somewhere?' Callum says, unconvinced. 'Okay, well let's just put them in a pile outside your door and we'll deal with that later. Okay?'

'Yeah, thanks.'

'Then we'll have a bit of space to work with and we can put all these books and tapes away, and *then* you can Hoover the floor.'

'Hoovering's a bit much.'

'I don't even know if you're joking.'

She wasn't.

They turn the radio up and work diligently. Every time Robin finds some torn-out music from a guitar magazine or some chords she'd jotted down on a scrap of paper, Callum slaps her hand away as she's instinctively reaching for the worn neck of her guitar. 'Later,' he laughs and she groans but knows he's right.

She barely sleeps that night, running through all the things to show her sister when she finally gets here. Robin's struggling to sleep a lot at the moment, thoughts of all the tomorrows and all the yesterdays clumping together and needing to be unpicked and sorted. Robin's not a planner, she's a doer, someone who lives in the moment and leaps off on tangents. But at night, her brain is so busy that she has to try to get some order in place. And there are so many questions too. Questions for Sarah, but also questions that maybe Robin should have asked a while ago. Questions for her dad like: *How could you let Sarah go?* Questions for Callum: *Why aren't you angry that your dad's deserted you and has promoted my sister to his daughter?*

But in the morning, all those questions get stuffed back into envelopes for other days.

Robin finally falls asleep in the early hours and wakes up to a cup of tea and an urgent shake of the shoulder from her dad.

'Wake up, sleepy head, we need to go in a minute.'

She reaches to her floor to grope around for her Therapy? T-shirt but comes up with nothing but a few strands of fluff. Ugh, why did she have to tidy her room so perfectly? She doesn't know where anything is now.

They buckle up in the Rover. Callum and Robin in the back, her dad in the front, Radio 2 on the stereo despite the groans from the cheap seats. Hilary stays at home to get the roast dinner cooking.

They'd decided that was the most English meal they could make for the prodigal daughter.

When Sarah half runs into the arrivals hall, she's pulling an expensive wheeled suitcase. Her hair is lighter and longer than when she left, her skin tanned. She's grown taller, and there's something about the way she moves that reminds Robin of a woman. Of their mother. Robin stays next to her dad until she can stand it no longer and then sprints at her sister, bowling into her and spinning her around.

Eventually embarrassment takes over and they grind to a halt.

'Hey,' Robin says.

'Hi.' Sarah smiles. Robin's relieved that her sister doesn't sound American. The girls walk back to their dad and Callum and Sarah hugs her dad while he strokes her hair and rubs her arms. 'Hello, girl,' he says, and his eyes are rimmed red, wet.

Sarah seems surprised to see Callum. This is a surprise in itself to Robin, who is so used to being a twosome with her stepbrother now that it didn't occur to her not to bring him.

'Good to see you,' Callum says.

'And you,' Sarah says, and the formality suddenly makes them laugh.

'Come on then,' their dad says quickly. 'It costs a bloody packet to park here.'

On the drive home, they all talk over each other. It flows freer than by phone, and despite the tiredness from the flight, Sarah is as excited as Robin.

'How's your mum?' their dad asks when they pull into Birch End, though both Robin and Sarah guess that he's wanted to ask all along.

'She's starting to refer to herself as a businesswoman,' Sarah mutters. They all pause for a moment and then burst out laughing.

'What?' Robin splutters. 'Does she even have a job?'

'She's selling Mary Kay cosmetics and she's bought herself a trouser suit.'

'Jesus fucking Christ,' Robin says, ignoring the tut from her dad.

'Yep.' Sarah laughs. 'Jesus Christ indeed.' Sarah never swears.

At least some things haven't changed, thinks Robin, smiling to herself.

The night before Sarah is due to leave, suitcase stuffed with sweets to take in to her new school friends (and there were so many, she hadn't stopped bragging about them), Robin can't find her sister. She isn't in the bedroom, or the bath. No-one is in the kitchen and only Hilary and her dad are watching TV.

'Where's Sarah?' Robin asks impatiently.

'Oh.' They look at each other. 'She's gone to the pavilion with Callum. Didn't they tell you?'

Robin marches out of the house, across the small lawn and out of their cul-de-sac. As she walks, hands in tight fists, she runs through all the reasons that it's wholly unacceptable for them to do this to her. Sneaking around behind her back, leaving her out. Sarah's only here for a week and she's already her old bossy self. Thank goodness she's leaving if she's going to be like this.

Robin turns into the cricket field, the sound of the sprinkler bringing her out of her thoughts and into the present. As she approaches the white wood of the pavilion building, she squints to see if she can make out the duplicitous pair. Nothing, it's abandoned. Maybe they'd lied to Hilary and her dad too, and gone somewhere else.

As Robin reaches the front of the pavilion, she can hear the sounds of urgent conversation. She rounds the building quietly, nursing her irritation, hoping to catch them talking. Maybe about her. As she pokes her head around the back – the place where she and Callum like to hang out, no less – she sees Sarah leaning against the wall and Callum standing in front of her with his hand on her arm.

'Are you sure?' he says.

Sarah looks irritated. She purses her lips and tries to push his hand off her arm. 'Yes. I keep telling you yes. Just leave it, will you?'

'I just want to make sure you're okay, that's all.' Callum sounds upset; he keeps his hand where it is.

'Right,' Sarah says. 'Well, I'm okay. And if he's that awful then you should be glad you don't have to put up with him any more and get to spend time with *my* dad instead.'

Callum lets his hand fall from Sarah's arm and turns around. He spots Robin just as she tries to jump out of view.

'What was that all about?' Robin asks them both as she rolls a cigarette in as nonchalant a way as she can manage. 'And why did you go off without me?' Her fire has cooled to mild curiosity.

'Don't worry about it,' Callum says.

Sarah stands awkwardly and eventually says, 'I'm going to go back and finish packing.'

They let her go.

'What was that really about?' Robin asks, taking a bitter drag and coughing at the sharpness.

Callum sighs, shuffles his feet in the grass and grit.

'I just wanted to check she was okay. Living with my dad, I mean. I know what he's like.'

'And?'

'And she thinks the sun shines out of him. She thinks he's a great bloke, great dad, great husband, bloody god among men.'

'Really?' Robin stubs her wet little roll-up out with her trainer.

'Yep. And you know what? Maybe he is. Maybe he actually is a great dad and a lovely bloke and whatever. And maybe the problem's with me. Maybe I was so unbearable to live with that—'

'Pack it up, Cal,' Robin chides. 'You know what you know. The guy's a prick.'

'Maybe I just imagined the whole fucking thing,' he snorts, ignoring her. 'Maybe everything bad just began and ended with me. Maybe I'm the problem.'

'Ah, enough, Callum,' Robin says, but he doesn't look back as he starts the walk home.

CHAPTER TWENTY-THREE

Present day

SARAH

I'm good at keeping secrets. When April and Evie, who run the B&B, ask me about myself, the cover story I've come up with is both banal and intricate. I wear it like a skin.

Yesterday I dressed in the smartest of my Surrey clothes and went into the most upmarket-looking estate agent and said that my husband and I were considering a relocation. I wondered which roads and areas were the most exclusive. From what Robin said at Dad's funeral, money isn't a problem. I was told that the houses around the green and the side of Chorlton closest to Didsbury were my best bets. I spent the day scouring those roads but, unsurprisingly, my sister didn't emerge suddenly from the houses I happened to be walking past.

When I got back to my room, feet and back aching, I lay on the bed and thought about Twitter. About the unused account I found a few days ago that might, at a stretch, be Robin's. I realise that I've been missing something very obvious: her bandmates. I met them once or twice and they should remember me.

I find them easily on Twitter on my phone and hastily set up an account to try to private message them, but realise I can't if they don't 'follow me' and I can't be public about who I am and where I am, just in case. So I'm stuck in a loop.

I could send an email to the record company, ask them to forward it to the band. But I've asked them to send messages to Robin in the past and it's not got me anywhere. Besides, they probably get requests like that all the time and just ignore them.

In the end I take a wild stab. I tweet the same thing to both Alistair and Steve: 'Please can I message you? It's about Robin. I'm trying to find her. I'm her sister.' Given Jim doesn't know about who I really am or who I'm related to, I figure it simply doesn't matter.

It's a long shot, but it feels like I've done something, at least, before dragging myself on another exhausting search around Chorlton tomorrow.

ROBIN

It's the middle of the night and Robin had been asleep when she heard the shout. It came from the back of the house, and as she slid into consciousness, she couldn't be sure it wasn't just a shard of a dream. Until it came again.

A man was shouting, in a thick and raspy Manchester accent. 'Oi, you, get down!'

Robin had sat up automatically and banged her head hard on the underside of her bed. With confusion rattling her sore skull, she scrambled out from under the bed and stood, heart thumping, in the centre of her bedroom. Her thin duvet was wrapped around her but her nakedness felt raw under shorts and a thin vest.

Whether it was the bump to the head or the fear, Robin struggled to navigate the room in the dark and was too scared to turn on the light. So she stood still, sweat soaking into her duvet, scalp contracting and head throbbing.

'Get down from there!' the man's reedy voice yelled outside. Robin dropped to her knees and crawled out through the door and into the hallway, sitting on the landing carpet where the mellow light was always on.

'That's right, clear off!' she heard the man call, stronger and less shaky than before. She leaned against the landing wall, straining to hear over the sound of her heartbeat.

All was quiet but after a minute or two she heard a woman exclaim: 'Oh, Albert!'

Robin crept back into the bedroom and looked carefully through the gap in the curtain. At first it was just a black soup, but then she heard a gate swing shut and could make out two figures heading slowly towards the apartment building, slipping into the patio doors of an apartment: Mr and Mrs Peacock.

Had someone really been scared off by a pair of old people? Or was the old man just losing his marbles? Robin had seen him shuffling around the garden, hunched over like he was looking for something. She'd seen his wife guiding him back inside, sitting him down and carefully taking his dew-wet slippers off.

It's two in the morning now and the old man has no business being out and about. And yet. Just because he's a bit muddled didn't mean the old man hadn't heard and seen something. Could Robin's determined visitor have tried a different, more troubling route?

Robin put the light on and slid back under her bed.

She woke up later than usual this morning, the top of her head tender from the bang when she sat up in the night. She'd laid awake for hours, trying to make sense of the circles her mind was racing in.

Robin felt foggy and slow. She shuffled her way to the window, fingered the fabric to one side. There was nothing to suggest there'd been anyone trying to break in, nothing broken, no big incriminating footprints painted in neon on any of the walls. She didn't know what she was looking for but she didn't see anything anyway. Maybe Mr Peacock was just one mad old man, seeing things in the witching hour. She tried to believe that.

Over the way, she can see the young woman raining little kisses on the sleeping lump of baby splayed on her chest. She can see the new tenant standing in his patio doorway, open just wide enough for his body. He's wearing a hoodie and joggers – it must be Saturday – and thick socks. In one hand he has a big mug of something steaming, in the other a cigarette. Robin still misses smoking. Smoking and playing music, they went hand in hand. Literally, a cigarette dangling between her fingers, pinched in place next to the plectrum. The last plectrum she used in public is still in her wallet. She'd hovered on the edge of the stage at the Manchester Apollo, fluffing her way through a practice set before fleeing. A familiar face among the roadies catching her eye. Smirking in the background in the black of the room. Cutting her dead.

She watches for a moment and then, just as the cravings for a cigarette get too deep, she flicks her eyes up to the Magpie flat.

'Good morning, Mr Magpie.'

The little boy is there. He's sitting at the table eating a dippy egg and soldiers. His father sits next to him, no food, just a cup of something. He cradles his drink and watches the little boy as he eats.

When he's finished, Mr Magpie takes the kid's plate away and picks the boy up from his chair and carries him out of the room, even though he's quite big now. One hand cups the back of his head and the combined Magpie shape dips out of view and returns in the little bedroom. The boy sits at the table and starts to make something out of Lego. Again, his father just watches. After a few minutes, Mr Magpie sits heavily on the bed, watching still and wiping his eyes on his dressing gown.

They both look up suddenly, Mr Magpie takes his phone out of his pocket and looks at it, puts it away again. He ruffles the kid's hair as he leaves the room and moments later he and Mrs Magpie are in the kitchen again.

Robin had been about to go and make a cup of tea, check the locks and start the day's belated steps. Now she goes nowhere, dares not close her eyes.

The Magpies stand at awkward angles, the woman leaning away from the man, him pointing at her and gesticulating. He steps towards her quickly, looks like he's shouting. Mrs Magpie slaps him across the face and runs from the room. He runs after her. Robin strains to see but they're not in view. Instead she realises that the little boy has climbed onto his bed and is curled up with his hands over his ears. What the hell is he having to hear?

Enough is enough.

Before she can talk herself out of it, Robin searches online for the local police station number and dials.

'I hope you can help,' she says as a voice answers. 'I'm worried about a woman and child who live near me.'

CHAPTER TWENTY-FOUR

1994

SARAH

'Fancy making me some breakfast?' Drew said when he trudged into the kitchen this morning. 'Angela's on strike.'

'Passionate' is the word Mum used to describe their relationship. I'd say volatile.

When I handed over the toast and eggs, Drew snatched the plate and ate so fast the yolk burst. I'd only ever seen him eat with restaurant manners, but as he leaned in to kiss me on the cheek, 'Thank you, angel', a strong, sour smell hit the back of my throat and I realised he must have been drinking the night before. That maybe he was still drunk.

Mum waited for him to leave, blazed into the kitchen – a smear of bright Lycra and make-up. 'He gone?' she asked, knowing the answer.

'Yes,' I said, loading the breakfast things into the dishwasher.

'Did you make him breakfast?' she asked, and I knew that 'yes' was the wrong answer.

'No,' I said, concentrating on the plates I was stacking in and the cutlery I was rinsing in bunches.

'Don't lie for him, Sarah.'

I do lie for him. It's just easier, it nips things in the bud. And the thing is, Mum wouldn't actually want me to tell the truth.

'What time did you come in last night?' she'll ask him over

breakfast. Choosing to make the question communal when she could have asked him in their shared bed first thing.

'Just before eleven,' he'll say, sipping his coffee and holding her eye like a poker player.

'Liar,' she'll say, standing up without eating her breakfast yet again.

'He did,' I'll say, breezily, 'I heard him.'

Afterwards, when she's gone to the gym with the answer she wanted, not the answer she suspected, he'll squeeze my knee. 'My angel, you got me out of a fix. I went for a few drinks with the guys from my department but you know what your mum's like. I owe you one.'

I've been saving up the IOUs over the months, tending to them, counting them, until I decide it's been long enough.

He's home from work now, sitting in the den watching a recorded game of American football. His tie is off and there's a heavy tumbler of whiskey in his hand.

'Drew?' I say, as gently as I can. He pats the couch next to him and I slide onto it, tucking my knees under me and – at his suggestion – leaning onto him awkwardly.

'I have something to ask.' I study my hands as I say it, my long fingers and neatly clipped nails. I'd put Mum's varnish on them once, but Drew hated it.

'Anything, angel,' he murmurs, his eyes and mind on the game.

'It's just…' I deliberately falter, to get his attention. 'I miss my sister,' I say, 'and I want to show her my new life here.' He doesn't look around but sits up a little straighter, listening. 'You've given us such a brilliant life,' I add, trying to get some warmth going before I take things further. 'I want to show it off.'

'Hmm,' he says, taking a thick sip of his liquor. 'I suppose it's been a while since you saw her. But do you think she'd want to come here?'

'Who wouldn't?'

I wasn't used to him asking questions he wanted answers to, normally he just talked into my silence, but he seems to like this.

'And I'm sure she'd come if Callum came.' He likes this less. It's something I've never understood and never dared ask. If I ever have kids when I'm older – and I hope I do – I'll never let anything or anyone keep them away from me. But for some reason, Drew and Callum don't see eye to eye. Callum says Drew was cruel to him when he was little, but I never saw it, and Callum is incredibly sensitive. I've heard Drew refer to him as a 'Nancy' before.

'Let me talk to your mum, see what she says, okay?'

'Thank you, Drew,' I say, knowing my time is up. I kiss his cheek and leave him to it.

ROBIN

Robin had swiped a bottle of Mad Dog 20/20 from the All Days store in the next village a few hours earlier, wedged between her belly and her waistband as she walked carefully out. She and Callum had sat on the swings in the playground and taken furtive swigs as the light faded. They'd talked about a boy at school that Robin liked. 'Well, I like him when he's by himself but he's a dick when he's with his friends.'

'Most people are,' Callum said, in such a sage voice that they'd both folded into hysterical laughter.

'Who do you like?' Robin asked, still chuckling a bit.

'No-one,' Callum said cautiously.

Still swinging side by side, Callum broke the silence. 'You know I like boys too, right?'

She'd pumped her legs to go higher and lied. 'Yeah, of course.'

Robin bit her lip as she swung. She could not let Callum see her disappointment. Not that he fancied boys – she didn't *like* him like that – but disappointed that she hadn't realised. She'd even thought about fixing him up with a few girls in her class. She hadn't gone through with it because she didn't want to be left out if he got a girlfriend, and because there was simply no-one good enough.

But, okay, he was gay. Her brother was gay. This was unexpected. Gay people on the telly were flamboyant and camp, but Callum was neither. Gay people liked disco music and Europop, didn't they? But Callum liked the Manic Street Preachers, Alice in Chains and Nine Inch Nails. He had an encyclopaedic knowledge of rock and its various sub-genres. He could play guitar like the Devil.

All Robin understood in that moment, as she pumped her legs as hard as she could, was that she'd have to pretend to understand a lot more than she really did. The questions she was desperate to ask were stuck in her throat. Robin decided that it was enough that he'd told her.

They'd swung until they got sick, then lay on the musky evening grass drinking the dregs from the bottle and talking in tones that suggested important discussions were taking place when, in reality, they were talking nonsense.

When they got home, lurching from side to side and giggling, they were asked to come into the living room.

'Shit,' they whispered to each other.

Hilary and her dad chose to ignore the obvious inebriation of their underage children and asked them to sit down.

'Your mum rang,' her dad said.

'So?' snorted Robin, a little too indignantly.

'She wants you to fly out to visit.'

Robin said nothing, glanced at Callum out of the side of her eye. He looked nervous.

'And your dad would like to see you too, Cal,' Hilary added, avoiding his eyes. He said nothing. 'You'd be with Robin,' Hilary added.

'And Sarah would be there,' her dad said.

Robin sat back heavily on the sofa, let her eyelids slide slowly down and tried to swallow away the queasiness and the taste of sour orange.

'My dad wants to see me?' Callum said, as Hilary had stood up to go back out into the kitchen for no real reason. 'Why?'

'What do you mean?' Hilary looked nervous.

'You know what I mean.'

The alcohol in his system seemed to be stirring him up, even Robin felt rattled by it. He stared at his mum until she looked away.

'You don't have to go, Cal,' she said.

'Good! Why the hell would you consider giving in to him? I put up with him for eleven years, his horrible words and his fucking cruelty. And now you want to send me back over there, just like you did with Sarah?'

Hilary shook her head. 'No, that's not it at all. I didn't want you to feel left out, that's why I suggested—'

'So he didn't even *want* to see me.' The sides of Callum's mouth twitched and his eyebrows furrowed the way they do when he's working on homework.

'Well, he—'

'Forget it.' The whole house shook with the force of Callum's long legs thundering up the stairs and slamming his door.

The next day, apologising to his mum, he'd avoided Robin's eye at breakfast.

'I'll go to Atlanta,' he said grimly. 'But only to keep an eye on Robin and check that Sarah's okay.'

'I don't need you to babysit me,' Robin said, trying to sound outraged despite being relieved.

'Are you sure?' Hilary searched his face but he drained the last of his tea and left for the bus without waiting for Robin.

A few weeks later, they were strapped into plane seats, buckled tight and nervous. Robin had never flown before, and Callum hadn't flown since his last family holiday with his dad years earlier. No happy memories.

She reached for his hand as the wings creaked and widened in preparation for take-off, and the chassis wobbled up and down as the big beast picked up speed. Once the nose tipped up and there was no going back, they sank back into their chairs and stared through the window in awe as the ground fell away.

They'd filled a bag with magazines at Heathrow, another with boiled sweets and toffees.

'When does the film start?' Robin asked, looking all around to see the nearest TV screen.

'Not yet, they'll tell you when it's coming on,' Callum said patiently.

'When do they bring food?' Robin asked.

'Soon! God!'

The film eventually started, a heavily edited version of a romantic comedy that neither of them would normally have watched.

'My headphones don't work,' Robin said, banging them on the seat in front so that the man sitting in it looked through the crack.

'Sorry,' Callum said to him.

Robin rolled her eyes but said sorry too.

As it approached Atlanta, the plane descended fast. A terrifying, clattering fall that Robin hadn't been expecting. When the wheels touched down with a bump that turned from fear to reassurance, some of the smokers at the back clapped and Robin looked at Callum to see if she should too. He shook his head. 'Don't do that,' he said.

They'd flown for over nine hours, were full of sugar and caffeine from the miniature cola tins, and wild-eyed in the strip lighting of the airport.

After heaving their heavy suitcases off the baggage carousel, they carried them out into Arrivals and stood, looking for a familiar face.

Suddenly Sarah ran at them.

'Robin!' she yelled but hugged both of them. It was an unexpected display and caught Robin off guard.

'Hey,' Robin said.

Sarah had stepped back, red-faced. 'How did you like flying?' she asked.

'My headphones were broken,' Robin said. 'But it was fun,' she added, because Sarah looked crestfallen.

'Where are they?' Callum asked.

'Your dad's at home but Mum's over there.' Sarah pointed to a woman nervously holding a railing. She had short golden hair rather than the long platinum perm she'd left with, and she wore an expensive-looking blazer over white jeans. She was pencil-thin.

'Why's she dressed like Princess Diana?' Robin asked.

'What are you all laughing about?' Angela said as she came closer.

'Nothing,' Sarah said.

They started to walk in the direction of the exit when their mother grabbed Robin and hugged her so quickly and tightly that Robin swung like a rag doll before slackening and eventually hugging her mother back. They stayed like that for a long moment, Angela stroking her daughter's hair and Callum and Sarah shuffling their feet.

For the last hug they'd ever give each other, it was a good one.

CHAPTER TWENTY-FIVE

Present day

SARAH

In my bedroom at Cornell Lodge, I have a map of Chorlton with the roads marked off as I've visited them. Every pointless pen line had chipped at my faith in the plan. I need a new approach; this is taking too long.

Early this morning I decided I had nothing to lose by trying The Spice Room that Robin – maybe – gave such a scathing review. Maybe she gave them another chance?

At the library, I'd printed off a picture of Robin from her record company website.

In the picture, her hair's the way she's worn it for as long as I can remember. Cropped short, black bouncy curls sticking every which way. Even in a still shot, her eyes burn with that same foot-stamping rage that she'd always had, her eyebrows knitted as she looks at the camera, daring it to capture her refusal to flirt with the lens, which I know the record company always wanted her to do. 'I'm the fucking guitarist, not a go-go dancer,' she'd said at Dad's funeral, when she'd had a couple of drinks and had been asked eager questions by second cousins.

I was fuming at her. Angry at her for turning up late, angrier still for turning up and being *her.* Being the black diamond that everyone stares at, listens to, talks about. *How dare she?* I'd thought. *How dare she be thriving when I'm barely surviving? How dare she have got away? How dare she have everything she's ever wanted, just by ricocheting her way out of our lives?* We spoke without really saying anything; she asked me questions about my life that only served as contrasts to hers. 'Oh, you've been working with Hilary and Dad?'

'We can't all be rock stars,' I'd said, my jokey tone a lie.

'What will you do now though, as the business will close?' she'd asked.

'I'd like to have a family,' I'd said, the truth in lieu of a ready lie. She'd nodded, blushing. No doubt embarrassed for me and my pedestrian desires. Then she'd turned to another second cousin to tell him more stories about life on the road.

In my blocky photo print-out, her lips curl in a practised sneer. If The Spice Room has messed up another order, they've probably been treated to this look.

The Spice Room is a few minutes' walk from the pretty triangle green, where I try not to look at the mothers pushing Bugaboos while they stare intently into their iPhone screens. I never looked away from Violet when I was with her. I want to call across to them, beg them to cherish these moments.

It's half past eleven in the morning. I hadn't thought it through but it's too early and the door sign says 'closed'. Inside, I can see a young guy folding napkins into swans at an empty table and the door to the kitchen swings open and closed as people come and go. The swan boy looks at me, tilts his head in confusion and my first instinct is to shuffle off in embarrassment but I hold my nerve and try a smile. He folds one more swan slowly, squirms under my continued eye contact and, begrudgingly, walks towards the door. When he unlocks it and pulls the door open, the hip hop playing over the speakers inside rushes out and takes me by surprise, so the words get stuck in my throat.

'We're not open yet,' he says gently as I stand there, mute. 'We open at noon,' he adds. 'If you're that hungry.'

'I, um...' I stare at his eyes, worrying about how much time is passing without me explaining myself. 'I'm looking for someone.'

'Okay?' he says, like it's a question. I fumble for the folded picture of my sister in my handbag, thrust it at him.

'This is my sister, Robin. We've lost contact and I need to find her.'

'Is she a fan of Indian food?' He smiles, and looks back at the picture. 'She looks a bit familiar, actually,' he says, 'but I don't think she's a customer.' He laughs. 'She's not famous, is she?'

'She is, actually, kind of. She's in a band. Was in a band. I'm not really sure now.' I realise that I sound manic and confused, that I wouldn't give information to me if I was him.

'I was joking,' he says, in a thicker Manchester accent than he had before. 'But she's famous, is she? Well,' he whistles, 'I wish I knew who she was then.'

'So you've not served her in here before?' He shakes his head. 'I don't think so but ... I dunno, let me check.'

He turns and calls behind him, the beat of the hip hop merging with his yell. 'Rav! Can you come here a minute?' The boy stands back and gestures me inside. 'You wanna come in for a bit? I'll ask the lads.'

I sit at the table and watch another waiter smooth white table cloth over white table cloth over white table cloth. Gradually a crowd of guys approach me; some of them seem shy and nervous but a few seem amused.

'You're looking for your sister?' a grey-haired man with a neat beard asks seriously and quietly.

'Yes.' I nod, over-eager, and spread the printed picture out in front of me so Robin's face is disproportionately large compared with all of ours.

'Is this her?' the man asks, flicking his eyes over Robin.

'Yes', I say and they all peer in, except for the older guy.

'Why do you think we'd have seen her?' he asks, suspiciously.

'She knows you like younger women, Rav', one of the tallest men at the back of the group says, loudly. There are snorts of laughter but Rav ignores him and keeps his gaze on me.

'She lives around here. I think she might have ordered a takeaway from you once.'

'Hmm', the older man says, lifts the picture of Robin and holds it up to the light. 'Hmm.'

'Not seen her, mate, sorry', says a tall guy at the back of the group, turning to go back to the kitchen, his friend following.

The older man shakes his head. 'I'm sorry', he says, and he really emphasises the words and pats my hand as he says, 'I've not seen this lady. But good luck finding your sister.'

The swan boy looks disappointed. I guess there's not normally much excitement on an early shift folding napkins.

'Thanks anyway', I say and ease myself to standing. Even though it was a long shot, I feel my eyes prickle. I cough it away. 'In case you remember anything, can I give you my number?'

I leave the young guy holding one of their own takeaway menus with my new phone number written on it, flopping in his hand. As I step down onto the pavement, the grey-haired man appears and relocks the door, holding up his hand to wave solemnly as I move on.

ROBIN

The morning after calling the police, Robin had woken up to see Little Chick in his room and Mr Magpie in the kitchen, doing laundry. Whatever happened that day, Mrs Magpie had left without the boy.

'Good morning, Mr Magpie,' she whispered, although really she should call him Henry Watkins now. Her Mr Magpie didn't exist.

Robin watched his apartment on and off all morning as she paced and tidied and checked her phone for nothing at all.

She'd done something. She'd actually done something. Something that might help. Beyond watching, counting and hiding, but nothing had changed yet. It was like she'd fired a warning shot that no-one had heard, and she was left itching to fix something.

The letterbox clattered, she took a deep breath and counted her way down the stairs, missing the final step so it was an equal number.

A bill from the gas board, a statement from the bank and a bright white anonymous letter. She bent and scooped them deftly. Took them straight to the office on the middle floor. The window overlooking the green was swamped by the heavy curtain and was never to be touched. The front of the house was not Robin's domain, that was his. The Caller.

She filed the bills in their envelopes. Placed the white letter on the desk, angled it so it was perfectly lined up with the edge and some more time had ticked by. She let herself study it for a moment, more than she normally would. It was thin, very light. Blurred postmark, looked like Maidenhead but she couldn't be sure. Stamp, not franked. Something about the brightness and the lightness transported her back to a time of official letter after official letter falling through her family's letterbox. As a youngster, Robin had loved getting post. They were generally birthday cards or, later, letters from America. Then the official letters had ruined that. And the letter in LA just before she'd imploded was the final straw.

You're a liar, it began.

There'd been a sweet spot without any post, a few weeks in this house before her address change filtered through and the letterbox started to snap again.

She turned this white envelope over. Looked at the gummed flap on the back. So thin, this paper. It would burn in seconds, tear in less. She needed to fix something. Robin's finger hooked into the gap by the gummed-down line.

This would be the first unexpected letter she'd dared open since that one in LA over two years ago.

She felt the scratch of its flap, pulling her into the present, shrinking the present to a moment. She closed her eyes, opened them, pushed her finger in more and was about to swipe it open when the knocks came. It was almost like he knew.

The Caller was back. The glimmer of hope that some vulnerable old man shouting had put a stop to it seemed ridiculously naive in retrospect.

She froze then wriggled the envelope off her finger and slid to sit on the floor, pushing herself slowly under the desk like a makeshift shelter. She felt closer and more exposed in the room at the front of the house.

When the bangs reached crescendo, then stopped dead, she resurfaced. The letter sat there, out of the question now. She threw it onto the top of the wardrobe with the others, slammed the door as she left the room and headed up to her bedroom.

From the curtain slit, she could see Mr Magpie and Little Chick still playing in the little boy's bedroom. It looked normal and it looked good but it was tarnished and made her feel worse than ever.

He was so good with his son. Was it possible that he could be a bad husband and a good dad and they could cancel each other out? Was saving Mrs Magpie from potential harm worth more than crushing the little boy when he found out what his father was like?

Robin reminded herself that Callum had said he'd liked his dad when he was a toddler too. His dad was loud and booming, tall and strong. Callum had told Robin that his dad had carried him on his shoulders and taught him to ride a tricycle, and as far as Callum could remember when he'd retold the story, he'd not smacked him once even when he'd fallen off. His patience hadn't lasted so long when he came to ride a 'big boy's bike' a few years later. He'd ended up being whacked across the legs with the belt for falling off after promising he'd manage it without stabilisers, and instead wheeling straight into the family car.

The Magpies weren't her problem, she tried to convince herself, it was for the police to decide whether to intervene. She had to let justice run its course without meddling further this time.

After lunch, Mr Magpie and Little Chick had walked off down the alley, the little boy on his scooter singing something indistinguishable. Mr Magpie had walked tall, swinging his arms. A bounce to his step that had been missing recently.

Later, Mrs Magpie had appeared in the kitchen. The two adults had sat at the table with mugs of hot drinks, a cosiness coming over the flat. Seeing that the little boy was playing in his bedroom and the two adults were at peace, regret nibbled at the side of Robin's mind and she was relieved to see that the police obviously weren't concerned or they would have shown up.

The sky was darkening. Robin was about to leave the room to run herself a bath when she saw it. The flash of uniform in the Magpie flat. Mr Magpie holding up his hands, tussling, Mrs Magpie pulling at his sleeves and the little boy running out and reappearing in his own room, throwing back his covers and hiding under them.

What had she done?

CHAPTER TWENTY-SIX

1994

SARAH

I'd been so excited to show Robin everything I'd learned to love about Atlanta. So excited to have my sister *there* in my life.

When we'd got home from the airport, Drew had been waiting inside. He'd shaken Callum's hand vigorously.

'You've grown!' he'd said, almost sounding proud.

'Yes,' Callum said, nervous.

'We'll make a real man of you yet!' Drew added. Callum said nothing and the rest of us held our breath, but Drew muttered, 'Just a joke,' and walked off to make a frothy coffee with his new machine.

That first afternoon, Callum and Robin wanted to sleep. After they'd gone to bed, I ate my dinner with Mum and Drew like I always did. The visit wasn't turning out how I'd imagined.

Still on English time, Callum and Robin had risen early the next day and were in happier spirits. They'd agreed to come and see the sights so, while Drew worked, Mum and I took them on a tour of the city. Everything was up for ridicule. Robin and Callum were constantly nudging each other, pointing. When I asked, 'What?' they said, 'Oh nothing, sorry,' and then carried on giggling.

That night, we went to The Varsity and when we pulled up and the voice crackled through, 'What'll ya have?!' they fell apart laughing while I burned.

I'd written Robin so many letters, had so few in return. Desperate for her to want to visit, I'd painted what I thought was a rosy picture. I'd exaggerated my credibility at school, talked about the horse-riding lessons and ballet classes that Drew paid for. Sometimes I said that if Robin lived here too then maybe she'd get guitar lessons and we'd be able to share a car when we were sixteen. She'd never responded to that.

The third day of the visit, Mum took us to the mall and insisted on buying Robin some new outfits. She refused to try anything on, of course, and insisted that Mum buy a bunch of T-shirts for Callum too. 'Your husband owes him,' was all she'd say as Mum rummaged for the credit card.

On the drive home, while Robin did bad impressions of my city's sweet and lilting accents, Mum turned up WSB Radio and stared forward while tears dragged lines through her make-up.

ROBIN

Robin doesn't understand why her sister likes living here so much. It's so tacky and loud, the sing-song accents sound fake and everything is big and ridiculous. Except for their mother. She's still ridiculous, but America has shrunk her.

She made her choice, Robin thinks, although something twists in her tummy when she looks at her mum. But Sarah hadn't had a choice, she'd been dragged here. Because of that, Robin thought her sister would be desperate to come home. *Home.* That they would plead with their mum to book an extra seat on the plane back when it was time to go. Turned out all it took were some new dresses, horse riding and ballet lessons and Sarah was in Drew's thrall. Like mother, like daughter.

Drew had eaten with them on a couple of nights, and then they'd all had to sit on the deep sofas in the den watching TV comedies with canned laughter. Most of the time he just stayed out of their way.

'He's not seen you for over a year,' Robin had said to Callum yesterday. 'Shouldn't he be spending time with you?'

'Believe me, I'd rather it was this way,' Callum had said, flicking his hair out of his eyes.

It's the last night and after a floppy pizza in a downtown Italian place that, despite herself, even Robin had loved, Drew asks Callum to 'watch the game' with him.

'Which game?' Callum asks.

'American football. A real man's sport.'

'That's like rugby, isn't it?' Callum asks cautiously.

'I think it's better,' Drew says. 'I didn't know you were into rugby, Callum?'

'I'm not.' Callum shrugs.

'I quite like rugby,' Robin adds, as she follows them into the den.

'This isn't for girls,' Drew replies. 'Apart from this one anyway.' He jokily jerks his thumb at Callum who stares at him.

'Don't say that,' Robin says, narrowing her eyes.

'Don't bother, Robin,' Callum whispers.

'You're like a little Jack Russell, aren't you?' Drew says to Robin as he sits himself in the reclining leather chair in front of the big screen. 'But you don't need to defend him, I was only joking.'

'Yeah but you've made digs at him since we got here,' Robin says. 'And that's when you've bothered to speak to him at all.' She doesn't move when Drew rises back up to his full height and stares her dead in the eyes.

'What did you say to me?' he asks.

'Robin, please,' Callum whispers, looking at the door.

'I said you've either picked on Callum or ignored him when you should be fucking glad he still speaks to you at all.'

'You're crossing a line here, young lady. You're in *my house*, lecturing me about *my son*—'

'And whose house were you in when you started shagging my mum? My dad's? Or Hilary's?' Robin shouted.

'You really are a mouthy little shit,' Drew says, shaking his head, the veins on his neck bulging.

'Yeah? And you're a big shit with a gold watch,' she says, fiercely.

'What the hell did you say to me?' Drew roars.

'Dad!' Callum springs up in front of Robin. 'Don't talk to her like that. You *did* start all this when you couldn't keep your dick to yourself, she's right!' Callum is trembling.

Drew's nostrils flare. 'How dare you? We invite you over, guests in our home—'

'Guests in your home?' Callum spits. 'I'm your *son*! I'm not supposed to be a guest in your home, I'm supposed to be part of your family. Loved,' his voice wobbled, 'and accepted.'

'Cal,' Robin says, tugging his sleeve, her own rage turning to something else. Anxiety. 'Let's just go,' she says quietly to his shoulder. Callum doesn't look at her, brushes her hand away.

'Oh look,' Drew says, to no-one in particular. 'The big guy here still needs his little girlfriend to look after him. Pathetic.'

'She's not my girlfriend, she's my sister,' Callum says crisply. 'And she's my best friend. Some of us are capable of being friends with the opposite sex without fucking them on the sly.'

'You pathetic little boy,' Drew says. 'As if you're capable of fucking any girl. As if you're capable of following through on this little performance. What are you going to do, fight me? Fight me for her *honour*?'

'Fight you? Fuck off, I wouldn't want to touch you, I might catch something. And yeah, Dad,' Callum is breathing hard, 'I'm not capable of fucking any girl. You got me. Congratulations. Consider this my coming-out party.' Callum turns to Robin quickly. 'Let's go now,' and she nods.

'You bloody what?' Drew says, the veins on his neck alert with anger. 'You bloody what? You're standing here in my house and telling me that you're a pervert?'

'Oh I don't care what you think any more,' Callum says, shaking his head. 'I really don't care.'

For a moment no-one says anything else. Angela and Sarah have edged anxiously into the doorway, drawn by the loud voices.

'I'm going to go and pack,' Callum says.

'You stay where you are, boy,' Drew growls as he stalks towards his son. 'I knew it. I bloody knew it. I tried everything to straighten you out,' he says quietly. 'But it was all for nothing.'

Neither say anything and Callum turns to leave.

And then, after five heavy seconds of silence, Drew Granger punches his son hard in the face. 'Fucking faggot,' he shouts as his fist connects.

It's the first punch Robin has seen in real life. It's nothing like on TV. Drew's wide knuckles hit Callum's face with a dull sound, like a meat mallet whacking a steak. Callum's head moves back slightly, his eyes startled, then he raises his hand to his mouth and cups it to catch a spoonful of blood.

The blood dripping through Callum's fingers spurs everything into action. Angela runs out and brings back kitchen roll for the carpet, Robin puts her arm around Callum, who shoos her away. Drew bellows, 'Clean this up!' at the back of Angela's head as she crouches to soak up the splatters of blood. 'You're a disgrace,' Drew says to his son's back, rubbing his sore hand, as Callum finally storms out of the room and up the stairs.

Drew marches out of the den, snatches his keys from the hall cabinet and slams the front door so hard plaster dust flutters to the floor.

Robin stands over her mother as she rubs at the carpet. 'How could you choose that man?' she says. 'How could you do this to us?' She starts crying and is furious at her body for it. 'How could you leave Dad for someone who hurts their own son like that?'

Angela scrubs harder and harder, pieces of kitchen paper sticking to the carpet, the dark red stain going nowhere.

'Mum!' Robin yells. 'I'm talking to you.'

Angela stops. Her head hangs inches from the sticky maroon patch.

'I'm sorry,' she says quietly. 'I don't know what to say.'

Sarah has slipped away. She's taken the stairs two at a time and gone into Callum's room without knocking. She's watching as he throws his clothes at and around the suitcase, not really getting many in there.

'Callum,' she says and he stops for a moment and then carries on. 'Callum, I'm sorry, I don't know what to say...' She turns to go.

'Does he do this to you?' he says. It's a matter-of-fact question asked in a trembling voice.

'No,' Sarah says.

'He doesn't hit you?'

'No.'

'He's never punished you? With his hands or his belt or whatever takes his fancy?'

'No.' Sarah shakes her head, her eyes filling.

'Honestly?' Callum says. 'Please, Sarah, be honest.'

'Honestly,' she replies. 'He's never laid a finger on me.'

'So it really is just me then.' Callum nods and carries on throwing clothes ineffectually. 'Right,' he says. His voice newly crisp, razor-sharp with anger.

'I'll go,' Sarah says.

Callum says nothing.

Sarah and Angela take Robin and Callum to the airport the next morning, the radio babbling on low and no-one managing to say very much. Drew stays in bed. 'It's his day off,' Angela says, 'and he works very hard.' Sarah, Robin and Callum glare at her, then Robin rests her hand on Callum's leg and looks up at the cut on his lip and his swollen jaw.

'Your dad's got a lot of work stress at the moment,' Angela says to Callum without looking back. 'So he's a bit tightly wound.'

'Tightly wound. Right,' says Callum, shaking his head to Robin. He doesn't say another word on the ride to the airport, briefly accepts Sarah and Angela's awkward hugs goodbye without making eye contact, and picks up both suitcases.

'I'll miss you, love,' Angela says.

'No you won't,' says Robin, unsmiling.

CHAPTER TWENTY-SEVEN

Present day

SARAH

I realise that the guy in The Spice Room is the only person who has my new number.

My old phone sits dormant and dismantled in the bottom of my holdall; its battery, sim card and handset lying separated and powerless. So much life suspended on that phone. Pictures and videos that it would crush me to watch. Phone numbers and names of people who never want to hear my voice again.

I dreamed last night that Violet had forgotten me. That I'd found her living with another family. That I'd said to her, 'I'm so glad I've found you.' She'd looked at me with her bright little eyes and said, 'Hi, who are you?'

My nights are peppered with dreams like this, but this one lay heavy with me all morning. I sat at the table like a zombie eating cold, dry toast and gagging. I have to do something.

I've found a phone box that still takes coins – a rarity. I've written down Jim's mother's number, and I tap it in carefully on the cold steel buttons. The smell of pee and the prostitutes' cards turn my stomach but I can't stop.

I put on a Georgia accent when Jim's mother answers, the only other accent I know. This will be harder than I thought. Just hearing her voice in my ear makes me close my eyes to scrunch away the image of our last meeting.

'Hey there, is this Mrs Galway?'

'Yes, it is, to whom am I speaking?'

Good, she doesn't know it's me. I take a deep breath, try to smile as I speak. Play the role. Just play the role.

'My name's Crystal and I'm calling from Robinson's Toy Company in Atlanta. You've been selected to take part in an exclusive competition—'

'I've what?' Her telephone voice is the most grating and haughty voice I've heard in my life but I ignore it. I pump more coins in just in case, I can't have the phone box beeps giving me away.

'You were put forward by the team at your local Waitrose, from a pool of their best customers.'

'Oh, I see,' she says, less frosty now.

'And with only one hundred entrants, you have a great chance. Did I tell you the prize?' I ask, knowing I didn't but trying to steamroller her cheerfully.

'No, but wait, who did you—'

'The prize is a hamper full of toys and beautiful dressing-up clothes for one lucky child.'

'Oh?'

'Yes, it's a glorious prize. I just need to ask a few questions to make sure you'd win the collection that suits you best.'

'Well, okay, but this won't be passed on, will it? I don't want junk letters.'

'Not *at all*. This is a very special thank you for your loyalty as a shopper, that's all.'

'Okay, well, I suppose—'

'So would you hope to win a boy's prize or a girl's?'

'A girl's.' For the first time, I waver. I could just about hold it together when the conversation was abstract, but now we're really talking about Violet. I take a deep breath, pinch the bridge of my nose and try to muster the will to carry on.

'Hello?' she asks. 'Are you still there?'

'Oh, it must have been a bad line,' I say, trying to keep my accent through the tears that have started to roll. 'I asked the age of your little girl.'

'She's nearly four,' she answers, not correcting me. *She's my little girl!* I want to shout. *Not yours!*

'She sounds like a darling. And she lives at the same address as you?'

'She does.' An emphatic answer. I hate them all.

'And does she attend school?'

'These questions are … why do you…'

'I'm just trying to ascertain if she'd like the prize bundle with books or with—'

'Oh, she's very bookish, like her father.'

'And does her father live with you too?' I ask, more snappy than intended.

'I'm sorry but that's a very personal question. What did you say your name was?'

'Oh my, I didnt mean to offend. Perhaps it would be easier if I could speak to Violet myself and get a sense of her interests.' I realise my mistake before she does, my heartbeat racing as I fumble to hang the heavy black receiver back up.

I hear her say, 'I didn't tell you her … Sarah? Is that Sarah? You listen to me—'

An avalanche of embarrassment, desperation and fury crushes me. I slam the receiver over and over on its holder, kick the plastic windows of the phone box and scream at the top of my voice. At least three people walk past me, quickening their steps. I don't care. I don't care about anything but getting my life back.

ROBIN

Robin has tried her hardest to stay away from the window. Her Mr Magpie didn't really exist, she doesn't want to see the real Henry Watkins, and she doesn't want to be seen by whoever was lurking in the shadows the other night.

She distracts herself in the gym room. She works harder, heavier, tries to make her muscles scream with pain every day. Ready, strong, able to protect herself.

She's ordered a shopping delivery, full of proteins and wholesome foods, watery green vegetables that she won't want to eat when they're here. The order should arrive in the next five minutes, according to the cheerful text message received not long ago. The delivery slot was chosen with precision, at extra cost. Well worth it.

Knock knock.

Robin looks through the crack in the curtain. She can make out the edge of the van just a little up the road. She walks to the front door, listens carefully for the delivery guy and is reassured by the tell-tale shuffle of heavy feet. She swipes the security chain out of the way, clicks open the lock, takes a deep breath and prepares for the weekly burst of small talk that means more to her than it could ever mean to the guy holding crates of shopping.

She starts to open the door carefully, just a crack at first while she builds up the nerve.

Suddenly, a thick black boot has been shoved in the gap and someone is pushing at her door from the outside. 'What the fuck?' she blurts as she pushes back against the door with everything she has.

The boot wriggles to get in further and the door is shoved roughly again and again from outside, the sound of a man grunting with exertion as it bashes against her. She uses every muscle in her body to push back. Every time the door inches nearer to the frame, her bare feet skid on the carpet.

'No!' she growls as she dredges every last drop of energy to drive the door back to a close, clicking it into the frame and fumbling to get the security chain back in place.

Whoever is out there kicks the door hard one last time but then Robin hears him running away.

She keeps pushing at the closed door anyway, her arms and shoulders locked in agony, her feet grazed and raw. She's breathing so hard she can't think over the sound of the air rushing in and out of her. After a minute, she lets go and creeps into the living room to look carefully through the smallest of gaps between the curtains. She sees the white van she'd mistaken for a delivery truck; it's reversing back into view and has the name of a hire company on it. Fuck. *Fuck.* She tugs her hair, bends over, can't think straight. All this paranoia coursing through her was right. *Fuck.*

Moments later, the supermarket van chugs into a space right opposite her house, a space they're not supposed to park in. The driver – one she's chatted to numerous times – is whistling obliviously as he stacks two crates on top of each other and carefully dodges cars to cross the road.

She ignores the knocks at first, but then her mobile vibrates. She answers, knows who is calling. Her heart is still thundering and she's pouring with sweat.

'Is that Robin Marshall?'

'Yes,' she whispers. Her name sounds alien and risky.

'I'm outside your house, love. With your shopping.'

'I'm sorry, I'm not well,' she says hurriedly.

'Well, you've paid for this stuff so I can't really take it back. I'll bring it through to your kitchen, if you like. Just come and open the door for me, would you?'

'I can't.'

There's a pause. 'Look, I really have to get this stuff dropped and move on. I'll be behind for the other customers otherwise.'

'Just leave it outside.'

'I can't do that here, it'll be nicked.'

'It's my stuff, isn't it?' she snapped.

'But you need to sign for it.' His voice with a new edge, she could hear it in duplicate through the living room window. She pictured his thick arms, his heavy boots. She didn't want more boots at her door.

'I'm contagious. Just push the thing through the letterbox and I'll sign it.'

'Okay, fine, whatever you want.'

The phone goes dead and the bulky handheld machine is shoved awkwardly through the letterbox. She grabs it, signs the screen with the stub of a nail and pushes it back through.

'It's for your own good,' she adds, trying a friendlier tone.

'Right,' he says. 'Thanks.' He doesn't mean thanks.

She goes back to the lounge, watches through the curtains as he reloads his empty crates and chugs off down the road. She looks around but can't see anyone else looking over and no black boots.

Outside, passersby help themselves to her milk, her bananas, her oats. Someone rifles through looking for booze but she hadn't bought any. They complain loudly to their friend. It takes under a minute for a small crowd to gather, safely coating her step. Unwitting protection. She pulls back the door and grabs what's left of her shopping as they skirmish away.

She slams the door shut again and sits on the floor of the hall surrounded by fruit, bottled water and vegetables in partly shredded carrier bags.

As her breathing finally slows and her heart stops leaping, Robin considers what just happened. She comes to two very important conclusions:

One: She's not just paranoid, someone really is out to get her. And being right about that is no comfort.

Two: Her best hope is that it's Henry Watkins, aware that it was her who called the police. Better the Devil you know. Better the Devil you can see.

Robin jogs upstairs gingerly, her grazed feet raw. She pulls up to the gym window and teases the curtain open a hair's breadth. She pushes her eye to the chink of light and looks straight at the Magpie flat. At first, she doesn't see him. Wonders, with creeping dread, whether he is still outside her house, standing angrily in his black boots, watching for an opportunity.

But then he appears in his window. He's wearing a towel around his waist, his wet hair scruffed. His chest is narrow and sunken. The towel slips down, showing jutting hips that used to have a layer of mid-thirties chub.

Even with superhero levels of speed he surely couldn't have been at her door and be back, naked and showered by now.

So it wasn't him. Someone is trying to get her and it wasn't him. Fuck.

Tears fall, a reaction Robin hates herself for, and she watches the equally defeated man pick up the mug of drink in front of him, stare at it for a moment and then hurl it at the wall.

As it explodes and showers everywhere, he crouches down on the floor and hugs his knees, shoulders shaking.

Robin doesn't see this. She's already crawled under her bed and is counting the bed slats to try to stop herself screaming.

CHAPTER TWENTY-EIGHT

1996

SARAH

I stand in the doorway of my mum's bedroom and watch her sleep. It's the middle of the day so Drew is at work but my school is closed for spring break and I'm hot and sticky in the house.

Before class broke up on Friday, some of the girls were talking about going shopping in Lenox Square but, despite my eager expression, none of them invited me so I kick about at home.

Our garden here in Atlanta is much bigger than both the gardens I had in Birch End. And it's more complicated too. There's not much grass but there are lots of rock sections and decks with lights rigged up and modern statues. There's a sprinkler system for what little lawn there is, and a water feature that bubbles around the clock. At night when it's still and quiet, I can hear it from my bed.

I think about Dad and how sad a garden like this would make him. 'There's nothing growing. There are no birds,' he'd say. There are hardly any flowers, but there are some reeds and grasses that make it look a bit like a desert.

Every year post-thirty, Mum seemed more agitated by what she saw in the mirror. 'You look great for your age,' Drew says, 'especially considering you've had twins.' 'I don't want "considering",' Mum says and he looks mystified. Often, like tonight, it falls to me to cobble dinner together while Mum's at the gym. I've been trying to get better at cooking, learning more dishes that Drew might like. Recently, I made macaroni cheese and put tuna in it, like I'd seen on TV.

Drew insisted on calling it 'a fine Italian meal', and ruffling my hair. The Drew I'd first met in England would never have dreamed of eating something bright orange like this. I was touched by his flexibility. 'Don't tell your mum,' he said, as he poured a slug of red wine into my glass. 'It goes with pasta after all.'

After a few more glasses of wine and another shot of it for me, my cheeks were pink and my stepfather was talkative.

'Angela's lost her spark, Sarah. I'm worried about her.'

I didn't say anything.

'All she talks about is the way she looks. She's still an attractive woman though, Sarah. I mean, she's got a few years on her since we met but she dresses very well and she's always made up. I said to her the other day, I said, "You're so beautiful now, Angela. I can only imagine how gorgeous you were before having children". You'd think I'd insulted her.'

He was getting more animated then, red-faced and frowning. 'I'm walking on egg shells in my own house here,' he suddenly exploded, and I'd jumped.

'Oh,' he'd said, rubbing my arm, 'don't mind me, don't mind me. I'm just worried about your mum.'

He'd opened another bottle by then and he'd poured himself a big glass and taken a gulp.

'Maybe she's homesick,' I said.

The corners of his mouth twisted down and he shook his head. 'Oh, I don't think it's that, I don't think it's that at all.'

'Maybe she's missing Robin and ...' I ground to a halt.

'She loves your sister but when she came here last time, your mum was as relieved as I was when she left. She's a handful,' he said, 'not like you. And as for that son of mine, well ...' Drew took another big swig, his lips purple when he pulled the glass away. 'Anyway, don't you worry about it. I'm sure your mum will perk up. We'll just have to give her some time.'

ROBIN

They're on their favourite spot: the wall behind the cricket pavilion, lined up like crows on a wire. Alistair and Robin, John and Callum. Smoking crumbly green weed in loose paper and laughing about nothing.

Callum is telling a story about John's mum nearly catching them together.

'We'd just, y'know, finished what we were doing and we hear footsteps up the stairs.' Callum's shoulders shake and John takes over.

'Cal was like,' John stage hisses, '"You promised me, John! You promised she'd be out!" and I really did think she'd be out for longer. Anyway, I'm lying there like a wally, butt-naked and trying to fumble around for my things, Cal's hopping about trying to get his clothes on and just before the door opens, Cal leaps into the wardrobe like something out of a sitcom, one leg in his trousers, and collapses on a pile of my clothes.'

'My heart's going like the clappers,' Callum takes over, 'and I'm lying there hiding in all his dirty kecks and trying to be silent while his mum walks over to him, puts a cup of tea down on the side and totally *ignores* the fact that John's lying there in bed, just wearing a T-shirt and covering his bits with a cushion at three in the afternoon.' They collapse into giggles, Callum leaning his head slightly onto John's shaking chest.

'She just thinks I'm lazy,' John adds.

'Teenagers!' Callum says, in a mock shrill voice.

Alistair and Robin laugh but Alistair looks away first. He and Robin still haven't done 'it' but now is not the time to bring that up. Especially in front of John, who is in the year above already.

'Seriously though, what would she do if she caught you?' Robin asks. 'I mean, you're practically an adult.'

'Yeah, but he's not.' John stops laughing and frowns as he takes the joint from Callum and takes a deep drag. 'And my mum is very traditional,' he says, as he blows out the smoke. 'She might not mind semi-nudity in the afternoon, but she certainly minds the idea of two men being together. Two *boys*, whatever.'

'She's a massive homophobe,' Callum adds, shrugging.

'Yeah, she is.'

Robin is passed the floppy damp paper and takes a lungful, coughing the smoke back out in bursts until Alistair thumps her on the back to help. They've been going out for a couple of months now, just a few weeks less than Callum and John.

Callum and John's friendship bloomed from a shared love of the same books and films, and into something deeper. They can't hold hands in public, they can't kiss, they can't really tell anyone outside of Robin and their closest friends.

When Callum first got together with John, he would spend hours lying on his bed, rambling to Robin about the various things that John had done or said. Analysing his own performances in the conversation, worrying that he'd belied his younger age or put John off. As the weeks passed, the analysis decreased and so too did Callum and Robin's time together. They played guitar together less, and she was often alone instead. She tried not to be hurt and decided it was time to act. Time to get a boyfriend of her own.

Alistair is in the same year as Callum and Robin, a short, baby-faced boy with a serious face but a kind manner. He's not exactly Robin's type, which is more in the region of Michael Hutchence, but he's an unassuming, easy-going lad, funny, trustworthy and willing to change. At her suggestion, he'd signed up for guitar lessons but has since switched to bass. It's a little easier to keep up with her that way.

They walk home from the park, arm-in-arm like a clothes line, stoned and sleepy, singing songs with patchy lyrics. As they reach a triple drain, they all sidestep it. It's unlucky. Although none of them understands why.

Robin had seen Alistair's look earlier. A look that she'd been ignoring for a while. But why not get it over with?

'I think I dropped my key behind the pavilion,' she mumbles.

'I've got mine,' Callum replies.

'Yeah but I still need to find it or I'll get bollocked. Come with me, Al?'

'Okay but I need to get home soon or I'll be—'

'You want to come with me,' Robin cuts him off, dropping her voice as they dropped back from the others. 'Before I change my mind.'

'Oh,' he says.

'Yeah,' she says. 'Why not?'

He presses his hand into hers and they jog giggling back from where they'd been minutes before.

Three months later, it had all collapsed.

Callum and John had been caught in the garden of John's house. It was late and John's parents were out. They'd laid in the back garden, shielded by trees and flowers, smoking and talking, wedged together on a big sun lounger. It had grown dark overhead, a deep grey sky yellowing at the corners where the spring sun was clinging on.

Callum had woken up to John kissing him. They were fully clothed, sleepy and stoned. And suddenly, standing over them and shouting unintelligible things was John's mother. She'd returned early with a headache, leaving John's dad boozing wherever they'd been. Callum had run out of the garden, ducking the furious waving arms as he skirmished away.

Over the following days, the quiet, gentle thing they'd grown had unravelled fast. Banned from seeing each other by John's parents, backed up by the school deputy headmaster, who had summoned both boys to the office to tell them in no uncertain terms that it would not be tolerated, that Callum's parents would be told if there were any more indiscretions. *Indiscretions.* John had stared straight ahead, nodded at the headteacher. After they left, Callum had tried to reach for John's hand and been shaken off.

After the 'intervention', John had stayed off school for a week and in the vacuum seemed to have shaken his feelings resolutely, or worked on a really good impression of someone who had. Callum, once encouraged into the upper-sixth-form common room by his older friends, was no longer welcome after a teacher-led clampdown on lower-sixth formers crossing the threshold. John had started to drive into school and take his friends into town in his Ford Fiesta at lunchtime. Callum had started to bunk off to avoid seeing him.

It was an insurmountable, iron-clad split.

Robin had called Alistair the day after Callum and John's break-up. 'I think we're just friends, really, aren't we?' He'd seen it coming; he could have made the call himself.

'We'll keep playing though, yeah? Still do the band we talked about?'

They'd agreed and met that night to hand over each other's stuff in the cricket field, to cement the plan. Made two scruffy little piles of tapes and borrowed hoodies on the stone steps as the daylight faded.

As they'd talked their goodbyes, their plans for new chapters as friends, they decided, well, just once more for luck. Behind the pavilion they'd pressed urgently against each other. His totally smooth face smelled of an aftershave he didn't need and the effort made Robin feel a tearfulness she'd never expected. They really would keep seeing each other as friends, she told herself. They really could start the band they'd talked about.

As they put their clothes straight, laughing at the uncharacteristic passion, Robin felt an urge to get back home. To get back to Callum, who finally needed her again.

She decided that she and Callum would stuff the latest guitar magazines up their sleeves at the petrol station, rip out the tablature and get playing. Just like they had through her upset years earlier, when Sarah didn't make it to visit.

And maybe they'd watch *Labyrinth* ten thousand times in a row, write nonsense poems, talk about writing a film but smoke too much weed to do anything but giggle. Same as they ever did. Sure he's upset now, she'd thought, but it will be okay soon. Back to normal.

Now Callum mashes at the PlayStation controller, sighs and flings it away. The wire loops over the arm of the sofa like a noose.

'Do you ever wish you could just press reset?' Callum says, huffing as he scoops the tossed controller.

'What, on this? You can. You're doing alright though.' Robin's tired of her stepbrother's tantrums just because he's bad at *Resident Evil*.

'No, not on this. Like, whichever way you turn you just make it worse. Like maybe you're just playing a bad go and there's a better game you could be playing. One where you get all the coins or all the lights are green or you beat every baddie or—'

'No.' Robin cuts him off.

'Forget it then.'

Callum leaves the controller dangling, slides out of the living room door and into the kitchen. He sits at the new mahogany-look table with his tin of tobacco and fumbles together a very skinny roll-up, a few scratchy odds and sods of weed dotted through it.

'That's a bit pitiful,' Robin says as she follows him and starts to make a mug of hot Ribena.

It's been two months and her patience is running thin. Callum's hers again, but he's battered and he's bruised. And he's very, very angry.

CHAPTER TWENTY-NINE

Present day
SARAH

I woke up to a notification on my phone, a type I've never had before. A direct message through Twitter from Alistair, Robin's bandmate and one-time boyfriend.

Message one:

Hi Sarah, I remember you. Sorry to say I've not seen Robin in a couple of years. She did a bunk in Manchester.

Message two:

Her email address is <u>robinmarshall762@gmail.com</u>. Kick her arse for me, we need to get back to work. Good luck.

I try to reply to thank him, but he doesn't follow me so I can't. I don't really care about that though, because I now know that my sister *is* in Manchester. Hilary was right, even if she was vague on the details. And, even better, I have her email address now.

I spend hours crafting an email on my phone. Stopping, starting, deleting. Going for a shower, starting again. There is so much to say but that doesn't mean any of it should be said, not yet.

In the end, after throwing up and having to sit with my face out of the window gulping in the syrupy city air, I go to an internet cafe nearby and buy myself thirty minutes of computer time and a thin grey tea.

I type out a new email:

Hi Robin, it's Sarah. I got your email address from Alistair. I hope you don't mind but the number I had for you doesn't work.

I'm in Manchester for a bit and I'd love to meet up. It's been too long.

I delete the last line, it sounds judgemental. I can't let her think I'm angry.

I'm in Manchester for a bit and I'd love to meet up. We must have lots to catch up on. Please call me on 076542275366 or reply to this and we can arrange something.

Take care,
Your sister, Sarah

I take a deep breath, sip the last gritty glug of tea and press send. Seconds later I have a reply.

Delivery to the following recipient failed permanently.

Before I can stop myself, I pull the keyboard out of its socket and throw it on the ground, chucking the empty tea cup after it.

'Hey!' the bearded guy behind the till shouts, the most engaged he's been in his surroundings since I've been here.

I feel a cold rage in my chest and snarl at him, 'It doesn't work properly.'

I troop back to the B&B. It wasn't a big hope but it's gone anyway. For one brief moment I'd felt a tiny thread was connecting me to my sister, wriggling its way down the streets and around the parks, tying us together so that I could tug it and find her. But that string's been cut.

ROBIN

Robin has not slept a whole night since the man with heavy boots tried to shove his way into her sanctuary. Instead, she lies sweating, whispering over and over to herself, 'Don't close your eyes.' With every extended blink, she slaps herself awake. Better to stay awake than be that vulnerable again.

She takes a flask of coffee upstairs each night but, despite her best efforts, she always falls into a restless sleep in the end.

Tonight, she even chewed some ProPlus energy tablets she found in her medicine cabinet, a relic of her late nights with the band while the rest of them took harder stuff. In those days, her form of night cap was often a frenzied and reckless dawn fuck with one of the hangers-on. The very thought is unimaginable now.

Despite the extra caffeine, she was still defeated and had started to nod off sitting upright on the bed. But now she's awake again. She doesn't know why.

And then she hears it.

Scratch, scratch.

It's a minute sound but it carries sharply through the blackness.

Scratch, scratch.

Rattle, rattle.

The sounds intensify and it becomes clear where they're coming from. Outside her bedroom window. Right outside.

Robin freezes.

The noises are so close and sharp that they fill the room like an echo chamber.

Fight or flight.

Robin is rooted to the spot, trying to catch hold of the thread of thought that will tell her what to do. She hears the movement of feet on the tiled roof below. The attic bedroom is set further back from the first two floors, which jut out in a dog-leg shape. Although it's on the top floor, it's the easiest window to reach. Despite the high roof, several cats have got up there before and yowled unsuccessfully to be let in.

She's not imagining this. She's not been imagining any of it.

Fight or flight.

There's no yowling, the sounds are deeper than a cat's paws on the tiles, heavier. Robin can make out the sound of distinct footsteps as they angle themselves and manoeuvre around. She thinks about that heavy, thick boot in her doorway, the rage that he threw at her door, the animal force she pushed back with. She was still spent from it, spent from days without proper sleep. But was he back for more already?

Fight or flight.

Her phone is charging downstairs but the thought of turning her back for even a moment, let alone making her way downstairs unprotected, terrifies her. Robin stays deadly still, frozen with the thought of his hands on her throat, her mouth clamped shut.

Up here, far from the street below, no-one would hear her scream.

Think, think. She tries to quieten the cold blood rushing through her ears, tries to review her options. She only has two and neither feel safe: try to slip out of the room and go downstairs to call the police – leaving the window unguarded until they arrive – or try to frighten him off. Threaten a racket.

She craves flight, but fight is the only real option.

Before she can talk herself out of it, Robin throws on the light and pulls the curtains back. All she can see is a slab of black night. She yells at the top of her voice, 'Get the fuck away from me or I'll fucking kill you!' She breathes hard, her knees knocking into one another, hands pouring with sweat. One second, two, three.

Suddenly a shape looms at the window and she leaps back. Dark clothes, pale skin and black holes for eyes. A monstrous snapshot.

The footsteps thump away, the old drainpipe groans and clangs as he climbs down it much faster than he'd climbed up.

She waits a few moments but has to check if he's really gone. She can make out the flats opposite, a lemony light still coming from the Watkins place but with no sign of Henry. The woman with the baby is shaking a bottle in her kitchen, swaying even without her baby in her arms. She pads away into the shadows. All this normality hangs like stage furniture, unreal to Robin.

Her small garden is silent. It's filled with black shapes that blend into the dark blue of the night. Wheelie bins, walls, the kitchen roof. There's nothing there. As Robin casts an eye along the alleyway, she sees a blur of movement as someone runs along and back out onto the road at the far right. He's gone. Thank god he chose flight. This time.

CHAPTER THIRTY

1998

ROBIN

Callum was shy about asking her, scuffing the toe of his trainer along the skirting board and staring at it, avoiding her eye. Robin pretended not to notice but her chest swelled with pride. The thrill of the upper hand.

'So would you?'

'Would I what?' she'd said, affecting a distracted tone as she lay ham carefully onto the bed of cheese, ready to layer another sprinkle of sharp cheddar on top.

'Like to meet him? Rez. My...' He trailed off, did a half-smile that made him look like a Levi's ad.

'Your booyyy-friennnddd!' Robin had teased, dragging the word out like a nursery rhyme and prodding his narrow chest with one finger.

He giggled, just a half-sound, easy to miss. 'Yeah,' he said, standing his six-foot frame upright and then booming like a town crier, 'My boyfriend!' They laughed. She didn't say anything for a moment and he understood. It was a delicate stage, applying the top slice of bread that had been buttered on the outside (the trick to perfect crust) and then closing the sandwich toaster lid.

'Yes,' she said as the lid snapped shut and the butter immediately sizzled under the hood. 'Of course I want to meet your booyyy-friennnddd!'

He didn't giggle then, just a small smile, dropped quickly. 'I really like him,' he'd said, that soft, low voice as ever.

'Good. Then I'm sure I will too. Right?'

'Right.'

Callum had been so crushed by the break-up with John, so hollowed out, that to see him even half filled up was a relief. But he wasn't the same. He hadn't been the same since. There were tatters at the edge. A slightly frayed temper. A quickness with his wit that, for the first time in their lives, could turn to cruelty. Which then turned to guilt. And the crushing fear of nature over nurture.

Callum was her control group. He was the true North. Robin had always felt safe pushing her own limits because she could always watch him to see the cut-off.

They'd smoked their first cigarette together, a dried-up John Player Special from a crunched-up pack that her dad had accidentally sat on and chucked to one side in his garage. They'd winced and coughed, eyes streaming.

'I don't like it,' Robin said, turning down the corners of her mouth and then taking another, more tentative drag.

'Me either.' Callum had grimaced, pecking at the cigarette like a little bird.

They'd drank their first drink together. A bottle of Babycham with Christmas dinner, when they were both thirteen. Robin's cheeks had gone bright red, Callum's ears the same. 'It's divine!' they'd joked. 'Simply spiffing!' There is a photo of that meal somewhere, taken by Hilary, Jack looking at the camera with concern, paper hat on his head. Robin and Callum laughing hysterically, food falling out of their mouths and hot pink faces.

First fag, first drink, first joint, first little pile of dust in a small wrapper.

Before John, Callum always used to say stop at just the point Robin was secretly hoping he would. Allowing her to sigh and roll her eyes and call him a big Jessie, or a 'Nana kid', and silently thank him in her head. Then the second phase of the night would kick in. Robin's paranoid phase.

'Check my pupils though.'

'You're fine, Robin.'

'My heart's racing too fast, Cal.'

A begrudging but gentle finger on the wrist, silent timing, confirmation. 'You're fine, you just need to sleep it off.'

'I can't sleep! I shouldn't have done it! It's getting worse. Why are your eyes alright? Cal? Why are your eyes alright – did you just pretend to bomb it?'

'Uh, enough, Rob.'

The tears. 'Why are you snapping at me?'

She was a nightmare on anything, but the more chemical, the worse it was. Callum seemed to be able to handle anything, his height maybe or his natural calm just absorbing and dissolving anything foreign that he put into his body. He'd be giggly to her wasted, chatty to her rushing, irritated to her wildly paranoid.

But after John he'd not had the same control. Going over his own line more and more. Noisy and aggressive or weepy and heavy, leaning his body on things and needing to be pulled up the stairs or wrestled into bed. As was her way, Hilary turned a blind eye and Jack was generally in a deep, throaty sleep by this point.

Robin knew he was seeing someone again. He'd been going out more. He'd come home wasted just as often – maybe even more – but seemed happier despite that. And this someone, she now knew, was a boy called Rez. Rez lived in Reading, he wasn't at school and Callum was obsessed with him. That's all she knew.

Callum invited Rez to the house when Hilary and Jack were out so Robin could meet him first. That was the plan, and yet at the last moment, Callum had gripped Robin's arm and whispered, 'Pretend we didn't plan this, okay? You just happen to be here, yeah? I feel a bit childish.'

'Sure,' she'd said, taken aback.

The doorbell rang, a dark shape blurred through the glass.

'I'll get it!' Robin sang, ignoring Callum's, 'No, wait, I'm coming.' She swung the door open with a big, jokey smile on her face.

'Alright?' Rez said.

'Oh,' Robin said, standing and staring. She hadn't meant to. She really hadn't meant to react that way. She'd expected to see someone who looked a lot like Callum, or like John, a smooth-faced, twinkly-eyed, slightly blushing lad. The man before her looked more like a crow than a smooth-skinned teenager.

'Robin,' Callum said behind her, his voice dipping in the middle.

'I'm ... no ... like...' Robin started and Rez looked over her head to Callum, who beckoned him in.

'Sorry, I, hi, I'm Robin,' she said as Rez squeezed past her and nudged up next to Callum.

'Hi Robin,' Rez said. He had shoulder-length dark hair and spiky features. His eyes were alert, flicking all around the hallway, taking everything in. There wasn't much to see: a small table from Argos with the phone on it, a shelf above that holding the Yellow Pages and the BT Telephone Book. Next to the stairs, the small hallway led to the living room and then the kitchen after that. A coat rack was weighed down with increasingly large coats that billowed out into the hall. Rez fought his way through after Callum, Robin trailed behind, stooping to pick up a denim jacket that had slumped to the floor.

'Tea?' she asked the room.

'Rez drinks coffee,' Callum answered, as if she should know that.

— —

'It didn't go well,' Robin told Sarah on the phone the next day. Callum used to stick around for the Sunday phone calls, sometimes he'd say hello. Not today. He'd been at Rez's since the incident yesterday.

'What did you do?' Sarah asked.

'Who says I did anything?'

'Didn't you?'

'Well, it wasn't … yeah, I did. But honestly, Sarah, you should see him. He looks like he works at the fairground. He's grim. He's older than Cal but he's a total drop-out. He smokes way too much puff, he reeks of it. And there's just nothing to him, y'know? Nothing special. And Cal's … Cal's special. He deserves someone special.' Robin was infuriated that she felt so tearful.

'You sure you're not just jealous?' Sarah asked.

'Oh fuck off!' Robin spat back. 'Rez is a total piece of shit and I'm looking out for my brother. How fucking dare you?' She slammed the phone down on her sister, even though Sarah had called them and was yet to speak to their dad.

Robin span around to storm into the kitchen and saw Callum standing in the doorway.

'I didn't think you were home,' she said quietly.

'Clearly.' He pushed past the coats, dropping a few, and then barged her out of the way as he ran up the stairs.

'I didn't know!' she shouted after him.

'That's not the point,' he snapped, slamming his bedroom door and turning his music straight on. 'From Despair to Where' by the Manic Street Preachers.

'Bit fucking obvious, Cal!' she shouted before she could stop herself.

The phone rang next to her. It would be her sister again. Robin wasn't ready to accept she'd over-reacted and taken it out on the wrong person. Instead she picked it up and, before Sarah could say a word, hissed, 'I'll get Dad.'

SARAH

Robin finished her exams last week. I didn't call to ask how they went – why should I? – but I know because Dad told me. He called on Sunday just gone. Mum lifted the handset and passed it quickly to me, walked off into the kitchen like someone had done wrong by her.

'So,' Dad had said after the initial routine of how are yous. 'Graduation next week.'

Words like graduation or Subway or soda sound wrong in Dad's mouth. He only uses them to mirror me, and the effort irritates me unfairly.

'Yeah,' I said, like it was nothing. 'The gown's upstairs, ready.'

It's crushed navy velvet with a dark blue cap and a mortar with gold tassels. It's hanging in my wardrobe in its dust sheet. I don't like seeing it there, its big, heavy shape looming like a monster every time I open the door. But knowing it's there, knowing I actually made it and I'm nearly onto my next chapter, that feels good. That's worth opening the door. I don't want to stand there on a stage surrounded by a sea of faces who never really liked me and will barely remember me. But I'll do it for Drew, who paid for it. Who likes to see me dressed up, likes to take pictures for his desk.

'And what's the name of the university you're going to?' Dad had asked.

I'd groaned a bit, because I bet he wouldn't forget which uni Robin was going to *if* she'd been going. 'Georgia State. It's only half an hour on the train, so I can stay living at home.'

Home. I know that still hurts him.

'Robin and Callum finished their exams last week,' Dad said after a pause.

'Oh right,' I'd said, trying to somehow get across both deep disinterest and blind fury.

'Did you want to talk to her? I could call her down—' he started to say.

'Nope, I have to go now. Love you.'

Graduation is tomorrow and I'm coming home after choosing a new lipstick from the drug store a few blocks over. It's not easy, choosing a colour to complement crushed navy velvet and gold tassels and I've been gone a while but I'm still surprised to see Drew's car is on the front drive already when I approach the house.

As I step into the hall, I hear my mum's voice.

'Everything gone to shit!' she's saying. '... dragging us down with you.'

I run up to get changed in my room and when I come back down it's quiet.

'Hey,' I say, as I step into the kitchen. My mum has her back to me, her hands gripping the side of the big sink, dangerously near the waste disposal. Her hair is held back with a headband and she's wearing gym clothes. She'd normally have been and come back by now, washed, dressed and fully made-up. She doesn't turn around.

'Hi, Sarah,' she says.

'Is everything okay?' I ask.

'No, Sarah, no, it's really fucking not,' my mum says, swearing like the old days. Before she held dinner parties.

I notice Drew is sitting nearby, his elbows on the table. His collar button is undone and his tie is in a little heap in front of him. He's perfectly silent, just raises his eyebrows to acknowledge me and then looks back down at the table. It's only five o'clock and he has a thick band of whiskey in a cut-glass tumbler. From the redness of eyes, I don't think it's his first.

'What's going on?' I start to ask but my mother cuts me off with, 'Drew's lost his job.'

'Oh no,' I say, and I look back at my stepdad. 'Why?'

'Yes, ask him,' my mother snaps. I say nothing, so she adds, 'Ask him about his "indiscretions".' She uses her fingers as quote marks.

I look back at Drew. He shrugs and one elbow slips off the table. 'It's a misunderstanding,' he sighs.

My mum puffs out her breath as if his words have just punched the air out of her.

'I'm going to the gym,' she says, to neither of us in particular.

I sit down next to him. 'Do you want a coffee?' I ask.

'Thank you anyway, angel,' he says, turning to me and patting my hand. 'But it's definitely a Scotch day.'

'What will happen now?' I ask. 'Where will you work?'

He looks up at me slowly, pulls his hand back onto his lap. 'I don't know,' he says, his eyes sad and droopy. 'My card's marked here now. Total misunderstanding but I'm done in this town.'

I don't know what to say but he likes it when I just listen so I try to look attentive.

'You know what though? My angel? My beautiful angel.'

Oh god, he's so much drunker than I realised. I humour him. 'What?'

'I'm so proud of *you*.' He jabs at my chest. 'And you know what else? We've had a good run at it here, but now you've finished school and I'm out of that hellhole of a company, I think it's time we went back home. Don't you? Back to England where you can get a decent drink and a good roast dinner. Wouldn't that be nice? Eh?' He squeezes my knee when I don't agree quickly enough. 'Wouldn't it?'

'Yeah,' I say and flash him a smile. I guess it would be good. I'd love to see my dad more, at least, though I push thoughts of Robin away. I'm still hurt by how easily she could take out her frustrations on me.

'Where will we live though? There are people renting our house.'

'We'll sling 'em out. We'll be able to buy a better house when we sell this place anyway.' I try to look happy. 'Yes,' he says, growing more emphatic, 'this is a good thing. Couldn't have come at a better time.'

I make us grilled cheese sandwiches and we eat them in silence. I try to imagine myself at an English university instead, maybe the one in Reading. I'd spent so long visualising my new start at Georgia State that the idea of a different new start makes me feel incredibly tired.

'Can I try some?' I say, gesturing to the whiskey. I've drunk alcohol a little before: some wine at home, warm beer in red cups at the few parties I've been to. But I've never tried hard liquor. It's what people have for shock though, and the longer I sit here, the more shocked I feel.

He grabs another tumbler from the set and pours a generous slop out of the decanter. I sip it and a burning sensation spreads from between my eyes and through my head.

'It suits you, sipping that,' Drew says. 'Very Wild West. Very cowgirl-esque. *Cool*, as you young women would say.'

Pretty sure I don't say that anything much is cool but I don't burst his bubble. I don't really want any more sips but I don't want to waste it so I try to swallow while bits of sandwich are still in my mouth to soak up the whiskey and mask the taste. When we were little, mum used to hide medicine in a teaspoon of jam so we wouldn't taste it. Robin would always gag on it anyway, but I tried to find the pleasure in the sharpness, knowing I'd done the right thing. Been the grown up.

We've drunk a little more. I've taken over the decanter for portion control but I still feel heady and a bit sweaty. A bit stumbly on my feet.

'Let's go into the den,' Drew says. 'I need to lie down.'

We flop onto the couch and I tuck my feet under me and try to look at something so I can practise looking in a straight line. The room tilts like a ship.

'You remind me so much of your mother,' he says, as he often does. 'Would you do something for me? Something she used to do?'

'What?' I ask nervously.

'Would you just rub my shoulders a bit? I'm so tensed up after today and I just want to shake it off, try to rest.'

I don't want to, not really. I've never done this before, but I guess I have hugged these shoulders. As I've touched them before, I think, *Okay*.

After a bit of clumsy rubbing and kneading, he lets out a long sigh. 'Your touch is wonderful, Sarah,' he says. I freeze, his shoulders in my hand. The whir of the room, tilting like it could slide into the sea.

I'm not sure how long I've been frozen. Long enough to think, *I've frozen, he knows I've frozen, what do I do?* or thoughts to that effect. Eventually I start to say 'thank you' but the words are lost somewhere and he's reached behind to where I'm leaning on the sofa and is rubbing my arms.

'Come round here,' he says. 'It's your turn.'

'No, it's fine,' I say. 'Thank you anyway.' But he pats the cushion next to him until I comply.

I sit stiffly on the couch. I don't think he should do this, but he's in charge so it must be okay. He rubs my head, but it's the way you'd pat a dog. Heavy-handed, open-palmed. Eventually he moves down to my back. It's been so long since anyone touched me that my body betrays me. It starts to tingle a little bit, just at the base of my spine. I realise that I don't *entirely* want him to stop. Well, I don't want the touch to stop, but I wish it wasn't from him.

He's still touching my back, moving up and down from the top of my knickers to the clasp on my bra, when he asks me about boyfriends. When I tell Drew that I don't have a boyfriend, he's pleased.

'Good,' he says. 'You save yourself for someone who appreciates you. Knows how special you are.'

He moves his hand back into his own lap. I hear him swallow. My skin feels the absence of his fingers. 'You really are special,' he says as I turn back to face him. He strokes my cheek so I close my eyes. When I open them, he's looking at me with sad eyes. I feel foggy, a little dizzy, but I appreciate the intensity of the gaze when, really, he should have better things to think about than me after today's news.

Right now, he's looking at me like I'm the only thing in the world. When he holds my chin in his right hand and moves my face towards his, I don't stop him.

I know his smell so well. Sandalwood aftershave and whiskey rush at me.

The room sways and swoops, the ceiling seems to ripple as I look up at it and I feel Drew's big hand teasing my ponytail loose and fanning my hair out under me. I wait for him to ask, 'Are you okay?' or 'Do you want me to stop?' I wait for permission to say, 'I'm not okay' and 'I do want to stop' but it doesn't come. The sofa sags under us as he climbs onto me and I feel an increased sense of panic. Not only do I not want to be lying under him like this, I'm petrified that I have to go through with something I absolutely don't want to do. And I'm terrified that I won't know what to do in the moment. I've only done things like this with one boy before and our mutual inexperience had set the pace. Will Drew laugh at my efforts? Will he stop, disappointed, shake his head and walk out of the den? Will I get in trouble?

I feel him grappling with the button on my jeans. So far there's very little expected of me except to just be here, this body, loose-limbed with liquor. I feel him tug my jeans down over my legs.

Moving seems like a hell of an effort now. I haven't had a sip of drink for a while but somehow I feel drunker.

He hoists himself up again, frees one hand to run it along my side, over my hip. He parts my legs, burrows into me with his heavy hips. I gasp. Maybe he mistakes my panic for excitement because he shoves into me roughly and his whole body lands on me, the weight making it hard to breathe beyond shallow gasps. He licks my ear, something I thought was an urban myth. I don't know what response is expected so I say nothing, do nothing. Grimace. I can hear how slimy it is. I focus on that. I'm too pinned down to do anything and in a way I'm glad to be anchored in this spinning room. His mouth is still close to my ear, his hot breath running through my hair. It's like he's in a horrible trance. 'Oh god,' he murmurs and he thrusts harder still until he stops, goes rigid, shakes a moment and then flops down again.

I lay in the spinning dark. Hot tears curl out from the corners of my eyes and fall heavily onto the sofa cushions under me. The blackness of the room makes my skin cold, like I'm lying outside on the soil. I feel heavier than I've ever felt.

I lay on the sofa long after Drew has eased himself off my body and staggered up the stairs, falling half-clothed onto the empty bed that he shares with my mum.

CHAPTER THIRTY-ONE

Present day

SARAH

When I get back to the magnolia room I look again at the map of Chorlton with its streets marked. Each pen scratch showing the places I've peered up at windows, imagining my sister looking back at me. The proverbial needle in a haystack.

And then before I realise what I'm doing I'm crying and ripping, ripping and crying, until my hands are riddled with paper cuts and Chorlton lies in pieces on the floor.

Just then, the phone rings. Only one person has the number but I still answer cautiously.

'Hello?' I can't believe it's actually ringing.

'Alright?' the voice says.

'Who is this?' I answer, although I know.

'It's Ryan,' he says, 'from The Spice Room. Listen, I think I know where your sister is.'

Apparently Ryan had mentioned me and my visit to everyone who worked for the curry house and all the regular customers.

'I just felt bad for you,' he said, and I could picture him shrugging his shoulders when he said it. 'Well, I told Dev, one of our drivers. I showed him the picture you left. He reckons he recognised her.'

'Really?' I ask, breathless.

'Yeah,' he said. 'He thinks so. I mean, it's not definite or owt but—'

'Where did he recognise her from? Did he know where she was?

Where she lives?' I'm panting and I don't mean to and I'm worried that I'm scaring him but when he speaks, he sounds excited more than anything.

'He'd had a run-in with her. I mean, y'know, a full-on row by his account. Dev does exaggerate though but, nah, don't get the wrong idea, he's not lying, he does think he's seen her but his idea of a big fight is probably more like a bit of mither.'

'Where did he see her?'

'Apparently he'd taken her order around for delivery, a while back, months and months ago. It's all one-way around there 'cos she lives near the green—'

He drops it in so casually that I almost miss it. She lives near the green. I can find my sister near the green.

'And 'cos it's all one-way around there, he couldn't stop right outside so he says he called the number he had from the order and told her he was around the corner and could someone come and grab it as there was a copper watching so he couldn't park up properly.'

'She lives by the green?' I ask again, scared I misheard.

'Yeah,' Ryan says, like this is a really small point getting in the way of the story, 'and she flipped her lid apparently. Wouldn't come and get it, wanted her money back if he wouldn't bring it to the door, all this.'

'Really? So what happened – did he see her?'

'Well, he didn't have a choice, he parked a few more streets away and walked it around. Said he thought maybe she was in a wheelchair or summat, couldn't leave the house, but when he got there, she opened the door and looked fine. Had another go at him and sent him on his way.'

'That does sound like my sister,' I say.

'I dunno, this is just what Dev says but he recognised her from the picture and said she was a right mouthy, well, whatever, but I think we might have found her for you anyway.'

'Thank you so much,' I say, still not fully believing it could be true. 'I'm so grateful,' I add. Robin or not, I really am touched that he bothered.

I'm about to put the phone down and head to the green, start knocking on doors, when he says, 'Do you not want her address then?'

ROBIN

The woman at the security company had spoken with such patience that Robin had to take a moment to compose herself.

She'd ordered a new alarm system, locks on the windows and bolts for the front door, back door and garden gate. The appointment time would be, she was assured, pinpoint accurate. In five days' time.

'I know I sound like a nut,' Robin had said, 'but it's really very important that he's exactly on time.'

'You don't sound like a nut at all, duck,' the woman had said, her voice giving away a history of receiving such calls.

Robin wished her dad was still alive. That she could just call on him to come and sort everything out. He'd have put new locks on for her, checked the gate was secure. Maybe even taken her home.

With one or two links missing from a family chain, the whole thing can fall to pieces. How long had it been since Robin saw Sarah? Was their father's funeral really the last time? Robin felt at once guilty for that and defensive. It took two to stay in touch, right, it wasn't just her job. But the truth was, she knew she'd pulled away. Let it happen.

The night of the funeral, she'd slept in her old room. Wide awake from jet lag, dried out from tears. She'd given up at five in the morning, gone to walk around the house, trying not to wake anyone. Eventually she decided to take a stroll to the pavilion, her and Callum's old spot. She pulled her coat on over her pyjamas, stuffed her bare feet into her trainers and went to the front door. An envelope was jutting through the letterbox, another card from well-wishers, except this one was addressed to her. Hand-delivered, just the name.

She leaned on the old telephone table, a strange comfort from seeing the latest Yellow Pages and BT Telephone Book, and opened the card.

A picture of flowers on the front.

In sympathy

Inside, in carefully Biro-ed letters, it said:

Who will you blame this time?

She'd stared and then read it again, as if her imagination had misfired.

She folded it in two and went to throw it in the kitchen bin, shoved it in deep among the cold teabags. She'd padded upstairs, shoved the rest of her things back into her suitcases and called for a taxi. She left a note of goodbye.

Afterwards, Robin used to check in with Hilary. Occasional phone calls and texts, postcards from abroad. The calls grew shorter and further apart. Each one stilted and sad.

One of the last calls with Hilary – what was it, three, four years ago? – that's when Robin learned that Sarah had moved away. *Good for you,* she'd thought, though it had made her feel more alone.

Now Robin's phone was unplugged, her number ex-directory. Her new mobile number wasn't listed anywhere. It dawned on Robin that her stepmother had no real way of getting in touch. For a brief moment, Robin's finger hovered over the 'Home' number on her mobile, unchanged for however many other mobile phones preceded this one.

Her finger stayed aloft. She wanted to reassure Hilary, to be reassured that her stepmother was okay, healthy, living a rich and full life. Wasn't dead. But the first question Hilary would ask is: 'How are you?' and the very thought of trying to answer that pushed Robin's phone straight back in her pocket.

How am I? Fuck, no. Robin is riddled with fear, coated in sweat, sleep-deprived and aching. There's nowhere she can feel safe any more. Where once she could sit in her bedroom, perched and observant, that room had been tainted. Watching children's TV in the lounge didn't make her feel safe any more, just small.

She sits at the top of the stairs, phone in hand, facing the front door. It's going to come, she knows it's going to come.

Knock knock. The fist cracks onto the wood with an angry force. If it really was him up there on her roof the other night, he was undeterred by her screaming confrontation. The door heaves and shakes on its hinges.

Another five days before the security people come. Another four nights fighting sleep.

The knocks are faster now. And lower, like some are actually kicks from a heavy boot. A boot imprinted in her memory. The door creaks and groans but stays firm and, eventually, the noise ends.

CHAPTER THIRTY-TWO

1998

SARAH

I don't remember going to bed but I wake up just in time to stagger into my bathroom to throw up. A rush of sour bile surges up my body, and I buck and buck until it's all out. A tangy sweetness in the air revolts me.

I splash my face with water and try to brush my teeth, but as soon as the bristles accidentally touch my tongue, I'm sick again.

Eventually, empty and aching, I tread lightly downstairs for a glass of water and some Tylenol. There's no-one in. I see the clock says ten o'clock and I see the blinking light of the answerphone.

Graduation.

The realisation of what I've missed tumbles away to nothing as the memory of last night looms larger. I pull open the dishwasher to get myself a glass for water. Someone filled it and put it on last night; the two glasses are side by side on the top rack.

I don't know what time my mother got home; she spends hours doing classes and then floating in the Jacuzzi. I don't know who cleared away the drinks, I only hope it was Drew. A memory of his big hands bursts into my head and I throw up in the sink and blast it away as fast as I can.

I stand by the phone for a long while, my eyes staring at the blinking light.

It's just gone three in the afternoon in Birch End. The time difference no longer a calculation, just absorbed knowledge after years. I imagine picking up the handset and dialling. Dad will be at work, oblivious and whistling. Hilary would probably answer. Would she know from my voice?

I imagine telling Robin, trying to find the words. I imagine Robin's disgust and rage travelling up the phone cable. I imagine her telling me to leave, to come home, to kick him in the nuts. I imagine her defensive of me, telling me without words that she loves me, that there's somewhere else I can go.

But then ... it might not work that way. How easily she can cut the strings between us, her defensiveness over Callum more vital to her than our twin hearts beating together. It's been weeks since we spoke, and she's made no effort to apologise for the way she acted when I asked a genuine, caring question.

I feel my stomach lurch again, imagine her telling me, 'Maybe this is what you wanted', like she says about America when she's angry. 'You love America, you think you're too good for England.'

I don't play the answerphone message or make the call. I go up and lie on my bed, sipping water and prodding the memories from every angle to try to make them right, make them smaller and fold them away.

By the afternoon, my sickness has dulled to a delicate stomach and my headache is a constant fuzz. I make my slow way downstairs, ready to attempt to eat something. Drew and Mum are at the kitchen table. Neither one of them mentions my missed graduation ceremony. They seem to have made up; my mother has turned her disapproval to the manner of the sacking. And has joined in the positive spin that Drew has given it.

'You look peaky,' she says to me as I lean on the kitchen counter and avoid looking at Drew.

'You should go to bed,' Drew says, sternly.

'Hang on though,' Mum says, 'we should tell her what's happening first.'

I don't care, I don't care, I just want to shove my head under the pillow and crunch my eyes shut and hope I see something different when I do. I don't want to be in the room with him, his body, his hands, his face, his smell, his nonchalance.

She tells me they've seen a realtor, that they can make a profit on this house and 'flip it' pretty quickly. We're going to move back to the UK, live somewhere 'nice and bijou' while we wait for this house to sell and for the tenants in Birch End to find somewhere.

'And you can go to uni there, and we'll be near Robin again.'

'Great.' I manage a small smile, still avoiding eye contact. My belly is emptier than it's ever been and it gurgles loudly. I can't face food after all. 'I need to lie down.'

As I walk upstairs, I hear my mum ask Drew what happened last night. I hear her mention the whiskey, the glasses. She must know. She must know and have folded it down like origami and slotted it away. Choosing a new 'bijou' house in England instead. Or maybe she just thinks that what happened is okay. Maybe that's what I'm supposed to think too. Who the hell is left for me to ask what I should think now?

ROBIN

It's after ten, but Robin can hear the raised voices as she approaches the house. Exhilarated from hours of frenzied band practice, her joy gives way to dread as she turns her key.

'You can't just do nothing, Callum, that's not the way the world works,' her dad's saying.

'I've got ambitions,' Callum's saying, in his soft voice. 'You're talking like I want to go on the dole for the rest of my life. I just don't see the point in going to university.'

'Fine,' Hilary says, 'we don't mind that. But you need to do *something*.'

'What's Robin doing?' Callum huffs.

'She's got the band—' her dad says and Callum hoots with sarcastic laughter.

'That's not a job! That's a hobby. *I* play guitar too, why doesn't that count?'

'It's kind of a job,' Hilary says. 'The band have earned a bit of money, they've played a couple of concerts.'

'*Weddings*,' Callum says, defiantly. 'And pubs.'

'Where have you played?' Jack asks, as Hilary tries to stop him.

'Well, nowhere, obviously, because I'm just a gigantic disappointment.' A chair scrapes and Callum appears in the hall, goes to push past Robin but stops. They're toe to toe.

She reaches up and puts her hand on his shoulder. 'Y'alright?'

They've danced around each other ever since the fall-out over Rez. Sliding in and out of rooms without eye contact, polite nods at dinner, bolting meals fast and without fuss. More often than not, Callum leaves soon after, a car waiting for him outside, driven by Rez or one of his scabby entourage. 'He can't exactly come in, can he?' Callum snapped at Hilary a few days ago. 'Robin made it very clear he wasn't welcome.'

Callum breathes in hard but let's it go again. 'Yeah,' he says, chewing the inside of his mouth and dropping his head onto her shoulder. 'Just a bit fucked off.'

It's the longest they've spoken in weeks.

'Want to play guitar?' Robin says, her face serious and hopeful. 'I can show you what I've been working on.'

He pauses. 'Okay, go on then.'

They troop upstairs, Robin heaves her Epiphone SG off her shoulder and props it in the corner, picks up her old acoustic and sits down. Its belly is covered in stickers, Tippexed band names and symbols scratched and flaking. She runs her fingers over them, blurred memories of summer days spent carefully painting them on together.

'So,' she says, putting her callused fingers on the strings and looking at Callum. 'This is something I've been working on but the bridge isn't right. You wanna help?'

'Sure,' he says, lies himself down on his belly to listen. Within a few chords, he's asleep.

Robin wakes up first the next morning, still wearing her clothes and arm sore from being cricked around a guitar neck all night. She goes downstairs to find Hilary at the kitchen table, neat stacks of invoices and receipts, a crunchy thick calculator and a pot of tea in front of her.

'Hey,' Robin says.

'Hi.' Hilary slides her thick bookkeeping glasses from her nose and shakes her hair a little behind her. 'Want some tea?'

'Yeah, thanks.' She waits a beat but can't help but interfere. 'Hilary, I'm really worried about Cal,' Robin says. 'And I don't want to be a grass but if I don't say something, I'll regret it.'

'What's going on?' Hilary frowns.

'He's just not himself, you know? All he does is hang out with Rez and smoke weed and drink. He's got this amazing brain and he's just doing nothing with it.'

'You're both eighteen, Robin, even I'd had the odd joint at your age, and I don't want to clip his wings and control him like his father did.'

'But he's not just experimenting, he's just drifting miserably along. And he's choosing to spend time with Rez over any of us. He's drifting *away* from us.'

Hilary takes a deep breath and pours them both another cup of tea.

'Maybe you're right and I don't like it either. But if I start putting my foot down, he's going to bolt.' She thought for a moment. 'Here's what I think we should do...'

Robin hadn't liked the idea but Hilary had invited Rez over for Sunday lunch anyway. Callum had agreed but wanted assurances that no-one would 'grill him'.

'I just want to meet the person you're spending so much time with, love,' Hilary had said. 'If he's special to you?'

Callum had looked down at his feet, shuffled about. 'Yeah, he is.'

'Well then,' she'd said.

'Well then,' he'd answered.

Rez had arrived dead on time at 1 p.m. that Sunday. He had some garage flowers for Hilary and bottle of Bell's whiskey for Jack.

'Where d'ya steal that from?' Robin asked and Rez had frowned.

'Robin!' Callum snapped.

'I was only joking,' she'd sighed, blushing and angry about it.

Rez had looked so strange there, sitting at the table in a shirt and trousers that must have been borrowed from someone bigger. Callum had given him encouraging smiles when he thought no-one was looking.

Rez had his greasy hair pulled back in a ponytail and smelled like he might have aftershave on. *Bad aftershave*, Robin had thought, *probably bought from some dodgy guy in the pub. Or stolen.*

'So,' Hilary had said as she loaded the plates with peas. 'Are you at university, Rez?'

Callum had coughed.

'I'm working, actually, Mrs Marshall.'

'Oh yeah?' Jack had asked. 'What do you do, Rex?'

'It's *Rez*, Dad,' Robin had prompted, trying to show Callum she was on his side but he glowered at her.

'What do you do, son?' Jack asked.

'I'm a welder.'

'Ah.' Jack looked pleased. 'It's a good line of work, that,' he said. 'I used to know a guy who made a killing welding, did it industrially. George Whassisname. Wato, was it, Hilary?'

'No idea, Jack.'

'George … George something. Greek guy. Do you know him?'

'No.' Rez had shrugged and smiled a little bit. His sharp little teeth flashing.

'Good bloke, he is. You ever meet a Greek George on a job, tell him Jack the gardener says hi.'

'I'll do that,' Rez said, swallowing a big forkful of meat and veg. The gravy dripped a little down his big shirt and Callum dabbed it off with a serviette while Robin smirked before she could stop herself. She saw Callum's eyes narrow.

'You got something to say?' he asked.

'Me?' Robin said, opening her eyes wide.

'Yes, Robin, you,' he said flatly.

'No, Callum, there's really nothing for me to say. Is there?'

'Well, I have something to say,' he said, more softly, turning away from Robin and looking to his mum. 'Well, we both do.'

Rez had carried on chewing, looking at his plate as Callum said, 'I got a job.'

'Oh that's great news,' Hilary said, smiling and nudging Jack.

'Great news,' Jack repeated.

'Shifts in a call centre in Reading. Four days on, four days off. Taking calls from the shopping channel.'

'Telesales?' Hilary had said, trying to disguise her disappointment.

'It's just a start, Mum, it's something to pay the rent while I work out what I really want to do.'

'Rent?' Jack had snorted a little. 'When have you ever paid rent, son?'

'We don't want your money, Cal,' Hilary added.

'Well, here's the thing.' He spread his long fingers on the table, next to his abandoned cutlery. 'The job's in Reading. And Rez is in Reading. So we thought, well, it makes sense really, Rez has the space—'

'Oh no,' Hilary said.

Callum flashed a look at Rez, then back at his mum who had stood up to hug him from behind. He stood up and hugged her back, wrapping his long arms around her narrow shoulders.

'It's just down the road, Mum. I spend most of my time there anyway.'

Robin felt sick.

'How are you going to afford rent *and* all that shit you smoke and shove down your neck?'

'I'll miss you too, Robin,' he said, and his voice broke and took the wind out of her.

'Are you really going?' she gasped, trying to keep her eyes dry.

'Yeah,' he said.

'I don't want you to,' she croaked.

'I know.'

When the meal was over, Rez shook Jack's hand and kissed Hilary's cheek. He pushed past Robin without saying a word and went to wait in the car.

Robin and Callum had hugged then properly. No sniping, no words, locked tightly together for the first time.

He came back for his stuff the next day.

As Rez's car bumped and banged down the road, loaded with Callum and his clothes, books and music, Jack held Hilary as she sobbed. Robin climbed back up the stairs, angry at her own tears, and kicked her way into her bedroom. There she found a shoebox of demo tapes and half-finished lyrics on her bed, and his acoustic guitar.

CHAPTER THIRTY-THREE

Present day

SARAH

Number 68 George Mews isn't a very impressive house for a rock star.

The windows are grimy and all the curtains are closed. It dawns on me that Robin may have only lived here for a short time before moving on, not bothering to tell Hilary that she'd left the city. I knock but there's no reply. I listen at the door but can't hear anything. Even if I did hear movement, it might not be Robin. Maybe she was never even here.

I feel like I'm being watched. Probably because I'm behaving strangely, and so I expect everyone around to notice that but when I look, I can't see anyone paying me the slightest attention. I hover on the step and look across the green. A few dog walkers, some teenagers sitting on the grass drinking Coke. I think I see a tall figure further away in the shade of the trees but the shadows make it hard to see clearly. A figure that makes me shiver. The shape of a long-lost ghost.

It's far more likely to be a drug dealer, or someone waiting for a secret assignation with a forbidden love. For all I know, it's one of the guys from The Spice Room laughing at me.

ROBIN

Today is a day like yesterday and the day before. Like last week too. But it feels different. It is different. At eight-thirty on the dot, a man called Kevin from the security company is going to knock on her door, be invited inside, and lock her house up like Fort Knox.

She'd still be living in a box, but it would be a safer box. A small, invisible thread would link her to people whose sole job it was to keep her safe. Alarms with automatic connections to security guards, panic buttons, military-grade locks and chains. Finally, she wouldn't be alone and vulnerable to whoever was targeting her.

She'd woken up about seven and scrambled out from under her bed, where she'd hopefully slept for the last time. She'd had a cup of tea while leaning against the kitchen counter and then made another, followed by a protein smoothie that made her gag.

She hovered in the kitchen for a while, scrolling through the workout apps on her phone. When her smoothie had gone down enough, she went up to the bathroom to brush her teeth and started taking her daily steps from there.

She'd only done three laps of the house when she paused in the gym room, glancing across at the backs of the flats.

The old lady was washing up but she wasn't looking in Robin's direction. The new guy was standing in his patio door with a mug in one hand and a cigarette in the other. He was rocking slightly on his heels and misjudged it, needing to correct himself or he would have fallen on his arse.

Robin moved up to Henry Watkins. He'd been up late. She'd seen a light on in his son's room when she had gone to the loo in the night, had seen the shape of him in there, as he often was. Had shaken her head and looked away.

Now he's in his son's window. He's not looking her way and he's sitting down by the looks of it. Perching, Robin thinks, on the small chair with its miniature table. The one they'd bought for the boy not so long ago and where Robin had seen him doing drawings and making Lego buildings.

Henry's profile faces the window, his grey streak more prominent than ever now his hair was longer. He looks at once wild and caged.

He stands up. Walks to the middle of the room and bends down. He's fiddling with something when the knock on Robin's door comes. It's only quarter past eight, and she was promised eight-thirty. She made it very clear she wouldn't answer at any other time. But ... she's desperate to get the work done, desperate for it to be Kevin from the security firm. She wavers but continues to watch the flats.

This knock is polite. It's gentle. It must be Kevin, mustn't it? She was so clear about the time though.

She hovers on the landing, listening for clues that don't exist. The knocks come again and still they're quiet and gentle.

Robin ignores the door, just like she told the woman on the phone that she would when she arranged the appointment. They'd really seemed to take her seriously, and this betrayal feels more personal than it should.

Irritated and anxious, she looks back at the Magpie flat. *The Watkins flat*, she corrects herself. Henry has pulled the little chair into the middle of the room and is stepping on it with one foot, like he's testing it. He stops, puts the chair back where it was and drags the small table to the centre of the room instead. He takes the Lego house from the surface, places it carefully on the floor.

When he takes the cord from his dressing gown, Robin realises what she's seeing. *Not this. Please, anything but this.*

There's another knock on the door but it barely registers with Robin. She's breathing hard, staring as Henry Watkins ties the cord carefully into a loop. His concentration is creating the same frown it used to when he built a new toy for his son, or when he took his wife's mobile from her bag and scrolled through it, stopping every ten seconds to check for her in the hallway.

He's tugging on the cord now, checking that the knot slides up in the way he wants it to. Testing it over his head, around his neck.

Robin can't think straight. Can't move. She's watching uselessly as he keeps screwing up the knot he's trying to make. The knocks come again. *Kevin the security man, please be Kevin the security man. He can go over and stop Henry Watkins.*

Robin runs down the stairs. Her knees shake, she's Bambi-legged and clumsy. She takes a deep breath and opens the door as far as the safety chain will allow. Pushes her eye to the gap of daylight and jumps in surprise.

It's not the security man.

CHAPTER THIRTY-FOUR

1998

SARAH

My mother knows, I'm sure of it. Knows what happened and what I did. She avoids me now or watches me carefully when I am in the room with her.

'Are you okay about moving back?' she asks me. 'Do you want to stay in Atlanta by yourself? Take up your uni place. I'm sure we could find the money when we've sold the house.' She looks away, fiddles with the scatter cushions. I know why she wants rid of me.

'Drew would do anything for you, you know.'

I turn to walk out. I don't know what point she's trying to make and I don't know what she wants to say. I don't want to hear it.

'You two have always been close, haven't you?' she asks, but it's not really a question. It's an implication.

'I want to go back to England,' I say. 'And I'm glad we're leaving because I want to live with my dad.'

'Are you sure?' she says, eyebrows raised.

'Deadly. And don't try to talk me out of it.'

I leave her sitting open-mouthed on the couch and go back up to my room to carry on packing.

When I come back down it's late afternoon and I can hear my mum on the phone to my dad.

'You don't have to gloat about it,' she says. A pause. 'Yes you are, Jack.'

I say I'll make my own dinner, just as I have for the last few weeks. I can't bring myself to sit at a table with them, not while they prattle on about their great English adventure and Drew rubs my mother's leg and pinches her bum when she stands up. I'd think that he's wiped it from his memory but he's barely met my eye since that night. I can't wipe it from my memory. I'll never forget.

I've stayed in my room watching TV endlessly.

The phone trills and I ignore it as I always do.

'It's for you,' my mum calls up the stairs.

'I'm not here,' I say, as I have since graduation.

'Yes you are. It's your sister.'

It's the first time we've spoken since we fell out. Neither of us mention it. My moving back is bigger, it pushes the argument into the past.

Still, Robin talks guardedly. She says she's excited about having me back but then she asks so many questions about my plans and the sleeping arrangements that I can't help but think she's the opposite of excited.

Just as Dad tells her to wrap it up in the background, she asks me, 'Are you okay?'

Am I okay? *No,* I want to say. *I'm pretty much the opposite of okay.* My mother has thrown me to the wolves, my sister doesn't want me home and I don't know if I should go to university in England, a country I barely remember, stay here on my own or try to get a job when I haven't the first clue what I want to do let alone what I'm capable of doing. But none of those things really stand up next to the big one. The one I can't possibly say right now. Not here. Not on the phone. Not to my sister.

I'm pregnant.

ROBIN

Last week, Callum came to the house for dinner and he and Robin got pissed together for the first time in a long while. Rez was working, though Robin was sceptical about the kind of work that a welder would need to do at night.

It started with a tense dinner, a shared bottle of red turned into raiding the spirits after Jack and Hilary went upstairs.

They lay on the sofa, heads at each end, jostling to get comfortable as the TV shimmered silently in the background.

'Want to hear a story?' Callum said.

'Sure.'

'Before I got the call centre job, I went for an interview in the sweets factory that Dad used to work for, back when he sold chocolate and stuff.'

'Mmm? Did you get offered it?' Robin had asked, her eyes closed.

'No. But I was a mess, I did a bad interview. I couldn't even get a job packing sweets. Fuck!' He laughed a bit, she didn't.

'Have I ever told you about the family fun day they held there when I was a kid?'

He had, but she let him tell it again. He seemed to need to. Hilary and Callum, then five, had been summoned into the grounds for a family day, before Drew moved into soft drinks. At the time Drew was a field sales rep for a confectioner, travelling with boxes of chocolate and boiled sweets in his car, pushing them on the small retailers of the south. His nearest rival in the sales charts had brought his own son to the company grounds too, a boy of a similar age who – in Callum's re-telling at least – was the size of a dumper truck.

The boys had been pitted against each other in an apple-bobbing competition. The other boy had grabbed three apples between his teeth, one-by-one, and then watched, dripping, as Callum bobbed two, then another. As he went back in for a fourth – the winning apple – the boy had grabbed Callum's head and held it under the water. The two men, watching their sons, had jostled each other rather than helped and by the time the dumper-truck kid had released him, Callum was crying, his T-shirt wet from the drum of water and his shorts wet from pee.

That night, Callum had been made to sleep in the garden: his father's method for toughening him up. Hilary had crept out after midnight, when Drew was asleep, and curled up with her son, his head in her lap, picnic blankets over them both.

The jeers of Drew's colleagues about his 'pansy son' forced him to leave the company, Callum was repeatedly told while he still lived with his father. After the split, Hilary told Callum emphatically that Drew had no choice but to leave that job, he'd tried it on with the boss's young wife.

Robin wondered if Drew was still up to those tricks, still sidling up to younger women while her mother turned a blind eye. Wondered if he was still willing to break up a family. She still remembered the way he'd looked at her mum, the way he'd touched her in the kitchen, the way he'd licked his lips when she spoke, the way she giggled. It had confused Robin back then, pressed on her mind. She knew it looked wrong, but had no root, no explanation. Looking back now, it revolted her. Every decision her mother had made revolted her, but at least there was one silver lining. Despite the animosity of recent months, despite his horrible choice of boyfriend and waste of talent, she really loved her brother. Almost more than anything.

CHAPTER THIRTY-FIVE

Present day

SARAH

Robin's front door finally opens. Just a crack. I hear my sister gasp. Her voice, even wordless, is just the same.

Now she's fumbling with something metal and the door clicks shut again before finally she opens it fully and I see her. God. I see her.

'Sarah!' she says, like she's seen a ghost.

'Robin, I'm so glad to see you,' I say. But I'm not glad to see the way she looks and I feel huge next to her. Her smallness frightens me.

She doesn't seem happy to see me, just shocked and agitated.

'I'm sorry to come here unexpectedly,' I say and I can feel my eyes filling up and I'm so embarrassed and hurt by her reaction that I want to shove her hard out of my line of vision and then run away and give this whole idea up.

'No,' she says, looking at me and looking behind her at who knows what. 'No, it's not that.' She's speaking fast. 'I'm shocked,' she pants, shaking her head, 'but I'm really happy to see you. It's just there's something awful happening behind me and I need to stop it.'

'In your house?' I ask and try to peer around her.

'No, one of the flats behind me. I...' she looks down at the mobile phone in her hand like she's surprised to see it and says, 'Hang on one sec, I'm sorry.'

She dials three numbers and lifts it to her ear. She starts to talk – she's calling an ambulance, saying maybe fire brigade too, for the ladder – now she's giving an address and it's not this one and she says 'hurry' and all the time I'm standing there, staring at my sister and trying to understand what the hell I'm seeing.

'The ambulance is going to take too long,' Robin says and her eyes search my face like she's adding things up.

'Ambulance for who?'

'Can you come with me? Can you help me do this?' she asks.

'Yeah, of course,' I say, but I still don't know what's happening. Even though she's only wearing a pair of shorts and a vest in March, she just shoves her bare feet into some trainers in the hall. She grabs her keys and after such a flurry of activity inside, she takes an age to step down onto the pavement. As she does, she reaches for my hand to steady her.

She looks so different to the last time I saw her that I look straight forward in case she thinks I'm staring at her. She's bent over, hunched and scrawny but with these lumpy little muscles on her legs, sloping shoulders and the palest skin I've ever seen, criss-crossed with scratches. She looks like something emerging from a hole, not really a person at all. Not a saviour. Someone who needs to be saved.

ROBIN

Robin can't take the time to consider why her twin sister Sarah is standing on her doorstep because, right now, Henry Watkins is standing on his child's table with a cord around his neck and he looks very much like he's going to step off and kill himself. Robin cannot let this happen, no matter what.

Robin's front door is wide open, the ambulance called. There are shoes on Robin's feet, shoes that have never stepped on this pavement. Robin reaches for her sister's arm; the weight of the world she's stepping into bends her in two. The sun is brighter than it had been in weeks. Unfiltered sun on her bare arms and legs. She squints into her sister's face, thinner and pinker than she remembered, her sister's concerned eyes, her spiky nose. Sarah. She would have to help. They move as one.

Robin's body is not used to any of this. The changing breeze, the sun, the noises all around. People, so many people, on bikes, on foot, scrambling buggies and dragging kids. People stepping backwards without looking, people so entwined with the world around them that they don't need to look.

As the sisters make their way along George Mews, Robin starts to straighten up. She has to focus on getting to that flat. She can't look at the big expanse of green, mustn't notice the battle of smells between exhaust fumes and spring grass. The rush of glass as the pub takes a delivery, the distant beeps of traffic that blanket this city. She just has to focus on getting into the flat and not dropping and curling into a hard little ball.

As her legs became used to the pavement and her eyes stop watering and adjust, Robin finally notices the warmth of the hand on her arm, how her sister is clinging to her too and not just propping her up.

'The man who lives behind me is trying to hang himself,' Robin says.

'Oh shit,' Sarah says. Sarah, who never used to swear. 'Do you know him?'

Robin falters. No, she doesn't. And yet. 'No, I just happened to see from the window. And if he steps off the table, I don't think the ambulance will get there in time.'

They go a little quicker. A three-legged race. Robin's legs and arms are goose-pimpled but she won't feel that yet. The sisters turn into Jewel Street, which runs behind George Mews.

Robin has never seen the flats from the front, but she knows which flat Henry Watkins is in. She remembers his address from sending his wife her gift, and starting all this trouble. She feels sick at the memory, and other memories too, which surface unbidden.

CHAPTER THIRTY-SIX

1998

SARAH

For the first month back in England, I lay on my new bed in my old room and tried to be glad I was home. Robin still tiptoed around me, still refusing to apologise but seemingly aware that she should.

Callum had gone, and Hilary seemed keen to forget his absence by concentrating on cooking and fussing over me. All I wanted to do was hide. And sleep.

Out of gratitude and duty, I tried to join in with the family meals Hilary had cooked, even though I felt queasy from mid-afternoon until bedtime. I lay still for many hours just expecting that my pregnancy would end. Remembering something I heard about how a high percentage of early pregnancies end in miscarriage, often without the woman even knowing. I tried to want that to happen, tried to will it. God knows, if any pregnancy deserves to fail, it should be one borne out of such a terrible moment. Moments.

What took my breath away, what made the tears roll into my pillow, was the pain I felt at the thought of it ending. An unplanned pregnancy, with a man that should never have so much as looked at me that way, growing in a body that was not his to touch. Jobless, without a plan, without a friend, and yet. The thought of being 'saved' from this catastrophe through the raw odds of loss punched holes in my heart.

This was my baby. Over three months now.

I got away with being quiet that first month. No-one expected much from me anyway. I was tired from the flight and then I was overwhelmed by the move. I was daunted by having to choose from the limited university options that clearing offered. I was looked at sympathetically, except by Robin, who didn't look at me much because she was out all the time.

After five years apart, our differences had hardened. I'd become an only child but she'd been one of a pair. Callum had gone, fled into an easier life with fewer questions, no expectations. But instead of seeing the twin-half now in front of her, Robin just retreated too. Staying out until all hours or hiding in her room.

Had I not spent so long lying on my side with one hand on my belly, feeling giddy and sick, I would have been more hurt. Perhaps I would have had it out with her, cleared the air.

For the next month, while my pregnancy became my 'baby' and I crept ever closer to that three-month mark that chose my path for me, I started to think about how I would explain it. To whom I should explain it. And I started to worry about the logistics. Unemployed, living in a small room in my dad's house, making excuses not to see my mother. How would a baby fit into that? I remembered distant talk about council houses for single parents, about benefits. I remembered them from snatched snippets of adult conversations, and they weren't favourable snippets. This world hadn't been one I'd considered before, certainly not when I lived in Atlanta, with a bathroom bigger than my current bedroom.

And yet, I looked out on the little lawn that my dad and Hilary were so proud of and I imagined a little girl or boy playing there. Squashy knees and dimples. I looked at the new table and chair set in the kitchen diner, and I imagined a little highchair pulled up to it, wedged between the chairs. I looked down at my body, and I imagined it swollen fully, and I put my hand there and wanted to see it sooner. And then I knew – I had to tell someone.

I asked Hilary and Dad if I could talk to them, and they nudged each other jokily. 'This seems very serious!'

When I first got to my dad's house after our flight from Atlanta, I'd been amazed at how much he'd aged. His curly brown hair had more grey strands than brown, his face was weatherworn. He moved slower than I was used to but he still had an impish excitement to him, a bubble of energy that Robin said, on one of our rare evenings together, was because I was back. 'Don't embarrass him by saying anything, but he's been like a bloody kid at Christmas ever since Mum told him you wanted to move back in.'

We sat at the new dining table. They were so proud of it that we seemed to sit here for everything. And now I was about to taint it. I swallowed hard. 'I have something to tell you.'

My dad asked, of course, whose baby it was. I'd got a story already lined up: a boy at a party in Atlanta; I didn't know his name. I don't think Hilary believed me but my dad did, I could tell by the way his face fell.

'Does your mother know?' Hilary asked, touching my hand lightly.

'No, and please don't tell her.'

'She'd understand, love, she wasn't much older when—' My dad had left it hanging in the air.

'And how far along are you?' Hilary asked, moving her hand to my dad's as he stared at his tea, looking a hundred years old.

'Over three months,' I said. 'Going from the date that it, you know, that—'

'I know,' she'd said.

'It's too late,' I'd added. 'There's nothing I can do.' Perhaps I'd said it too soon, but they didn't push me.

Ever since I told him my news, Dad hasn't known how to be with me. He never asks about the baby directly, but offers me warm drinks and makes me sandwiches. He bought me herbal tea at

Hilary's suggestion, but didn't acknowledge why I was off caffeine. Hilary's asked about tiredness and sickness a few times but I can tell she starts to think about her own pregnancy with Callum, and his name carries a black cloud now. He hasn't been back to visit since I got here. He doesn't know about his nephew or niece. And he'll never know that this mound under my baggy sweaty actually holds his half-brother or half-sister.

It's getting late but I can hear Robin crashing about in the kitchen so I go down. She's making hot squash and a toastie, smears of melted cheese trailing between the Breville machine and the sideboard. She's drunk.

'Been out?' I say.

'Just practising with the band,' she slurs. 'Few beers. Sorry, I should have thought. You could have come.'

'It's fine,' I almost laugh because *imagine*.

There's a smirk breaking on her face but I don't think it's at my expense. Something about the way she adjusts her clothes and runs her fingers through her tangled hair.

'Are you seeing someone?' I ask.

The smirk flickers fully. 'Not *really*, just a guy who works behind the bar at the Purple Turtle. We...' She rolls her eyes and giggles, a sound I've not heard for many years. 'Have a connection. Of sorts.'

She breaks her toasted sandwich in two, hopping around with it as it scalds her hands. She slops her hot squash out of the mug so I take it from her to help before she ends up with third-degree burns.

We go into the living room and flick on the TV. A different set since I was last here.

We put on *The Word* and I lay down carefully, sighing as I ease myself into a comfortable position. She looks at me, her head to one side. 'What's going on with you?' she says. 'Are you alright?'

So I just shrug and say it: 'I'm pregnant.' Just like that.

Her mouth falls open like a cartoon character and she repeats what

I've said like she's trying to make sense of it. 'You're … pregnant?'

'Yeah,' I say and I rub my stomach as if that proves something.

'Um, what? Seriously?'

'Yeah, seriously.'

'Did you just *smile*, Sarah? Are you *happy*?'

'Well,' I say, because that's the first time anyone's asked me that. 'Yeah,' I say and then I let myself smile properly. 'Yeah, I guess I am. I shouldn't be, but I am. I mean, it wasn't planned.'

She bursts out laughing. 'No shit!'

I told her how far along I was. I answered the questions only she'd asked me. About how it felt. About what Dad had said, Mum. When I told Robin that Mum didn't know, she said I should tell her with my head held high. That Mum was a bitch whose opinion I shouldn't care about. I said it wasn't just her, I was emphatic that I didn't want Drew to know. Or Callum for that matter.

'Why? Who gives a shit what Drew thinks?'

'I just … I don't know. Not yet, okay?'

'It's up to you.' She shrugs. 'But I don't get why you care what anyone thinks.'

She was right. Drew certainly didn't deserve my concern but it wasn't that simple. If Drew had known I was pregnant, he would have known it was his. My biggest fear of all was that he would want the baby. Or worse – me and the baby. I knew I wouldn't be strong enough to say no. I'd watched my mum snared in his tractor beam for long enough to know that.

'I just…' I fumbled. 'I just don't want the earache,' I said.

Robin was silent for a good minute, while the sound of Terry Christian's grating little voice blathered in the background.

'You know I don't believe you, don't you? But if you don't want me to tell them, that's up to you,' she said. She stopped asking questions and fell asleep with toastie crumbs sprinkled around her mouth.

CHAPTER THIRTY-SEVEN

Present day
SARAH

Robin's ringing the bell for the man whose trying to kill himself but he's not answering. Her left hand is still in mine and the heat makes our palms sweaty but she grips it tight.

'He's not going to get down and answer, is he?' Robin says, more to herself than me.

She starts ringing all the other bells. I worry about annoying people. A man's life is at stake but it still rattles me.

Eventually a voice comes over the buzzer: 'Yeah?' We don't know which buzzer but Robin puts her mouth to the microphone and pleads for them to let us in. 'One of your neighbours is trying to kill himself,' she says.

'What?' The voice is sceptical rather than alarmed.

'*Seriously, please.* We've called an ambulance but it'll take too long.'

Bzzz. The door opens a crack and we push ourselves through. As we're about to jog up the stairs, still holding hands but looser now we're inside, one of the ground-floor flats opens up and a young guy comes out. He's dressed smartly but his face is ashen.

'I just buzzed you in,' he says. 'Can I help?'

We're already thundering up the stairs but Robin beckons for him to join us. He's out of shape, puffing with every step, but he catches up with us.

Robin stops outside a door that has a big bristly welcome mat and two pot plants either side. It looks too cheerful to contain someone with a cord around their neck but Robin drops my hand and starts hammering on the door anyway.

'Henry!' she's shouting. 'Henry, I'm sorry! Please don't do this!'

My sister said she didn't know him but I don't believe her. She seems to be taking an awful lot of responsibility for a stranger. I think he's probably someone she's fallen out with or maybe a jilted boyfriend, but I stay quiet and put my hand to my belly while I think what to do next.

Something occurs to me at the same time it occurs to the neighbour and we both reach for the handle. I pull my hand away again, to let him do it. He turns it to the right – nothing. Turns it to the left, the door opens. In any other situation, our stupidity not to try that first would have been funny. Not today. We pile in.

Robin seems to know the way, which confirms my suspicions that she's been here before. She winds down the hall. To the right is an open-plan room that seems to be the living room, dining room and kitchen. I step in to it briefly to get out of the way for the neighbour. It's sparkling clean. Even the hob has no marks of grease, no tiny little specks that normally don't come off. The floor is immaculate, right up to the kick board. The sterile perfection makes the hairs on the back of my neck stand on end.

Signs of a child drip from every surface. Arthur: his name peppered around the room, spelled out in magnetic letters on the fridge. I step back into the hall and see little shoes taking pride of place on the shoe rack. By the size of them, I'd say he's probably the same age as Violet. I suck the air and look away.

How could this man, with a loved child the same age as Violet, want to kill himself? Unless the child is gone? Some terrible accident that I can't let myself think about because I don't know what this child looks like so my mind plasters Violet's face over the idea and

I already can't look at her memory even though she's alive and well with her dad and grandparents. Alive and well, as far as I know. No. Stop. I have to shake myself out of this spiral.

We pass two doors on the left that we don't open and then head for the last one. Robin takes a deep breath and reaches for the door. Just then, we hear the scream of an ambulance outside.

'I'll go,' I say, before they can stop me. I'd rather never see behind that door.

I rush back out of the flat and down the stairs. As I make my way to the front door to let the paramedics inside, I realise an old lady is standing in the doorway to one of the flats. She's wearing a tabard and twirling a duster in her hands. 'Is everything okay?' she calls, in a thick Manchester accent.

'Yes,' I call back as I run, even though it's not.

As I open the door to the uniformed medics and point up the stairs, the old lady comes right up to me and touches my arm.

'Careful, love,' she says, 'you shouldn't be running around like that in your condition.'

I put my hand on my belly. An instinct to touch, to protect, to check it's still there.

'Oh,' I smile at her, 'it's okay, I'm being careful.'

'How far along are you?' she asks, running the duster along the banister as she steps up after me.

'It's early days.' I smile. 'About fifteen weeks.'

'Well,' she says, 'good luck to you. Mine are all grown up now. I miss them being little but I don't miss carrying them. I was sick as a dog.'

'I've been quite lucky,' I say.

'You look it. You're blooming,' she says and smiles for the first time.

'Thank you.' I smile back, but then I remember the darkness upstairs and bid her good day.

On the way up the stairs after the uniforms, I take it slower. I feel the old lady's concerned eyes on the small of my back and I put one hand there and rest the other on my bump. The adrenaline of the morning has washed away, leaving gritty sediment in its place. It slows me down and by the time I get into the flat, I can hear Robin yelling.

'What the fuck?' she shouts. 'How could you even think about doing that to your kid?'

He's alive then.

I hear the male paramedic telling her to go and cool off. Robin arguing. I stand awkwardly in the hallway of a flat in which I don't belong. The guy from the downstairs flat comes out from the back bedroom, his skin is white and clammy. His neck is just a bit too fat for his collar so it looks like a plinth for his head.

'I think a cup of tea is a good idea,' he says. I follow him into the kitchen. Neither of us know where anything is and we destroy its perfect condition as we shamble around, opening cupboards, shaking loose dust off the teabags, spilling slops of milk.

'Stick some sugar in his,' I say. 'It's good for the shock.'

'Yeah,' he says, 'I think I'll have some too.'

His hands are shaking and he scatters sugar everywhere. I take over.

'Thanks,' he says. And then he holds out his hand. 'We've not properly met. I'm Sam. I live downstairs.'

'I'm Sarah,' I say, shaking his clammy hand. 'I'm Robin's sister.'

ROBIN

Robin looks at Henry Watkins, slumped on the small bed. He's still in his dressing gown, which flaps open without its cord. Underneath, he wears flannel pyjama bottoms and an old vest she knows well. His hair is longer than she's ever seen it, the Magpie stripe as wide as a fist. He looks wrung out. His eyes are hidden among a scribble of wrinkles, his skin is pale but not, she knows, as pale as hers.

He is sitting in his son's room, surrounded by strangers, and he doesn't seem to care. Just stares at nothing.

The paramedics have checked him over. He hadn't taken that final step. Just stood there, on the table, with the cord around his neck. Whatever he was waiting for, it didn't come. But they did: Robin and Sam.

She'd rushed in first, locked eyes on his. His neck wore the cord loosely, his dressing gown flapping. He'd inched his bare toes over the edge of the table, which wobbled slightly when the door burst open and Robin and Sam had rushed in.

'Fuck,' Sam had said.

Robin had slowed to a stop, pulled Sam behind her and held her hands out to Henry, showing him her palms. 'I'm not going to do anything,' she said, 'but you know this isn't the answer so we've come to help you down.'

He'd bowed his head, pulled the small stuffed mouse from his pocket and held it to his face. 'I just want my boy,' he said. 'I can't live without him.'

'I know,' Robin said. 'But he can't live without you either, not properly.'

She'd offered her hands and he'd taken them, but at first he didn't move. Stood holding them, noose in place, like an exhibit.

Behind him, through the window, Robin could see her own house staring back at her.

'Please,' she said to Henry, 'please take the cord off and we can have a chat.'

The little room wasn't designed for any of this, not for this many people, not for this much sadness. When the paramedics had checked him over and accepted that he was not going to actually go through with it, they agreed to leave once Henry called his mum and asked to stay with her for a while. It was a short conversation, no detail.

'She's coming to get me,' he said.

'We'll wait until she gets here, mate,' Sam said.

'You don't have to do that,' Henry said, without looking up. There was silence. The room still felt small with three adults standing and one sagging the little bed down in the middle. Suddenly Henry looked up, stood up. 'How did you know?' he said.

'I saw you,' said Robin, stepping forward. 'I saw you from my window. You must know that I did, because you've seen me too.'

He wrinkles his forehead and sits back down, but keeps his eyes on her. Dark brown eyes with very little white. 'I've never seen you before in my life,' he said.

'I wasn't going to do this now but as you've asked: I saw you look at me the other day,' Robin answers, standing a little taller, 'not long after you'd punched your wife.'

Sarah and Sam flash a look at each other but say nothing.

'Punched my wife?' Henry screws his face up like he's swallowed something sour. 'I've never punched my wife. What the hell are you talking about?'

Sarah looks nervously at her sister now and Sam lifts his free hand like he's about to separate Henry and Robin, but let's it fall to his side.

'C'mon,' Sam said, and then takes a sip of his tea like he's not sure what else to do.

'No,' said Henry, quietly. 'I want to hear this. You think I punched my wife?'

'I saw you,' Robin says, holding his gaze. 'I saw you make a fist, and I saw you throw a punch. And then I saw the argument after that, saw your little boy covering his ears. I didn't see what you did, but—'

'And you think you saw me punch my wife?' Henry says, shaking his head. He doesn't sound angry, the words come out slower than that. Like he's doing sums.

'It was you, wasn't it?' he finally says. 'You called the police.'

Robin stands planted to the floor, breathing in and out like a bull preparing to charge. 'Yeah, I did. And it was the right thing too.' Only Sarah can see how fast Robin's knees are shaking.

Henry stares at her, his mouth open slightly. Just as Sam says, 'Look, I really don't think this is the time,' Henry stands up and walks towards Robin. Robin stays still. Feet to the floor, hands on her hips. Henry looms over her, wraps both him arms around her shoulders and starts to sob. She looks at the others, panicking, but then pats Henry's dressing gown, wraps her arms back around him and holds him.

Sam has left for work now and Sarah and Robin are left with Henry, sitting at his table while they wait for his mum to arrive.

'I thought Karen had called the police and lied to them. I was so fucking angry, I can't tell you. I thought she was trying to paint a picture of me so she could take my boy away.'

'They won't let you have your son if you've hit your wife,' Sarah says carefully, the first time she's addressed him directly.

'But I didn't hit my wife. I'd never hit my wife. I'd never hit anyone. I know when you're talking about, Robin. I threw a punch, look.' He gestured to a crack in one of the wooden cupboard doors. 'I regretted it straight away. But I didn't hit my wife, I never would. She was cheating on me and she'd left me and I thought she was trying to take my boy away completely, but I would still never hit a woman. We had some blazing rows and I hate that Art heard them. I'll never forgive myself for that, but I would never hurt Karen. Not like that.'

Henry had been hoping to sell the flat, find something cheaper so he could afford to get a part-time job and share custody of his son Arthur with his wife.

'I know she did the dirty on me, but I wanted us to live close by, try to do it right. I wanted to be a proper dad to him still, even if I only had him part of the time. But then the police got involved and it blindsided me. Even after the cheating, I trusted what she'd said about Arthur. That she would share custody and try to keep things as easy for me as possible. So when I thought she was trying to stitch me up with the police, paint me like that to get custody...' He trails off, fiddles with the toy mouse in his hands.

He still had a chance to put things right. Arthur's mum hadn't turned against him, hadn't dismantled his chance with his son. It was Robin's meddling that had nearly done that. But now, finally, that meddling had saved Mr Magpie's life.

CHAPTER THIRTY-EIGHT

1998

SARAH

Chalk and cheese, that's what our dad used to say when we were little. And we still are but my sister has been kind to me. Maybe it's because I'd been knocked flying from my high horse. Maybe it's just because Callum has left and she needs a distraction, but for the last few weeks, Robin has helped put the air back in my lungs. She doesn't treat me like the elephant in the room. She talks about the baby like it's an actual living thing, who will grow and have a name and wear little clothes and run around in the playground with his or her auntie.

She refuses to let me be ashamed at growing such a thing, even though I am embarrassed. I was going to be a normal girl who went to college, got a nice safe job, met a nice guy, got married and had two planned children. I was embarrassed that I'd believed that, and ashamed that I'd blown that.

Most importantly, my sister takes the mickey out of me to help keep everything as normal as possible. And I've noticed she's spending more time at home now, sitting next to me on the sofa like a guard dog, giving my dad warning looks when he says something she thinks might offend.

Robin came with me to the midwife today. My first appointment at the village surgery. As soon as we were in the room Robin asked the midwife if she was going to give me an internal examination and then added, 'Because she's not had any action for about four months.'

'I hope you're not going to be too much trouble, young lady,' the midwife had said.

'I'll be on my best behaviour,' Robin had said, wide-eyed.

'So,' the midwife had said, clapping her hands together, 'I can see that you're a little further along than we'd expect at a first appointment.'

I told the midwife the date that I got pregnant.

'Are you certain that was the day?' she'd asked, filling in a little card with notes.

'It was a one-off,' I said, and I saw Robin's brow knit, her dark eyebrows curling in thought.

'I see,' the midwife had said. 'And was this a surprise, then?'

'Yes,' I'd whispered, 'a big surprise.'

'Well,' the midwife said quietly, 'shall we see if we can hear your surprise's heartbeat?'

I looked at Robin. I hadn't expected this. She nodded in encouragement.

I'd laid down on the paper-covered bed and lifted up my top as she gestured. The midwife dragged my stretchy jogging bottoms down so the waistband sat below the small bulge that had sprung up in the last few weeks. I instinctively wanted to bat her hand away. She squirted something cold on my tummy and then put something called a doppler on my belly, jiggled it roughly until a beat filled the room. It was real. It was alive. It was mine.

Robin stood up from her chair and came over to me, slipped her hand into mine.

Afterwards, my belly was wiped clean with a scratchy tissue and my blood pressure was taken. After that, vials of my blood were siphoned by the midwife while Robin still held my hand, then I was given a narrow jar to pee in.

When I came back into the room, I heard Robin say, 'You should ask my sister that, not me.'

Whatever it was, the midwife didn't ask it. Instead she told me that I had already missed one standard scan at twelve weeks and was already due the next one.

'Can she find out if it's a girl or a boy, then?' Robin had asked.

'If she'd like to know,' the midwife said. I just sat numbly while they talked about what would happen, and that I'd get a letter with a date and time, that I'd need to arrive with a full bladder. That Robin – or *someone* – could come if I wanted them to, but that only one person could come in with me. 'So you couldn't bring your mum *and* the baby's dad or—'

'I'll be going with her,' Robin had interrupted.

We walked back from the surgery in silence. Robin's jokes had run out and she seemed distant, almost anxious. As we turned into our road, my sister turned to me and said, 'Who's the dad, Sarah?'

I'd stared dumbly. It was a reasonable question. 'The boy at the party,' I answered, and the third-person script of it hung in the air.

'Okay,' she said after a moment. 'You don't have to tell me.'

I'm awake. It's still black outside and my heart races with the shock of being conscious. I look at the alarm clock next to me: it's just gone two. I don't understand why I'm awake until I hear voices downstairs. I get up, wrap my big dressing gown around me, and tread carefully onto the landing. Robin's heading down the steps, and Hilary and Dad are already downstairs talking quietly to each other and someone else.

Callum. Apparently he's been dropped off at the house by Rez's cousin. Even by peering down the stairs I can see he's far thinner than before. Tall, like his dad, he still has a skinny child's body. As I take a few steps, I realise the sour smell rising up is from him.

In the dim hallway light he looks pale and yellow. He's slid down the door so he's squatting on the floor, leaning back. His eyes roll around like loose marbles and when he focuses, he screws his nose up and spits at whoever he's focused on. I've never seen him like this. I've never seen anyone in this state.

Dad saw me on the stairs and told me to go to my room, a chastising voice I'd not heard since I was small. I don't argue. As I walk back up to bed, Callum asks whose room I'm staying in.

'Her room,' Dad says sharply. 'This is her home.' As I shut my door, I hear Callum's garbled protests.

He's been in Robin's bed for two days, sweating and raging. She sleeps on the sofa, as there's no room in my bed. When he emerges from his pit, Callum's different. Apologetic, embarrassed, he avoids all our eyes.

'I'm really sorry if I said anything to you,' he says to me as he makes instant coffee and offers me tea. 'I was on something. Mum said Rez didn't know what to do with me so he brought me here. I don't know. I'm sorry.'

'You didn't say anything to me,' I lie. He looks relieved and stands up a little straighter.

'How are you?' he asks quietly, stirring sugar into his mug.

'I'm okay.' I wrap my cardigan around me, hug my belly to obscure the small bump.

'How come you're living here? Had enough of my dad?' he asks, without looking up from his work with the spoon.

'Both of them,' I say. He grunts in recognition.

I want to ask him so many things. I want to ask so many questions to which, maybe, I didn't really want answers. But instead we just sit at the table together in quiet understanding.

He stayed another two days, calling in sick to his call-centre job and having angry calls with his boyfriend that he thought we couldn't hear. With every hour that passed, he and Robin giggled more, played each other songs they'd found in their time apart. They warmed up old jokes, and colour filled in both their faces.

Robin was less interested in me, partly because I'd sworn her to secrecy about the baby, so her chief source of interest was off-limits. She wasn't unkind to me though, and I found myself tearful with gratitude.

When Callum disappeared again this afternoon, collected by his grubby-looking boyfriend Rez, who was hanging out of someone's Vauxhall Corsa with a joint in his hand, Robin was inconsolable.

'Every time Cal pulls himself out, he gets sucked back in. I don't know what the fuck he sees in that rat-faced little weasel. He's not even funny. He's got shit taste in music. He's nothing.'

ROBIN

Nobody says anything in this family, that's the problem as far as Robin can see. They didn't speak up fast enough when Callum started giving up on who he was, started sliding down this shitty road instead.

They've not asked Sarah anything about her unexpected pregnancy, and no-one is looking at the future. Only Robin has a plan, only Robin has the spirit to get out of here.

It's not that she thought *she* would be the one to fuck up and get pregnant, god no, but Sarah? It doesn't sit right. And now her sister just lies around, or makes lists of things she needs for a few months' time and nobody asks how she'll pay for them. Where will the baby sleep? What will Sarah do for money? Why won't Sarah tell their mum and ask her and that piece of shit for some money? They have more than they need.

Robin likes the idea of being an aunt, loves the idea of some fresh untainted blood around the house, but the inertia of the adults turns her stomach.

What will it take them to *do* anything?

Robin's band is picking up traction, getting tighter, getting a following. A few more eager faces popping up time and again, jumping around to the songs they recognise. Working Wife make a bit of money playing at weddings, which Robin hates as she has to wear smart clothes and play middle of the road rock by middle-aged men, and they try out their own stuff at the Purple Turtle and in an assortment of scruffy, smoky pubs.

The sickly scent of yesterday's smoke as they set up, the semi-darkness punctured by tiny red lights from cigarette ends all facing her, the slap of her trainers on the wooden stage of the floor, that's what Robin lives for. That's what courses through her and where her energy spikes.

And then, arriving back home still pumped up and drunk on adrenaline (and whatever drinks she's cadged from the landlords), she'll hit the concrete wall of inertia.

There are a lot of questions that aren't being asked.

A lot can change in five years but people don't fundamentally change. Callum's acting like a tool but he's still Callum. Beneath the attitude and the bloodshot eyes, he still likes books, likes the music that has always made him smile, he's still funny, sweet, kind.

Sarah is still a good girl. She still lives to please. She rushes to lay the table for dinner, washes up without being asked, melts under the warmth of praise for such simple acts. The idea that good girl Sarah went to a party and got nailed by a stranger doesn't fit. It just doesn't fit. But no-one is asking the right questions and Robin doesn't think they ever will. And it makes her want to fucking scream.

SARAH

We watched a comedy re-run tonight but neither of us were in the mood to laugh. Robin was tired, a bit grumpy. Had that heavy forehead she gets, loaded with things she wants to say. I just hoped she wasn't going to ask me – again – about the baby's dad. Every single day, I choose to be happy about the baby and I choose to smear a thick black line over the memory of its creation. That's the only way to survive, to keep my baby pure.

Robin's been spending more time with her band recently, rehearsing in bedrooms and garages and occasionally village halls that I'm not entirely sure they have permission to be in. Some weekends they play at weddings and she comes back with pockets full of tenners and slices of cake.

She'd nodded off at one point tonight, mouth open and warm breath catching in her throat.

Dad and Hilary are out, dinner with a regular customer of Dad's who has a big enough house and garden to need regular landscaping. Robin and I peeled away from each other on the landing and went to bed early, plodding into our respective rooms. I felt full and warm, my scalp beating with the central heating, my blood thick and heavy. Robin has dragged herself into her room. I heard her putting music on, I think Jimi Hendrix but I don't know, that's not my forté.

I don't know if she's fallen asleep yet but I haven't, my eyelids heavy but my brain twitchy. Too many things squirming to climb out from under thick black lines.

— —

Suddenly, the front door bangs open downstairs. It's too early for Dad and Hilary. There are heavy footsteps crashing up the stairs and I sit up, instinctively putting a pillow over my belly.

I hear the flurry of footsteps crunching along the landing and someone pushing a nearby bedroom door open. I hear Robin yell with that gale-force voice: 'Hey, what the fuck do you want?'

I hear a male voice snipe. 'Wrong room, you idiot!'

Robin's bed springs squeal urgently. I don't know what to do or who it is. And then I hear her say: 'What the fuck do you *want*, Cal?'

Mumbling, moaning, swearing. The thud of feet along the hall to Dad and Hilary's room, doors banging open, male voices mumbling, Robin yelling now. 'What the fuck are you doing, Cal?'

'Get back in your box,' I hear a voice say. I can only guess it's Rez.

My knees tremble, I feel a sloop in my gut that I think could be, *could be* the baby. I don't want my baby's first fluttering movements to be out of fear, so I swallow the thought away. That has to come on another day. Another thick black line.

'The fuck you say to me?' I hear Robin spit. 'You pair of dicks barge into my house and tell me where to go? Get the fuck out of here.' She sounds weary but the dismissive tone is replaced with something else and she cries: 'Get off me!'

I hear Callum's voice clearly for the first time. He sounds relatively calm. 'Don't, Rez. Robin, just let us get this stuff and we'll go.'

Should I hide in my room with my baby bump or help my sister? I don't know what to do but inaction feels worse than action, so I stand up and step out quietly into the hall. A few feet away on the landing, Robin and Rez are tussling in the dim light. He's much taller than her and bending like a reed. Callum, exasperated, is trying to separate them.

'Give that stuff back!' Robin's screaming, grasping at Callum's pockets while he tries to prise her fingers away, Rez looking panicky.

'How could you, Callum?' Robin yells.

'He's owed it,' Rez says, his voice soft but cold.

Robin struggles free, kicks back wildly and catches him somewhere near the crotch. 'You're not though.'

Rez and Callum both reach for Robin, I don't know what they're going to do but without thinking I run at them, pushing Rez.

I hear Robin pleading with me not to and Callum yelling at me to leave it. I realise he's drunk again, or maybe stoned. I feel hands shunt me around. I feel fingertips on my fingertips and it not being enough. The feel of the top stair carpet under the arch of my foot, the swooping tickle of it, the lurching sickness in my gut.

I open my eyes at the bottom of the stairs, and close them again.

I open them again in the bright light of an ambulance.

I see Robin's tears. I see her rage. A twin fury that passes through me too and burns so hot and so bright that I pass out from it.

'I shouldn't be in hospital yet,' I croak. They just look at me, big-eyed and nervous.

My appointment isn't for a couple of days. My scan, it's not yet.

'Too soon,' I hear my muffled voice, the words drawling slowly from a mouth that doesn't feel like it belongs in my head.

The sea of faces around the bed just nod. Red eyes, hands on my arms. Dad, Hilary, Robin.

I try to sit up and it hurts so badly that I slide back down even further under the sheets and blankets than I'd been before. And suddenly Robin is on me, stuck to me, her skinny arms around my neck and her lips on my face, kissing me, resting her forehead on mine.

'I'm so sorry, Sarah, I'm so sorry,' she breathes into me.

Dad's pulling her off and whispering to her, 'She's too sore, you need to be gentle,' while I'm trying to sit up again and failing.

I hear myself: 'The baby?' A quieter voice than I knew I had. . And the tiniest shake of Hilary's head and the power of Robin's rage slamming into me like a bulldozer.

In two days I was due to go for a scan where I would have found out in a more routine way that my unexpected baby was a little girl. I would have realised then just how much I could love her, in spite of her creation. Instead I'd found out too fast and too late, just as I tumbled down the stairs.

She – *she, my god* – was eighteen weeks. They called her a 'miscarriage' and put her in a special box. But she was my baby. *Was.* The worst word in the dictionary.

When I was able to sit in a wheelchair, they took me down to the chapel, where we all stared numbly at a priest I'd never met who read words I hadn't chosen about a heaven I didn't believe in. And slowly, with each word, every single piece of the girl I'd once been seeped out of me.

In that girl's place, my family wheeled back a shell. They placed the shell carefully on the hospital bed, kissed it goodbye and turned out the light. And I lay there, this shell I now am, and I tried to understand how any of this stuff could have happened.

Callum and Rez had been there that night by the stairs, I remembered that. They were taking Hilary's jewellery, tangling it up as they shoved it in their pockets. The bright gold stuff from the Drew days that *might* have been worth a little bit but was probably just gold-plated costume junk.

Robin told me later that they hadn't even taken the jewellery, just dumped it on the landing and fled from the house.

'He's dead to me,' she'd said. 'He's fucking dead to me.'

I'm home now. My bruises and cuts have faded a little and my belly gives nothing away. Everybody except Robin seems either relieved or oblivious. Dad can now forget his daughter had ever shamed herself like that, with a fictional boy at an unlikely party. Hilary can get back to saying nothing and doing nothing about her son and the path he's taken. And Mum and Drew could stay insulated in ignorance.

But me? I'll never forget and Robin will never forgive.

A baby girl. My baby girl. Robbed from me.

ROBIN

Robin paws at her anger in private. Where once she'd been the only one to take a positive interest – touch Sarah's belly, laugh about the size of her swelling bust, make up nicknames for her niece or nephew like 'little bean' – now she avoids her twin sister. In their brief conversations, Robin looks down at her shoes. When she's home, Robin locks her bedroom door, creates a wall of sound to keep everyone out.

Despite promising Hilary she wouldn't, after three sleepless nights in a row made her feel crazy with indecision, Robin called the police.

She gave them Rez and Callum's name. Told the police that they were selling dope, that at least Rez if not both of them were shoplifters, told them that they'd tried to burgle the family home. Told the police that they'd pushed her sister down the stairs. Told them to check with the hospital, see the records for themselves.

Nobody else had wanted to involve the police. Not even Sarah, who just wanted to forget and to channel her anger and grief in her own way.

Instead, Sarah had to give a stilted statement to two uniformed officers, who came and perched on the sofa and drank tea politely. While Robin sat next to her, closer than they'd been in weeks, Sarah could hardly get the words out.

The policeman jotted down Sarah's patchy statement and the policewoman looked at the sisters with concern as Robin hugged her stomach like it was her body that had been hollowed out. Like they'd done it to her.

The police went to call at the flat while Rez and Callum were out. Their flat, which they shared with odds and sods of Rez's extended family and network of shoplifters and rat-eyed drug dealers, was an Aladdin's cave of minor crime. But honour among thieves, no-one told the police where to find Rez or Callum.

The police can't have tracked them down yet because Callum and Rez have just arrived at the Marshall house, their car exhaust banging an announcement as they pull up and crush the edge of the lawn.

Robin thunders down the stairs and flings open the front door, her dad shouting after her to wait.

'What the fuck are you doing here?' she rages, marching up to Callum and Rez so they both take a step back on the small lawn. Jack and Hilary have followed her out, Hilary small and exhausted, her cardigan wrapped around her like a swaddling blanket.

'You called the police, Robin,' Callum says quietly and looks at Rez. 'Do you know what you've done?'

'Callum, please, you need to go,' Hilary is saying and she's put her arm around his waist to try to nudge him back to the car but he's just twirling away from her and refusing to leave.

'The damage you've caused, Callum, you need to get the fuck away from here,' Jack is saying. The loudest voice Robin had heard from him in years. *You should have acted this bravely years ago,* she thinks through the red fog in her head.

'Please, Jack, don't do this here—' Hilary tries.

'Enough, Hilary! Don't you defend him,' Jack snaps and Hilary sags even more.

Robin stands there on the lawn, barefoot in her shorts and T-shirt. She cannot say anything. She can't catch a clear thought; they jumble in a ball and hurtle around her brain. She's so angry, so upset, that she feels like her whole body is on fire and she's just burning there on the grass, chest heaving.

Rez is trying to tug Callum away but he's shaking him off too. 'Robin,' Callum says, with no fight in him. He's shrinking under the glare of Jack and Robin's anger, Hilary's shame.

Robin looks away from him and up at Sarah's window where she sees the outline of her twin. The flames pick up even more and she stares at her beloved brother through them, still mute.

'I'm so sorry about that night,' Callum's pleading now, new tears catching in his throat as Rez puts a hand on his shoulder. 'I said I was fucking sorry, but you didn't have to go to the police, Robin, you'll ruin our lives!'

'Ruin your life, Callum? *Your* life?' Robin shouts. 'You pushed my sister down the fucking stairs!'

Rez is shaking his head, opening his mouth to argue but Callum says: 'I've said I'm sorry. She's alright, isn't she? She's alright, she'll live. We didn't even take anything in the end.'

'That's enough!' Jack yells again. 'You've got a bloody nerve coming round here after what you've done. The pain you've caused my daughter.' He tries to move his stepson off the grass by force, pushing his back and pulling both his arms in turn. Tries to get him and Rez back into the rusty old car they'd arrived in.

'You took everything!' Robin screams and she starts to thump Callum's chest. 'She was pregnant. And you two killed her baby!'

Callum sucks the summer air and wobbles on his feet. He stares down at Robin, his chest still absorbing her thumps.

'She's pregnant?'

'Was!' Robin says, stepping away from him and leaning over panting. 'Was,' she says again.

'I'm—' He stops and looks at Rez, whose own face has also just drained of all colour.

'Shit,' Rez says. 'Look, I'm sorry too—'

'Both of you need to get the fuck off this lawn, now,' Robin says. 'Your sorrys are worth shit to us. Your sorrys won't bring that little baby back, they won't piece Sarah back together and they won't make me love you again, Callum. I hate you. I hate you from the top of my head to the soles of my fucking feet. Now, *get away from this house!*' Her voice is broken, feral, louder than bombs.

Callum stares at his mum, who nods, stoney-faced. Rez backs

away, pulls Callum's sleeve so he follows dumbly. They get into their car, sit for just a moment staring at each other, and then roll slowly down the road.

Just hours earlier, Robin had stood on their postage-stamp lawn, in her shorts, and shouted things into her brother's face that she hoped would destroy him. She'd *wanted* to destroy him. To annihilate what he'd become. To crush the love she'd had for him, grind it to dust and blow it into the wind.

She'd wanted to. But she'd calmed down a little as the evening ploughed on. Had even managed to slip into a thin, watery sleep until the sharp ring of the home phone slashed through the stillness.

Hilary is up, phone in hand, by the third or fourth ring. Robin turns her pillow over to the cold side, burrows her face into it. Waits. It'll be about Callum; he'll be drunk, high, in some kind of dramatic state. Rez will have had enough of him, will have given up trying to prise his deadweight spaghetti limbs off the pavement and out of harm's way. *Let him stay there. Let him suffer.*

Robin sighs, heaves herself up and shuffles to the bathroom. Sits down harder than she should on a toilet seat that constantly breaks, pees while she tries to listen. Hears the word 'ambulance'. Stomach pump? Even though Callum's been in big messes before, after the last few weeks and the argument, perhaps he'd pushed himself too far. Taken too much, washed it down with the wrong thing. She wants to say 'good' like she would have a few hours ago, but she can't. There's been one too many ambulances recently.

In the room next to the bathroom, Sarah is stirring. Her mattress creaks as she rolls to the edge. Two dull thuds follow as she steps out of bed.

Robin wipes, flushes. She wouldn't normally at night but everyone is up, she can hear her dad and Hilary downstairs, talking over each other. Robin splashes herself with the tap by accident as she reaches for the soap. Curses as she dries her hands, T-shirt dripping.

Sarah is already on the landing when Robin leaves the bathroom.

'What's going on?' Robin asks. Sarah is leaning over the top of the staircase, listening. She spins around, grabs Robin by the shoulders.

'I think we should go into your room,' she says.

'Why? What's he done now? What's he taken?'

Robin doesn't want to push past her sister, especially at the top of these stairs but the front door is open and her dad and Hilary are leaving. It's only been a minute or two since the call came and they're already wearing coats over night things.

'Dad!' Robin calls but he ignores her, the door closing.

'Sarah, let me past.'

'You shouldn't go, don't—'

'Let me the fuck past.' It's a growl. Sarah steps aside, head bowed, hand on her stomach.

Robin thunders down the stairs, grabs her coat on the way out of the door and runs barefoot after the car's rear lights.

They had to stop and let her in of course, as soon as they saw she was there. No time to stop and argue. The cold quiet of the car rushes at her while she buckles up. An embarrassed held breath that means nothing when Robin realises Hilary has her head in her hands, is breathing hard and crying.

'Faster, Jack,' she pleads. The car lurches forward, swings out from the estate and flies up the high street towards the A road to Reading.

'What's happening?' Robin asks quietly.

'You shouldn't be here, Robin!' Hilary shouts. 'You slowed us down.'

Robin can't remember the last time Hilary shouted. Her dad ignores her, concentrates on the car, which is shaking along the outside lane of the A33, topping a hundred miles an hour. The mess of traffic lights by the football stadium start to flip yellow then red but apart from a quick look to the left, Jack doesn't slow down.

The car pulls up outside the small block of flats and stops across two spaces. Hilary and Jack unbuckle, shove their doors open and run to the front door. As they press the buzzer repeatedly, Jack grabs Hilary's hand, holds it to his chest. Robin is out of the car and following behind, her feet sore from running along the road minutes earlier. Her chest burns with a nameless feeling. Hilary and her dad are inside already.

She can hear shouting, crying. Rez comes running out of the front door, shoves past her as he heads to the car park. He gets into his banged-up car, starts the engine and then covers both his eyes with his hands. As Robin goes into the block and starts up the communal stairs, she hears the tell-tale cough of Rez's old engine as he drives away.

But mostly she can hear Hilary. Hilary isn't crying, she isn't shouting. She's screaming. A sound Robin hasn't heard before or since. Neighbours are rattling their doors open, poking their heads out. Robin takes a deep breath, walks up the last set of stairs to the top floor.

The door to the flat is open. She's only been here a handful of times and each time the place has been filled with people, laughter, smoke. Tonight the place is still and black.

Robin steps inside, follows the noise that Hilary is making. As she walks into the living room, Robin hears the ambulance pull up outside. The air in here smells male. Sweat and old clothes, beer and bad food. And even though he hadn't been his groomed and particular self in a while, there's still a top note over it all. A tang of shower gel and the aftershave that baby-faced Callum didn't really need.

As the paramedics' boots rush up the stairs towards the flat, past the dull hum of neighbours talking to each other, Robin steps into the bedroom. At first, she doesn't see the real focal point.

Instead, she sees clothes scattered across the floor. A guitar with only three strings propped against the chipped window frame. And Hilary siting on the unmade bed. She's motionless, the sheets bunched into balls under her rigid hands. Suddenly her thin shoulders start to pulse up and down under her jacket and nightie. She pulls the wrinkled sheets up to her face and screams into them again.

Robin stays rooted to the spot, squinting through the dim light of a swinging bulb, scanning for her dad. She realises that he is merged with the wave of clothes spraying from the wardrobe. He looks at first like he is holding back another wave, but no.

'Oh god, no,' Robin scrambles over, bare feet skidding among crunchy socks and sweaty T-shirts. It's all too late.

Her father is half in the wardrobe. He's swaying slightly and panting with exertion. His arms shake as he holds up Callum's body. Holds his head up closer to the high wardrobe rail.

Callum's long arms and legs are dangling and his eyes are closed. His toes twist and point among the clothes, just skimming their surface. As his weight slips from Jack's grasp, his desperate stepfather heaves him up again. And again and again, with shaking arms. All for nothing.

The paramedics rush in and take over. Jack protests. 'I need to hold him up,' he croaks, grinding himself into the floor. They prise the dead weight from Jack's hands gently and firmly, guide Jack to the bed as they lay Callum down among the discarded jumpers and blim-burned jeans. It's a practised move, all in one, wordless and graceful somehow. Like a ballet.

Jack shuffles closer to Hilary. Now he has relinquished Callum, he notices his next task. Snaps to and wraps himself around his partner until she disappears into him, their bodies shaking together.

Robin is silent. Her knees are shaking, her hands feel icy, but she doesn't move. Can't move. She didn't even move as the paramedics pushed past her, carving a small curled path in the fabric on the floor.

The light is dim but as the paramedics unwind the rope and attend to Callum – another fruitless gentle dance – what little light there is outside shakes free through the wonky blind and rushes to outline him.

Still Robin stares at his neat, slim body in disbelief. He's wearing only boxer shorts. His long limbs with their dusting of golden hair, taut and surprisingly muscular. An almost-man.

The matching tattoo they both have is just visible from her angle. The quote from *Labyrinth*, mirrored on her own arm: 'It's only for ever, not long at all.'

This is the last time I'll see his skin, she thought, clapping her hand over her mouth in case her thoughts broke free. Even through his size and his emerging man's shape, you could still see how he looked as a kid, could follow that line all the way to imagine how he looked as a baby. When all of this was still to come.

And a baby must have been what Hilary had seen when she burst through the door and saw that it was already too late. That her life and everything she had done with it was gone for ever. Her boy was gone for ever.

'I'm so sorry, Mrs Marshall,' the female paramedic said after laying a stained duvet cover over Callum from his face down. 'There really was nothing anyone could have done.'

Ashtrays overflowed and abandoned pints of squash were stacked up on old bits of furniture. There were books everywhere, the most Callum thing about that room. He died surrounded by books so, well, it didn't mean anything because he was still dead. None of it had meant enough and nothing that could be said or done would change that.

Everything is cold and slow now. Hilary shakes herself free from Jack, wipes her eyes and nose on her jacket and walks gingerly to where her son is laying. She kneels down next to him, pulls the duvet cover back so his face is no longer hidden. She strokes his cheek, brushes his hair away from his eyelids. Her shoulders shake and she wipes her eyes again, the tears pouring faster than she has any hope of catching.

Hilary lies down next to her son, on the uneven fabric-coated floor. He's so much taller than her, somehow elongated in death.

The spell on Jack breaks and he realises Robin has been there the whole time.

'Oh, love,' he says, and she stumbles and falls to him, her eyes springing with tears that seem too small, too pathetic, so that she starts to beat her own head with her fists but that's still not enough.

'He's gone?' she asks no-one. She knows. They all know. Rez knew, when he fled, the others too no doubt.

'I'm so sorry,' Jack says, the words catching. 'You shouldn't have been here tonight.'

'*He* shouldn't have been here tonight. *I* should have been here for him, Dad. A long time ago. Fuck.'

He doesn't argue, doesn't console. Just holds her until she can stand by herself again.

There are formalities, papers, calls to make. Robin wasn't really listening to the calm words from bright uniforms. As one paramedic leads Jack out and into the living room, Robin goes into the kitchen to get a drink of water, splash her face, paw at her new emptiness in solitude.

That's where she sees it. The note.

It is the only clean thing in the room. Dirty plates, bowls and takeaway trays teeter on every surface, while ash piles sit next to overflowing ashtrays. The note is written on lined notepad paper, the kind they once wrote their songs on together. It's held in place by a half-empty cup of black coffee that isn't completely cold. His cup. The last thing his mouth touched. Robin traces her finger along the edge, collecting his dust.

She reads the words quickly without touching the paper.

She reads it again. And again. Again. Eyes spiralling helter-skelter from top to bottom, lurching back up.

Now it's inescapably committed to memory. Stamped into her like animal flesh under a branding iron.

As the words tick over, she claws at them, to their soundtrack. She thinks about who he'd become and whose fault that was. She thinks about Hilary lying on stinking clothes next to her only child, touching his skin for the last time. She thinks about how much worse this note could make everything.

Robin picks it up like it's poisonous, folds it carefully and slips it into her pocket. She takes it into the bathroom, sits on the watermarked toilet with the door locked. And the words still tick through her.

I'm so sorry, he wrote, in his beautiful neat writing, just curly enough.

I didn't know that Sarah was pregnant and I can never forgive myself for what I've done. I've made so many mistakes over these last years but I can't come back from this one. My greatest fear was turning out like my dad, and what I did to Sarah is far worse than anything he ever did.

I love you all but I don't deserve you. It wasn't Rez's fault, it was my idea to steal that stuff and it must have been me who pushed Sarah. So it was all me, all of it. I'm so sorry.

For ever is too long after all. I love you always.

It's three in the morning. Back at home now, Robin spreads it on the bed in front of her as Hilary frantically vacuums every inch of the house, howling, and Robin's dad paces the living room, hiding from all the women he doesn't know how to help.

CHAPTER THIRTY-NINE

Present day

SARAH

So here we are, back at Robin's front door. A couple of hours after we were last here.

My twin is spent. Utterly wrecked by bashing doors and standing up to a suicidal man who she'd thought was a wife-beater. It's just so Robin.

Once inside her hall, my sister bends down to pick up a card from the hall carpet. While she reads it, she leans on the wall, exhausted, and I click the door closed behind us.

It's just a normal family house. Nothing special, nothing fancy. It's solid, neutral, a bit old-fashioned. There's not a trace of personality.

'Damn it. I just missed them,' Robin says, finally moving down the hall. 'Sorry,' she adds, 'come in. Let's get a cup of tea or something.'

We walk into the kitchen and she puts the kettle on. She pulls down two chunky pastel-coloured mugs. The kitchen is a basic wooden affair; it's so normal it makes me feel sad.

She slides the card towards me along the counter.

'It's from a security company I called. When you were knocking, I thought it was them. I...' She stops. 'I missed them.'

'Oh,' I say. And automatically open the fridge to get out some milk. It takes my breath away. Everything in there is organised into coloured sections, in Tupperware boxes. Robin's certainly changed. In fact, unlike the grime of the outside, the whole house is spotless.

'Why did you need security?' I ask quietly. I wonder if she's having trouble with fans, maybe a stalker. It seems a bit much.

She doesn't answer. Just suddenly turns and hugs me. I'm nearly knocked over.

'I'm so glad to see you,' Robin says, and she looks up into my eyes in a way that no-one else has for weeks. 'I'm sorry I didn't answer the door before, I didn't know it was you.' She laughs, and I don't know why but I'm so happy that we're finally together that I hug her again. We uncouple and then she laughs again. 'And you're pregnant!'

I smile. 'Yeah,' I say aloud for the first time. 'I am pregnant. My second baby.'

'You mean, you have a child?' she asks.

My voice catches in my throat. 'Yes, I'm so sorry I didn't tell you before. I have a little girl.'

'A little girl,' she repeats, nodding. 'That's … That's really good. You deserve to have a little girl. I'm so happy for you. Oh my god, that means I'm an auntie.' She's gleeful and I feel guilty. Because how can you be an auntie to a child who doesn't know you exist?

'Yep, you're an auntie. Violet's nearly four, and she reminds me of you.' She does. It's the serious eyes. The compact strength. I'd never told Violet, of course. Never told anyone. Just silently enjoyed it.

'How far along are you?' She gestures to my belly. It shows more on me because I'm slim. Slimmer than I should be, maybe, but all I've tended to eat has been toast at breakfast and the odd chocolate bar. I've been too worried and felt too queasy and nervous to eat, and who knows how long my money will last.

It was getting to the point in time where I would have had to tell Jim. I wanted to get to that point; too late for him to make any rash demands. I knew he thought we weren't ready. I wouldn't have been able to keep it secret much longer. But he took care of that.

Robin is throwing back tea and asking questions, and she's so happy to see me that I'm knocked for six. She thinks this is a happy visit. I can almost reach up and touch my guilt. It hangs around my neck.

The adrenaline has swept away and Robin has slumped on the sofa, two hands on her mug, third cup of tea nearly drained. The questions have slowed and her eyes are droopy. She's asked enough questions about Violet to recreate her out of clay and she's the first person to ask questions about my bump.

'Do you know what you're having?'

'It's too soon, but I think it's a boy.'

She's been silent now for a few minutes.

'How long have you lived here?' I ask.

'A few years.'

I want to ask why. Why Manchester? Why Chorlton? Why this family home that is so at odds with Robin. But I just say, 'It's really nice.'

'Where are you staying?' she asks.

'A B&B in Sale. It's about – oh.' I smile at my stupidity. 'I was about to tell you how far away Sale was, like you didn't know.'

Robin smiles without looking up from her mug. Her chin is getting closer to the table; she looks like she's about to fall asleep and it's not even lunchtime.

'So,' I say, in as cheering and rallying a way I can manage a few hours after being reunited with my sister and being dragged headfirst into a suicide rescue. 'How about you show me around your city? I've not really seen much of it and you can give me the locals' tour.'

Robin looks up. 'Yeah, sure, not today though, I'm so tired. Is that okay?'

'Of course.' I don't have any interest in seeing Manchester, I just wanted to gel myself into her life, try to make plans to buy myself time to say what I need to say, do what I need to do.

'How long have you been here?' she asks.

'Oh, not long, a few days,' I say, trying to play down how hard I'd looked for her.

She frowns. 'A few days?'

'Well, a bit longer than that.' She's still looking at me, reading my face for specifics. 'I mean, I got here a couple of weeks ago.'

'Just a couple?' She looks sceptical.

'Yeah, why?'

'Oh, no real reason. It's just that someone's been trying to get hold of me. Like, really trying. And for a moment I hoped it might have been you. It doesn't matter.'

Knock knock. A quick rap from the front of the house makes her jump. It's such a normal thing that I wait for Robin to say something or to move, but she just stares wild-eyed at me.

She whispers: 'I need to go upstairs.'

'But there's someone at the door.'

'I need to get something under the table. Just stay sitting right there, okay?' She lowers herself down off the chair, crouches and shuffles under her kitchen table. I don't know whether to laugh or what.

Knock knock.

'Just stay still,' she whispers.

'Who is it?' I ask, trying to understand if this is a clever joke I'm too tired to understand. 'Is this who's been trying to get hold of you?'

Knock knock knock. The sounds are getting louder.

'I don't know,' she whispers hard. 'Just hang on, just be quiet, can you?' She doesn't seem annoyed, or amused, more anxious than anything.

'Are you hiding from someone?' I ask. 'Do you owe money?'

'No, it's fine. Just, shh.'

This is ridiculous. This whole thing is ridiculous. I can't help myself, I stand up sharply and go out to the hall.

Robin scrambles out after me. 'It's not safe,' she says urgently, 'not in your condition.'

I have no idea what she's talking about but it's her house, her rules. I tuck behind her and prod her gently as she moves towards the door.

'Come on,' I say, trying to be rallying. 'This is ludicrous. There are two of us and it's broad daylight!'

She grinds to a halt as the bangs on the door step up tempo.

Who is it?

I hold Robin's hand from behind, guide it up to the lock. She's shaking but takes over. She unbolts it and twists the Yale lock as I reach to swipe the chain open.

ROBIN

'Oh my god,' Sarah gasps and she climbs backwards up the stairs, sits halfway up, breathing hard and holding her stomach.

Robin breathes in, draws herself up to her full five-foot and shouts, 'What the fuck are you doing at my house, Rez?'

He's staring at her. His thin, greying hair in a snaky little ponytail, his dark eyes tracing every line of her face.

The front door shakes in Robin's hand as she holds it to steady herself, breathing hard.

Rez is breathing hard too, as he continues to study her, holding his silence like a weapon. He's taller than Robin remembered. She'd crunched him down to rodent-sized in her memory. He'd looked smaller than this in the dock, childlike. Not that she'd allowed herself anything approaching sympathy.

He doesn't say anything. She doesn't say anything. Seconds pass. Someone has to make a move.

'Shall I get Sam from the flats?' Sarah says from behind Robin's head.

A bit more of the old Robin crackles to life. 'Fuck that, Sarah, I don't need a hero. Come on then, Rez,' Robin says, pushing her breath into her words to force them out. 'You've been trying to get this door open for weeks and now you're just staring at me.'

He looks down at his feet, sniffs hard and then – quick as a fox – he's stepped forward and is looking Robin dead in the eye from point-blank range.

'I've waited so fucking long for this, Robin,' he says. Even in anger, his voice is softer than she remembered, more like Callum's, but she stops that thought.

'Oh yeah?' Robin says, her knuckles white and trembling.

'Yeah. A long time. I've had so much to say to you. I've gone over and over it in my head but now I'm here, looking at you, I can't remember any of it.'

'Well, how about you fuck off then, Rez. There's nothing we can say to each other to make anything better. You know what you did. I know what I did. I hold my head up fucking high.'

A quick laugh shoots from Rez's mouth. His breath is sour. Roll-up fags and cheap fortified wine.

'You really think you're holding your head up high? I've watched you. Watched your sad little life, Robin Marshall. The pint-sized warrior. The great rock star. The loyal sister. You're a joke. Maybe that's why I can't find the words. It's hard to be that angry with someone so pathetic.'

'Me pathetic? You're the one sending tonnes of poison pen letters!'

'Letters? What letters? I don't know what you're on about.'

Robin ignores this, carries on shouting. 'You tried to break into my house! And before that you were scared off by an old man. And you couldn't even push your way in an open door. So yeah, the pint-sized warrior and all that shit but this pint-sized warrior kept *you* out.

'And now you're standing at my door after hunting me down but for what, Rez? What are you even here for? You want to deliver some speech to me? Go ahead.' She fans her arm behind her. Not really meaning for him to come in. It was a figure of speech, a common gesture, but he comes in anyway. Pushes past her, grabbing and nearly tosses the door closed as he does so.

Sarah stays sitting on the stairs, hand on her belly, tucking her knees up and making herself small. Rez pokes his head around the living room door, hesitates, then goes in and sits down on the smaller of the two sofas. Robin follows and sits on the larger sofa, in her dip. She hasn't taken her eyes off Rez. Watching him like an unpredictable snake. Sarah eventually moves into the doorway of the lounge and contrives to watch Rez carefully.

'You cost me everything,' he says finally, looking at his hands in front of him.

Robin laughs. 'You? You think *you* lost everything?'

He waits for her to finish, then says it again. 'You cost me everything. You lied about me. You lied about me knowing that there was no chance of anyone believing my story. You lot thought you were the bloody royal family compared to me but you didn't know anything about me.'

'You think you were innocent? You really don't think you deserved to pay?' Robin asks, eyebrows risen so high they disappear into a tangle of curls.

'I never said I was innocent. I did a lot of things wrong. There's a hell of a lot I'd take back, before and since. But I didn't do half the stuff you said I did, and you were dead wrong on one thing. I loved that boy.' He pauses and takes a breath. 'I loved him. And I'd not loved anyone like that before and I sure as hell haven't since. And you made him into an angel. And what did that make me? The fucking devil, mate.'

Robin's eyes fill with tears but she wipes them angrily. 'Don't talk about him, you've not got that right.'

'Why? 'Cos you own the rights to Callum? I loved him too and he loved me. Everyone else looked at me the way you're looking at me now but not him. I wasn't anything to write home about before, but I got by. I was young and desperate, I nicked a few things, made some dodgy decisions. But I could have been okay. I could be alright now. I could be sitting there, like you two, nice house, bit of money. No chance of that with a record.'

Robin goes to speak, to argue, but he shakes his head and carries on.

'Did you know my mum died when I was sixteen and I had to drop out of school to look after my brothers? Did you know that? Course you fucking didn't. I was always going to work with animals. That was my dream since I was a little kid. And instead I had to beg, borrow and steal to put food on the table. My cousins helped, got involved. We got through it. We lived, we ate. My brothers might not have flourished like you lot, but they were happy enough. And then Callum came into my world, my dirty little world, and he didn't see it like that. He got it. He understood me. And I understood him. 'Cos I'd been alone too. And he was still alone.'

'He wasn't alone, he had me,' Robin says fiercely, wiping away angry tears.

'He loved you so much, you stupid cow, but he couldn't open up to you like he could with me, couldn't rely on you. You were a little girl. You liked him when he liked what you liked. You liked him when he was fun. Do you remember telling him to tell his dad that he was gay? Do you? If you understood what that man had really put him through, you wouldn't have sent him within a hundred miles.'

'And what about my sister? Just 'cos Callum loved you, did that give you the right to rob her of her baby? To kill something tiny and vulnerable?'

Sarah lowers her head, tears falling onto her top and catching on the bump.

'You've told that story so many times you actually believe it, don't you?' Rez searches Robin's face but she keeps her lips pursed, eyes on fire.

'She fell down the stairs and you know she did. I didn't push her. *He* didn't push her. He thought he did because he was off his head and believed everything you told him. You put his neck in that rope the second you told him that. And you know it. That's why you're holed up in here like this, licking your wounds and hissing at everyone like a cornered animal. What is it? Guilt finally got to you?'

'That's not true,' Robin says quietly.

'She fell,' Rez says, keeping his eyes on Robin. 'I told him over and over, all night, that it wasn't his fault but your word was gospel.

He couldn't cope. I went out to get some drinks, I didn't know what else to do. Came back and it was too late.'

Robin is shaking her head: 'No, no.'

'Yes, Robin, *yes*. He believed the best in you and the worst in himself. It was too much for him; he was too sensitive, too *good*. And yeah, if we hadn't been there that night on the landing, none of it would have happened. I'll take that guilt with me to my grave. But you stitched me up. You laid everything at my feet. When I was already on the floor from losing Cal. I couldn't fight. No-one would listen to me anyway. Why would they?'

'No,' says Robin, softer this time, 'that's not what happened.'

'Then you all just went about your business. He was gone, I was banged up. I hadn't done half the stuff you said. And I don't say this easily. But like it or not, Callum wanted to take that stuff. It was him who asked his mum when they were going out. He wasn't taking it to get at you lot, or his mum, it was stuff his dad had bought her. It was to get back at him. But you lot were fine. You got fame and fortune, yeah? And you...' He turns to point at Sarah, who shrinks away. 'Well, I know you had your problems but looks like you're alright now.'

Sarah just shakes her head, stays curled against the wall.

Robin's breathing hard, staring intently but not saying a word. Rez's story is not how she remembers it, not at all. But to accept it would be to unravel spools of rope she can't risk getting caught in. So she shakes her head dismissively, gets up as if she's going to tell him to go. Rez stays where he is and she sits back down.

'But do you know who I used to hate most of all?'

Robin stays quiet.

'Your dad.'

'My dad didn't do anything!' Robin blazes.

'Oh yes he fucking did. You weren't there in court every day. You did your bit and ran away. You didn't hear what he said. About

Callum, about me. And Callum's mum stood by and watched. Just like she'd sat by and watched Drew tear lumps out of him when he was a little boy. Mute. Mute the whole time. In court. Before, after. And you all put me in that prison.'

He pauses, wipes his eyes and clears his throat. 'Can I have a glass of water?'

'No,' says Robin.

'I'd never done time before. You can't even imagine what it's like in there. You think Drew Granger had a problem with homos? You try being a faggot at Her Majesty's pleasure. I ended up in the infirmary more times than you've had hot dinners.'

'For someone scared of going to prison, trying to break in here so many times seems pretty fucking stupid,' Robin snaps.

He says nothing, shrugs his shoulders. 'I wasn't going to do anything.'

Robin laughs, but her eyes aren't smiling. 'Bullshit.'

'I really wasn't. I just wanted to check I'd got the right house, the right person. Thought I could take a peek, that's all, thought I could barge in and then if it wasn't you, then, I don't know, I'd have legged it, but if it was, we could finally settle this shit that I've been carrying around with me for a lifetime.'

'Yeah, right,' Robin says.

'The more I knocked and you didn't answer, the more I thought I might be wasting my time, that maybe she'd given me the wrong address.'

'She?' Robin looked at Sarah and back at Rez. 'Who do you mean by she?'

'Callum's mum.'

'Why did she give you the address?' Sarah says, her voice louder. 'She only told me Manchester,' she adds, 'said she didn't remember the rest. Why wouldn't she tell me?'

Rez shrugs. 'I dunno. I knew you were up here. I'd seen your band practising. I said I wanted to write to you and clear the air. She gave it up straight away—.'

'Look,' Robin interrupts. 'What do you want, Rez? Money? I don't have as much as you think.'

'I don't want your money. What good would money do me? I don't give a shit about that. I work up here now, in the Apollo, happy coincidence, eh?'

'I earn enough to keep me in puff and the odd curry. I don't want much. When I needed money was when the boys were younger; they're all men now. They learned to stand on their own feet when I was inside. So no, I don't want your fucking money.'

'What *do* you want?' Sarah asks, her voice quiet again.

'I want to hear Robin admit what really happened. I want her to acknowledge that Callum wasn't just a saint and I wasn't just a sinner. I wasn't expecting to see you, Sarah.' His voice softens. 'But I really didn't push you down the stairs. I'd never do that. My old man used to push my mum around. I'd never do that to a woman. I'd never do that to anyone.'

'I didn't lie,' Robin says. 'I mean, not really, it wasn't...' She grinds to a halt and swallows hard. 'Maybe I did unfairly load the dice but wouldn't you have done the same in my place?'

Rez sighed, opened his mouth to speak.

'But,' Robin interrupted, 'you would have gone down for something eventually, even without me. Your flat was full of shit; it's not like I planted anything.'

'Yeah, maybe. But we'll never know what might have happened, all I know is what did happen. Everyone who relied on me lost me. And I'd lost the one person I could rely on. Do you know what that's like?'

'Yeah,' Robin says quietly. 'I know what that's like. But Sarah, the baby, I had to do it for them. They deserved some justice.'

'Robin, I never wanted you to go to the police,' Sarah interrupts.

'And I love you for wanting to protect me and to get revenge – or whatever you want to call it – for me, but I didn't want any of this.'

'You were too broken up by what had happened to know what you wanted,' Robin says, turning to look at her sister.

'You've got to stop making decisions like that for people, Robin. Callum didn't want you to intervene between him and his dad, but you stirred things up in Atlanta. I didn't want you to do any of this, not in my name. I'm sorry, I know you did what you thought was right, but Callum loved Rez, *clearly*, even I saw that and I barely saw them together. You told me he loved Rez enough to mention him in the note.'

'Sarah,' Robin says, eyes pleading with her sister.

'What do you mean, Sarah?' Rez says. 'Robin, what's she saying?'

'Nothing. You've made your point, I get it. I'm sorry, okay?' Robin says.

'What do you mean, Sarah?' Rez asks again.

'The note,' Sarah says. 'Callum's note. Did you see it?'

'He left a note? That night?' Rez's eyes are wide and he looks between the two sisters in disbelief. 'What did it say?'

Robin sighs, her shoulders drop and she whispers, 'Okay, wait there.'

Outside the dining room, she pauses. It's been months since she opened this door, years since she touched the things in here. She turns the handle and forces herself inside. The brightness of the room surprises her and she goes straight to the specific box she needs. It's the one that says 'filing cabinet' in someone else's writing, the house packers loading and dumping things into boxes with no idea the damage they were dealing with.

The letter is two-thirds down, among the other paperwork: old rental agreements, guarantees. She touches it, the lined paper worn and soft like old cotton. The folds are still in place from the night she found it and took it home. She doesn't need to read it, it's scorched through her like rock.

'Here,' she says to Rez as she walks slowly back into the living room.

'Is this what I think it is?' he asks, breathing hard again.

'Yes,' she says. 'I'm sorry. I'm sorry, okay?'

He opens it carefully using the tips of his fingers and sits back in shock. 'It's been so long since I saw his handwriting,' he says, to no-one in particular.

Robin takes a deep breath and looks at Sarah, while Rez stares at the paper in his hands.

'He says it wasn't my fault,' Rez says, 'but you ... He says it was his idea to steal the stuff but that's not true. The minute he mentioned his mum's jewellery I started to think a certain way. We were always skint and it was just sitting there. I dunno who finally said it but it was not just his idea.' Rez is wiping his eyes with his right hand, holding the note away with his left.

'He says he pushed Sarah,' Rez reads, looking up in confusion. 'But he didn't. No-one did, she fell. You fell, didn't you?' he says to Sarah.

'I still don't know,' Sarah says, quietly and emphatically.

'My poor Cal,' Rez says. 'And you've had this the whole time?'

Robin hangs her head. 'Yeah,' she says. 'Maybe you should have it now. I'm sorry. I just wanted to do right by him.'

'You might not believe this, Robin, but that's all I wanted to do too.'

He left, cradling the note like a newborn. It was a strangely flat feeling after weeks of anticipation and fear, years of mutual loathing.

Robin knew she'd been blinkered, knew she'd laid everything at Rez's feet. Knew it wasn't fair but it had felt fair. She hadn't known her dad did the same.

And she believed Rez. Believed he wouldn't come back. Believed the anger and grief he'd carried around had boiled over in his frenzies at the door and his attempts to get in. Believed that he had thought she was out each time and went crazy in frustration.

As the front door clicked back into its frame, the two sisters hugged wordlessly. Too many words had come out already that they didn't have the energy to pick up and tidy away. So they didn't.

CHAPTER FORTY

1998

SARAH

Nobody else has ever seen the letter. Just Robin. She won't let me read it, has just given me a patchy summary that I don't believe. And no-one else knows it exists. Not Hilary, not Dad and not the police. Robin carries it with her, clutching it to her in bed as she cries silently every night. I watch her through a crack in the door and creep away, my own grief stealing my tongue.

Robin plans to speak at the inquest, whenever it is arranged. She plans to tell the panel of strangers that her stepbrother had been led astray by Rez, his resistance low because of the brutality and rejection from his father, Drew Granger.

Drew and Mum came around the day after Callum ended his life. They sat on the edge of the sofa in silence, across from a half-conscious Hilary, who had been given something, and Dad who was silent, still shivering in shock.

Nobody knew what to say and everyone felt responsible. Only some of them should have, but that's not the way it works.

Robin had refused to come out of her room to see them and Mum sent Drew to the car while she went up to speak to my sister. I expected her to reappear seconds later but Mum was gone a little while. Perhaps Robin was desperate for comfort while Mum still didn't know that I'd loved and lost, that I needed comfort and couldn't possibly seek it from her. She must have known what happened that night in Atlanta, and she just left me to hide it and deal with it all by myself. If she'd known the outcome, the loss, she'd probably just be relieved. The surface would still look the same. And isn't that what matters?

ROBIN

They all nursed their grief in different ways. Hilary had emerged from the sedation she'd been given and trailed like a ghost around the house. She would go into the garage and sit among the spiders and the dust, leaning against the bin bags full of stuff Callum had left behind. Unable to open or touch inside the sacks.

She spent hours in the garden. Dug holes in it for no reason, filled them up again. Jack just watched from the window, made her cups of tea that went cold as she drove her shovel deeper into the lawn, scarf slipping from her hair.

Everything Callum had ever touched became an artefact. An old toothbrush was wrapped in tissue paper to preserve it. There was a bag of laundry he'd never picked up. Cleaned of his scent by the machine, Hilary would hug the clothes and take deep sniffs, throwing them across the room because they smelled of detergent and nothing more, then gathering them all up, mumbling apologies into them.

Robin hid. She hid in silence, because there was so much music that was out of bounds now and she hadn't yet found anything untainted. Callum oozed out of her record collection whichever way she thought about it. Bands he'd got her into, music they'd loved together, albums they quarrelled about, those early chords they'd learned. It was too knotty to try to unpick, every note would strike her heart, so she didn't risk it. She lay on her bed, staring out of the window and watching the clouds tumbling slowly like playful animals. Watched the scratches left in the blue by planes heading to and from Heathrow.

When Robin slept, she dreamed of Callum. Dreams in hyper-real colours, rich textures, smells. Dreams so real they taunted her into trying to stay awake. She lay at night with her arm slung over the acoustic Eastman guitar he'd left. The only physical reminder she could bear to see.

She knew her mother and Drew would come over. That in grief, Drew would claim an ownership of Callum that he'd surrendered in real life. She wanted to lock the house down to keep him out, instead she just continued to hide.

When her mother knocked lightly on her door, 'Robin, it's Mum,' Robin fully expected to tell her to go away. 'Can I come in?'

'Okay,' Robin said, choking on the word in surprise.

Angela had come in and sat lightly on the bed. Robin didn't look at her. She stayed where she sat, leaning against the wall with her fingertips just reaching to brush the strings of the guitar.

'I'm so sorry, love,' her mother said, and Robin's face creased in on itself and the tears came so suddenly that her face and hands and arms were soaked with the wet heat of them.

The eruption passed quickly. Robin wiped her nose and eyes on her sleeve and looked up. Her eyes were bloodshot and swollen.

'I don't know what to do, Mum,' she said. And then the hot wet tears came in waves again, her small chest lurching with the force of them. When she looked up again, she saw the tears coursing down her mother's face and her own tears turned to anger.

'It's his fault, you know. All of it.'

'Whose fault?' her mother asked.

'You know who. Your husband. I heard him downstairs just now, heard his empty words in the hall. How dare he come here and act like he's upset.'

'Of course he's upset! We both are, we all are. God, Robin, how could you say that?'

'He hated Callum.'

'He did n—'

'He *hated* him. He hated that he was soft and gentle and kind. Hated that he was like Hilary, that Ca— That he ... wasn't some red-blooded, macho philanderer like Drew. And my brother knew it. He *knew* his dad felt like that and it had messed him up since he was a little boy. Even when he was happy here and accepted and loved, he still dragged that around with him.'

'He may not have been the best father—' Angela started.

'He was a terrible father!'

'He was traditional and he was impatient, yes. He probably was a shitty dad the first time around but he was still Callum's dad and he's lost him just as much as any of you. More, maybe, because he never got the chance to put it right.'

'Neither did I,' Robin whispered.

'What do you mean?' Angela lowered her voice, tried to reach across to stroke Robin's hair but she inched away. 'He knew how much you loved him. You two were always thick as thieves.'

'It doesn't matter,' Robin said. She said it to her knees, without looking up.

'Robin, please.'

'It doesn't matter, just get out.'

'Robin,' Angela said, her voice still soft and low.

'You chose Drew. You chose him and look what happened. But don't ever ask me to feel sympathy for him.'

'Just you listen a minute, girl,' Angela said, sharper, holding Robin's gaze until she looked away. 'You need to take a step back because you do not know where your anger is going to lead you. You need to bloody well humble yourself in the face of other people's heartbreak. You don't own grief. Do you understand me? Because if you don't control yourself, you will regret it.'

'Just get out, Angela.'

'Please don't do anything rash,' her mother said, softer again.

'Get the fuck out of my room.'

— —

It was only after he was arrested that the family found out how old Rez was. He was twenty-three. It had been bad enough when everyone thought he and Callum were both a pair of kids but they'd got together when Callum was seventeen and Rez would have been twenty-two. A man. A skinny, immature, rat-faced man, but still a man. And dominant, they believed, despite the pathetic figure he cut.

Robin faced down that man. Stared into his rat face as she gave evidence at Rez's court case for theft, possession and actual bodily harm – outraged that he wasn't charged with grievous bodily harm and refusing to hide while she said it all. 'He pushed my sister and he said, "I hope you die". He definitely meant to hurt her.'

What she said changed from the original statement she'd given before Callum's death. She blamed anger for clouding her memory. Claimed she'd heard Callum trying to stop Rez, claimed it was Rez grabbing the jewellery, Rez leading everything. Gentle Callum being swept along. It was deeply and deliberately untrue.

Sarah didn't give evidence. Instead, Robin read a witness statement. Growled it out across the courtroom, choking on several of the words.

None of it mattered. They'd found enough at the flat to stick Rez away for eighteen months, a combination of crappy little charges from a petty life.

No-one felt vindicated. For ever stretches far ahead and those left behind have already scattered to the wind.

CHAPTER FORTY-ONE

Present day

ROBIN

'What else do you have in there?' Sarah asked, peeking curiously around the dining room door.

Robin took a deep breath, sighed and shook her head. 'I don't even know. Not all of it. I've lugged it around from flat to flat. Demos, old notebooks, guitars, my first amp. The little Park amp, do you remember?'

Sarah shook her head. 'You must have got that when I was in Atlanta,' she said and Robin tried to ignore the bitter note.

Sarah opened the door wider, put her hand on the small of her back and stretched into it.

'You okay?' Robin asked. 'Is it the baby?'

Sarah smiled. 'I can't feel it yet,' she said, 'I'm just sore. A bit tired.' She stepped in further, tentatively, and beckoned for Robin to join her.

'I don't know,' Robin said, 'it's been a fucked-up day as it is, I don't think I can handle this too. I'm sorry.'

'Well, how about we look at it tomorrow? Together?'

'Maybe,' Robin said. 'But what are your plans tomorrow and, y'know, after?'

'That's not an easy question to answer,' Sarah said, moving her hand self-consciously to the small bump under her baggy top.

Robin waited for more of an explanation but it didn't come.

'Would you mind if I went to bed?' Sarah finally said, bustling back out of the room and leaving Robin to hurriedly shut the door firmly again lest some stray memories burst out after them.

CHAPTER FORTY-TWO

Present day

SARAH

At Robin's insistence, we're sleeping in the same room for the first time in years. Top and tail. Twenty years have dissolved and we're jammed together at a sleepover. All that's missing is Callum.

Robin's smelly little feet are in my face and both our heads are filled with ten thousand crazy stories. I need to add one more. She asked earlier what my plans are, and I know my sister, she'll be filling in the gaps herself.

So I take a deep breath and tell her what happened with Jim, about the list. I tell her wide eyes again and again that I'd never hurt a child. That he'd misunderstood and misread everything and that I'd not helped myself. That it was the perfect storm. I tell her I need somewhere to stay.

'If Jim finds out too soon about the baby, I'll have no hope. But if Jim knows at the right time, he'll feel differently. He'll listen to my side because he'll have to. But he can only know when it's too late, you know? When I'm too far gone and there's no going back. And then he'll have to let me see Violet too; he can't keep siblings apart. God knows, we can't let that happen again. Maybe he'd even let me bring her up here to stay. And then—'. I slow down, I don't want to get ahead of myself. Robin says nothing.

'I just need to get myself straight before I try to get Violet. You have money. I know, I know, that's gross of me but I'd rather be honest and ask outright—'

Robin, propped up on a pillow, holds up her hand to stop me. Pulls at her dark curls. 'You can have any money you need,' she says. 'But Sarah, this is so fucked-up.'

'I know.'

'I mean, I just don't understand what you're asking from me. We've not spoken in years and we have no idea what's happening in each other's lives. How do you see this working? What are you actually saying? Do you want to live here? Do you want me to write you a cheque? Do you want me to talk you out of this?'

If she doesn't understand this, how can she understand the next part of the plan?

'I just need help to make a new life for Violet to come back into. And I need some support, from the only person I've ever really had support from—' My voice cracks. 'You're stronger and tougher than me and always have been. You know why I am the way I am. You know I'd never hurt a child, never hurt anyone. I don't expect Jim to believe me just like that but there's no way he'll even hear me out on my own.'

'So you want to stay with me while you get straight?'

'Yes. I mean, I'd love to.' My heart soars. My sister. I knew she'd help.

'No, that's not what I mean,' Robin starts and the caution in her voice chills me. 'I mean, you think it's best if you hide up here while you're pregnant but then you'll spring it on Jim that you're having his baby and want to try to get custody of the daughter he thinks you hurt?'

'When you say it like that it sounds crazy but...' My smile fades again.

'It is fucking crazy, Sarah. It's the kind of crazy that would get anyone's kid taken away. You won't get custody like that but I don't think you're talking about formal routes. You must realise I won't help you snatch your daughter.'

'Well, what would you do then, Robin? What would you do in my situation?'

Robin swings out of the bed, comes and sits at my end. She lifts a wiry arm up and drapes it on my shoulders. It feels good. My sister. My twin.

'What I'd do is probably far crazier,' she says. 'That's why I'm not thinking about what I'd do, I'm thinking about what you *should* do. You haven't hurt your daughter but you've told Jim enough bullshit that he thinks you're mental. And you're pregnant with a baby he doesn't even know about, and you've run off to Manchester to see your equally mental sister. Like, Sarah, this shit is not going to work. You need to stop. You need to just stop and tell the truth. We need to tell the truth about *everything*.'

Robin sits up in her bed, leans against the wall and crosses her legs. We could be six years old again. 'Okay then, let's do this,' she says. 'It's my turn to tell you the truth.'

Robin tells me that she hasn't left the house in years. Not months, *years*. She hasn't recorded with her band, or even seen her band, in just as long. She isn't writing music, she isn't working. She spends her days walking in circles around her own house, counting her steps or doing way too many weights in her gym. Or she watches the neighbours and grows more paranoid and crazy by the day.

She tells me that she didn't know who it was but that Rez had been knocking on the door for weeks. And that she'd woken up one night to hear an elderly neighbour shouting as Rez tried break in, that he'd tried to push through the door when she opened it for a delivery and that, more recently, he'd even made it up onto the roof outside of her window and looked in. That, despite all of that, she still hadn't gone to the police because she was terrified they'd make her leave the house, to go to the station or eventually to court. That's why she was due to have new locks and alarms installed, but they'd visited while we were in the flats behind and she'd missed the appointment.

'But you *are* strong, Robin. You faced Rez. You faced him today and you made things better.'

'Only because you were here. I'd have fallen apart by myself.'

'That's not true. I'd just clung onto the wall and tried not to faint. You handled it, just like you always did.'

She'd stepped up to him because she's strong and tough and slightly nuts, the Robin I've always known. But she seems to have forgotten that. I ask her what she wants now.

'Well, I'd like to meet Violet. And I do want to help you with all of that but I can't even get out of my front door unless it's literally life or death. I can't even sleep in a bed most nights. Usually I'd be lying under it. So I need help too. I'm so fucking embarrassed, Sarah.'

I ask her why this has happened, why she's receded into this tiny shell, miles from home. She says she doesn't know. But without needing to highlight the segue, she says: 'I loved him, Sarah. But I hated him for what happened to you and then before we all had a chance to start again or try to find a way forward together, we lost him.'

She's still self-censoring the name, Callum. Just like she did after he died.

'I blamed him for what happened to you, and what happened to him, to be honest. Then I blamed Rez for corrupting him, I blamed Hilary for not kicking his arse and I even blamed you for distracting me from him—'

I look down at the small bump under my borrowed pyjamas.

Robin squeezes my hand lightly without making eye contact in the dim light. 'I just want to be honest. But most of all, Sarah, I blamed myself. I all but tied that rope. I should have saved him years before so he shouldn't have needed someone like Rez.' She lowers her voice, picks her words more carefully than I'm used to.

'Callum was lonely and different, yeah? But I'd lost my twin, my other half, and I felt different too. Together we hadn't been so lonely. It's not that I didn't miss you, but it helped having him there and we fitted together. And you know the worst thing? I think it was because I was jealous when he got a boyfriend, that's when we started to grow apart.'

'Rez?'

'No, not Rez, John. A boy at school who broke his heart before Rez. John was his first proper boyfriend. Callum was head over heels with him. And when they got separated by John's parents and the school, I guess I didn't see what a hole that had left because I was excited to have him all to myself again.

'But he was never the same after that, Sarah.' She puffs all the air from her lungs and flops onto her side. 'So there it is. I could have prevented all this if I'd been a better friend, a better sister, but I didn't. And if I'd saved him, then what happened to you wouldn't have happened because he wouldn't have been there with that shithead nicking his mum's stuff. And you know what, maybe Rez wasn't even that much of a shithead. Maybe C—' She swallows. 'Maybe Callum could be a bit of a shithead too.'

I don't know what to say. There are whole years of my sister's life that I only knew about in postcard-sized bites. I never told her what was happening below the surface of my life in Atlanta, and she never told me what was really going on in Berkshire. A lot of empty letters.

Robin tells me that she's been getting letters now, at this house. That she's been struggling to cope with anything unexpected. That while she's filed the unopened bills away, chucked junk mail in the recycling without a thought, that these bright white letters have haunted her. She'd thought they might be connected to the knocks on the door. 'But if they were, Rez would have admitted to them, right? Anyway, the postmark was from down south and he says he lives up here now.'

'Down south?'

'Yeah. It sounds ridiculous,' she adds, 'but it's how plain they are that bother me. Someone's typed my address on a plain white envelope and used a proper postage stamp, not one of those office franking machines. Like it's a person sending them one after the other. It's just … odd. It spooks me.'

A lot spooks you, I want to say. And she was always so brave. When we watched *Jaws* as a kid, I'd had to sleep in with Mum and Dad, while she made the boys at school play shark games in the swimming pool before the council closed it because it was leaking and filled with slime.

'Go and get the letters,' I say. 'I'll open them for you and we'll handle it together.' I want a chance to be strong for her. How hard can it be? It's just opening a few letters. But like pulling the wardrobe doors open to check for ghosts in a child's bedroom, the moment just before the doors part, your adult heart still beats a bit faster.

Robin gets out of bed slowly and trudges downstairs to the spare bedroom she uses as an office. She returns with a small, neat stack. I open the top one carefully, using my finger briskly like a knife. I pull the letter out. The light is bad but I scan it quickly. It looks official. Warning Robin about someone who may be a risk to her. It says that this person has attacked another family member some years ago, that they had been treated but required to register their whereabouts. That they had stopped.

It says to remain calm but be vigilant. To call if she has any questions. That they'd like to receive confirmation that she's seen this letter. And the others.

'It's just an advert for a fashion magazine subscription,' I say, being strong for her. 'Weird how they'd bother to put it in an envelope.'

'Seriously?' she says, but she doesn't reach for the letter and I put them all on the floor before she can think to.

'Yeah,' I say and I hop out of bed. 'Just going to the loo.'

She laughs. Throws her head back and laughs. As I go out of the door, I cast a glance back and see my sister throw herself backwards on the bed and take a long, deep breath. She looks just like she did when we were young, a tiny little scruffy thing making big gestures. I've discreetly brought the letters with me, down the stairs and into the kitchen. I find the key on a hook and open the back door slowly, like a safe cracker. I step outside with my bare feet. The ground is gritty and cool. It's a relief after the stuffy house. I ease the lid of the wheelie bin open, stuff the letters in as deep as I can, and snap it closed. I lock the kitchen up quickly, rush up to the loo and then back into bed.

'You okay?' says Robin. 'I thought I heard the door.'

'Yeah,' I say, trying to keep my voice and breathing steady. 'Just wanted to get a bit of fresh air and a drink.'

'Did you lock up properly?' she asks lightly and I know she's not asking lightly.

'Yes, don't worry. You really don't have to worry about anything, Robin. I promise.'

There's a pause. 'I'm so fucking relieved,' Robin finally says.

'Good,' I say, a little triumphant. 'And I really appreciate you letting me stay. I'll get the rest of my stuff in the morning, if you're sure it's okay?'

She sits back up and reaches her hand for mine. 'Of course it's okay. You're my sister.'

We fall asleep still holding hands and as I drift away, somewhere deeper than I've gone in weeks, I allow myself to think that maybe me and my sister, and Violet too, that we might be okay. Even after all.

ROBIN

Sarah sleeps soundly now, her steady breath in and out transporting Robin back to many nights in childhood, crammed in the same room for one reason or another. But Robin's relief has given way to questions. Lying on the bed and not under it still doesn't come easy. Sarah's hand is curled around Robin's fingers and she slips them free, one-by-one. Sarah murmurs and rolls onto her side.

Robin stares at the ceiling and tries to wrap her head around everything that's happened today. All those paths colliding in her life, in one day. Henry. Rez. Sarah.

But things aren't resolved, not really. Henry was off to stay with his mum and hopefully that would be okay. Rez had shrunk back down to size. His anger washed away to reveal sadness and vulnerability, feelings she was battling to stay detached from. But Sarah, her poor sister who always tried to do the right thing, be the good girl, all those lies had torn her life apart. A life she deserved to live. A life she deserved to get back.

Lying has caused enough damage. Leaving those lies in place and hiding up here wasn't going to help Sarah, and only the truth held some hope for any of them.

Giving up on sleep, Robin treads lightly on the stairs. Sarah's phone is in her hand. Robin uses the light of the screen to find her way. She creeps into the living room, turns the lamp on and scans the room from the relative safety of the doorway. It's all as she left it. Neat, clean, warm. She closes the door quietly and goes to sit on the smaller sofa.

There are fewer than a handful of numbers on this phone. Literally, four. A curry place, somewhere called Cornell Lodge, Jim's mum and Jim.

Jim's is a mobile number. It's late but it's important. Tomorrow's sun might scare Robin's resolve away, and she owes it to her sister.

She presses 'Call'. There's a terrible pause and then the ringer crackles into life. Eight rings. She's about to hang up, half relieved, when a man's voice answers.

'Hello?' He sounds sleepy but she doesn't apologise for waking him. Bigger truths at stake. *Just get on with it.*

'Hi, Jim,' she exhales. 'You don't know me but I'm Sarah's sister. I'm calling because there are some things that I need to clear up. About my sister.' Robin hears the breathing at the end of the line grow faster.

'She didn't lie to you for bad reasons, Jim. She's not done the things you think she has. She loves Violet more than anything but she was covering up a lot of stuff that happened in her – in our – past and she dug herself into a hole.'

Jim doesn't say anything for a long while. Finally he asks, 'What's your name?'

'I'm Robin. Robin Marshall. I'm Sarah's sister. And she's with me in Manchester right now because she had nowhere else to go and she was scared and didn't want to make everything worse.' Adrenaline is causing Robin to waffle, but she has to keep going or she'll lose her nerve and hang up.

Jim remains silent.

'But I promise you that everything you think about her is wrong. She'd never hurt a child. Please, Jim, please give her the chance to explain it all. She misses you and she misses Violet and she wants to put everything right and I promise you, *on my life*, she deserves a chance to explain.'

There's a long pause.

'Sarah,' he says. 'You're *Sarah's* sister?'

'Yes.'

'She told me she had no family.'

'She had her reasons, but they weren't the reasons you might think.'

'I don't care. I needed to be able to trust her. She was looking after the most important thing to us, to me. And she lied in the most despicable ways. Did the most despicable things.'

'No,' Robin says, realising she's making everything worse. 'No, she would never do anything to hurt anyone, it's all a horrible misunderstanding. She still loves you—'

'She's not supposed to love me!' he says, louder than before. 'She was just supposed to take good, *safe* care of Violet.'

Robin can't help herself, the old flame bursts into life again. 'That's a horrible attitude to have towards your *wife*,' she says. 'Doesn't she deserve a loving relationship too?'

'My wife's dead,' he says, his voice strangled. 'Sarah was our nanny.'

Robin is silent, her heart banging around in her chest. She's heard only fractions of what Jim is saying, but she's trying to put it into the right order. She can't make it fit, because it makes no sense.

'I mean, Sarah *was* a godsend after Elaine died and Violet adored her but she crossed so many lines, even before...' He trails off.

Sarah is not Violet's mother. She is not Jim's wife. She is not desperately seeking help to win her own family back. In fact, Robin doesn't know what, who, her sister really is. A cold wind runs up and down Robin's legs. She hasn't seen her sister in years. But she didn't think to question any of what she said. Who was the woman upstairs?

'Are you still there?' His voice is impatient, confused.

'Yeah,' Robin gasps, 'I just ... this is news to me. I don't really understand. So you're really not married to my sister?'

'No. Absolutely not. She was our live-in nanny.'

'Just your nanny,' Robin repeats, trying to make the word fit comfortably in her mouth.

'Look, she was great at first but she got way too attached and her behaviour got stranger and stranger. I kept her on for the consistency and, honestly, because I had my own stuff to deal with, but then she crossed a line. More than one. Lots of lines. My daughter is my priority.'

'And Violet? She's your daughter. But not—'

'She's *my* daughter. Sarah is absolutely *not* her mother. No matter what she liked to tell people, as it turned out.'

'And your wife, she ...' Robin feels her cheeks colour, can't bring herself to say it out loud.

'My wife is dead,' he says.

Robin says nothing and Jim says nothing.

'We had to sack Sarah,' he says finally. 'I'd let it all go too far and Violet paid the price. My parents wanted me to go to the police then and there but I couldn't bear for Violet to go through that. Being interviewed, going to court. God, no. That little girl has been through enough.'

Robin imagines someone watching her from behind but when she turns around, there's no-one there, the lounge door is still closed.

After apologising to Jim and hanging up, Robin opens the door and steps into the hall. She listens at the bottom of the stairs but everything is still. She walks into the kitchen, quietly opens a bottle of beer from the fridge and leans against the sideboard.

As Robin sips, she goes over Sarah's story in her head, tries to believe it. But Jim's words push it away and take over. He had no reason to lie to her, especially with such a tall tale. But Sarah did. If she wanted Robin to help her keep this secret baby, even try to snatch Violet or God knows what, she'd tell her anything she needed to. Robin looks at the back door.

Why would Sarah come down into the kitchen and open the door, when she said she was going to the loo?

Robin goes to listen at the bottom of the stairs again, hears nothing. She pulls on her trainers and goes back into the dimly lit kitchen. Using the light from Sarah's phone as a torch, she fumbles with the back door and opens it as quietly as she can. To get out there, she tells herself it's bin day. She manages to put the rubbish out sometimes, under cover of darkness. She'd manage it now.

Bin day. The letters.

Her heart bangs harder in her chest as she steps out on shaking legs. Two steps, three. The bin isn't far but the sky over the garden is as big and grey as death.

She flips the lid open quietly, shines the screen light inside. Two neatly tied black bags sit in there from last week, but to the side of one of them, something white catches the screen light. It's very white indeed, reflective almost. Robin looks up at the flats ignoring her, leans in and grabs it.

She closes the bin, practically jumps back through the kitchen door and locks it quickly. She pulls the letter out of the opened envelope; it feels even more of a ticking bomb than it had lying in a stack for months.

She reads it.

A family member attacked by Sarah Granger, her sister. It says that Sarah should have been in contact, registering her whereabouts. That's she's missing. That the woman upstairs in Robin's house right now is a possible risk to other family members. It gives a number to call, not open now until morning.

Robin knew Sarah had had some trouble before she left Birch End for good, it was hinted at in the stilted calls with Hilary that Robin had neglected for months, maybe years. But violence? Sarah was never a violent person, never a risk to anyone. *At risk*, more like.

Robin doesn't know if anything that Sarah has told her since arriving today is true. Her compulsion to run from all of this is strong, but there's nowhere to go within the house that is any safer than right here, armed with only a phone that isn't hers.

Her only hope of making sense of this night is to fill in any blanks she can, try to understand what she's actually dealing with. She can't think beyond that. Robin calls the number still etched in her mind, after all these years. It's late, but she would answer. Their generation always answers late-night calls.

A click the other end. 'Hello?'

Robin's throat is sore from using her voice more today than she has for over two years. Her voice croaks out the name.

'Hilary?'

A pause. 'Yes?'

She clears her throat but speaks barely above a whisper. 'It's Robin. I'm sorry to call so late.'

'Robin!' Hilary's voice is thinner than ever. 'Darling! Are you okay? What's going on?'

'Hilary,' Robin says again, feels her eyes spill sudden tears down her cheeks. For a moment, she just sobs. A sound she's not made in a long time, while her stepmother listens and waits as she always did.

'Sorry,' Robin splutters.

'Shh, shh, what's wrong?'

'Sarah's here, Hilary, she just turned up today and I don't know what to do.'

'Sarah's there? With you, in Manchester?'

'Yes, she turned up out of the blue this morning—'

'Oh, Robin.' Hilary pauses. 'This is my fault. I tried to put her off, I told her you were in Manchester but I didn't give her your address. She must have found it herself, I'm sorry.'

'But I want to see my sister, I just ... there's more—'

'Are you alone with her?'

'Yes, why?'

'Just be careful, give her room to move, okay? She's changed a bit since, well, when did you last see her?'

'Dad's funeral,' Robin whispers.

'Mmm,' Hilary says, pausing as she always does at the mention of Jack. Seconds tick by. 'Well, between then and leaving Birch End, you know she had a few difficulties, don't you? And she's worked very hard to put them behind her, so just be gentle with her. We don't want her to slip back. And I don't want ...' The seconds tick by again. 'You just be a little careful, okay? She can be a bit unpredictable.'

'Did she hurt you?'

'Me? No, never, why did you think that?'

'I had a letter. Saying Sarah had hurt a family member and was supposed to register her whereabouts or something. Who did she hurt? Was she in trouble with the police?'

Tick, tick, tick. 'No,' Hilary eventually says, making the word as long and thin as it could be. 'Not exactly. Sort of. She had a bit of a crisis, couldn't really handle a lot of the things that had happened, maybe things we don't even know about that she hinted at, and she... I suppose the expression is that she snapped. But she got help and she got better.'

'Why didn't you tell me?'

'Well,' Hilary says, 'we didn't want to worry you. And you and Sarah hadn't been close for a while, it seemed better for us to just contain it and get her some help.'

'Who is "us"?'

That deathly pause again. 'Your mother and I.'

'Who did she attack?'

'Robin, you should probably call your mum. She can help you.'

'When has she ever helped me?'

None of this made any sense to Robin. After bidding goodbye to Hilary, promising to call with an update the next day, she dialled before she could overthink it. A number she was surprised she still knew, years and years after she'd last rung.

It rings for so long Robin has time to panic. She does not want to call this house. She does not want to hear either of the voices that might answer. Eventually, a woman's voice says uneasily: 'Hello?'

'Angela?'

'Yes. Is this—?'

She clears her throat. 'Yes, it's Robin.'

'Oh, Robin.' There's a pause. 'I'm so pleased to hear your voice. Is everything okay?'

It's been seven years since we saw each other's faces. Is everything okay?

'I need to know something.'

'Okay.' Her mother sounds wary, but not surprised.

'Did Sarah attack Drew? Did she assault him for all the harm he caused our family? And did you and Hilary keep it from me?'

There's a pause. Robin fills it with angry thoughts.

'No, Robin,' Angela eventually says. 'No, she didn't.'

Robin rocks on her heels and rubs her temples with one hand. 'Don't lie to me, Angela. I know she hurt someone in our family and I know you and Hilary "dealt" with it. I've been sent a letter. So who was it?'

Angela takes a deep breath. 'Sarah asked to stay with us a couple of years after Dad died.'

'Really? Why?'

Angela ignores the question. 'I was surprised but obviously delighted. Drew wasn't keen but I stood up to him. I'd let him dictate when my children could visit too many times.' She left a pause but Robin refused to fill it. 'Anyway, she came here and we had a meal. She was staying over and we'd had a few glasses of wine so we all went off to bed quite early. The next thing I know...' Angela paused. 'Do you really want to hear this? It was a few years ago now.'

'Yes,' says Robin firmly. 'And I should have heard it then too.'

Angela takes a deep breath. 'Okay. Well, we must have been asleep for an hour or so and I woke up with Sarah on top of me, hitting me. She was going crazy, like a wild thing. I've never been so scared. She started clawing at my eyes—'

'What?'

'I think she would have killed me if Drew hadn't come back in. He'd been in the bathroom.'

'What a hero,' Robin spits.

'Hardly,' Angela says.

None of this made any sense to Robin, but neither did the conversation she'd had with Jim.

'She wanted to hurt him just as much as me, maybe more. She probably would have killed him if he'd been the one in the bed.'

'Why?' Robin asks, trying to keep her voice hard.

'Because she thought I knew what he'd done, Robin. And I swear to you, I didn't know. She didn't believe me and you probably won't either but I didn't know.' Angela takes a deep breath.

What he'd done? What had he done?

'It was only after she'd been arrested and released to stay with Hilary that I got to see her. Drew begged me not to go. It didn't make any sense. He was pleading. He should have been angry but he was scared. So I went to the old house and I sat with Sarah and Hilary, and your sister told us everything.' Angela's voice breaks and falters.

'What do you mean?' Robin says, louder than intended. 'Everything about *what*?'

'That he'd *seduced* her – that was the word she'd used, I'd use a different one – how he'd—' Her voice cracks. 'How he'd got her *pregnant.*' The word sticks in Angela's throat.

'That was his baby?' Robin gasps, an eighteen-year-old question finally put to bed in the worst way.

'My poor girl,' their mother says. 'She looked at me like I was insane for asking, like I'd known it all already. I really didn't. I felt sick to my stomach. Of course Hilary hadn't been that surprised, not after everything he'd done to her and Callum.'

Robin winces. She avoids ever using Callum's name and it had been brandished freely today. Every mention hurts.

'I've never felt so guilty or so angry. Sarah still didn't believe me though,' Angela adds.

'And yet you stayed with him?' Robin says quietly, her mother as low in her estimations as she's ever been.

'Jesus Christ! Is that what you think of me? I threw Drew out that night. I threw him out and I begged Sarah to tell the police what happened in Atlanta but she refused. Said she was eighteen at the time, that he'd confused her, got into her head, that she didn't want to relive it. It was her decision. I had to give up in the end and she swore me to secrecy.'

'So what happened to Sarah after that? Surely you didn't press charges against her for the attack?'

'I wanted them to drop it. Hilary and I both begged them. But I'd already given a statement, before I'd known any of this stuff. They said I couldn't withdraw it, that it was on record. They said she'd get help if it went to court. That it would be in her best interests. I promise, Robin, I promise I didn't know what had happened. Sarah doesn't believe me and I understand why but I didn't know. I'd never have let that happen to my child.'

'And where's Drew now?' Robin isn't prepared to believe her mother on the strength of one phone call.

'I don't know and I don't care. The last I heard, he was in Scotland, bobbing from job to job, probably from naive woman to naive woman. I haven't seen him since the night I threw him out.'

'That's hardly a comeuppance for everything he did.'

'What do you want me to say, Robin? This isn't a fairy-tale. As far as he was concerned, anything less than a glowing reputation, a fancy job title and a thin wife equalled failure. I have no doubt he thinks that his life is over.'

Robin shakes her head, says nothing.

'Look, the priority was Sarah,' Angela continues. 'Even if she still thought I was her enemy, Hilary and I had to make sure she was looked after and that she got better, and then Hilary helped her find a new job away from here. A fresh start. And she's still there now. She's working as a nanny for a family in Surrey.'

'No, she's not. She's up here with me and I don't understand why you didn't tell me any of this. I shouldn't be finding it out now while my sister sleeps upstairs,' Robin hisses.

'What difference would it have made if I'd told you? You already hated me. Anyway, it was Sarah's story to tell.'

Robin says nothing. Her mother was right.

CHAPTER FORTY-THREE

2013

SARAH

She's perfect, Violet. Exactly the kind of baby girl I always dreamed about having. I always knew I wanted children, for as far back as I can remember. Two children, a girl first and then a boy.

Jim, my boss, is pleasant enough but he's distracted right now and goes days without so much as kissing his daughter's little head. I kiss her constantly, wrap her in cuddles. She shouldn't suffer just because his late wife was lacking as a parent. I know Jim will re-emerge, he's a good dad. But right now, she's all mine. My responsibility and my joy.

When I first moved here, I called Hilary once a week to check in. I have to check in with several people. I tell them that I'm working at an accountant firm, typing up letters. I don't tell them about Violet. My mother said it wasn't such a good idea. But Hilary knew I'd be good at this and she was right.

I mean, I certainly don't always get it right first time. I've made some mistakes along the way but with every day that goes by my confidence grows and so does my bond with Violet. And that's what she needs more than anything right now. Someone who loves her more than anything else in the world. That's a job I can do for the rest of my life.

CHAPTER FORTY-FOUR

Present day

ROBIN

Robin cracks open another bottle of beer, holds its cold body to her head to help her think clearly. Too much today, too many shocks to think straight. She listens out in the hall – nothing. Sarah is sound asleep. Pregnant women get very tired, Robin reasons. Robin's tired too, but a couple of questions have just fused together in her head and she has to find out the answer before she can decide what to do next.

Robin goes to the recent call list on Sarah's phone and presses Jim's name. It only rings three times.

'What now?' he says when he answers.

'I'm so sorry,' Robin says, 'but there's something else I really need to know. Then I promise I'll leave you alone.'

'Go on,' he says, sounding a hundred years' tired.

Robin takes a deep breath. 'Jim, how did your wife die?'

'That's none of your business. I don't know you from Adam.'

'I know, but please. It's very important,' Robin whispers. She can almost hear him thinking, deciding whether to share this private pain with a stranger on a telephone late at night.

He takes a breath, says quietly, 'She fell down the stairs while she was on her own with Violet. Violet was a few months old and asleep in her cot at the time. For obvious reasons I don't like to talk about it.'

'I'm so sorry,' Robin says, a grim stillness settling on her shoulders.

'That doesn't help,' he replies. 'I have to go now. Just keep your sister away from my family, and I won't go to the police.'

'I will, I promise, but I just need to know one more thing. Did you sleep with Sarah?' Robin says. Jim doesn't reply, not even in outrage. That tells her enough. Robin says, 'It was a few months ago, maybe a bit more. Yes?'

'Oh shit.'

'Oh shit's right.'

'It was just once. We had too much wine and it got out of hand. But it was just one time, a mistake that I apologised for profusely.'

'That's all it takes.'

'What are you saying? Are you suggesting she's *pregnant*?'

'Well, yeah, what did you think I was suggesting?'

'That I'd made things worse. Which I did.' Jim paused. 'But she can't be pregnant.'

'Why?'

'Because I can't have any more children.'

'How come?' Robin had blurted it out before she could stop herself. 'I mean, I'm sorry, but are you sure? One hundred per cent?'

'Yes, I'm deadly sure. I'd always wanted two children but it would be impossible for me to have any more. And Violet was conceived with a lot of help.'

'Does Sarah know that?'

'Of course not, why would she? I wouldn't tell my nanny something that private. Is she seriously claiming that she's pregnant with my child?'

'Yes,' Robin says. 'That's exactly what she's claiming.'

'Well, I don't care what she's told you, that's physically impossible. So if she's pregnant, it's got nothing to do with me.'

Robin rubs her hand through her hair, pulls on the curls and presses her forehead to the wall. If Jim's not the father, who is? How many more people are holding secrets about Robin's sister? How many more secrets is Sarah holding?

'What are you going to do now?' Jims asks. Robin wasn't sure if it was simple curiosity, genuine concern or seeking reassurance that someone would do *something* to keep Sarah away from his family.

'Honestly, I don't know. But she needs my help, especially if she's got a baby on the way. And I really don't believe she would ever hurt a child.'

'Believe that all you want but if she ever comes near Violet—'

'I know, I'm sorry.'

Robin ends the call, turns to lean on the sink and splashes her face with water.

All this time apart and she'd thought she was the one in the biggest pit. Her sister, her poor, fucked-up sister. Lying upstairs with god-knows-whose baby growing inside her. But a baby she could actually give birth to, could raise, with help. A baby she deserved to have a chance to mother, finally.

Robin didn't know if her sister even knew she was lying any more, that was the problem. And that bastard Drew Granger. That vile pervert. The whole thing was far worse than she'd ever realised.

Robin leaves her beer, creeps into the hall and takes off her trainers. She starts up the stairs. It's dark, after midnight now. She would have to crawl under the other bed and try to sleep some sense into this. She reaches the first landing, still holding Sarah's phone in her hand. As her feet feel their way onto the larger expanse of carpet, she feels Sarah's breath on her neck.

'You called Jim,' she says.

SARAH

I stand in the dark, shoulder to head with my sister. My interfering sister.

'I came to you for help,' I say.

'I was trying to help,' she says. All the usual bluster is gone. 'I was trying to make things better for you.'

'You've made everything worse. Just like you always did. I don't know why I thought you could help me.'

I can't see her properly, it's dark and I don't know where the light switch is. I've been nervous at the top of stairs for years, but alien stairs in the dark is pretty much the worst place for me to be. I feel sick.

'Sarah.' Robin's voice is as thin and croaky as when I first arrived this morning. 'You're pregnant, you need to calm down and come away from the top of the stairs. I'm worried about you.'

'Ah yes,' I say spikily, before I can stop myself. 'I forgot that it took a pregnancy to get your attention.'

'That's not fair, I was interested in you before...' She pauses. 'Before and after your pregnancy. I just didn't know how to handle it. I was eighteen.'

I step back from the top of the stairs. 'I was eighteen too, Robin, and I lost everything. Including you.'

She reaches out, I feel her fingertips and start to make out her shape in the dark.

'Why did you lie, Sarah?' Robin asks.

'We all lie, Robin. Everyone lies. I wanted to get what I deserved, what I'd had stolen from me. I wanted the chance to be a mum. I don't apologise for that.'

'But did you hurt that little girl, Sarah?'

The rage shoots through me. How could she even ask that? I loved Violet. I loved her from the moment I held her, when she was just a few weeks' old. I loved her and I looked after her day and night while that woman lay around and talked about how tired and miserable she was. I fed Violet in the night and the day, I gave her everything she needed. And the one night I was supposed to go out on some online date I was dreading, Elaine had begged me not to go. Jim was at a work thing and the woman had clung to me, pleading. Violet was asleep in her Moses basket, softly snuffling after I'd rocked her to sleep.

Elaine had grabbed both my shoulders and looked into my eyes and said, 'I can't do this. It was a mistake, I'm not cut out for this. Please.'

It wasn't my fault, I didn't mean for it to happen, but when it did, when she lost her footing, a calmness came over me. An opportunity presented itself, a chance to be there for my new family in the way I'd always wanted.

'I would never hurt Violet,' I say to Robin. 'I love her. You can't possibly understand what it's like to love someone like that.'

'But her father thinks you hurt her.'

'Jim doesn't know anything. He's a weak little man who doesn't know anything.'

'He knows he doesn't want you near Violet.'

'He can't keep her from me!' I shout. It's the first time I've shouted in so very long and my throat stretches around the words. I grow with them. A new anger makes me sway.

'Come downstairs,' Robin says. She's using the kind of voice you'd use to coax a nervous animal. 'Let's talk about this downstairs. I just want you and the baby to be safe.'

'No,' I say. 'I don't want to talk about this. I don't want to open this up. I want Violet and I want a boy baby and I want what I should have had all along, what everyone else has taken from me.

'No!' I say again, and I reach out to push at Robin but she's already making her way down to the hall.

She turns the light on at the bottom of the steps and I see her looking up at me, and looking nervously behind her at the front door. She's trapped, and she knows it. She's not going out the front unless it's life and death, she's told me that before. I don't want it to be life and death for her. But what life is this? She's a hermit, a recluse. Living here in a home built for a family. Who would know, if she wasn't here? Who would know if someone with a family moved in? Violet and I. We could be happy here. I thought we could be happy with Robin, thought she could help me get my girl, that I could find my boy, give them a life together, but I was wrong. For all her rebel talk, Robin is the biggest snitch of all.

'Why did you attack Mum?' Robin asks, looking up at me. She thinks I don't notice that she's stepping into her trainers in the dark of the corner. I see everything. Just like Mum did.

'Why do you think?' I say. Really? I really have to explain this?

'Because you thought she let everything happen to you?'

'I thought she saw it all. She'd watched the way he looked at me, the way he planned it all. She says she didn't but I still don't know whether to believe her. The same thing he'd done to her, he did to me. How could she miss that? Only Hilary was truly there to help me afterwards: she got me some help, came to visit me. Picked me up when I got out, helped me start a new life in Surrey. Helped me find a nannying job.'

'You tried to claw Mum's *eyes* out,' Robin says. That's a huge exaggeration, but I see from the way she's screwed up her face that she will never understand how I felt that night, and for all the years that ran up to it.

'I'm not here to talk about that, that's history. I came here to ask your help to get Violet back.'

'You need to forget Violet,' Robin says softly, 'and focus on the baby that's *yours*. I understand why you lied about Violet, I get it. You were still upset about the baby you lost and I understand why you got attached to her but you have your own baby on the way. I can help you with *this* baby. I can still help you.'

There's a pleading whine to her voice. I've never heard Robin on the back foot before. But she doesn't get it. She doesn't get any of it. That the baby idea was only there to get Jim to take me back, to seal the deal. To let me back in and accept that what's best for Violet, what's best for all of us, is for me to be Violet's mother. Just like I've been for the last three years. That it didn't matter what it took to get back to that; any lie, any deception, anything was worth it.

I start to tread down the stairs, carefully, but the baby thing is history now. I lift up the pyjama top and vest, pull at the tape and throw the bump on the floor. That plan is ruined now. I need a new plan.

'You're not even pregnant?' Robin asks, but I ignore her. 'What the fuck is going on, Sarah?'

I don't answer.

CHAPTER FORTY-FIVE

Present day
SARAH

Robin is too hung up on this fake baby thing; she's seeing everything in separate pieces, not the whole picture. I ball up my fists. There's no getting through to her and I can't let my frustration cloud my thinking. I need a new plan. I have to get things ready for Violet, I have to get her back, find somewhere for us to live. It was going to be here but Robin isn't going to help me, that much is clear.

I need to think fast, come up with a new plan, but Robin won't shut up and it's hard to think.

'What the hell, Sarah? You've lied to me constantly since you got here. Why didn't you tell me the truth?' Robin asks. 'I could have helped. And now I'm wondering what else you're keeping from me. What do you want from me?'

She's backing away down the hall, into the kitchen.

'You? You only wanted to help me when Callum had left you and you needed a project. You never wanted me, you never wanted your sister back. I'd missed you for so long but you just moved on to a replacement.'

'I'm sorry,' she says. 'But that's just not true.'

'Now you've gone behind my back again,' I say. 'But it's not too late. You can still help me.'

'How?' she asks, that new nervousness still creeping into her words.

We're in the kitchen now. She's reaching for the key in the back door, and I reach for the knife on the side. I don't want to hurt her, I just need to make sure she stays here while I think up a new plan, get it straight. I've never wanted to hurt anyone but I have nothing. I thought I had a sister, but she's just going to stand in my way. I chant it quietly: 'I don't want to hurt you, I don't want to hurt you, I don't want to hurt you.'

She looks at the knife, looks at me. She doesn't understand that I just need time to think.

'Robin, please, I'll ask you for the last time: will you help me get Violet back? I need to come up with a plan. Will you help me?'

I lift the knife in my open palm, show her I mean no harm, but she's shaking her head.

'No, Sarah, you attacked Mum and you've lied about serious fucking stuff. You don't need a plan to get Violet back, you need help.'

While she was talking, I realise too late that she was fiddling with the back door and now she's opened it and is stumbling out backwards. No! I need time to come up with a plan, this has all gone wrong. I rush out after her.

ROBIN

Robin plunges out into the cold air and trips over her own trainers. Her sister is bigger but Robin is stronger, scrappy. Through the tangling limbs, Robin manages to push herself back up onto her feet to scramble away.

Someone is panting hard and it takes a moment to realise that the sound is coming from both of them.

'Please!' Sarah is saying, but she's swinging wildly with the knife. Robin ducks and runs down the garden.

When Robin dreams, which is rare, she dreams about running outside. About throwing the door open and flying out, scything through the air, light and fast instead of rooted and heavy. She wakes from those dreams drenched, feeling sick. But Robin finally feels fast now. She can hear her sister's footsteps behind her, running unsteadily on the cobbles. Sarah is barefoot, but almost keeping up. Driven by last chances.

Robin sprints as fast as she can into the black of the alleyway and thuds straight into something. Someone.

'No!' she cries but they move around her and grab Sarah's arms. The silhouette moves into the light and Robin sees that it's Sam from the flats. He pins Sarah to the wall and Robin knocks the knife from her hands and kicks it somewhere into the shadows.

'Fuck!' Sam says. 'What's going on?'

Robin and Sarah say nothing and the gate to back of the flats swings open. Mrs Peacock pokes her head out, torch in her hands.

'Call the police,' Sam says, his voice shaking like he's trying it out. The old lady disappears back into the garden.

Sarah had been limp against the wall but starts thrashing and crying. Robin rushes at her, grabs one of Sarah's arms. When the moonlight catches her face, Sarah wears a look of desperation and panic.

'Thank you,' Robin says to Sam, who looks even more frightened than he did this morning.

'What the hell's going on? Isn't she pregnant?'

'No,' Robin says grimly.

Sarah slumps down to a crouch, sobbing and mumbling sadly about needing a plan, needing help. Robin and Sam are still holding her tightly. They stay that way, taut and tensed around an exhausted body, until the police finally arrive; three officers running full pelt down the pedestrianised alleyway, illuminated by the squad car parked askance at the end.

'You'll be okay, Sarah,' Robin says as her sister is handcuffed. 'This is for your own good. I promise, you'll be okay.'

'Since when does our family keep promises?' Sarah says, as she's pulled barefoot along the cobbles.

CHAPTER FORTY-SIX

2017

I lead my sister through the double doors, into the rose garden and out to the car park. She's nervous, not used to the outside. The wind lashes at us and makes her jump. It's been months since she's left the grounds but the time has finally arrived. She's as ready as she can be. The rest is up to us.

I get into the back seat with her. The two women in the front cast nervous glances at us but don't say anything.

'Did you tell her where we're going?' they ask.

'I did,' I say. 'I told her about the new house and she's excited, aren't you?'

'Yes.' She smiles, a little uneasy.

I'm not sure if she really is excited. I think it's more a sense of giving in, of going along with the plan. But that's enough for now.

The engine starts up and we rumble down the drive and out through the gates. I see her thin fingers digging into her jeans, her tight jaw clenching as the trees and hedges start to whip past faster, blurring into streaks.

She has pills and tools to help with the transition. She has support and a safe place waiting for her. But it's new and she's still raw. The outside is so big for her, just like it was for me.

'Did you tell Sarah about the album?' Hilary asks, breaking the silence.

'No,' I say, embarrassed. I look down at my own jeans, pick at a speck of something on them. Paint, I think, from the kitchen. Since getting the keys, we've been pushed to get everything finished in time.

'You should be proud,' our mother says, as she slows to indicate into our new road. There's a staccato to her voice still; it gives away how nervous she is around us. How much she wants to get everything right.

'Robin's releasing an album.' Hilary leans back to try to make eye contact with Sarah.

'Have you got back together with the band?' Sarah asks, taking her eyes off the window for a moment to look at me. 'That's good.' She smiles thinly.

'Not with the band,' I say. 'This is ... different. I'll tell you later.'

We pull up outside the house, a family home in Maplesden, a village a few miles away from Birch End. Sarah stays in the car for a moment while we all get out. I see her chest rising and falling, see her looking around as she takes in the newness of everything.

Hilary and my mother talk with their heads close as they walk from the car. I hear them admiring the front garden, joking about what our dad would have had to say about the height of those bushes. They smile together, bow their heads briefly. I wonder what it's really like when it's just them. So many mistakes over the years, so many things said. So many losses. If Hilary holds my mother responsible, she hides it well. Beneath the layers of gentle words, her creamy coffee advert voice, her nervous distraction.

When I first said I'd come back to Berkshire, finally ready to get the help I needed, they'd come together to rally around me. My mother had driven me from Manchester to Berkshire. A long journey for such a nervous driver, but she didn't complain. I was glad to only be travelling fifty miles an hour on the motorway, my head in my hands for most of the five or six hours. She'd taken me to Hilary's house, the house I'd grown up in. Mum visited every day, talking in low voices with her one-time friend, casting glances at me and touching each other's arms in quiet agreement.

While Sarah was being cared for, perhaps they both needed a project. Perhaps that project was me. They often took me to my appointments together, me with my eyes closed, panting and saying, 'Oh fuck, oh fuck' like a mantra.

It had been Mum's idea to do music therapy.

It had been Hilary's idea to send the album that had emerged to my old record company.

I'm not cured; I still struggle with towns, shopping centres, supermarkets, the list too long to finish. People en masse feel like a swarm, the open air can feel choking. I have panic attacks where I still believe I will die if I don't take exactly ten thousand steps before nightfall. But the space between them has grown. I'm ready to be the strong one again.

'So here we are,' I say, as I pull Sarah's suitcase out of the boot and we trudge up the front path. 'Our new house.'

Sarah stands and stares at the front door.

'Just the two of us,' I say.

'Just the two of us,' my sister agrees as she slowly reaches for my hand.

Sleeve notes from *Only For Ever*
by Robin Marshall and Callum Granger

I didn't write these words and I didn't dream up this music. The heart of this album was created by the best friend I ever had and the only brother I knew.

For years, I was too scared to listen to the demo tapes he left me or read the words he'd written so carefully. To see and to hear was to acknowledge the gap he'd left behind. Its vastness swallowed me whole.

It took my sister to hold my hand, to twist my arm up my back, and to push me into the place where I could finally honour these memories. I hope you like what my brother started, and what I finished. But I hope you won't be offended if I say that it doesn't matter either way.

For ever is too long to hide from memories, good and bad. So here are ours: hers, his and mine.

For my brother and sister, for ever.

Acknowledgements

Before I thank the many, many people I need to thank, there's something that I'd really like readers to know.

There are some very difficult and sensitive scenes and characters' experiences in *Don't Close Your Eyes*. Please know that I agonised over each of these and desperately wanted to be sensitive and respectful to those affected by suicide, family separation, sexual assault, pregnancy loss and mental health issues.

At this point I'd also like to mention one charity here, CALM – Campaign Against Living Miserably. They do valuable work in understanding why male suicide accounts for 76% of all suicides and is the single biggest cause of death in men under 45 in the UK. They're working hard to help drive these numbers down. If you'd like to know more, please check them out. (www.thecalmzone.net)

But for the thanks, the need for which is swelling with every book.

To the incredible team at Corvus – especially my wonderful editor Sara O'Keeffe, whose insights shaped this book immeasurably. With special thanks to Francesca Riccardi, the absolute peach that she is, Louise Cullen (who will be missed), Alison Davies, Lucy Howkins and Nikky Ward – but really, everyone there is awesome. I could not have hoped for a more brilliant bunch of book lovers working on this novel.

Thank you to everyone at Ballantine in the USA. And especially huge thanks to my lovely new editor Julia Maguire, whose enthusiasm and notes gave me several late nights and many, many improvements.

Thank you also to the publishers around the world who are releasing *Don't Close Your Eyes* in translation.

As ever, my deepest gratitude to my intrepid, inspirational and incredible agent, Nicola Barr. The whole team at Greene and Heaton are the bomb. Special hat tip to Kate Rizzo.

Thank you to my parents and my family, including my sister – who I swear neither of the Marshall sisters are based on – not to mention bro-in-law Mark and my beloved little cherub of a niece, Eva.

Thank you (and sorry) to my adored children. I love you guys so much. Thank you for putting up with my glazed-over expression when I'm there in body but in 1990s Berkshire in my head.

I dedicated this book to my friends. I'm very lucky when it comes to friends and I love them all dearly, even if I'm way too English to say that to any of their faces. I'm slowly realising that friendship and its importance is something that runs through everything I write. And those friends who have been lost will never be forgotten.

And to my best friend of all. My champion, my matinee idol, the Franco Columbu to my Arnold Schwarzenegger, my beloved husband James. I love you mate. Thanks for everything.